BRIGID'S CHARGE

BRIGID'S CHARGE

CYNTHIA LAMB

Bay Island Books

Bay Island Books

P. O. Box 485

Corte Madera, CA 94976-0485

415-924-9026

The information in Brigid's Charge *on medical treatments using herbs
and other methods should not be taken as advice or instruction.*

Brigid's Charge / Cynthia Lamb.–1st ed.

ISBN 0-9654694-0-9

ISBN 0-9654694-1-7 (softcover)

1. New Jersey—History—Colonial period, ca. 1600-1775—Fiction.

2. Witches—Fiction. 3. Goddess religion—Fiction. 4. Society of Friends—Fiction.

813'.1   LCCN: 96-78573

Manufactured in the United States of America

First printing, on acid-free paper

THE LEGEND
of the
LEEDS DEVIL

DEBORAH SMITH LEEDS was called Mother Leeds in part because she had odd powers. She could heal almost anyone of anything, sometimes with touch alone. She was a Quaker. And a witch, some said, though not in her hearing. Deborah's troubles began in 1735 with the birth of her thirteenth child. A child which never should have been born—a child which never was born, some say.

Perhaps it's true the Devil wouldn't have come at all if Mother Leeds hadn't cursed the child. "I will not bear this babe!" she called out when the pain of birthing grew too strong. "Devil take it, should it come!"

The infant did come, and was just as normal as you please at first. But as the knife severed the cord, the child grew at once to the size of a man. Its skin turned green and scaly like a serpent's. Its head became a horse's head. It stretched out huge bat wings and flew about the room, thrashing its dragon's tail. Some of the women dove under the bed, while others hid behind furniture.

The beast circled the room wildly, its breath hot as Hades. Then with a horrible strident screech, the likes of which had never been heard, it flew up the chimney and into the night.

Before day had dawned again, the creature ate chickens and goats and a cow. It trampled corn, overturned milk, spoiled butter. When the women who had attended the birth told of Deborah's curse, the beast was named: THE LEEDS DEVIL.

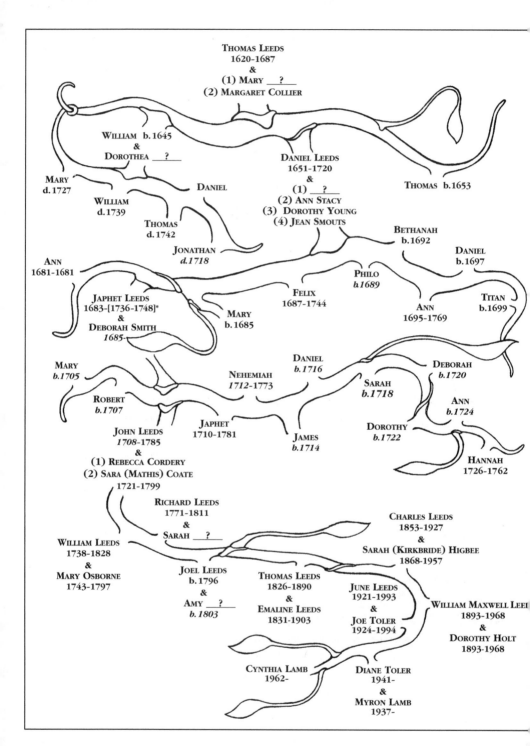

THOMAS LEEDS
1620-1687
&
(1) MARY ___?___
(2) MARGARET COLLIER

WILLIAM b.1645
&
DOROTHEA ___?___

DANIEL LEEDS
1651-1720
&
(1) ___?___
(2) ANN STACY
(3) DOROTHY YOUNG
(4) JEAN SMOUTS

THOMAS b.1653

MARY
d.1727

DANIEL

WILLIAM
d.1739

THOMAS
d.1742

JONATHAN
d.1718

BETHANAH
b.1692

DANIEL
b.1697

ANN
1681-1681

PHILO
b1689

FELIX
1687-1744

ANN
1695-1769

TITAN
b.1699

JAPHET LEEDS
1683-[1736-1748]*
&
DEBORAH SMITH
1685-

MARY
b.1685

DANIEL
b.1716

DEBORAH
b.1720

MARY
b.1705

NEHEMIAH
1712-1773

SARAH
b.1718

ANN
b.1724

ROBERT
b.1707

JAPHET
1710-1781

JAMES
b.1714

DOROTHY
b.1722

JOHN LEEDS
1708-1785
&
(1) REBECCA CORDERY
(2) SARA (MATHIS) COATE
1721-1799

HANNAH
1726-1762

RICHARD LEEDS
1771-1811
&
SARAH ___?___

CHARLES LEEDS
1853-1927
&
SARAH (KIRKBRIDE) HIGBEE
1868-1957

WILLIAM LEEDS
1738-1828
&
MARY OSBORNE
1743-1797

JOEL LEEDS
b.1796
&
AMY ___?___
b.1803

THOMAS LEEDS
1826-1890
&
EMALINE LEEDS
1831-1903

JUNE LEEDS
1921-1993
&
JOE TOLER
1924-1994

WILLIAM MAXWELL LEE[
1893-1968
&
DOROTHY HOLT
1893-1968

CYNTHIA LAMB
1962-

DIANE TOLER
1941-
&
MYRON LAMB
1937-

*Japhet's will was written in 1736 and proved in 1748.

Italicized dates are approximate.

All information is based on records at the Atlantic County Historical Society.
Discrepancies in birth and death dates in secondary sources are common due to the ear[
Quaker observance of March 25th as the beginning of the new year.

Leaving

EBORAH HELD the doorjamb and leaned her head against her hand, unable to step into her grandmother's candlelit room. She knew her grandmother was waiting for her even before her mother shouted for her to come. But that was all the more reason to linger, for soon after Deborah crossed this threshold, her grandmother would die.

And so she stood and watched her mother, Catherine, move anxiously around the room—pouring cider from a pitcher into Granna's wooden mug, straightening a dried flower wreath on the wall. Finally, Catherine noticed Deborah and waved her over. But Deborah still didn't move, couldn't seem to pick up her right foot and step, couldn't release her grip.

Catherine came over and grabbed her arm, yanked it away from the jamb. "You are who she desires with her," she said.

Deborah met her mother's glare and thought, Why vexed? For you have got what you hoped for. Granna's time hath come.

Deborah pushed past her mother into the room, and Catherine left.

Granna lay propped on the three feather pillows she and Deborah made together years before. Her coarse grey hair was loose and disheveled, flattened against the pillow. She was sleeping, or so it seemed, her breathing audible. Unable to believe this was happening, Deborah sank onto the stool by the bed. Her Granna, who had always been so powerful, was dying.

Granna's eyes popped open, as an infant's do just after birth, a moment when Deborah always wanted to cheer, and she had at the first birth she'd attended with her grandmother. The newborn's eyes opened and suddenly a new person was there. When she whooped with joy the eyes shut. Granna had admonished her for frightening the babe, but Deborah thought later there were worse fates than being first greeted with a heartfelt cheer.

She smoothed the hair around her grandmother's face as her own eyes filled with tears. She hadn't known that eyes could pop with the last bit of life as well.

"I know 'tis troubling to see me," Granna said, her voice low and rasping, "but worry not." She smiled and her bottom lip cracked. Blood ran toward her chin.

Deborah dabbed at the red splotch with a cloth, then rubbed a mixture of beeswax and calendula over Granna's mouth. The ointment soaked right in. She applied a thick second coat, biting her own bottom lip.

"Will you go?" Granna asked.

Deborah replaced the ointment on the bedside table and stared at the shuttered window above the bed. Cracks of daylight shown through. She wiped her nose with the back of her hand. How could she remove? How could she leave England? She looked back at her grandmother, who had pushed down the quilt and was drawing out her hands, holding them aloft in front of her, palms facing her granddaughter.

Deborah knew what she meant and glanced down at her own hands. Like her grandmother's, they were large with broad, flat palms. The better to sense the ail, Granna had told her.

I may be a healer, Deborah thought, but why must I follow Mam's wishes and journey to the New World to marry a man I have yet to meet? A man who could be a brute or rogue.

"He is neither," her mother had said, and then told her she was fortunate to be offered such a match, that she ought to be grateful for the rise in station. For Japhet Leeds was the eldest son of a man of great repute and wealth in New Jersey. And since the son was of a certain age and had found none he fancied, the father had sent back to relations in Leeds—relations with whom Catherine was acquainted, and who agreed that despite the questionable grandmother Deborah was a strong and comely girl who would make any man a pleasing wife.

Catherine spoke with great enthusiasm about the match, but Deborah knew the real reason she wanted her to go. Regardless of her mother's best efforts to the contrary, if Deborah remained she would take her grandmother's place as a healer and priestess of the Old Religion. She would become a witch, and the family would be ostracized for another generation.

But you, Granna, Deborah thought as she brought the quilt up over her grandmother's chest and tucked it around her. You desire me to remove as well. You have told me before, but still I do not understand. "Why must I be transported to the colonies as if I were a thief?"

Granna gestured for cider, and Deborah held the mug for her while she sipped it down.

"Our line hath survived thousands of years on this soil," Granna said, her voice barely above a whisper. "And though they ne'er hanged me on the gibbet, no longer are we welcome here. The men of schooling and the clergy do as once did we. They sit counsel, tend the ill, pass the soul on at death. I am known by some, and birthing is left to me, but most think me an old fool, as you know, or worse. In the whole of England you can ne'er be what you are. In the New World, mayhap. 'Tis a large country, with few physicians." Granna gasped for breath and motioned at the empty mug.

Deborah poured more cider from the pitcher and held the drink to Granna's lips. She hated to press her grandmother with questions, but had to be sure. If she was to get on that coach for London and leave the farm and woolens-making to her mother, two brothers, and sister, she had to know it was right.

"In the trunk," Granna said.

Deborah put down the mug, crossed the room, and opened the lid of an old chest. A gift wrapped in faded blue silk lay on top of folded linen. She brought it back and sat down again. "For me?" she asked. Granna nodded.

She untied the cloth and saw a small volume, its cover a bright seaweed green.

"A book of receipts and stories of our line," Granna said.

Our line, Deborah thought, which is pledged to Brigid, Mother of our ancient people, the Brigantes, who lived in northern England. She traced her finger over the cover, not certain she wanted it. She was afraid her mother might be right—that she should forget what Granna had managed to teach her, that she must not remember or she would die.

Granna reached out and gripped Deborah's hand, took several loud, gasping breaths, then said, "When you are gone from your mother and the memory of me, you will have more ease. Here you can be neither Christian nor witch. A'ways we would tear at you, rending that cleft in you larger still."

Her breathing became more labored, and when she spoke again her voice was lower. Deborah leaned over her. "In the New World, you will find your own way. And though the cleft may never be fully mended, you will build a bridge o'er it to bear your weight." Deborah's ear was at Granna's lips now, straining to hear. "Under the bridge are the waters you heal with, which issue from the cleft as a spring. And in this Brigid's well swim the fish, which are sacrifice: what you give and are given."

Deborah kept her head there, waiting for more, even though she knew her grandmother had spoken her last words. Her sweet, ferocious Granna was dead. She lay her head on her grandmother's bony chest and reached her arms around her. "I will go, Granna," she said as she started to weep. "I will honor your final wish."

MAIDEN
1704

1

HE COACH halted at the inn, wheels skidding on the bricks, and Deborah jerked awake. She drew back the curtain and looked out at the setting sun, a brilliant, pulsing scarlet shot with orange. It was unsettling somehow, unnatural. "Lovely though it be, I do not like the looks of that," she said.

"Indeed, 'tis queer, is it not?" The driver's head appeared in the window hole as he yanked open the coach door. "The setting sun grows e'er fairer, while the days in this dreaded city grow dingy and grey."

They had arrived at the Pool, the center of maritime activity in London, where the air was choked—and Deborah as well—with acrid vapors of tar. A thousand vessels from every nation clustered on the River Thames, their flags flown high as if in battle. On crafts setting sail in the morning, lines of butchers like red ants carried salt beef and pork aboard. At the bank of the river an execution dock stood black against the purple sky. A woman swung from a noose, her body stiff-jointed, her rotting odor strong.

"Wapping's where they hang them," the driver said. "At low tide. They leave them there till three tides flow o'er. 'Tis a lesson, to those needing one."

"What did she?" Deborah asked in a low voice.

"Her? Coulda robbed or killed, or e'en bewitched, for aught I know." He hoisted Deborah's trunk to his shoulder and carried it toward the inn.

Deborah remained in place, staring at the woman hanging on the gibbet. She crossed her arms protectively over her chest.

"Good luck to you," the driver said when he returned.

"As well to you."

He clucked to the horses and was gone.

Deborah opened the inn's door, the image of the hanged woman still in her mind. "Preserve me," she whispered as she stepped inside. "Deliver me safely to the New World."

The interior smelled like fish. When her eyes adjusted to the diminished light, she saw the proprietor watching her from behind a desk across the room. She stepped forward more confidently than she felt. "Prithee, sir, I require a small room for tonight, mayhap longer, till the *Willow* set sail. Will you show me to one?"

He looked her over, then called toward the back, "David!"

A gangly boy with blackened, rotting teeth and a pox-marked face came from the kitchen and picked up her trunk. The proprietor silently led them up the dark narrow staircase with a candle.

When they reached a room at the top of the stairs, the proprietor pointed to two empty beds. "Likely as not they'll be none other for the night." He gave her a hard look. "You do have the means to pay, do you not?"

"I have a purse," she said, surprised, and touched the satin stomacher that covered her chest. Beneath the cloth, a leather pouch hung from a hemp string between her breasts.

"Nay, lass, stay. You may pay in the morning. Pray forgive my discourtesy. Rarely do we see honest ladies alone in Wapping. Shall you come down now for some supper?"

She looked around the spare room and thought, 'Tis the last bit of comfort I shall see for some months. "I think not. I will sleep without and eat heartily in the morn."

"As you wish." He left, pushing the boy ahead of him.

Exhaustion struck suddenly, weighing Deborah down like wet sand. In slow motion she removed her modesty piece, unpinned her stomacher, took off her gown and bustle, and untied her petticoat. She left the pouch on, as well as her shift and cotton stockings—for what little protection they would give against the fleas.

After several hours of deep sleep, Deborah woke with a start and sat up, calling out "No!" She looked in fright at the adjacent bed and then glanced around the room, her heart pounding, her shaking arms braced against the mattress, but didn't see anyone. I was only dreaming, she told herself, then opened a tinderbox on the bedside table. She struck the steel and flint together and lit a piece of cord that had been dipped in melted brimstone. As she held this match to a candle's wick, she remembered that the hanged woman had been in the dream, and at the time had seemed familiar. She sat awhile, watching the candle burn, trying to remember more. At last she gave up, thinking grimly that the dream will surely return but she shan't. She had left her home forever. Damn me, she thought, as the tears came. "Granna, why did I have to go?"

And then her grandmother was there in the room, squatting as if in her garden at home, pulling weeds. Deborah imagined their barn in the background and the River Aire beyond that. Granna's maternal line had inhabited the area just south of Leeds for centuries—before Kirkstall Abbey was built, before the Romans came, even before the Celts. "Descended from the faeries we are," Granna used to say, not always in jest.

"But no longer," Deborah said to her image. "With me gone the land passes out of our hands."

Granna leaned back on her haunches and nodded sadly. "Death comes eventually to all. But you've a new world to take our line—to plant it, watch it grow." As the image faded into nothing Deborah heard, "Fear not, for you shan't be alone."

"Granna," Deborah said, her voice ringing in the empty room. "Granna." Do I go mad? she wondered, then walked to the window and looked out over the deserted quays of Wapping. The vessels were a murky yellow, cast so by the inn's candle lantern mounted above the front door.

Soon now, she thought, I shall be on one of those. I wonder which 'twill be? She craned her neck, looking as far up and down the quays as she could. Imagine, she told herself, I shall soon sail on the Atlantic as Pappa did. She felt a stab of anxiety, then frowned. He had many a voyage ere he perished. Worry not and trust Granna. All shall be well.

She turned away from the window, sat again on the edge of the bed, and emptied her pouch's contents on the table. "Nine guineas," she marveled as she counted the gold coins. "And shillings besides." She heard a noise outside the door. Quickly she replaced the coins and put the pouch on. It bounced against her ribs and jerked on her neck. She listened, but didn't hear anything. No one there. She shook her head in self-amusement and climbed back in bed, scratching. She'd been bit several times.

Deborah stood in the doorway of the narrow, smoke-filled pub where the proprietor had said she would find Captain Hughes. She wore a pale purple damask gown her mother had made, and her honey-colored hair was gathered into two long curls which fell over one shoulder. To any passerby she would appear poised, but she felt frightened, aware of this moment, this doorway, as a crossroads. She could almost see Hecate of the Three Ways stirring her cauldron, asking her, "Yes, Deborah, what shall it be?"

But there was no goddess there, only the barkeep who had stopped wiping the counter and was watching her. I might still turn about, she told herself. I might still return to the farm. The keeper resumed his wiping. No, she thought, I am going. Indeed, I have left a'ready.

She walked to the bar. "Might you tell me where I may find Captain James Hughes, shipmaster of the *Willow*?" she asked.

The barkeep peered curiously at her, then pointed to a table where three men sat: two in velvet coats and long powdered wigs, and the third whom Deborah presumed to be the captain—a tall, well-muscled man about forty with shoulder-length auburn hair. His chair was turned sideways, back against the wall. As Deborah approached he raised his eyebrows and the other men stood.

"Good day." She curtsied. "Pray pardon my intrusion, Captain, but Daniel Leeds, the father of my betrothed, hath sent me hither to purchase passage for myself to Burlington, New Jersey, where I shall marry his son Japhet and travel with him across the colony to Leeds, New Jersey."

He looked her up and down, settling on her bosom. "Indeed, lass, what be thy name, and whence doth thee hail?"

She cleared her throat loudly and the captain's eyes rose to her face. "Deborah Smith, of Yorkshire."

He reached for a nearby stool and dragged it next to him, motioning for her to occupy it. She pulled the stool to the end of the table and sat, her hands clasped in her lap. The other men were still standing.

"We shall take our leave now," the taller one said to the captain. "Foul winds beside, you'll leave on the morrow, yes?"

"Aye, that I shall, and to be sure, shall be a most fruitful journey. Most fruitful indeed." He watched the men as they made their way to the door, then addressed Deborah somewhat accusatively, "You have arrived with little time to spare."

"'Tis my good fortune, then," she said, "for I have arrived in time."

"Hmm. Your good fortune is the tars' ill—that's the crew. Bad luck having women aboard, and you will make five."

"I am familiar with the appellation," Deborah said indignantly. "They are so called because they coat their breeches with tar to keep off the water. My father was a tar ere he died at sea." She cocked her head and added sardonically, "And not a woman aboard upon whom to fix blame."

The captain smiled. "You are handsome, and a wit besides." He picked up a quill and began figuring on a tablet. "Danny Leeds sent you, did he? A most august statesman, they say." He put down the quill. "Ten guineas it shall cost you to cross. Best brigantine on the Thames, the *Willow* is. Quick for a cargo ship but weatherly as well. Some would take three months and cart you by way of the West Indies, but not she. Six weeks is all. Then you'll lay your head on your husband's pillow."

Deborah swallowed. "If you please, Captain, Mr. Leeds said your price would be but nine guineas, and 'tis all he did send." She started to plead, but thought better of it and waited.

"Ten guineas is a good price. For bed and board, you'll find none better. You'll have a room in the hold with only four others. Fine ladies they be, like yourself." He reached over and touched her hand.

Deborah yanked it away. She had a sudden urge to run out the door, but steeled herself. "Captain Hughes, Mr. Leeds sent but nine guineas for passage on your vessel. I have no more. Shall you bid me passage or do I find one who will?"

He took a sip of his ale, then eyed her coolly. "You rob me, lass. But you may pay your nine guineas."

Deborah stood up. "I'll bring it with me in the morn."

Captain Hughes told her where the *Willow* was moored and bid her be waiting no later than dawn. She left the pub feeling both relieved and ill at ease. *Had I been delayed just one day,* she thought. *Or should he not have taken my price . . .* She shuddered at the memory of his hand on hers. *I'll keep my distance is all,* she told herself, quickening her step.

2

N THE PROW of the ship, Deborah and the other women were to share a small triangular room that smelled of accumulated sea water. Six hammocks hung from ceiling beams along the room's rounded sides—shaped so by the curve of the bow. The base of the triangle, a thin plank wall, separated the quarters from the rest of the hold.

Since Deborah was the first to board, she had her choice of hammocks. She took the one farthest aft, along the larboard wall. Mounting the hip-high hammock proved difficult—she tried first to put one knee on it and then pull herself up, but the hammock swung away, forcing her to hang on to keep from falling. Then she stood on her trunk, held the hammock tightly with both hands, leaned forward, and landed on her stomach. She whipped her legs around and turned onto her side, laughing. What a vision I must be, she thought. As well is that dirty chest. I must find a cloth to clean it.

The piece of furniture stood in the center of the room, next to a vertical wooden ladder that led up to the main deck. Steps sounded on the ladder rungs. Deborah saw feet, legs, and then rumps as four women climbed down. She slid off the hammock and stood before it, straightening her gown.

"The captain did not speak truthfully," one of the younger women said. "'Tis quite a dreary room, is it not, Mother?" She looked about and settled on Deborah, as if she were part of the bargain and found lacking as well.

"I'faith," her mother agreed, "we'll spend as little time here as God shall allow."

They walked around the room—unsteadily because of the ship's swaying—and selected their hammocks. The second young woman pointed at the one next to Deborah's. "I shall take this, if it shan't trouble you," she said, smiling.

"Please do," Deborah answered. "You may use my trunk as a perch, if you wish, till yours is brought down. It eases the climb." She pushed it in place.

The woman stepped on, holding her arms outstretched, pretending to be more precariously balanced than she was. "I always liked to climb trees," she winked at Deborah, "when no one was about."

Despite her drab dress—an umber broadcloth gown and petticoat, and a white cotton kerchief crossed over her chest—Deborah thought her comely. She had fine brown hair dressed to frame her face in short curls, and a generous smile. The intelligence and mischievousness evident in her dark brown eyes belied the dress's temperate effect.

One of the older women joined them. Deborah found her striking as well, with bright white hair and blue eyes. "My name is Mrs. Spencer," she said. "You've met my mad daughter, Charity. This is my other daughter, Hope, and my sister, Mrs. Moore. We sail to Boston."

"My name is Deborah Smith, soon to be Deborah Leeds." She smiled. "I meet my betrothed in Burlington, New Jersey."

"*Burlington*," Mrs. Moore said. "Is not that a *Quaker* town?"

Deborah knew nothing about Burlington, but she resented her contemptuous tone. "I 'spect that 'tis."

Mrs. Moore frowned, turned her back on Deborah, and addressed the others. "Let us go above and see about our baggage. We must remain watchful o'er our manservant, or he shall be reduced by this rogue crew, especially as he must bed with them." Mrs. Spencer and Hope followed her.

Deborah tried not to snicker at the sight of them waddling up the ladder. It reminded her of a family of badgers she'd once seen at dusk, hurrying away across a fallen log. She glanced at Charity, who was grinning on her hammock.

"Pay no mind to my aunt," Charity said. "She believes Quakers yet run naked in the streets."

"Did they ever? I think them a sober bunch, at the least in their dress."

"So have I heard," Charity said, "but methinks no longer. Mayhap with land of their own in the New World there is no need for them to expose their parts."

Deborah laughed though she was a bit surprised by Charity's saucy tongue. "I hope 'tis no longer a practice, for though my betrothed only greets me in the city, I don't wish for such a shock."

Charity giggled. "You do not remain there, then? Whither do you go after he meets you in Burlington?"

"Eastward, across the colony to Leeds." Her chest constricted and she felt dizzy and slumped onto her trunk. She had the disorienting sensation of talking about herself as if she were someone else—that paradoxical experience that strikes at moments of deep realization. She *had* left home. She *would* soon meet her husband.

"Are you unwell? Shall I get you a cool cloth?"

"Nay, nay. I am well, only . . ." Deborah looked up and noted Charity's kind, attentive eyes, her genuine concern. She had to tell someone. "I am frighted," she said, "truly frighted, it seems."

Charity nodded her head slowly. "I'faith, so should I be were I alone. I am frighted now and I've my family with me and more await in Boston." She sat beside Deborah and patted her hand. "But do not trouble yourself about it. To be sure, all shall be well. You will soon meet your betrothed and you will be married. See, you are beyond me on that score."

Deborah smiled; she was starting to feel better. He will be a fine match, she thought, utilizing her mother's argument. I only hope I find him pleasing.

"Forgive me for being so bold," Charity said, "but your dress is lovely. I have ne'er seen such a contrast—the pale purple of the gown against the black petticoat and the darker purple stomacher. 'Tis startling a'most."

Deborah looked down at the gown. "My mother is quite accomplished. I have in the main refused her creations—I prefer simple clothing—but this gown is indeed fair. She told me she would sew it for me and one day I should be pleased to have it, and so was she in the right."

"To be sure, it shall serve you when you meet your betrothed."

"I do hope that is so." Deborah felt her stomach clench. "I must own I am all stirred up. I can hardly believe I shall marry a man I have yet to meet."

"The family is good, to be sure."

"Yes, and my betrothed is the eldest son. The father is a member of Lord Cornbury's council as well as a writer of an almanac. The town where he resides bears his name. I warrant 'twill be a felicitous union. And yet . . ." She paused uncertainly.

"And yet you are frighted. Methinks you are courageous, leaving your home, traveling to the New World alone. I'faith your fright proves the point. Without fear there can be no courage, and no satisfaction. For if we ride easily to victory, what have we won?"

"You are in the right, of course. I only wish it shouldn't feel the way it doth. One minute I am well, the next falling upon my trunk."

"You shall be well, I am certain of it. And who should not fall a time or two when she stands on a thing that pitches and rolls?" Charity stood up and held out her arms, rocking back and forth. "You see, 'tis merely the vessel. You are quite well."

Deborah laughed. "And you are a wit."

"Yes, and it causes my mother no end of grief. Speaking of her, I ought to attempt that ladder and join them above. Though I fear," she grinned at Deborah, "that you will find me amusing, as you did my family."

Deborah started to apologize, but Charity shushed her. "Nay, nay, I found it humorous as well. We will at the least have mirth this journey." She stood up and headed for the ladder. "We will speak anon."

"Yes," Deborah agreed. "We've a long voyage ahead of us, to be sure."

Later that morning, Deborah stood on the main deck just aft of the foremast by the galley's entrance. A piece of sailcloth that acted as a door was pulled back. Inside, the cook chopped carrots next to a brick fireplace where a kettle of pea soup simmered. Dressed more or less as the other seamen, he wore a blue-and-white checked linen shirt, tar-coated breeches, and grey wool stockings.

"If you please," Deborah called in, "might I have a cloth for cleaning? We have the most horrid chest in our quarters."

Without looking up he pointed the knife over his shoulder to an old, fraying sail stretched over a cask. Deborah walked past him into the dim room and picked up a corner of the sail, then looked around for something to cut it. Wooden boxes, casks, and kegs holding food, water, and rum were stacked all around. Just a few feet from her on the floor lay a fat, contented-looking sow.

The cook walked over and handed Deborah his knife. Her breath caught when she saw his withered left arm bounce against his side, but she quickly covered her reaction with a smile.

He mumbled something she didn't catch and turned away.

As she left she could think of nothing else to say except, "I thank you for the cloth." She didn't want to go below just yet, and so put the cloth in her apron pocket, leaned back against the rail, and watched several tars adjusting the sails above her. Among the foremast's rigging hung two canvas sacks, each containing a hindquarter of beef. Nearby, a boy of about fifteen in a Monmouth cap applied a coat of tar to a coil of hemp rope.

Squinting against the morning sun, Deborah turned to look at the river. Gravesend, the last town along the Thames, was up ahead, and beyond that the open sea.

"Damn me!" the young sailor exclaimed. He held one of his hands, which he had burned with tar.

Deborah rushed over. "Be still," she said, taking his hand and examining it. "'Tain't a bad burn, but stay and I'll bring you a poultice."

The boy didn't answer. He pulled his hand away and stared at the deck.

She climbed down to her quarters and took fresh comfrey root and a mortar and pestle from her trunk. Quickly, she returned to the galley and asked the cook, "Might you have some warm water?" He looked at her as if irritated by another intrusion. "That I might make a poultice for a burn."

"Aye," he said finally. He ladled water over the black roots in the mortar and stood by as she mashed the comfrey into a grey, clammy paste.

She thanked him, left the galley, and squatted next to the boy. "Give me your handkerchief." She used the pestle to spread the comfrey onto his cloth, then positioned the paste against his palm. "Your first voyage?" she asked, as she tied the handkerchief.

"Second," he answered defensively.

"My father burned his hand like this." She smiled at him. "More than once."

His features softened and he allowed himself a small smile.

"There now." She pulled on the knot to be sure it would hold well, but not too tightly. "I'll change it when it dries. 'Tain't such a bad burn. You'll scarcely notice it soon enough."

The boy lowered his head, apparently embarrassed that some of the crew had stopped to watch them. He picked up another rope.

"Back to it, ye lazy skulking sons of bitches!" the captain cursed, shocking and startling Deborah, who hadn't realized he was behind her. "Well, well," he said sarcastically as she whirled about, "you ought to have told me you were a Doctor of Physic. Then I'd have charged you but eight guineas to cross. Aye," he continued in the face of her nonplused expression, "'tis a boon to have a person of your skill aboard. Only slavers get the physicians." He snickered.

Deborah glared at him, angry and flustered at being spoken to with derision. "I should think you would be truly grateful for the help. Indeed," she added, mocking him, "mayhap I will take back that one guinea."

He surprised her with a loud guffaw. "You hear that gents, she wants back her coin. Why do you not ask your friend? How 'bout it, Jake. You think she's worth a guinea?"

Deborah reddened and clenched her hands into fists.

The captain laughed. "Have I trodden upon your honor? What a pity, and with no one about to defend it."

She looked toward the mainmast where her quartermates and their servant watched. Mrs. Moore especially eyed her with disapproval. Charity seemed as if she didn't know what to think. Deborah glanced about at the crew. Many stood watching with smiles on their faces, enjoying the scene. Jake stared at his rope. The cook stood in front of the galley, expressionless. There is no way out of this except to continue, she thought, composing herself.

"Methinks you are in the right, Captain, for no one steps forward. Though how could they when you would but gather your might and your mates to pitch them overboard, dare they try. Thusly am I left to my own defense. And so I say, Captain, that I have served you and your crew by tending an injured member, and I will continue to do so if I am needed. That being the case, I deserve your gratitude and not the abuse you have heaped upon me. I might add, sir, that you may believe you have won this day, but truly you are undone. For you have shown yourself to be a bully. Good day."

She gathered her skirts, walked the five paces to her quarters ladder, and descended it.

When she reached the bottom, her composure vanished and she collapsed next to her trunk. "Granna you were wrong, wrong," she cried, hitting the lid with her fist. "'Twill be just the same for us in the New World."

"Child," the voice of a familiar spirit said as it appeared, "I cannot continue to visit."

"Granna," Deborah whispered to the image, "are you really here?"

The old woman shrugged. "What doth it matter? Listen, for I shan't remain long. I own 'tis a hazardous road we walk, but 'tain't all 'tis. You recall when Mrs. Jones lay at her death, frighted beyond all that she would burn in hellfire? Do you recall how you held her hand and talked to her, as if she were trapped up a tree too frighted to come down and save herself? Too frighted to let go of this life."

Deborah nodded. Mrs. Jones had clutched her hand so tightly it hurt. Her huge, terror-filled eyes, begging for comfort, fixed on Deborah's. So Deborah laid her hand on the old woman's cheek and spoke of love, of a mother's arms waiting to receive her, of a tired, ill body soon to be at rest. There is no hell, she said, only a painless, purifying fire for the soul. Then she tried the reason that always had worked for her. Why should an all-powerful god have need to send you to torment? To what end was that? It sounded more like the revenge of a human than the wish of a god. Mrs. Jones blinked, then blinked again, and Deborah asked if she could tell her what she believed, and the old woman nodded, looking up at the ceiling. Deborah spoke of all creation as one body, thus no one is ever alone. She said she believed Mrs. Jones would go to the Mother's cauldron and be purified, then await her next life surrounded by family and friends on the Isle of Apples. Mrs. Jones smiled at the ceiling and let go of Deborah's hand. "Oh," she said, then she was gone.

Gazing at Granna's image, Deborah said, "I remember Mrs. Jones."

"There will be more of that, child, in your life. You dip your hands into Brigid's well itself and bring those waters to the world. You cannot turn away from that, and I know you will not. Do you remember how you felt after you helped Mrs. Jones go in peace?"

Deborah smiled.

"A life lived in awe," Granna said, just before she vanished. "Who should not desire that?"

Deborah stared at the place where her grandmother had been, sensing she might never see her again. Not till the Isle of Apples. From her trunk she took out the book Granna had given her. Deborah had watched her make covers for other books. To make this one, she would have pounded raggy linen and plant matter to break it down, then boiled it in a cauldron for several hours. After washing the pulp, she would have beaten it again, added green dye, then woven in pieces of silver thread into a pattern that looked like the night sky. Finally, after forming the paper with a mold and letting it dry, she would have sewn and glued the green sky with silver stars onto a stiff piece of sailcloth to form the cover.

Deborah pressed it against her belly, trying to feel her grandmother. Tears fell on the book and rolled down. The cover absorbed them nearly without trace.

She glanced up at the ladder and thought of the captain's attempt to humiliate her. Then she smiled, remembering how she had come to her own defense. She clutched the book and pictured Mrs. Jones, her eyes blinking away terror as if it were dust. Might I simply blink the captain away? she wondered. He hath clearly fixed on me as one to torment. How might I dismiss him? She started to pace the room. I will keep a good distance between us on all occasions, if I might, and turn a deaf ear to his derisive banter. And this above all, she decided, I will endeavor to be not hooked on the line if he again tosses it for me.

3

EEP IT for your quarters," the cook told Deborah when she attempted to return the cleaning rag. "You'll have occasion to make use of it, to be sure." She nodded and turned to leave. "Tell me," he said, before she had reached the sailcloth door, "what is your name, so I'll know how to call you?"

She turned to face him. "Deborah Smith."

"My name is Richard Massey."

He was younger than she had thought him at first glance, little older than she, about twenty. His short, wavy hair was light brown, his eyes almost the same hue. His skin—which had led her to think him older—was thick and tanned. "Metal-colored," her father would have said.

"You're kinder than most," Richard said. "Most folks look the other way like you done, then never look back." He picked up his limp left arm and dropped it against his side. "The Devil's arm, they say."

"I dare say not," she retorted. "Methinks the Devil hath no more interest in the left than he doth in the right."

"You think so? I might well agree with you." He smiled, then looked down, seeming boyish and shy.

Again she started to leave. "Don't go," he said. "I was about to make some chocolate for the captain. Might you have a sip with me?"

She glanced anxiously toward the doorway, then back at him. He *seems* a good-hearted sort, she thought. "Yes. I should like that."

Richard gave the soup another stir and put a three-legged kettle of milk and water on the fire. He handed her a stool, then leaned against a cask.

"How many years you been out to sea?" she asked.

"Seven. Five ere I lost the arm." He slapped it with his other hand and Deborah saw a small blue light flash and disappear near his left elbow. There must be life yet in that, she thought.

"'Twas caught in rigging jerked by a fierce wind. Never been of use since. Captain Hughes made me cook after that. Lost another man that night. Wind blew him into the deep."

The milk-water began to steam. Richard took out a roll of solid chocolate nearly the length of his forearm and, resting it on his lap, shaved long pieces into the liquid. Then he tossed in a few handfuls of sugar from a canvas sack.

"Hath it had any doctoring?" Deborah asked.

He frowned. "There was a surgeon aboard, a passenger, who stabbed it with his knife, then told me to strap it 'gainst my side to keep it from flailing about." He shrugged and Deborah thought she saw the arm twitch.

He picked up a cup and dipped it into the kettle, tasted the drink, then handed the cup to Deborah. She took a sip, noticing the beauty of the porcelain as she gave it back to him. He drank the rest, dipped again, and passed it back.

She held the cup against her mouth and watched him through the rising steam. "I might be able to heal your arm," she said.

"What is that?"

"My grandmother tended some of the ill in our hamlet of Hunslet. She taught me more than simply the healing of burns. I might be of help to you." She offered him the cup.

He seemed afraid to touch it. Then he snatched it, drained the contents, and put it on top of a cask.

"Shall I return on the morrow?" she pressed.

"Aye," he said suddenly, seeming to surprise himself. "Do come."

"Tomorrow then." She smiled and stood up.

As she turned to go, she picked up the cup and rolled it back and forth between her hands, playing with its weight. It was round and full with a broken-off handle, and had specks of blue against a rose-colored background. Turning it on its side, she rolled it with her palm on top of the water cask.

Richard said, "Captain Hughes broke it again' a tar's head a voyage back. Not so certain I like to keep it about, bad luck and all. But 'tis a treasure—made in China. My mother gave it to me after my first voyage."

"'Tis lovely," Deborah murmured, mesmerized by the cup, still rolling it back and forth, feeling the rough broken part bump on the surface of the cask.

"I have just thought . . . "

"What is it?" She stopped watching the cup and gave it to him.

"How shall you not be noticed by others when you arrive and leave?"

"Hmm. I must be wary. 'Tis to our advantage that the galley is tucked into one end of the ship and that the door as well faces the bow, but do keep the sailcloth down on the morrow. Thus I might stand to the side between the galley and rail and slip in when no one is watching. If ever I am seen I shall say only that I was collecting water for a remedy. All know that of me now. If we are caught I shall say I am healing you of an injury to some other part, which you might then feign."

"Let us have care and hope it doth not come to that."

"Indeed."

When Deborah returned the next day, she asked Richard to heat a small kettle of water. As soon as it boiled, she dropped in bruised comfrey root and let the decoction cook awhile before adding ribwort leaves. "When they're soft," she told him, pointing to the leaves, "remove the kettle from the fire."

After the water had cooled she took his left hand in both of hers and immersed it. The hand was like a dead fish. It slipped away from her unless she held onto it tightly; it didn't respond to her touch, though Richard bit his lip as if feeling something.

She began with the little finger, kneading from its tip to where it became hand, moved to the left into the valley, then up the fourth finger, the ring finger. Some still believed a woman had a vein or vessel which ran from her heart to her left fourth finger. A ring placed there bound her magic and claimed her heart.

Deborah rubbed each finger in the same fashion: up one side then down the other, going back and forth for more than an hour. Sometimes she saw tears in Richard's eyes. Sometimes she saw blue in the water. Both are good omens, she thought.

When she was finished, she dried his hand on her apron and gently placed it onto his lap. He looked at it, as if unsure it was his.

"I'll return tomorrow," she said, "and so on, as long as you wish."

He opened his mouth to speak, but seemed too overcome. His eyes were bloodshot and his face pained. Lowering his head, he took one of her hands and brought it to his cheek, leaning his face into it in thanks.

4

HE CAPTAIN had said they were experiencing the longest streak of fair weather ever on a trip, and standing at the rail, as she did almost every evening, Deborah believed him. How could it be much fairer? The temperature was so perfect it had no feel. The sunset was lovely as well, with varying shades of orange and red stacked like steps to a lavender sky.

There must be an island nearby, she thought, for a gull was there, bouncing on the wind before her. Its white head and black eyes darted from the sea to the ship to her. It seemed to want something. She remembered the rest of her biscuit from supper in her apron pocket, and threw a piece of it into the air. The gull swooped and caught it. She threw a few more pieces, which the gull caught, then she held the rest of it in her upstretched hand. The bird flew toward her and back, toward her and back, timidly. She began to hum, then sing to it. Most of the words were lost in the spray, but the melody went through and the bird hovered again, staring at her; music filled the space between them.

A sudden wave crashed against the ship, dashing the song. Deborah grabbed the rail to keep from falling and the biscuit dropped into the sea. The gull dove for it.

As she pulled herself up, she heard her name being called. Charity hurried toward her. "Are you harmed?" she asked.

"Nay, I think not," Deborah replied, brushing off her gown, "only more pitching and rolling." She noticed people gathering on the other side of the ship, on the quarter-deck. "What is that?" she asked.

"'Tis the reason I have come to fetch you. The captain hath invited us to witness an extraordinary event. I'faith, you shan't wish to miss it."

"To be sure," Deborah said, though she wasn't at all certain she would enjoy anything the captain would want her to see. Nevertheless, she picked up the red wool blanket she'd brought from her quarters and followed Charity. On the raised quarter-deck Captain Hughes leaned against the rail, his long hair flat and stringy with spray.

Charity accepted a hand up the ladder, but Deborah paused. She felt touched by something, a hint of movement, a shadow across the topsail. Mystery, she thought and smiled, looking toward the setting sun and the gull who hovered again, as if in its wake.

"Minton," the captain ordered, "give her assistance so we might begin." Deborah looked up at the first mate who reached down to her. She accepted his hand and climbed the seven steps.

Hughes watched her until she was settled between Charity and Mrs. Spencer, then began, "Nautical tradition holds we seamen dunk a tar at his first crossing of the 'quator, for then he hath become a true seaman. As you surely are aware, we shan't cross the line on this voyage, but the crew determine 'tis bad luck having women aboard, and adding to that two left-handed uninitiated crew..."

"Methinks 'tis we who have brought the fair weather," Deborah whispered to Charity.

"Shh," she chided.

"Hence," the captain went on, "they will dunk Jacob and Manny and wash away the Devil in the briny deep. 'Tis superstition, I grant, but great sport. Like a hanging, save no one dies. Usually, that is."

A shiver went through Deborah as she remembered the hanged woman in Wapping. I'll not dwell on that just now, she thought, and turned to watch the crew. In service only to themselves, their pace seemed decidedly more lively as they hurried about the ship, gathering accouterments. One man placed a woolen cap on top of a mop. About its wooden body another tar had tied a rope to which others were attaching items: knives, caps, flasks. The carpenter tied a kerchief, cravat-style, around its neck. They have fashioned a sea god, Deborah thought, intrigued.

When the mop was sufficiently adorned, two of the crew carried him up the ladder and leaned him against the rail near the captain. Hughes crossed his arms and moved away as if afraid of it.

"'Tis naught but a mop," Charity whispered.

"Yes," Deborah said, pretending to agree, then looked toward the foremast. A rope had been reeved through a block of wood fastened to the larboard foreyardarm. One end of the rope was held by some of the crew, while the other was tied about the abdomens of Jacob, the boy who had burned his hand, and Manny. Deborah couldn't see their faces but sensed their terror.

"Ho!" the crew shouted and up went the boys, Manny above Jacob, into the air. The crew held them there, level with the foreyard, laughing and shouting taunts. The boys flailed their arms and legs, floppy as puppets.

This is no ritual, Deborah thought angrily, but only a pretense to torment them. I must do something. After taking a deep breath and letting it out slowly, she said in her mind: With the air of thy breath and the fire of thy will, hold us in the waters of thy belly, our feet rooted in thy bountiful earth. Using her imagination, she drew a circle of protection—with pentacles in each of the four directions—around the ship. Brigid, she prayed, I invoke thee, enter this circle now. Keep these boys from harm.

The crew let go of the rope and the boys plunged belly-first into the Atlantic. Deborah held her breath.

With a shout, the crew hoisted the boys up to the yardarm again, where they coughed and kicked. Deborah started for the stairs to be closer if her help were needed, but the captain grabbed her arm.

"Remain," he said. "I assure you, they shan't be harmed."

His tone was almost kindly and she stepped back. The boys dropped again, their shrieks shrill in her ears after the water had consumed them. Finally, after a third dunking, the crew pulled them, soaked and cursing, out of the violet sea.

Captain Hughes climbed down the ladder and handed Jacob a flask of rum, then went toward his cabin below the quarter-deck. The carpenter retrieved the adorned mop and leaned it against the mainmast.

"Thrilling, was it not?" Charity asked, as she stepped down the ladder.

Deborah looked down at her. Thrilling was not the word she would have chosen. She glanced at the crew. Jacob and Manny were laughing now, taking swigs from the flask while the others gathered around. 'Twas an initiation after all, she thought. The male sex displays its mettle.

"Are you not coming?" Charity called.

"I'll be along."

Charity hurried away and caught up with her mother.

When all but the helmsman, aft of her, had left the quarter-deck, Deborah sat down on her blanket next to the edge. She disinvoked the goddess Brigid and opened the circle of protection she had drawn. The crew was seated now as well, around a candle lantern made of horn. She was too far away to hear their words, but their laughter reached her. Swirling around her like a cloak, it pulled her into memory, while the sky, ever-darkening, deepened past indigo.

She was no longer aware of her surroundings, only the movement of time going backwards, stopping finally at the night of the ritual honoring her first blood.

Granna and her four coven sisters had packed pomegranates, red apples, and cranberry bread, and were trudging with Deborah through a field of browning clover. The only light bobbed from Granna's candle lantern, making goblins of the nearby trees. Deborah would jump away in fear only to find the goblin gone the next moment.

Millicent, a widow with greying black hair which hung to her waist, caught her hand. "Are you frighted?" she asked.

"Yes," Deborah admitted.

Millicent pulled her off to the side. "You have naught to fear, Deborah. Tonight, we will give you gifts. We'll tell you what you must remember, and we'll sing and dance. 'Tis your first blood. We must teach you about male callers and how to ease the pain the blood sometimes brings."

"Might we sing the spiraling song?" Deborah asked.

Millicent squeezed her hand and they began, their voices uncertain at first, taking some time to find the melody, to allow the notes and words to connect with deep feeling for this moment, this rite of passage for a girl who was becoming a woman.

> "Life and death and birth we go
> dancing the spiral 'round.
> Death and life renewed again
> the spiral shall never end.

Circle of life
We are thee.
Spiraling 'round
We are thee.
Life unending
We are thee."

The other women joined in, taking hands to form a circle, singing the verse again and again, and then beginning the dance. They swayed toward each other and back, moving from the hips, their shoulders loose, heads rocking, eyes closed. They danced clockwise, slowly, invoking with their song and movement a place that was sacred and safe. A place for magic.

Granna let go of Deborah's hand and nudged her toward the center. Deborah didn't know what to do, then stretched her arms out to the side and let the music move her. Her body was tingling and warm. Her heart pounded out the beat of her steps as she danced. She raised her arms over her head, her fingers outstretched, reaching for the new moon. Then with a charge through her body she would never forget, she felt for the first time the subtle, shimmering connection, like a spider web, among all living things.

She dropped to the ground and the song lowered to a whisper like decreasing rain. Granna stepped forward, wrapped a red wool blanket around Deborah, and kissed the top of her head. "Welcome sister, daughter of my daughter. Welcome to the circle. This blanket shall protect you. Thou art loved."

Oh, Granna, Deborah thought, suddenly aware of herself sitting on the blanket on the quarter-deck. Can you really be gone? She looked down and stroked the blanket's red wool.

A hoarse voice intruded. "Why do you not go o'er? To be sure the crew shouldn't mind."

Deborah got to her feet as quickly as she could and moved away from the captain, who was climbing unsteadily up the quarter-deck ladder. He stopped at the top, blocking it.

"I should think one such as yourself should not wish to witness such unchristian acts, tippling and idolatry." His words were slurred.

Deborah didn't respond. She didn't want to say anything to antagonize him, for it seemed to her that he had been tippling as well in his cabin.

He gestured behind him toward the crew. "That mop they adorned is a demon, you know, from heathen times. The fools used a demon to cast out his brother." The captain's grip slipped and he almost fell backwards.

Deborah feigned a light voice. "Captain, methinks you mistake their meaning. The crew only makes merry. 'Tis nearly the first in these weeks that I have seen them idle."

Instantly she knew that wasn't the right thing to say. He stepped toward her and growled, "And how spend they such time as I give? With idolatry!" He looked at her piercingly, then glanced away as if he'd seen something that repulsed him. "You are in on it as well." He staggered back down the ladder.

Deborah watched him go, but his look stayed with her. The wind was cold now and she shivered. She wrapped her blanket around her and watched the crew, still sitting around the lantern telling tales. There seemed nothing left to do. She climbed down the stairs to the main deck, crossed toward the bow, and went down the ladder to her room, hoping her quartermates were asleep.

For hours she lay awake in her hammock, replaying the scenes: Jacob and Manny hitting the water, and their later acceptance as tars, and as men. Then the captain's look of repulsion. She could tolerate his rudeness, but his inconsistency disturbed her. He was surely the rogue, but he had a bit of the pious as well. He had understood the mop represented something more. And he knew she understood as well. The thought evoked panic.

All shall be well, she tried to convince herself. He was in drink—he'll not remember it on the morrow. But he's in the right, she heard her mother's voice say inside her head. Your deities are really demons.

Be still! Deborah commanded the voice. You are wrong.

Her throat caught. It did not used to be this way, she thought. It did not used to be. The air was dense, choking her. She had to get out. She slipped off the hammock.

After grabbing her blanket and Granna's book, she climbed the ladder. As she neared the top, her eyes level with the main deck, she looked for the right place. There it was. The lifeboat just a few paces away. She glanced around for the tar who was supposed to be on his watch and saw him passed out against the larboard rail. She tiptoed to the boat and got in. A piece of sailcloth beneath her, she lay on her back, and looked up at the moon.

The May air felt luxurious again, with just enough chill to warrant the warmth of her blanket. The masts were like trees: tall, swaying, angled as if in conversation. She closed her eyes and saw the same night sky the cover of her book depicted. Then a woman dressed in green was beckoning her through violet gates. Deborah followed her and began to spin in a vortex with other women, some familiar and some not. There was Granna planting in her garden; a hooded woman on her knees in a cave, wailing; a young woman gathering herbs while her mother waited in a clearing; a hundred women joining hands and jumping off a cliff with a city burning behind them; an old woman walking to a pyre, hands bound, jerking away from those grabbing at her.

Still spinning, Deborah realized she was only a small part of what always had been. But she was a part of it—this was her lineage. She felt overcome with joy and reached out to the women around her, but they vanished. Then she saw an older woman running, being pursued through unfamiliar woods. No! she shouted, realizing it was herself. The image disappeared but left a feeling of terror. She was flying and falling at the same time, end over end, and side over side. She knew her fear was justified. She understood she was being warned. "I must have care," she said, and the vision ended.

Deborah gradually became aware of herself in the lifeboat. She felt her feet crammed into leather shoes too small for her. The tree-like masts swayed above. The smell of fish filled the air. She breathed in deeply, happily. It is sweet, she thought, as she climbed out of the boat. It is real.

5

HEY SMELLED LAND before they saw it—the New World's sweet perfume—pine, spruce, and balsam. Lured by the aroma, passenger and crew left whatever they were doing and stood at the rail. Even Captain Hughes seemed moved, though surely he had experienced this many times before: the strong scent of forest, like that just after a rain, while they were still many miles out.

Deborah recognized the opportunity and hurried to the galley. She checked to be sure no one was watching, then ducked behind the sailcloth. Richard was in the back of the room, his left arm chest-high on stacked wooden boxes. A look of despair crossed his face when he saw her, and he reached with his other hand to remove the arm.

"No," she said, understanding that he was frustrated. "Attempt it again. I know you can raise it."

He frowned, but put his arm back on the boxes. His brow furrowed, the veins in his neck stood out, and the arm began to rise, slowly, a few inches. It hung there, suspended as if by string, then dropped. He winced as it hit the box.

"Pain is the best mark of all," she said.

He brought the arm to his side and scowled at the floor.

"You can move it," she said. "One month before you could not." He was still staring at the floor, sullenly, but also seemed afraid. "What troubles you?" she asked.

He looked at her. "At the first movement of my arm weeks ago, I decided to desert this ship when we landed at Philadelphia. I thought I should be well by now. But we turn up the Delaware River in a matter of days. There's little time."

"You can go if you wish it," she said. "No longer do you need me. Move the arm about every day as I have taught you and it shall improve." He eyed her suspiciously. "It shall," she insisted. "In one year's time you shall be well."

"One year?" He cradled his arm and stared at it.

Deborah listened to the creaking of the wooden walls, sensing he had more to say. Finally, he raised his head and asked, "How have you done this?"

She swallowed. "I listened to my hands."

"I have heard of those like you."

Deborah leaned back against the cask and waited for the ostracizing look which had burned hatred in her mother for the Old Religion and its rituals. The look which said: You may heal me, but then be gone. Which said, I loathe and fear you because I do not understand. To which Granna had sometimes replied, "You once did."

"Deborah." Richard reached out and took her hand.

This was not what she expected. A warm, heavy sensation in her chest moved down. His eyes fixed on her, seeming for the moment to be her own.

"I shan't e'er be able to thank you."

She couldn't believe what was happening—her heart was beating fast, and her sex . . .

Richard brought her hand to his mouth and kissed it. "Come with me, Deborah."

"What?"

"I do need you. As my wife."

"Wife?" She stared at him, disbelieving.

"I know this is of a sudden, for I have hid my feeling well. I do love you, Deborah."

He is grateful is all, she thought. Granna told me this might occur.

"You know naught about the man you will marry. He could be a scoundrel." Richard grimaced. "Pray forgive me for I ought not use fright to win you. There's just so little time and . . . Do you share any of my same feeling?"

Deborah turned aside and leaned against her arms on another cask. Why wasn't she saying what she knew she should? That his sentiment was common enough. That she could not return it. She rubbed her forehead with her palm. Talk to him, she told herself. Tell him the truth. She faced him again. "I own I feel—I do not know what 'tis I feel."

He stepped closer.

"No," she said. "I cannot go with you."

"Do you trouble yourself about the money paid for your passage? For I vow that I will repay every guinea."

"That is not the reason in the main." She took a long breath to clear her thoughts. "I have never healed anyone before as I have you. To be sure, I have healed scratches and cuts and burns, and I have assisted at births, and there was one death. . . ." Healing Richard, she realized suddenly, had been inevitable, as was this journey. She was being guided. She had a destiny to fulfill. She went over to a stool and sat down.

"Richard," she said, "since I was a child my grandmother hath told me I am a healer, and I wished to believe her. I agreed to this journey because . . . because 'twas her final wish. And though I left, I did doubt her. I wondered how she could be certain of what lay so deep inside me. So deep I didn't see it. I was afeared she was wrong about me. And I was afeared she was right. Do you not see? She was not wrong. I am a healer. I am a daughter of Brigid, goddess of poetry, smithcraft, and healing. My life is not fully my own." She paused, feeling the weight of what she had said, feeling the burden and opportunity.

Richard hit the top of a cask. "How do you not know 'twasn't this Brigid who put me into your path? How do you know you are not destined to leave with me?"

"I know my Granna was in the right," she said softly. "I must continue to follow what she set for me."

"But why are you not permitted to choose your own mate? You're not some damned queen or lady. You're a commoner, like me. You ought to be able to choose."

This point reached its mark and she had no easy reply. No one she knew had an arranged marriage. She realized she was supposed to feel pleased about it, that it meant she truly was rising in station, but Richard was right. She wasn't pleased. She was merely bowing to what her mother and grandmother wanted. And yet, she argued the other side of the matter, mayhap 'tis my mother's view that I ought to be grateful for the rise in station, but that was not Granna's. She sent me hither so that our line might survive. I must continue to walk forward. I must not turn aside.

"I see the answer in your face," he said. "I'll not press you further."

Deborah got up and took his left hand and clasped it in both of hers. "You shall have a good life, Richard Massey, you may be sure. And if you desire it, you will desert this ship at Philadelphia." She smiled warmly at him.

He returned her smile with a wan half-grin. "When you look at me like that, how can I despair? I will leave at Philadelphia, and I will remain fore'er grateful to you."

"And I to you, for what I have learned from your healing." They held each other's gaze, then she said, "May I ask how you will leave the ship?"

"The captain will send me for provisions, as is his wont. And I shall make my way northward to Providence, where my sister resides."

"But how shall you manage it?" She imagined him without means and alone, the captain's men hunting him down.

"I know a widow who owns an inn. I'll go to her for a bed and a loan. She will hide me till the *Willow* sets sail."

"Oh." Deborah let go of his hand. "Can you not ask for your pay from the captain and be gone ere they know it and come after you?"

He shook his head. "A seaman ne'er gets his pay ere the end of a voyage, sometimes longer. The bloody cheap masters try to halt desertion, but to no avail. I shan't have my pay, but I shall have the bit of change he gives me for provisions." He glanced down at her hand which had recently held his. "I fear I have told you more than you wished to know."

"I have no call," she said, and headed for the sailcloth door. He followed her and caught her arm. She turned slowly to face him. As she reached up to touch his shoulder, he bent down to her.

"I'll ne'er forget you, Deborah," he said just before they kissed.

6

AN YOU believe it?" Charity asked as she put an arm around Deborah at the rail. "We have been on the Delaware nearly three days. Soon we shall be at Philadelphia."

"Yes," Deborah said, facing her, "and I feel curiously sad about it as well."

Charity smiled. "In truth, I feel the same. How can it be I was in England not long ago, and now I stand here with you whom I know not truly, and very soon you will be gone to your betrothed, and I shall be also in the New World, but very far away."

"'Tis something about the travel," Deborah said. "I know not whether I have the words, but methinks we are meant to move by walking, and the world is ordered around that speed. Carriages and ships change that order, so we run along as if trying to catch the conveyance. Yet we cannot truly. Thus we feel odd for a time, somehow left behind."

"Yes," Charity said. "That is why I am weary after a ride in the carriage. I never understand it, since 'tis the horses who pull, but 'tis this. We feel the ride as if we had walked ourselves, because 'tis proper and right that we do. But what of this travel from one world to another?" Charity raised her eyebrows. "Shall we *ever* recover?"

They both laughed, then Deborah said, "We must. Methinks 'tis our daily work that puts us to right. A few weeks of churning and spinning and we shall again be just as we ought."

"To be sure," Charity said. "Though I have not missed those chores on this journey."

"Nor have I."

"Ah!" Charity exclaimed, squeezing Deborah's waist. "There 'tis."

Deborah watched as the town of Philadelphia came gradually into view. She was surprised to see such a thriving seaport. The city looked like a giant millipede at the edge of the river, with its leg-like piers reaching into it. As they neared their destination, High Street Wharf, she could distinguish people working amidst the warehouses and docks. Their activity disquieted her, and she understood then what had drawn her father again and again to the sea: its solitude was precious and its spirit palpable.

The ship approached the wet wooden posts of the wharf. Deborah noticed a girl of about fourteen standing just outside the flurry of dock workers. She wore a dark blue gown and a white apron. She held a basket and was staring at Deborah. The *Willow* docked with a dull thud and a long deep scraping sound which scattered gulls from the posts.

The girl reached into her basket and took out a foot-long fish that flashed rainbows as it flapped slowly in her hands. She held the almost-dead fish over her head for a few moments, then threw it into the water. After wiping her hands on her apron, she saluted Deborah and ran quickly away.

For some moments Deborah stood dazed, uncomprehending. She didn't notice some of the crew behind her, lifting the wooden covering of the cargo hatch, or that Charity was no longer beside her. But soon the pungent odors of fish, tar, and brine brought her back.

She glanced toward the gangway and started. Richard was bowing to the captain. He is leaving! she thought. This is my opportunity.

She forgot about the girl on the dock and hurried toward them, calling, "Cook, oh, Cook! You are going to town? By your leave, Captain." She pushed her way between them. "I wish to ask the cook if he might purchase paper for me in town. I have exhausted my supply." She pulled a bundle out of her apron pocket. "Here is a note with specific directions as to correct shade and stock." She tried to push the note and coins into Richard's reluctant hand. "I trust this shall suffice."

"Really," he protested, "I should be pleased to purchase paper for you, but I shall collect after, when I know what to charge."

"Not another word on it. Methinks this shall be pretty near the mark. No cause for you to put out your own pence or the captain's on my account." Their eyes met, and she handed him the money.

Captain Hughes turned and bellowed at the crew, "You fat-gutted chuckleheads! You can do naught without me!" He rushed away with three other men to stop a cask rolling down the deck. "Grant, secure that rope, I told you. Come hither, you whorin' knave."

"I would rather have you than your money," Richard said to Deborah, "but I thank you." He put the coins and her note into his pouch.

"I wish I had more of it to give you."

"You have given me more than anyone else e'er. You have sprung me from my cage. I have naught to give you in return, but I do desire you to have this." He pulled out the porcelain cup from under his cloak. "'Tis all I dared bring with me. Keep it, to remember me."

Deborah took the cup and rolled it back and forth between her hands. She still loved the balance of its weight. When she looked up, Richard said, "Farewell, Deborah."

"Farewell." She blinked back tears.

He gave her one last long look of love and gratitude, then walked down the gangplank. When he stepped onto the dock, his pace quickened. Deborah watched as he grew smaller and less distinct, becoming at last just another fleck of color among the crowd at High Street Wharf.

"Go below now." The captain had returned.

With feigned casualness, she brought the cup to her side and took a step back from him.

He ran his fingers through his hair. "'Tis dangerous on deck. Go below whilst we break bulk."

Deborah nodded and turned away, walking slowly toward the hatch.

As the captain had ordered, the women remained in their quarters while the ship was unloaded and reloaded, then they went topside again that evening. No one said anything to them about Richard's desertion, but Deborah saw the crew whispering about it as she sat with her quartermates eating salt pork and bread.

When they had finished their meal, the first mate, Minton, walked up and stood in front of Deborah, his bulk blocking the setting sun. "The captain wishes to see you, in his cabin."

"Me?" she asked, giving the women a quizzical look to hide the anxiety she felt. She followed the mate through the doorway of the quarter-deck, past the pantry and parlor, to the open door of the captain's cabin, where she hesitated.

"Come hither," Hughes called.

With a quick glance at Minton, who was walking away, she stepped just inside. The cabin was small but bright. Hughes sat at a mahogany table with a map on it, covered with glass. A porthole above the table admitted the last of the sun. Behind him a set of built-in shelves with a raised lip bore books and ivory and jade figurines. Deborah wondered why the figurines were pushed together.

"Sit." He motioned to a stool across the table from him.

"I wish to stand, if you please."

The captain's face reddened. He stood up and looked out the porthole. "We believe the cook hath deserted the ship." He whirled around to catch her reaction.

"That scoundrel!" she said with convincing indignation. "And with my coins, no less." Before he had a chance to respond she added, "Why, I hope you're looking for him."

Hughes walked to the shelves and picked up a jade elephant. "We're looking. 'Tis a pity you did not listen to his protest about taking your pence. Makes him less the rascal, doth it not?" He put the elephant back and turned toward her again. "Jake's hand hath healed well. There's nary a scar. You *are* quite the physic, now, are you not?"

Deborah blinked. "Like many women, I learned about the healing herbs from my mother."

"Ah, yes." Hughes faced the shelf again. Behind another carved elephant, he pulled out the porcelain cup Richard had given her.

Deborah's breath caught, and he smiled at her astonishment and fright. He walked toward her holding the cup before him. Deborah backed into the doorpost.

"Minton found this when he searched your quarters during supper. You didn't see him, did you? He's nearly as slippery as you, ducking in and out of the galley. Ah, but I run ahead of myself. When Minton showed me the cup I must say I asked myself why he should give you such a treasured piece. Then I thought, 'Mayhap in payment.' That is it, is it not?" He dropped the cup to the floor and it rolled toward the threshold. "Minton hath seen the cook move his injured arm. You healed him and helped him to desert."

Deborah turned to go, but Hughes rushed forward and grabbed both her arms and shook her. "Witch," he smirked, "what spell shall save you now?" He pulled her against him and kissed her violently on the mouth.

She struggled to get away but the captain held her tightly. Then he reached down and grabbed her buttocks with both hands. She screamed, and using all of her strength and flexibility, twisted out of his grasp. He went for her again, but tripped on the cup and fell into her instead. She brought up her knee and hit him hard in the groin. He went down. She grabbed the cup and ran, passing Minton who stood just outside on the deck. His laughter followed her as she crossed to the bow.

She hurried down the ladder to her quarters, halting part-way and forcing herself to climb slowly, to conceal what had happened. At the bottom, she looked around. Her quartermates were readying themselves for bed and only Charity glanced at her for a moment. Deborah wanted to run to her, put her head in her lap and cry, but she denied the urge and went to her trunk instead. Blocking her quartermates' view with her body, she took out her knife, unsheathed it, and placed it under her pillow. Then she climbed into her hammock and sat, willing herself to calm down, her eyes not moving from the ladder. After a few minutes she was reasonably certain he wouldn't come after her, so she lay on her side facing the entrance, her hand under the pillow, gripping the knife. Eventually she fell asleep.

"What?" she called out and sat up, her knife raised. The room was silent. Everyone seemed to be sleeping. Nothing was amiss. She lay down again and closed her eyes. A woman's bloody face appeared.

No! Deborah thought, and sat up again. No. The knife still under her pillow, she put her face in her hands but could not banish the image, the same that she'd seen in her dream in London. The woman's face was clear now, insistent. She had long, greying black hair. I don't wish to remember it again, Deborah cried. Pray not . . .

I do remember. I remember trees and the river and the warm June day. I was fifteen, lying on my back, watching the trees form a cone above me.

The sunlight flickered through the leaves like thousands of fireflies, lighting the clearing in the grove. My grove.

I could hear the River Aire through the trees, but I could not see it. I remember. I wore my yellow broadcloth gown with no stockings. The grasses were cool and soft on my legs. I lay beneath an old oak with one of its roots under my head. Then I heard something. Human voices, hostile, accusing, growing louder. I leapt up and ran to shelter among my trees.

Four men half-dragged, half-carried an older woman into the clearing, while a fifth man walked behind. They threw her on the ground and her head struck the base of the old oak with a loud deep thunk. The sound echoed up the tree, shaking the leaves. Deborah bit her tongue until it bled.

"What will we do with her now?" one of the men asked.

"Toss the witch in the water. That's what you do with them, I say," replied the largest man.

"Then her body will float, be found. Let us leave her to the wood. Nature created her, let she dispose of her."

"No."

They all glared at the man who had spoken. He cowered a little, then said, "'Tis wrong what we've done."

"Wrong, Jeremiah? She's the one done wrong. You saw Hester's babe, face crushed, only one arm."

"We do not know 'twas her doing."

"She birthed him, did she not? Birthed and bewitched him."

"Mayhap Hester had a fall. 'Tis happened in this way before."

"What folly is this?" The large man peered into Jeremiah's eyes. "Mayhap you've a bit of the Devil as well. Shall we check you for his marks?" He grabbed his arm.

Two others pulled him away. "Come along," one said. "Let us take our leave. Naught can save her now."

They walked out of the clearing in a line, without looking again at the old woman lying at the base of the oak tree, or at Jeremiah who stared at her.

When they were gone, Deborah dashed from her hiding place and knelt next to the woman. "Millicent," she pleaded. "Millicent. Wake up." She stroked the woman's hair which was just beginning to mat with blood. Seeing it on her own hands, she became enraged. She bit into the seam of her thin cotton apron and tore the garment into strips of cloth which she tied around Millicent's head.

"I did not know," Jeremiah whispered, "I did not know we would do this."

Deborah glared at him. "Have haste and help me. We can tend to her, carry her to my grandmother. Hand me that wood."

Jeremiah put his hand on her shoulder. "Child, she is gone."

Deborah shook off his hand and looked at Millicent. Her eyes were vacant and staring. Fighting tears, Deborah said, "I shan't just leave her here. Give me that wood."

With two branches and Jeremiah's cloak, they fashioned a stretcher and lifted Millicent onto it. Deborah walked backward over the narrow path. Jeremiah's eyes darted back and forth from the old woman to the path. Millicent's limp hands hung over the sides of the stretcher, palms up.

Now in the darkness of her quarters, Deborah gasped for air, feeling a hollow space like a cavern in her chest. She imagined the captain standing over Millicent and laughing. "Witch! Witch!" she heard him accuse.

The image made her body shake and her chest heave. She panicked, struggling for air in the midst of too much air. She pressed her face into her pillow, held it over her nose and mouth. Take the breath slowly, she commanded herself. Breathe, breathe.

By degrees, her body settled and her breath calmed. She took the blunt wooden end of her knife and pressed it into her solar plexus to feel something there. Millicent. She remembered holding her hand during the first blood ritual, the two of them singing, dancing.

Tears came then, light as mist. The drizzle grew slowly to a downpour which fell onto parched brown earth. In the earth were seeds that waited to grow. Deborah saw the seeds hidden from light in the cavern in her chest. She saw them but felt utterly alone.

7

HE RIVER was quiet, the only sound the flitting calls of swallows and robins as the vessel glided calmly up the Delaware. It moved so slowly it seemed to be scraping the river bottom. Charity wondered aloud how deep the water was.

Captain Hughes laughed loudly behind her and Deborah. "No need to trouble thyself about it," he said. "Deeper hulls than the *Willow's* have landed at Burlington City." He pointed to Deborah's trunk by her feet. "You planning to desert, as did your friend?"

Her hands shook but she glared back at the captain's angry, mocking eyes. "Methinks only those who are ill-treated should desire to leave."

"Hmph," he grunted, and moved away.

Deborah turned toward the river again, vowing to keep track of him out of the corner of her eye. I have only minutes left on this voyage, she thought. I'll not be trapped again.

They rounded a bend in the river, and up ahead their path appeared to be blocked. A large island nearly spanned the Delaware.

"There she be!" the captain called.

"There she be?" Charity asked.

It was another minute before they saw the outskirts of town: a row of brick houses and a road lining the river. Charity put an arm around Deborah. "Burlington," she said, "at last." She squeezed her waist and laughed. "Mind you, be wary of those unclothed Quakers."

Deborah laughed and put her arm around Charity's waist as well. Am I truly here? she wondered. Is this really Burlington?

A flash of blue light caught her eye, and she watched as it faded on the trunk of an enormous sycamore growing by the bank of the river.

"An ancient tree," Charity said.

"Aye," agreed the captain, who'd returned. Deborah moved still closer to Charity and did not turn around. "'Tis the one which first moored the *Shield* from Hull. A mighty tree, is it not?"

More than mighty, Deborah thought, watching its lobed leaves bounce in the wind.

The ship glided on toward the dock, bouncing gently against its posts, and Deborah looked around for someone who might be Japhet. He didn't seem to be there. The men at Town-Wharf busied themselves with cargo to load or other tasks and were paying no attention to her. Seeing that the captain was occupied with the crew, she said good-bye to Charity with a kiss on her cheek, sad to be leaving her.

"I am loathe to say farewell," Charity said, smoothing back Deborah's hair. "For I know we shan't meet again. God be with you and keep you." She had tears in her eyes.

"I thank you, Charity, for your good company these weeks. Farewell."

They kissed cheeks again, and Deborah pulled herself away, calling to one of the tars to help her. She followed him down onto the dock, then to a grassy area beside it where he set her trunk. As she watched the tar hurry back aboard, she tried not to panic. Japhet Leeds will be along presently, she told herself. To be sure, word of our arrival went out as soon as we were sighted.

She looked toward the ship again, hoping to see Charity, but she wasn't at the rail. The *Willow* seemed forlorn, rocking gently against the pier. Suddenly she felt dizzy and nauseated. She sat on her trunk and put her head in her hands.

After awhile, something wet and warm touched her forearm. She jerked up her head. A yellowish brown dog was nosing her. "Well, hello, old boy." She petted the hound between the ears.

"Yonder, hast thou found her?" A young man was walking toward her, his stride smooth and graceful.

"Mr. Leeds?" she asked.

The man reached her and offered his hand to help her up. She hesitated, staggered by the realization that after all she had been through, this was Japhet Leeds, the man she had agreed to marry.

He laughed nervously, obviously taken aback by her expression, but said in a light tone, "Come now, I am not so terrible, am I?"

The veil of his jocularity was thin, and she saw him there behind it: a gentle man, kind and eager to please. The sun glimmered off his chin-length, straight black hair. His grey eyes watched her, waiting. He is comely as well, she thought, then quipped, "Methinks I find you fair enough."

He grinned and offered his hand again. When she was standing, he hoisted her trunk to his shoulder and they headed toward town. Deborah walked as if still on board—her body swinging somewhat like a pendulum from side to side. She attempted to walk normally but could not.

Yonder trotted next to her, his big tongue hanging out. "Why have you named him so?" she asked, petting the dog.

Japhet stopped. "Because that is whither he goes: way yonder, hunting about for scraps . . . and wives for me."

"Well then," Deborah joked, "if you have more than one wife, you ought tell me about it, for I shan't share my home with another."

They laughed, looking at each other happily. She had hoped her new husband would be kind, but hadn't expected to like him right away. It was his easy way with her and their banter. She walked on, content.

"Mr. Leeds!" Captain Hughes shouted. He hurried toward them on stiff legs, one arm raised before him. From a distance he looked to Deborah like a wooden doll: dimunitive and breakable.

"By your leave," he said when he reached them. "Mr. Leeds, I wish to say farewell to your betrothed." He bowed and Deborah stiffened. "My dear, it hath been my pleasure. If e'er I catch that thieving cook–" He grabbed her hand and kissed it before she could pull it away. Coating her skin with his breath, he whispered, "God be with you."

Deborah yanked back her hand and spat out, "Good day, Captain," and turned away, heading toward town.

"She is firey, now, is she not?" Hughes said.

Japhet caught up with Deborah and strode in silence beside her. As she walked, she held an image of the *Willow*, spent and rocking against the dock. Suddenly nauseated and dizzy again, she reached out to steady herself with Japhet's arm. He caught her just before she fell to the dirt of Water Street.

8

EBORAH WOKE with one eye covered by a lukewarm cloth hanging halfway off her forehead. She turned to the side and watched the cloth fall onto the bed, limp and crumpled. Precisely how I feel, she thought, as she sat up to see where she was.

The room was large and painted white. The sun shone through white lace curtains onto a polished mahogany table beside the bed. She ran her fingers along the varnish—impressed by the luxury—then touched the bottom of a glass vase holding a bouquet of wildflowers.

Also on the table was a small tray bearing black bread, porridge, and tea. She leaned over and tried unsuccessfully to dip a crust into the solid mass of cold porridge. She gave up but kept the bread and chewed it slowly, letting each bite soften in her mouth.

When she was done she pulled back the quilt and walked unsteadily toward the window. Pushing it wide open, she leaned out and let the warm breeze catch her hair, which floated around her face, buoyed by the wind.

Two stories below and at a distance, villagers converged around a market in the middle of the road. From here it appeared that most of the people were dressed similarly: men in grey or snuff brown breeches, coats, and waistcoats, with cravats about their necks; women in ankle-length grey or brown gowns, some with wide-brimmed suede hats.

Deborah noticed a woman walking by, just below the window, who was singing. Her long brown hair was worn in a thick braid which bounced against her back as she walked barefoot. She was about four months pregnant.

Suddenly she paused, shading her eyes from the sun, and peered up at Deborah. Then she hastened toward the building.

Puzzled and fatigued, Deborah sat back on the bed. Steps sounded on the stairs. The door opened and a stout woman with white hair entered carrying a cloth. Behind her, the young woman she had just seen carried another tray.

"Thou art indeed about," the older woman said. "Grace said she saw thee at the window."

The woman picked up the lukewarm cloth lying on the bed and helped Deborah prop herself against the wall with pillows. Then she put the fresh cool cloth on Deborah's forehead.

The younger woman placed the tray tentatively on the bed. "I trust I didn't fright thee when I rushed so toward the door. I was startled to see thee at the window with thy hair so lovely in the wind. I thought mayhap I saw a vision, then I knew it must be thee, so I hurried hither."

Deborah smiled at Grace. "I am no vision, to be sure." She felt nauseated and closed her eyes. In her mind she saw herself standing by the wharf, someone's breath on her hand. "What did happen to me?" she asked.

"Thou fell faint," the older woman said. "Japhet Leeds says thou went down with no warning. He hath been quite bothersome with his worrying, listening to no one that thou shalt be well. Many are those coming hither whose first days are occupied with such a condition as thine."

"How long was I asleep?" Deborah removed the cloth from her forehead to check for fever. There was none.

"Only one day." The woman poured hot tea from a copper kettle. "Ah, I have yet to tell thee—I am Elizabeth Basnett, and this is my tavern. Grace Kirkbride will be a neighbor of thine."

Deborah nodded at Grace. There was something sweet but sad about her, in her eyes.

"Japhet hath taken a liking to thee a'ready," Mrs. Basnett said. "'Tis a good sign, methinks. None have seen him so perturbed since last he left Burlington."

Deborah smiled, trying to remember what he looked like. She recalled him walking toward her, his gait languid, cat-like. "Where is my betrothed?"

"I can send for him now," Mrs. Basnett offered.

"If you please, ere I lose my strength again."

Japhet followed Mrs. Basnett into the room, smiling broadly when he saw Deborah sitting up. "Thou look'st well," he began.

"I am nearly so, methinks."

"Elizabeth Basnett says 'tis expected the body might collapse after a long sea voyage."

"I must rest here a time, another day."

"Yes, thou must."

They looked at each other. The ease at their meeting seemed to be gone. What doth one say to one's future husband? she wondered.

"I'll leave you twain and see to dinner." Mrs. Basnett left the door open behind her.

They smiled at each other tentatively. I am marrying this man, she thought, and I know little about him.

He fiddled with the hem of his grey muslin coat, his eyes downcast. She had always believed she could sense the true character of a person right away. But what of the captain? she thought. Well, there have been times when my desire for one thing hath blinded me to another. Mayhap my resolve to leave obscured the captain, though I did understand to keep clear of him. And what else might I have done? Turned about and left the tavern? Pappa a'ways said shipmasters are not to be trusted. Another might have been worse. Be that as it may, though I wish it to be so, methinks this Japhet Leeds is a good man, albeit a bit nervous.

He was still worrying his coat. "I say," she tried again at conversation, "you were born here? In the New World?"

"Yes, at my father's farm just outside Burlington City."

"May I ask? Do all persons of the area use the old speech: 'thee,' and 'thou?' I knew not the custom prevailed here."

"All those who are of the Society of Friends do so. We Friends—Quakers some call us when our backs are turned—hold no person above another, thus we don't recognize the singular *you* which came into use to indicate a person of rank. Of course, we still say *you* when speaking to more than one person. As well we do not use any title when addressing another. We have been despised for this—for refusing to bow and call a man 'Lord' or 'Master,' and for calling a person by his naked Christian name."

"Indeed, I should imagine that many would take offense. But you say 'we.' I was told your father was Anglican and you lived eastward, across the colony in Leeds."

Japhet frowned and his face reddened. "My father is Anglican, but he was once a Friend, as was all my family. We dwelt here on our farm where my cousin Mary remains, till we removed to Leeds, a town in the east he was given after he surveyed the area. He was the first Surveyor-General of West Jersey, which was the name of our colony till we were united with East Jersey but two years ago."

"I was told your father hath many accomplishments."

"Yes. Yes he hath." Japhet seemed flustered suddenly and disturbed. He went to the window and looked out for awhile. Finally he faced her again. "I fear I must tell thee plain. I wish to remain here in Burlington County with thee."

"You wish to remain?"

"Yes, Burlington is the home of my youth, as is The Society of Friends. I wish to return to the Society."

Deborah leaned back against the wall, alarm creeping in. Was he saying he will betray his father?

"Thou must not trouble thyself about it. I will purchase his farm here, and I will repay him for thy passage, for he expected me to return to Leeds and assist him there with his plantation."

Deborah found no words to reply. What he proposed felt dangerous, but she was too tired to consider it. She pulled the quilt up to her neck.

"Forgive me," Japhet said, "for I see I have troubled thee despite my intentions. We will speak on it again when thou art stronger."

"Yes," she said, grateful for the reprieve. "To be sure, I shall be well on the morrow."

"I'll return then, if I may, tomorrow eve and carry thee to the farm."

"Tomorrow then," she agreed.

He left quickly, closing the door behind him.

That was my future husband, Deborah remembered, incredulous at the thought. But what of his desire to remain here near Burlington? What if his father refuses to sell the farm? Nay, I cannot think on that just now. She lay down and turned onto her side. On the morrow, she told herself. I'll think on it on the morrow.

9

EBORAH WALKED onto the flagstone porch of Basnett's Tavern the next morning and was surprised by the freedom she felt in her shoulders. She swung her arms and felt as if more constraining weight were leaving her upper body. Trepidation, she decided. Although I deigned to keep a good distance betwixt myself and the captain, I did not know I held my body stiff like armor. Nor that I required that level of protection. But I did. And though I had not foreseen his torment of me should lead to assault, my instincts had. They knew all along.

With a final, loosening swing of her arms, she stepped off the porch. In front of her the river was a bright, clear, and cloudless blue—reflecting the sky. And there in the middle of it was Burlington Island. Its banks, strangled with scrub pines, rendered the interior as impenetrable as the island itself made the river.

Deborah turned the corner onto High Street where the market house in the center of the road bustled with barter. Plainly-dressed Quakers clamored for goods, some of which had come in on the *Willow*. Clad in her flamboyant purple gown, she felt like a flower among stems and that shamed her. She crossed her arms over her chest.

"'Tis a lovely day, is it not?" A woman passed her with a nod on her way to the market.

"To be sure," Deborah replied to her back. As she started to follow her, she noticed women at the market gathered together as if to repel strangers. So she watched awhile longer from the side of the street before walking on.

Soon she came to a hexagonal building and stopped short. The white-painted wooden structure, faced with brick on the front, rose to a white spire with three small windows at its base. A low white fence surrounded the building. Deborah smiled, pleased by its odd, honeycomb shape. Whistling, she continued her walk.

After a couple of right turns she ended up back at the river again on Water Street and saw the huge, ancient sycamore. Large patches of bark had peeled off, exposing pale red wood, but the grass beneath the tree was free of debris. Reverently she approached and looked up through its branches, leaves, and ball-like seed clusters. She placed her ear against the trunk and heard a low roaring.

"Lass, go not so close. 'Tain't a tree for good Christian souls."

She turned around quickly to see a very old man sitting on a stump about twenty yards away. He leaned on a pale wooden cane and his clothes hung on him as if he'd once been much larger. She walked over to him, trying not to stare at the drooping folds of his facial skin, or at his eyes, so slit-like she couldn't tell what color they were. She had never seen anyone so old. He frowned, because of her examining gaze she supposed, so in a jolly voice she said, "Methinks that is not so. Else why should it be so well tended?"

He winked and tapped his cane. "Aye well, thou hast caught me in a falsehood a'most. 'Tis true, she is a beloved tree. I tidy up the bark myself. But she's no Christian tree, to be sure."

He motioned for her to come closer and held out his hand. "I am Isaiah Whyte. But thou need'st not trouble thyself to tell me about thee. Thou hast come to wed Japhet. It so pleases me he hath returned to Burlington. He was not yet a man when his father, Daniel Leeds, that slanderer, took him away to the swamps and barrens of the East. Poor lad, he wished to stay, pleaded to remain, but his father turned a deaf ear. Packed him up with his seven brothers and sisters and bade this town good riddance. And we him, shames me to say." Isaiah took a breath. "Daniel Leeds is a man of great power, and through his writings he hath turned many away from the Light and toward the Church of England."

"What is the Light?" Deborah asked.

"The Light of God which lives within each of us. Through the Light, the Lord speaks. Come to a meeting if thou hast desire to know more." He closed his eyes.

"I know little regarding my future husband," she said quickly to regain his attention, "only his relations in Yorkshire. They're fine folk but not Friends, though my mother did say Japhet's grandfather had been a Friend, but his father was not." She frowned. "However, no one told me I should be walking into a battle."

"Yes," Isaiah said sympathetically, opening his eyes wide.

They are the dark blue of the sea when clouds pass over, she thought.

"There's a pity in that, to be sure," he said. "But think on this: Japhet hath called on thee for help. Ere he left with his family, he came to this buttonwood and promised to return. He hath returned, God bless him, but without a helpmeet he shan't resist his father's desire that he return."

Deborah nodded her head slowly. Though she was concerned about going against the wishes of Japhet's father, she had decided—upon waking this morning, or perhaps when she first saw this tree from the ship—that she wanted to remain in Burlington.

Isaiah passed the cane to his other hand as though confirming her decision.

Deborah looked quizzically at him and surmised that he had somehow understood her thoughts. She decided to test him. "I heard a roaring," she said, "when I placed my ear against the tree."

"A roaring?" Isaiah laughed. "To be sure, many folks have heard that and much more. We call her the 'Witches' Tree.' More than a few have seen crones here circling its branches."

"Here in town?"

"Aye, 'tis strange, is it not? You would put the witches a ways off from town, I understand?" He winked and tapped his cane. "In the barrens may-hap?"

"You spoke of that before. What is it?"

"The barrens are to the south and east. Thou mightst have seen them as the ship rounded the colony to enter the river. If thou wert awake." The blue of his eyes shone again for a moment.

She flushed. "Is it the knowledge of the whole of Burlington that I fell faint?"

He waved his hand between them. "I was merely poking thee in the ribs. Spend no time in worry about it, or us. We shall bring thee no harm." He paused. "Shall I tell thee about the barrens or the tree? I shan't have the strength for both." He considered. "Thy husband will tell thee about the barrens, to be sure. I will tell thee about the tree." He stretched out one leg and began.

"One morn, many a year ago, when I lay resting beneath its branches, I too heard a roaring... well, more like a buzzing it was. First I thought 'twas a mosquito, but I neither got bit nor did it cease. I opened my eyes, saw no sign of any pest and closed them again. Then I heard a low whisper. I kept my eyes closed. The whisper grew louder till I heard my own name within it. My own name the tree was saying: 'Isaiah Whyte, wake up. Listen to me, Isaiah.' I was too frighted to open my eyes but I half-whispered, half-stammered, 'I am awake, buttonwood, what hast thou to say?'

"It answered me in a loud voice, 'Isaiah, tell thy neighbors thou art to be my caretaker. And before thou art gone, thou must select another. For so long as I am tended, I will live fore'er. And so long as I live, Burlington will prosper.'

"I knew not what to think of this, but I took the tree's words to the next Friends meeting and respoke them just as I have to thee. Friends are not superstitious, but was it not agreed I would do as the tree asked. And so have a few come to me since with their own tales of the tree having spoken to them as well. So thou must see, Deborah, why I thought it not queer it would roar in thy ear." He looked toward the old sycamore; its button seed clusters bobbed in the wind. "'Tis a friend, Deborah, but not a *Friend*. She belongs to a tribe much older than we."

Isaiah clicked his tongue as Deborah helped him to his feet. "Aye, yes, 'tis very good thou hast come to Burlington." He started up the road, limping slightly. "Very good indeed."

10

Y GRANDFATHER'S second wife was a minister," Japhet told Deborah as he cut a bite of pork and ate it with his knife. "She was jailed in England for heresy as was my grandfather, Thomas Leeds, before they knew one another."

Japhet's cousin Mary nodded. "The former Margaret Collier had equal measures of daring, piety, and beauty. 'Twas a combination which drew enormous crowds when she preached, and she was jailed several times. After the fourth detainment, when she was but twenty and three, her father bade her go with him to the New World. She told me she hadn't wished to go— methinks she rather enjoyed her fame—but she feared being an orphan, having no brothers or sisters and her mother long gone, so she left with him, eventually residing in Burlington."

Deborah glanced at Japhet, sitting across the table from her. He had told her Mary was his favorite relative. And though she was only twenty-six, she was the keeper of the family's history. She loved to tell stories, and Deborah liked to hear them. With her own family so far away and Granna gone, the details of Japhet's family—soon hers—helped her feel increasingly at home.

"After the death of our grandmother," Mary continued, "our grandfather removed from Shrewsbury in East Jersey to Burlington, West Jersey, and married Margaret. Their union was the first recorded marriage of

English Friends here, and it hearkened an era of new hope. It proved the Society did exist, that we might have families and communities, that we might live in peace."

Mary looked at her cousin. "My Uncle Daniel, Japhet's father, never recovered from the death of his mother—my grandfather's first wife. He seemed even to blame her for it, for in some manner his grief turned to spite. He speaks falsely in that tract of his, 'News from a Trumpet Sounding in the Wilderness,' that his mother, a Friend, forced him to get off his knees and renounce Christ. 'Tis a ludicrous accusation—for we are Christian as well—and one which made him many an enemy."

"If I may be so bold as to inquire," Deborah asked, "if he is thus opposed to the Society, how is it you have come to tend his land?"

"Someone must," Mary said. "He didn't wish to sell the farm, and he trusted few others. As well, 'twas a favor to my father, who of late had become an Anglican, sold his holdings here and bought land near Leeds, very close to Japhet's father. All my family save for me were to remove thither at the same time as Japhet's family. I wished to remain as I was betrothed to a Friend here. My father began to worry I should be poor, since my intended did not have much means, so he asked his brother to allow me to reside upon his farm. Soon after their departure, my dearest betrothed passed on. I might have removed then, but chose to remain. The farm pleases me. I cannot imagine leaving it."

"You have a'ways resided here alone then?" Deborah asked, surprised. "And managed the farm yourself?"

Mary nodded and smiled, as if accepting the compliment. Since her arrival, Deborah had been impressed by the independence of the Quaker women she'd met. She knew of widows in England who managed their estates, her own mother included, but never a woman as young as Mary— or as winsome with her wild black hair. Uncontainable in the loose knot she wore, it frayed about her face. Mary was also quite large. Tall like Japhet, but not thin, she had the muscled build of a farmer.

"I trust we don't tire thee with the family history," Mary said.

"Oh no," Deborah protested. "Though I feel I ought mark down all the names and relations, for 'twill be some time before I remember who is who."

"Thou canst write and read then?" Mary asked.

"Yes, my family hath a'ways had the skill."

"That is most unusual." Mary raised her eyebrows.

Damn me, Deborah thought. I must have more care about what I reveal. Granna told me Brigid taught the first priestess in our family to read and write, and it was passed down.

"Thy family is most enlightened," Mary continued. "I endeavor now to help found a school for all children of the township, girls as well as boys. Very soon 'twill come to be." Deborah let out her breath, relieved. "More cider?" Mary asked. She poured at Deborah's nod.

Deborah sipped and scratched thoughtfully at the wood of the mug. "I must say, it pleases me to learn about your Society, which in the main is extraordinary. In England I once saw a woman Friend preach in the city center in Leeds, and 'twas a marvelous event." She smiled. "I own I have grown fond of Burlington a'ready. And it astonishes me how quickly I have left England and my voyage behind." She thought of Richard and wondered if he got safely to his relatives.

"'Tis very well indeed thou canst move along so quickly," Mary said. "A lifetime of mourning is a bitter life." She looked down and cleared her throat. "'Tis better, if thou canst, to fill the loss with what is new. Thy intended husband, for one." She put a hand upon her cousin's arm, then said, "If you twain are finished with your dinner, prithee go and pick whortle-berries whilst I whip up the cream."

They got up without hesitation. It was clear Mary wanted to be without company for awhile. Japhet took a pail from the corner and they stepped outside.

"'Tis sad about her betrothed," Deborah said as she raised the hem of her calico gown to cross the hay field. "You knew him?"

"Yes, he was a fine man."

"'Tis pitiable to think she may remain alone. She is strong and handsome. I should think she might have her choice of suitors."

"Some of us give our hearts but once," he said quietly.

She shot a glance at him. Was he saying what it sounded like? How could he possibly feel such affection for her already? She stumbled on a rock, and he reached out to steady her. She could feel the warmth of his hand through her sleeve. His fingers trailed down her arm and took her hand. He brought it to his lips and kissed it, looked at her with desire. She moved her hand to touch his cheek, and he bent and kissed her gently on the lips. She reached up with her other hand and spread her fingers through his shiny black hair. The pail dropped to the ground. He wrapped his arms around her and pulled her against him.

Suddenly the pressure reminded her of someone else. The captain was there, smelling of sweat and brine, moving his hands down her back. She pushed Japhet away.

He looked at her, surprised, hurt, then contrite. "Pray forgive..."

She stared at him. Japhet Leeds, she told herself. This is Japhet.

Tears filled her eyes. He stepped toward her slowly and cupped her face with his hands, his palms soft for a farmer's. "Thou art so lovely," he said and kissed her lightly, briefly on the lips.

She reached up and touched his hair again. Black gold, she thought, the way it shimmers.

"Shall we pick?" he asked. Deborah nodded.

They started again toward the berry patch. Japhet swung the pail back and forth. He is indeed fair, she thought.

"You never told me," she said, "whence came the name 'Quaker'? I know only I must not use it." She smiled in his direction.

"No, thou must not. I know not whether the story be true, but 'tis said George Fox, the founder of our sect, was standing in court telling the judge he ought quake before God for his ill usage of the Society of Friends. The judge laughed at him and said, ''Tis you who are the quaker, not I.'"

Deborah chuckled, then stifled it, not wanting to offend him. "'Tis queer enough to be true, do you not concur?"

Japhet nodded in agreement, but didn't seem to be listening. She wondered if he was thinking about his father. Would Daniel Leeds really sell them the farm? Japhet insisted he would and asked Deborah to trust him to it. Of course I will, she thought, but I cannot help but be troubled by it. They were nearing the berry patch. "Japhet, how did you come to the desire to rejoin the Friends?"

He halted and the pail banged against his knee.

"What is it?" she asked.

"The story is a bit fantastic...."

She smiled. "Then to be sure, you must tell it. Fantastic stories are the best ones."

"But what wouldst thou think if I told thee 'twas true?"

"My goodness, that frighted, wary look on your face—I warrant whatever you experienced, others have as well."

"That is precisely my concern. If I tell thee and thou believest it, then I should be adding to belief in superstition, which is a danger in the populace. Belief in fairies and haunts—we fright ourselves out of our wits, when in the main there are rational explanations. It can be e'en more vile, for belief in witchcraft alone hath caused the murder of many a poor old woman with no more magic in her than in me."

Deborah averted her shocked expression. She had never heard anyone speak like this before—to say that witches were humble innocents. But the argument also felt dangerous. If she convinced him that some were true witches with power, would he then insist they deserved to die? Would she be revealing herself? She hadn't even thought about how much, if anything, she would tell him. She could feel his eyes on her face. He must be curious, she thought, wondering what hath silenced me of a sudden. I must turn the discussion back on him.

"Doth there exist a rational explanation for your experience?" she asked.

He shook his head. "Thou hast gone to the heart of it. Only a part of it can I explain, and I know not how to think on the part I cannot."

"But are there not many things we cannot explain? 'Tis the height of arrogance and folly to deny the existence of a thing only because you cannot explain its origin."

"I might concur were it not the case that most of the populace would blame the occurrence, whate'er it may be, on the wee folk and the like."

She cocked her head. "If I do not insist the wee folk had a hand in your tale, will you tell it?"

He smiled and matched her light tone. "I will. But thou best keep to thy word." He led her to an oak tree where they sat on exposed roots. After they were settled he began, "When my father snatched me from Burlington I was like a tree without roots, naught to hold me. After I reached twenty and one, he told me I needed a wife. Since there was no one I fancied, he sent back to his relations in England.

"When we received word of thine acceptance, I packed a little more than I needed for the time I should await thee in Burlington—mayhap in some manner I knew I should stay. Mayhap my father knew this as well, for he was troubled about my living for e'en a short time amongst Friends. At the time, I entertained no notions of becoming a Friend again, so I assured him I had no such intentions. 'Twas then the truth. I had no mind for anything aside meeting thee and carrying thee back to my father's house.

"But soon after my leavetaking, my heart became troubled. I traveled alone on horseback, following the Lenni-Lenape Indian trail across the colony. I began to fear I should perish and no one would know what befell me. Every tree branch was a rogue to me. Every rock a beast. Though the trail is well marked, 'tis narrow, and I was frighted even to stop. I was amongst the trees on the edge of the barrens, they call it, where there is sand, pine, and cedar swamp."

Deborah touched his arm to signal him to pause. "Thou hast knowledge of the barrens?" he asked.

"Isaiah said you would tell me about it."

"He did? So he knew better than I. 'Twas in the northern part I traveled. 'Tis said even the Lenape do not go in amongst the trees lest it be with a hunting party and while the sun yet shines. I was thus, as I said, in a fearful state, my heart troubled as I rode along the trail, the sun close to set. I rode till light was gone and my mare began to stumble. Then I walked her a ways farther till I found a clearing in which to make a camp. I dismounted, then of a sudden the moon shone, full and round, and I was astounded. For it was as I have ne'er seen it before, large as a house and cherry red. I looked about, and though I stood on level ground, I was above the nearby trees. I found some courage and asked aloud, 'What goes here?' And a voice answered me." He paused, seemingly to gauge Deborah's reaction. She leaned closer to him.

"I know not if the voice came from the moon herself gazing upon me, or from within my own heart. There was no difference for those moments. The voice said I must remain in Burlington. That I must return to the Society, and if need be, fight for acceptance. It said thou wilt be a fair and fine wife for me. And it told me I will be called upon to speak. Of what it did not say, only that I must listen for the call."

He combed his fingers through his hair. Deborah listened in tense astonishment. "The next I remember," he said, "I awoke lying down, the sun beginning to touch the sky. I thought I was yet entranced, and leapt up, for again I stood over the trees. All around they grew no higher than my middle.

"Since arriving in Burlington I have told this tale only to Mary and Isaiah, and he says he knows of such a place. 'Tis a forest of dwarf trees. But he said I must not disown what I heard, for the Light hath spoken to me and I must not turn aside." He smiled warily at Deborah. "Thou hast heard it now. Dost thou think me mad?"

"No, but 'tis as you said, a wondrous tale. What did the voice mean to say about fighting for acceptance?"

He stood abruptly and looked down at her. "I shall tell thee when we return with the berries. I fear Mary's cream may have curdled in our absence."

"As you wish," she said, but had a feeling she wasn't going to like what he had to say.

While picking berries, they spoke of nothing consequential, then walked back to the house in silence, Deborah becoming more and more uneasy. She wished Japhet would just tell her. He was only making matters worse. She thought for sure he would answer once they were seated at the table, but he seemed intent on eating and didn't even look up from his bowl.

Finally, Deborah said curtly, "You planned to speak to me when we returned."

"So I did." He put down his spoon and cleared his throat. "At the first monthly Men's Business Meeting after my arrival, I told them the Light had reawakened in my heart and I wished to rejoin the Society. I then asked for permission to marry thee. At the first, many among the men were opposed to my return. They shall ne'er forgive my father for his scathing tracts, and said no child of Daniel Leeds shall be welcomed by them. Others argued 'twas a fitting bit of justice for Daniel: his eldest son rejoining the Society. But some of that mind said I may not marry thee, for a Friend marrying a non-Friend is a marriage out of unity, which is not allowed. Thus if I were welcomed into the Meeting, I might then be read out of it. Still others said since I was not a Friend when I contracted to marry thee, I am not subject to their censure. I could marry thee and soon thereafter be welcomed into the Meeting.

"My head was awhirl with these complications, but eventually the men decided in the usual way to form a committee to determine if I am sincere and acceptable. They decided as well to consult with the Women's Business Meeting, because the procedure the Society follows to judge a couple's clearness for marriage does not readily apply to our unusual situation. At the next Men's Business Meeting 'twas determined that I should be welcomed, save for the issue of my marriage out of unity. They said then that both the men and women had agreed if I were found otherwise acceptable that thou and I should stand before the women, who will determine whether the answers to rather delicate questions are sufficient to grant an exception and allow our marriage."

Deborah looked out the window at the sun which sat just above the forest. Standing before the trees and rendered orange in the slanting light was the small cabin she and Japhet would share after they married. Mayhap.

"Should the women decide not in our favor, what then?" She saw herself alone in the colonies.

"Thou art vexed, I understand, but do not be troubled. I will marry thee regardless of their decision. Should they refuse to sanction our union and thus not allow me to rejoin, they shall still permit me to attend meetings. And eventually they will welcome me—such is common enough." He frowned at the table. "Though all I have said is truthful, I do wish to be part of the Society now. I long for what I felt here as a boy. If they bar me from that . . ." His voice caught.

"I cannot believe they would do so," Deborah said. "When must we stand before the women?"

"On the morrow next."

"Thou ought to have told her before," Mary chided him.

Japhet took Deborah's hand. "Wilt thou stand with me before the Women's Business Meeting and request their blessing?"

Her stomach tightened and she turned away from his eyes. What would the women ask? she wondered. Questions about her religion? She had to think about this, but Japhet was waiting.

With her other hand she took a spoonful of whortleberries without cream, tasting their tangy sweet juice, feeling their bitter skins coat her teeth. She put down the spoon and placed her hand over his. "Yes, Japhet," she said, "I will stand with you."

11

N THE HEXAGONAL Quaker meeting house, one hundred women sat on two sets of yellow-pine benches placed at right angles. Facing them was a third set of benches, where the twenty female elders sat. There was no pulpit, only a triangular space in the middle formed by the benches' confluence, where Deborah and Japhet stood, facing the elders. The room had no decorations of any kind.

Deborah thought she couldn't be much more anxious. Her throat was dry, her hands shook, and she felt nauseated. She turned her head to look for Mary. There she was, gazing out the window, seeming pensive or grave. Mary glanced then in Deborah's direction and smiled. 'Worry not,' she mouthed. Deborah smiled wanly and again faced the elders.

One of them, a woman with greying brown hair, spoke first. "We Friends have no quarrel now that Japhet's expressed desire to rejoin our Society is sincere. However, a marriage out of unity is not permitted. Thus as a Meeting we face a certain difficult situation that I trust you might appreciate. For we cannot sanction your union. All that we might do is to allow it without repercussions to Japhet. With this intention, we have a few questions to put forth to Deborah Smith. Art thou an Anglican?"

"No, I am not."

Another elder stood. "Thou art not an Anglican? Art thou Popish?"

Deborah hesitated. Their next question could be her undoing. She attempted to prevent it. "My mother is Anglican, but I do not follow after."

This was received in silence. With a smile, she said, "I do know something of your Light. My grandmother and I, we have a'ways listened to the voice which speaks from our hearts."

The silence sweetened, wafted around the room. Deborah glanced up toward the spire where a dense cone of sunlight dispersed as it settled toward the floor.

Elizabeth Basnett, of Basnett's Tavern, stood and spoke. "I'faith, the Light of God shines in us all. I welcome thee to Burlington, Deborah, and I wish to welcome thy husband to our Society. We have held counsel amongst ourselves and many are convinced this union ought to be permitted. I urge the rest of our Society to concur." She smiled at Deborah and sat down.

Another elder rose. "To be sure, the Light of God shines in us all, but that doth not mean we are all Friends. Thou dost not mean to say thou art a member of our Society a'ready?"

Before Deborah could answer, Elizabeth spoke again. "Methinks she says she hath come to the Light from another way. And if we allow Japhet to marry her and remain in our Society, when she is more knowing of us, to be sure she will become a Friend as well."

"Indeed." Mary stood. "If we refuse to welcome him because of this union—the betrothal of which was entered into before he decided to become a Friend—what do we say about the tolerance of our Society? We ought not speak of marriage out of unity, for the Lord hath seen fit to return Japhet Leeds to us and hath offered to our fine town another woman to grace it. Let us not trouble ourselves over her. My cousin shall be a good example to his wife, and she shall soon find value in our ways. Let us trust in God's wisdom as revealed to Japhet Leeds. Let us rejoice that God hath reclaimed, that we have reclaimed, a soul we thought lost to the Anglicans."

"Mary Leeds speaks eloquently," another elder said, "but we have rules to follow. If we do not act in accordance with them, will anarchy not reign?"

"Anarchy?" Mary asked incredulously. "Eloise, methinks thou art merely prejudiced against my cousin because of his father. We all know Daniel Leeds betrayed us. I concur with the opinion that admitting Japhet is the best justice for the deeds of the father."

"I agree as well," Eloise persisted. "But Deborah Smith is not a member of our Society, thus their marriage will be out of unity, and we cannot permit it. We ought to do what we have done in the past—wait to see if Deborah and Japhet attend meetings together, and when 'tis proved they both are sincere, we admit the family."

"Thy suggestion is indeed sound," Elizabeth Basnett said, "but what if Deborah doth not desire to join? Methinks we would put an unfair burden on this young pair and doom their marriage to discontent. We must come to the Light on our own, not because our husband pushes at us. Besides, we have not disowned others of our membership who married out of unity. Therefore, why should we in effect do so here, when I can think of no other situation that speaks out more clearly for exception."

There were murmurs of assent, then an elder with white hair spoke. "If we are to allow the union, we must have more understanding of the intended wife. Thou hast said thou art not Anglican, but thou didst not answer: art thou Popish?"

"No, I am not." From the corner of her eye she caught Japhet's smile of approval.

"Neither Popish nor Anglican," the elder said. "But still we do not know what faith she holds. If we are to welcome Japhet, and I would like to do so, must not we know this at the very least?"

Heads nodded, and Deborah thought, Damn me, I am undone. What say I now? She looked around the room and settled again on the elder who had spoken last.

"Dear," the woman said, "what faith dost hold?"

She remembered Millicent lying dead at the base of the oak and began to panic. Whatever the cost she must avoid that fate. She said, "To be sure, I find value in what I know of your ways. I have been told of female ministers, and even now, this Meeting—women holding counsel together—it draws me and pleases me."

She paused, remembering the blood matting Millicent's hair. She knew she had not yet said enough to save herself. "I own," she lied, "I am yet unformed in my faith. But 'tis as Elizabeth Basnett hath said, mayhap when I am better acquainted with your Society, I shall wish to join it."

Many of the elders nodded, seemingly satisfied. Eloise stood up as if to lodge a protest, but a large florid woman with red hair spoke first. "I am pleased thou mightst one day consider us, and I too welcome thee to Burlington. Thou hast traveled long, and to be sure thou hast thy reasons for it, as did we. Understand that we question thee because we must concern ourselves with the souls of the children thou shalt bear. Eloise," she said, "if Deborah gives thee assurances, wilt thou be willing to allow the union?"

"As I have stated," Eloise said, "the correct course is to wait and allow their marriage to come into unity. Then we might admit them both."

"But Eloise," Mary said, "to be sure thou must undestand the burden that places upon this fragile union. Prithee consider it and listen to Deborah's answer. And remember as well, we have other marriages out of unity among our membership." She gestured toward a woman near the back of the room, who nodded, seeming to acknowledge hers was one.

Eloise looked Deborah over for a full minute, then agreed with a nod.

Japhet let out a faint sigh of relief.

The red-haired woman looked around at the others. "If we welcome Japhet, we must consider 'tis possible Deborah Leeds will not in the end desire to attend our Meeting. If we have blessed Japhet's union with her and she doth not join our Society, we do require assurances on the matter of children." She addressed Deborah. "We do not believe in making vows and cannot ask thee to do so, but canst thou assure us that regardless of thy eventual faith, thou shalt allow Japhet to raise thy children as Friends?"

Deborah jerked back involuntarily. She had assumed she would have children, but hadn't thought much about how she would raise them, except to hope that one of her children would be an heir to her knowledge and craft. But what of the rest? she thought. How can I say how I will rear them? How can I hurl them yet unborn into the laps of these people, whom I know not?

She closed her eyes, feeling wretched. I have no choice, she decided. If I say no, they will not sanction our union, Japhet will rage at me, and the Society will fore'er look at me askance—might e'en guess at my true faith one day. But if I say yes, Japhet shall be welcomed, become part of their community, and I will as well. And I desire that. They do not seem very different from the women of my religion. Can I not then simply tell them the truth? That I follow the Old Religion and insist I must have leave to teach it to my children? Would they accept a true witch in their midst? Never! However tolerant they may be, they are yet Christian. I have no other choice. I must give them my children, then they will be appeased.

She cleared her throat to speak and felt the cleft within her that Granna had said was there. She felt she was not building a bridge over it with what she was about to say, but was widening the cleft, tossing her children and herself into its depths. "I have no quarrel with thy faith or thy teachings, and believing that will continue, I will allow my children, if I am so blessed, to attend your meetings with their father. As well, I will not in any manner thwart his attempts to teach them your ways."

It was done; she could feel it. Japhet took her hand and squeezed it. The first elder stood and asked if there were any other concerns. There were none. It was agreed that Japhet Leeds would be welcomed by the Burlington Friends Meeting and suffer no consequences for his marriage out of unity. He and Deborah could enter the state of wedlock before a magistrate, but not in the meeting house, for there no Friend could marry a non-Friend. "But we do welcome thee," the elder told Deborah, "to attend our meetings."

Deborah and Japhet walked out of the building into bright sunlight, and she shaded her eyes. Japhet embraced her suddenly. "Thou hast done it!" he said. "I am pleased!"

Deborah couldn't bear it. She pulled away gently and continued walking, watching red dirt kick up and color her leather shoes, her eyes beginning to blur with tears. She tried to blink them away.

He caught her arm. "Art thou not pleased?" he asked, confused and concerned.

She averted her face and wiped her tears with one hand. Then she looked at him and feigned a self-deprecating smile, as if to say: You know a woman and her tears.

He smiled sympathetically. "Thou art overcome. I understand."

She nodded in assent.

A sudden burst of yellow raced toward them. Japhet dropped to a squat and caught Yonder as he shot into his arms, knocking him over. He struggled to a squat again and grabbed Yonder's big head, tossing it back and forth between his hands while the dog bit at his fingers. Then he hugged the dog against his chest and almost sang, "I'm home, Yonder. Good dog! I'm home."

Still holding onto the squirming hound, he glanced up at Deborah. His expression was so tender and childlike, the tears returned to her eyes. Must I conceal the truth even from you, my future husband? she asked herself. The tears slipped down her cheeks.

He let go of Yonder and embraced her. You are the one who shall know me best, she thought as she wept into his shoulder. I must conceal especially from you.

BURLINGTON

12

HEY SLEPT as they often did: rumps touching, feet exposed and intertwined before the large stone fireplace. In late July—much too hot for a fire at night—only the coals were kept alive with a covering of ashes for the next day's cooking.

Deborah woke just before dawn, her hip numb from sleeping with only two blankets between her and the packed earthen floor. It shall please me mightily when Japhet finishes that wooden bedstead, she thought as she rolled onto her other side and rubbed the sore spot. She raised herself to her elbow, careful not to pull the light blanket off Japhet, and looked around for Yonder. The hound lay near their feet, shaking his head at a small swarm of insects that pestered him. Flies, she thought, frowning at the window. That greased paper keeps out naught and lets in only enough light to make me lonesome for more.

Indeed, Deborah's love of color and beauty found much challenge in the decaying log cabin. Japhet's father had built it more than twenty years before with the intention of it lasting only one or two years until the large house, now Mary's, could be built. Though in no danger of falling down, the cabin offered scarcely enough protection from the elements. The pole and bark roof had many small holes. Some of the clay mortar between the walls' logs had worn away, and the wind whistled through. The aging chimney, lined hazardously with unplastered wooden planks, required regular sweeping.

There was no floor save the Jersey dirt and little furniture in the two-room cabin. Three stools fashioned from sections of tree trunks stood near the spinning wheel. The top of a trestle table—a wide oak board—leaned against the wall next to its frame. In a corner across from the fireplace, a small maple cupboard held eating utensils. From a loft beam above the hearth hung the drying pole, not yet laden with fruit, herbs, and strings of sausages. A second small room had no furniture at all; it would house the loom come winter.

And then there was the wooden door, the result of their first quarrel. Before they moved into the cabin, Japhet promised they would live there only one year, long enough for him to build a new house. But few things had been more distasteful to Deborah than the reality of living in the dark, bare, doorless cabin.

"It *hath* a door," Japhet said when she had asked him to hang one.

"A blanket is not a door," she countered, sitting at Mary's table a week after their wedding. Her arguments for a wooden door were practical. "Wolves, panthers, bears, rogues, tax collectors, horses, flies, mosquitoes, and ants."

"There's no door that'll keep out ants."

"Japhet, shall you or shan't you fashion a proper entry?"

"Deborah, that heavy blanket shall keep out the cold better than any wood slab. The cabin hath shifted too much for me to hang one across it."

"Oh," she considered. "Why did you not say so at the first?"

He didn't answer and they finished the meal in silence. Deborah conceded the point, but the dreary cabin continued to oppress her. She could not bear living in it. One afternoon while Japhet was working on the new house, she studied the door frame and came to believe that a panel *could* be hung across it. A blanket on the inside would cover any gaps and could be tied back like a curtain most of the day. She told him about her discovery the next morning while they sat at Mary's table.

"Why shall you not let the matter alone?" he asked. "The new home will have a lovely door. Why canst thou not wait on it? I do not wish to waste labor on the cabin for that will only extend the time we must live in it."

"We? 'Tis I who live in that cave. You merely rest your head there. I would not press save you are a carpenter; otherwise, I'd build the door myself."

He snorted and looked down at the trencher they shared. "My father and his second wife lived in that cabin just as 'tis. I expect we can as well."

"The cabin was newly built then, and is she not the wife who perished at the end of that year?"

He glared at her. Without another word he went outside.

She sat there a minute, then went to look for Mary in the pantry. Not finding her, she peered down the vertical, winding staircase to the basement kitchen. Lifting her skirts and following the faintly-sweet smell of corn porridge, she climbed down.

Mary and her servant were just about to bring up breakfast. "Deborah, what–? Carry up the hasty, Constance, I'll be along." Mary eased Deborah onto a stool and sat on one herself. Deborah leaned her head on Mary's shoulder and began to cry.

Mary stroked her hair. "Dear Deborah," she said, "thou hast no need to tell me what's the matter. 'Twas on thy face. Life is harsh here, more trying than thou hadst imagined, to be sure. Mayhap, as did we all, thou thought 'twould be easy and romantic. Life in a New World. Pretty thought, eh? And to be sure, Japhet is a fine man, mayhap as fine as any, yet . . . I have it, do I not? He is not always the kind gentleman thou dreamed he would be?"

Deborah raised her head. "I do not understand why it hath come to this weeping. I naturally assumed that Japhet should hang a wooden door in the stead of that old blanket. Why, the winter cold in these parts should be our death in a fortnight. But he says a heavy blanket or skin holds faster on a frame that is out of kilter. I own I am no carpenter, but I looked at that frame and it seems straight enough to me. And there need be no wasted labor, which he fears. When the new house is built, the new door could then be rehung. But Japhet shall not e'en have a look at it."

She took the sip of cider that Mary offered her. "I despise that cabin, Mary. 'Tis vile, dark, and dank. I spent six weeks a'ready in one dungeon; I don't wish to trade it for another. A door, only a door, would make it in some part a home."

"Have you spoken about it in this manner with Japhet?"

Deborah looked down at the mug. "We have not spoken, only quarreled."

Mary shook her head. "I fear my cousin falls prey to pride a'times. His father lived in that cabin, and so shall he. I told him you twain might live in this house with me till yours is built but he would hear none of it. I barely succeeded in convincing him to eat several of your meals with me. And yet he is no ogre. Say it plain as thou hast to me. Methinks he shall listen."

"I have heard it," a man's voice said.

Deborah watched Japhet warily as he continued down the stairs, then noticed he carried one of Mary's red roses. She felt some of her hard feelings soften. As she accepted the rose their fingers touched and he said, "I will look again at the frame."

Lying on the floor before the hearth, Deborah smiled in the direction of the wooden door Japhet had eventually fashioned, then faced his back. She wondered if it were a Leeds trait, his abundance of body hair. It rose thick and black from his groin up his torso and over to the wings of his shoulder blades. She pulled one long back hair gently, and he swatted at her as if she were a fly. Chuckling, she slid a fingernail slowly down his spine. He quivered. She started to do it again, but before she reached his mid-back—a particularly sensitive place she had learned—he grabbed her arm and rolled her onto her back.

"Now," he said, releasing her arm and reaching beneath her, "'tis my turn to play with thee."

It had been more painful the first time than Deborah thought it would be. She had seen her fair share of animals coupling and observed neither pleasure nor pain in it. But that first time had been only pain and had ended with her wondering why there was so much ado about it. The times after, however, had been different.

She wrapped her mouth around the end of Japhet's nose and made as if to eat it.

"Have care," he said, entering her again.

The hard earth beneath fell away and they rode each other like waves. She felt herself falling back, back. Her pelvis was in the air, her back arched; her hair was growing heavier and heavier. She looked up and was shocked to see a woman with long, dark hair holding her, leaning over her.

"My pretty," the woman said and disappeared.

Deborah felt herself dropped, then falling through space. She called out and suddenly the sensation of falling ceased. Japhet was kneeling with his arms clasped around her hips, lowering them both to the ground. Down they went until the small of Deborah's back scratched against the wool blanket. She sighed, and Japhet twisted over onto his back, rested his arms above his head.

She lay there, her breath settling. Then she looked toward the only spot of color in the cabin—the mulberry-painted, carefully-crafted wooden door—and began to laugh.

13

HE Delaware River was calm and the wind cool as Deborah and Japhet stood at the rail of the ferry, watching the sun rise toward the silver sky. Only two months ago she had sailed up the Delaware, but standing there, it seemed as if a year had passed. At the same time, everything reminded her of the *Willow* and her voyage: the swooping gulls; ferry owner Charles Snowden parading the deck, like the captain he once had been; even her anxiety.

"I know naught about selecting a servant," she said to Japhet.

"As thou wouldst a horse." He suppressed a laugh at her appalled look. "I merely jest," he said, "but thou must have care—look her o'er well. Examine her muscle to determine that she is strong. Talk to her to discern how well she speaks English. Watch her eyes to be certain she meets thy own, to be certain she is forthright."

Charles Snowden broke in, "The ship hails from Ireland, so thou must have extra care to assure she is not a drunkard. They will have exhausted their supply of rum and beer on their months-long journey, but breath holds the stench of spirits. A drunken woman is e'en more vile than a man. She walks about at night, forsaking her children, behaving with impropriety. 'Tis a pity, but the Irish are the worst. If you would but wait, you might purchase a family of German redemptioners. They are the most loyal, to their families and to the ones they serve." Someone shouted his name from across the deck, and he hurried away.

Deborah's knuckles were white on the rail. Their callous words disturbed her uneasy assent to be part of this purchase at all. In England, most servants came from her class, farmers' sons mostly, and daughters. So when Japhet told her she would need a servant, she was surprised. She couldn't imagine herself as a mistress and told him so. He finally convinced her that such help was vital in the New World, and reluctantly she agreed.

But here they speak of them as if they were barely human, she thought. In England, there's no shame in going out to service.

"Thou art cold," Japhet said. "Let us go thither for a lesser wind."

He took her arm, but she didn't move. She stared at him, dismayed. 'Tis all so different here, she thought, looking into his puzzled eyes.

"Come along," he urged, pulling on her arm.

"Yes," she said, taking a step. "This wind leaves me cold."

Familiar tar and fish odors met Deborah on the wharf, but as they neared the servant ship *Dalia*, another smell reached her, this one putrid but also familiar. She halted, remembering the woman on the gibbet at Wapping. "I smell death, Japhet."

He glanced at her, then looked away, his expression inscrutable. They continued to walk but more slowly than before. Her legs felt heavy. She held her arms stiff and straight.

When they reached the ship, she stared aghast at the two hundred malnourished and ill men, women, and children lining the rails. Some hunched as if no longer strong enough to support their shrinking weight. And yet, despite their poor health, they all wore new, clean clothes, given as part of their indenture agreements. They seemed like corpses to Deborah, dressed prettily in their coffins, denying their deaths—looking all the more dead for the denial.

She gripped Japhet's arm. "They have been starved, have they not? Where is the shipmaster? Captain Hughes fed us like queens compared to these."

"'Tis a servant ship, Deborah," he said in a calm, controlled voice, as if comforting a child. "Such is the lot of those who cannot afford their keep."

"You knew it would be like this! This doth not strike at your heart?"

"Y– yes," he stammered. "It doth. But we can do nothing about it. Profit masters these ships."

She turned away and looked at the servants again. The injustice of their condition was so evident she wondered how he could dispute it. How could anyone dispute it? She faced him again. "You excuse this lot, Japhet. You who decry slavery! Look at them, Japhet. Look!"

He followed her angry gaze to the ship. Despite their weakened conditions, most of the servants actively searched for buyers, jostling each other for the best position. One purchaser squeezed the arm of a teenaged boy. Another probed the mouth of a young woman while she smiled, tight-mouthed, at the sky.

Japhet looked back at Deborah, blinking. "We shall treat her well," he said. "She'll have a good home—to be sure better than what she left—and twenty-five acres at the end of her term."

"It shall not undo their ill usage."

"No," he agreed, "but we shall treat her well."

Deborah sighed heavily. "And how do I select a maid from among them? I want none of them, and all of them."

"Thou shalt know when thou hast found her."

He offered his arm, and Deborah took it. They stepped onto the gangplank and climbed to the deck. As a woman's hand reached out to her, a mate's broom fell upon it. Deborah glared at the mate and examined the woman's thin wrist. It wasn't broken, only bruised. "Have no fear," she said. "Thy limb will soon cause you no pain." She released her arm. The woman frowned as if disappointed Deborah was not purchasing her indenture.

Deborah walked on, feeling increasingly dismal. Finally she stopped and let go of Japhet's arm. "I desire no part in this."

Just then she heard a soft, shrill sound like a bee buzzing near her ear, but from farther away. She looked around but saw no insect. Then it was there again, a whistle in her ear but at a distance as well. She looked straight ahead toward the stern and saw a woman about her age with a half-smile on her face. Unlike the other women in tan or blue, she wore a green gown. But something else was different about her. The calling tone.

Deborah darted for the woman. "You," she said when she reached her. "Did you make the whistle?"

The woman smiled; her pale blue eyes were bright despite her malnourishment.

"Dost thou speak English?" Japhet asked, coming to Deborah's side.

"Yes," the woman said, "very well, you will find."

"What is thy name?" he asked.

"Erin." She smiled again at Deborah. "I am able-bodied, missus, strong and sensible. Have no interest in marrying. 'Tis a maid you wish?"

Deborah nodded. A matronly purchaser stepped up and quietly advised her, "Don't choose a comely one, dear. Too trying on a young marriage." This woman was dressed in a cherry gown decked with gold ribbon knots. Atop her coifed hair she wore a tall frontage, which she pointed at Erin. "You are a cook-maid?"

"No, ma'am." Erin grinned as the woman hastened away.

Japhet suppressed a chuckle, but said nothing.

Deborah reached out to touch the sleeve of Erin's gown. She had rarely known anything so clearly in her life. Erin it must be. "Shall you come with me?" she asked.

Erin nodded. "Aye, missus."

"My name is Deborah, please call me so, and this is my husband, Japhet Leeds."

"Thou shalt assist my new wife in the care of the house, Erin, including cooking." Japhet gave her an amiable look. "And other common tasks. Yes?"

"Aye," she said. "I'll soon return to my normal frame and there will be no slack in my step, you will see."

"Well 'tis done then." Japhet clapped his big hands together. "Let us dine at the Blue Anchor while we await Charles and the others. Go with thy mistress, Erin. I will retrieve thy indenture from the shipmaster and we shall be gone from this place." To Deborah he added, "Wait with Erin on the dock. I will speak to the responsible party about their conditions, then meet you twain there."

Deborah nodded, somewhat comforted.

The Blue Anchor, surrounded by whortleberry bushes at the mouth of Dock Creek, was a small, single-story wooden building with a brick facade.

On this summer day the interior was hot and noisy, tightly packed with Scotch-Irish, German, and English men and women, and Quakers. At candle-lit tables, gossips gathered around letters and pamphlets. Near the bar, a hindquarter of venison roasted on a turnspit over an open fire. Two little dogs in a cage next to the spit ran on a treadmill to keep it turning.

Japhet left the two women sitting across from each other at a table in the back and went to the bar to order. Erin tucked her dark brown hair behind her ears. A play of freckles spotted her nose and cheeks.

"It pained me so," Deborah began, "to see that dreadful ship and the manner in which you were kept. The journey must have been horrid."

Erin nodded. "'Twas. They shoved us into the steerage, and before the next moon we started dying. One a day, or two . . . some days more. They'd toss the dead o'er at sun's set, and the rest of us would pray—we'd pray we weren't next." She put her elbows on the table and rested her head on her hands. "They said on the ship that Quakers make the kindest masters. I saw you and your plainly-dressed husband and knew him for a Quaker. So I whistled, and you heard it." She smiled.

I did, Deborah thought, wondering how she had managed to produce the odd sound. "You do speak English very well. Japhet says most of the Irish redemptioners speak very little." Erin responded with a silent glare. "What I . . ." Deborah tried to take back her words.

"I learned as a child." Erin left it at that, her anger seemingly gone.

Deborah felt unsettled, not only by Erin's sudden emotion, but because she just didn't know how she was supposed to behave. Erin will be my servant, she thought, but I feel a'most as if I know her a'ready, and I desire her to be my friend.

"You are newly married?" Erin asked pleasantly.

"Yes. Not even two months. How do you know it?"

"You are mindful of each other, not yet at ease." She turned to look over her shoulder at Japhet, sitting at the bar now, talking with Charles Snowden. "Your husband seems a good sort."

"Methinks that is so. I did not know him ere we were betrothed."

"*Cinniúint*," Erin said. "Every now and again a thing is fated."

She winked and Deborah had a feeling she wasn't just talking about her and Japhet. Doth she feel as do I? she wondered. Doth she feel she knows me?

Erin glanced again at Japhet, and Deborah realized in a flash she did so because she was hungry. "Our victuals will arrive soon methinks," Deborah said. "I wish I had a piece of something to offer you now. I did not know they would starve you."

Erin looked back at her. "I thank you, missus, and I shall be well again when I have eaten. The birds never sang for me since I left."

"What was that? I did not hear you."

"The birds. 'Tis the reason I left my home. My mam died when I was too young to know her. Pappa died last spring. Death was waiting on me as well. I heard them in the trees. My Aunt Gwen is from Wales and she told me of Rhiannon's birds. They were singing for me every time I walked to the garden. Singing my death they were." Erin put her hands on the table, fingers spread. Sharp-looking bones pressed against the skin; blue-green veins ran along the bones. "I waited for the birds to sing on the ship, but I never heard them. They never sang for me again. Not since I left." She put her head on her hands.

She needs food now, Deborah thought.

From the bar Japhet and a boy carried wooden trenchers bearing bread, sweet corn, and venison. They put them down on the table and Japhet sat at the end.

Erin lifted her head and began to eat slowly at first, as if she'd forgotten she was hungry. After a few bites she picked up her pace, wincing once from a burned tongue, but barely pausing.

Deborah watched her, her stomach clenching. "Don't eat so hastily," she warned, "or you will fall ill. 'Twill be a day or two ere you might consume as much as before, so go slowly now and allow your stomach to tell you when 'tis full." Erin nodded and checked her pace. Deborah picked up her slice of bread but wasn't hungry. She set it aside, speared her piece of venison with her knife and put it on Erin's trancher. "Only if you require it," she said.

Japhet watched Deborah, grease on his lips, his mouth full and chewing. "'Tis the only cure she needs, is it not, wisewoman?"

Deborah met his eyes, suddenly struck with gratitude for her lot. It might have been horrid, she thought with a shiver. Her husband might have been a rogue or scoundrel or otherwise cruel.

She picked up her corn—she had never eaten the vegetable on its cob—and spread butter on it the way Japhet had. Tentatively, she took a bite. It was sweet, delicious. She took another bite, then several more. Too soon the ear was empty. She put it down. Suddenly, a whole one appeared on her trencher.

"A swap of meat for that." Erin gestured toward the corn. "I have the better of the bargain."

"Oh, I think not," Deborah said, as she reached for the butter. "This is the best tasting food I e'er ate."

14

ow is it?" Deborah called down the chimney. "Have you collected up the coals?"

"Aye," came Erin's muffled response. "Drop her down."

Crouching on the roof she had recently patched, Deborah awkwardly lifted a goose, made passive by a blindfold, and stroked its back. "Forgive me, Sophie," she said, "for this ill usage, but 'tis the only manner in which to clean this old, small flue." She held the rope tied around its middle and lowered the goose into the chimney.

Sophie's honks deafened as she thrashed wildly down the flue. Loosened soot formed a cloud which rose up into Deborah's lungs. She held onto the chimney and coughed.

"Ugh," Erin grunted below, then called out, "Pull her up!"

Deborah took a moment to straighten the burlap sack she wore to avoid soiling her clothing, then pulled hard and steadily on the rope to bring the heavy fowl back up to daylight. As the goose appeared, she reached out with gloved hands and held it below the wings. "Soon, Sophie," she said, breathing hard, sweat running down the backs of her thighs, "your trial will be done." She leaned over the chimney and called down into the darkness, "Here she be!" then dropped the bird. The smoke was just as thick this time, but Deborah moved back before the cloud reached her.

"Now!" came Erin's cry.

Deborah pulled hard on the rope. She was tired now, her arms sore, and she bent her knees for better leverage. As the goose reached the top of the chimney, she shouted, "Once more!" and let the rope go slack.

"I have her," Erin called.

After the soot cleared, Deborah looked down the flue. 'Tis cleaner, she thought, but I shall be pleased when we remove to the new house with its grand fireplace. Then, none will do this nasty job. Japhet will hire a sweep.

Carefully, she crouched her way down the roof's easy pitch toward the ladder. Erin, also clad in a long, soot-covered burlap sack and holding onto the goose, waited for her at the bottom. Deborah grinned as she climbed down. "You are nearly as soiled as Sophie."

"As are you," Erin said.

Deborah reached out and stroked the bird's blackened back. "Enough for you now, is it not, old girl?" She took the goose from Erin and carried it toward the stream.

When they reached the bank, Deborah put Sophie down and untied the rope. As she took off the blindfold, the goose whirled about, neck flattened, and bit her gloved hand before she could pull it away. Deborah cried out in pain. Sophie padded forward and back, hissing, her head still outstretched, now swinging from side to side. Finally, she flew to the water and flapped wildly, cleaning herself.

Erin eased off Deborah's glove and they looked at her hand. It hurt, but no bones were broken and neither was the skin. "'Twill be well," Deborah said as she knelt by the stream and put her hands in the cool water. Though well before midday, the August sun was merciless. The burlap sack roasted her. She sat on the bank and put her feet and legs in as well. Erin waded toward the center of the stream.

Deborah wiggled her fingers in the water and thought of Grace Kirkbride's son Caleb, whose arm she had splinted last week. I'll check on him tomorrow, she thought, and bring dandelion leaves and purslane to shore up Grace's blood so the unborn babe doth not drain her. As well, I'll brew her another batch of red raspberry leaf tea. She doth not drink enough of it to ensure a smooth labor.

"Come in, Deborah." Erin was waist high in water, the sack clinging.

Over the hill, Japhet and some neighbors were working on the new house. He carried drink with him, Deborah thought, thus he would have no need to return to the stream for water. Yet . . .

"I lived near the River Aire," she said. "But Mamma ne'er permitted me to swim in it, no matter how hot. She said 'twas not proper for a girl."

Erin grunted and splashed around. "You English."

"But on the hottest days when Mamma was away, Granna dressed me in my thinnest shift and walked me down to the river. She didn't like the water herself, so she sat on a rock or picked herbs and flowers by the bank."

"Come in then," Erin said.

"It hath been long . . ."

Erin paddled toward the bank. When she stood again, she was in water just over her knees. "Firstly, we toss aside these sacks." She struggled out of hers and threw it toward shore. Then she took off her shift.

Deborah raised her eyebrows. Erin had filled out to her normal frame, and Deborah found her lovely: full hips and breasts, dark hair against fair skin. Without taking off her sack, Deborah stepped off the bank and followed Erin toward the middle of the stream. The water's coolness shortened her breath as she dunked up to her shoulders a few times. She could feel the burlap shrinking. She looked around for Sophie. The clean goose squatted peacefully in the shade of an oak.

When Deborah turned back around Erin was gone. "Whither–" she started to say, but hands grabbed her waist and pulled her underwater.

Erin was laughing with her hands on her hips as Deborah came up sputtering. She sprang at Erin, but the clinging sack slowed her. Erin splashed handfuls of water and Deborah leapt after her again, but she was too quick.

"You!" Deborah said. "No mother kept you from the river!" She was instantly aware of her mistake and sorry.

Erin stared at her, breathing hard. Ringed waves flowed away from them, collided, then lapped back. Deborah stepped closer. The sack rode at her thighs. It wasn't so cold now; the water felt good. She reached Erin and touched her shivering shoulder. "Forgive me," Deborah said. "I spoke ere I thought."

Erin's eyes softened, let her in. They were mesmerizing, those eyes, so pale they seemed bottomless. Cool water hit Deborah's stomach. She looked down. Erin was taking off Deborah's sack and shift together. Deborah helped her by raising her arms over her head.

"*Níl ann ach sin*," Erin said as she threw the sack and shift toward shore, then scooped a handful of water over Deborah's bare shoulders. "Now you have the right suit."

15

EBORAH LAY curled against Japhet's back, her hand resting on his thigh. She could tell he wasn't asleep yet, and he had been unusually quiet, almost sullen, at supper. "What troubles you?" she whispered.

He rolled onto his back. "Thou art too familiar with the girl," he said.

"What do you say?"

"Thou ought to treat Erin with kindness but not allow her to lord thee about."

"Shh, or she will hear you." Deborah looked over him toward the other room of the cabin where Erin slept. She didn't sense any movement but didn't hear Erin's light snore either.

"Erin ought to hear me," he said. "I have naught against her; she works hard and well. And I'm glad thou dost find her pleasing, but thou look'st on her nearly as a friend."

"She *is* nearly a friend. And what is the harm in that? I have none other, 'cepting your cousin Mary. And Erin doth not lord me about, as you say. We do our work together, is all."

He sighed in exasperation and turned over, away from her. "Deborah, forget I said a word about it. 'Tis clear thou shan't listen to me. Not as if thou ever dost."

"Oh, listen to the master speak." Deborah sat up. "You are a Friend, are you not? Your people permit women a role in directing the course of the Society, so do not trouble me about holding to my own mind." Japhet mumbled something. "What is that you say?"

He turned over, snickering, and pulled her down on top of him. "I say I understand now why my father turned away."

"Oh, do you now?" She pushed his shoulders playfully.

He started to tickle her, but Deborah drew away. "Erin is awake, methinks."

He frowned and closed his eyes. She sat there, watching his chest rise and fall. Why was he questioning her about Erin? What was the harm in their being friends?

"Japhet," she whispered, not wanting him to go to sleep angry. "Japhet," she said a little louder. He opened his eyes. "Why *did* your father leave the Society?"

"Thou woke me to ask me that?"

"You ne'er told me. I know only of the ill will since, not its cause."

"There was a large event. The Philadelphia Quarterly Meeting was offended by his second almanac and bought all unsold copies from the printer and destroyed them. My father at the first apologized to the Meeting but later was bitter about it, and took up with George Keith and his followers in speaking against the Society. But methinks in the main 'twas an accumulation of discomfort that erupted. My father desires the comfort of one way. It frighted him that one's own inner Light might be valued above scripture."

"Is that so?"

"Dost thou not concur that God's direct revelation to me hath more merit than his revelations centuries ago? That is if they conflict, which may or may not be."

"I understand how that might fright your father."

He sat up a little. "What dost thou mean?"

"What if you are in the wrong," she said, "and 'tis not God but the voice of the Devil whispering in your ear?"

He squinted at her. "Hast thou been reading my father's pamphlets?"

"I do not say I agree—to be sure, I do not—but many would feel alarm at that sentiment. My mother would feel the same as he."

"But thou hast yet to speak of the Society. When we minister, we carry the Meeting with us from town to town. The Meeting provides what is called a 'traveling minute,' which includes the means to travel as well as an introduction of the bearer. If a Friend seems to have gone astray from the Light, the Meeting could withhold the minute. But my father doth not trust in the Society, nor in the goodness of each person." Japhet paused and sighed deeply. "If I speak more of my father I shall lie raging a'night. Let us sleep now. We can quarrel again in the morn."

He smiled at her disapproving frown and kissed it several times quickly until it was gone. Then he winked and turned onto his side, his back to her.

Deborah shook her head. I do like this man, she thought, even if he doth mock me a'times. She lay down, remembering their conversation. Her thoughts rolled back to Erin. "There is naught wrong with our being friends," she said and turned over, her buttocks touching Japhet's. She closed her eyes. This was her favorite moment of the day—when her body gave up its toil, when she was free to dream.

The night sky turned bright green and a loud voice beckoned. Deborah followed it. The voice led her down red stairs, into a huge orange room, then toward two enormous yellow, pulsing doors, which opened as she approached. She passed through them into a second room and the doors slammed behind her.

The second room was smaller than the first and its walls were green. She followed the voice to a pair of blue doors. They opened to allow her to pass, then closed behind her as well. The third room was indigo. She walked through its cool darkness toward a pair of violet doors. These she had to open herself. She stepped over the threshold into a blinding fog.

It swirled away and she found herself on the coast of a rocky beach. The voice she'd followed belonged to a woman—the same one, she realized, that she'd seen during relations with Japhet. The woman sat just offshore on a boulder, her hips and legs hidden by splashes. Deborah turned around and saw the huge violet doors closing. She looked back toward the beach, then down. The hem of her gown turned bright purple in the water. She raised her eyes to meet the woman's. I have seen you before, she thought, but who are you?

The woman laughed and her legs rose out of the water. They were green and joined. Deborah moved out of the way as the woman's tail uncoiled smoothly like a snake, bridging the distance between boulder and shore. It was clear what had to be done. Deborah climbed onto the tail, kept her eyes on the woman to avoid the crashing sea below, and crawled to the boulder.

When she was sitting across from the woman, she felt dizzy and grabbed the sandstone beneath her and one of the woman's hands. It felt rough, but human. The woman smiled, suddenly took hold of Deborah's arms, and pushed her to the edge of the boulder. Then she leaned over Deborah, bracing Deborah's lower body, and arched her backwards toward the spray.

Deborah felt as if she were floating down. She sensed the woman's firm grip on her and caught a scent, her own. Deborah's slow descent ceased just as she felt her hair grow heavy with water.

Upside down, feeling the woman's strong hold, Deborah breathed in deeply. Her torso relaxed and lengthened. The water climbed her hair, lapped lightly at her scalp.

The woman laughed again. The sound wound up Deborah's spine, shaking her. She became frightened, jerked up and tried to sit but the woman held her down. Nearby she heard splashing and looked for its source. She saw a fish leaping frantically, as if hooked.

Deborah breathed deeply again, gathering her strength, then pushed suddenly from her belly. All resistance evaporated and the vision ended. She sat up, astonished, in front of the hearth. A voice whispered, "You shall see me again."

She looked at her arms and thought she saw red imprints fading. She touched her hair; it felt damp. Her neck and back ached, although her belly felt stronger somehow. She put her palm over it and felt the life she had suspected was there.

Japhet stirred. "What is it?" he asked groggily.

"Only a dream," Deborah whispered, lying down again and pulling the covers up to her chin. Her hand trailed back to her belly and probed it gently. Not simply a dream, she thought, but a visitation. By whom? Who is that fish-woman? Granna would know. Mayhap there is a mention of her in my book.

Her fingers traced a spiral over her lower torso as she imagined it swelling. Soon, she thought, I shall be a mother. How can that be? I am but a child myself. She remembered her promise to allow her offspring to be Friends. The Society can have all of them but one, she decided. One of my daughters shall be my heir. Mayhap not this first child, she sensed, but she will come. I have only to watch for her and to wait.

16

MOOTH WHITE birch slivers fell to the dirt floor of the cabin. Deborah leaned over a long stick, running her knife down its length, removing all the bark below a mark she'd made near the top of the birch. The slivers began to cover her gown and feet as well, so she took off her shoes and sat cross-legged in the chair.

She wore a loose linen gown she had dyed purple with woad leaves and madder root. Her fancy gown was much too impractical for the life she led here and long since had been put away. And though she had done so willingly, there were times when she was alone that she would go to her trunk, open it, and touch the gown's fine patterned damask.

"What way is it with the broom?" Erin asked. She stood at the hearth stirring a large kettle of corn, potato, and mutton stew.

"Nearly done, methinks."

More slivers fell to the dirt floor, like lines of cream in cocoa. Deborah thought of the wood floor they would soon walk on and wiggled her toes. A tingling pain shot through her legs and she tried to uncross them, but they were asleep.

"Assist me, Erin, shall you? My legs."

When Deborah was standing again, stamping her feet to return them to normal, she had a wild thought. She extended one end of the birch to Erin, who seemed puzzled for a moment, then grabbed it with both hands and leaned back. Deborah leaned back as well.

They began to walk in a circle, slowly, with quick glances to the right and left. When they had mastered that pace, they leaned farther back and walked faster, then still faster, until they were spinning. Their backs were stiff and arched, their necks craned forward. But it was too much to sustain. Erin's grip slipped. Deborah kicked the well bucket into the spinning wheel, and Erin fell against the wall.

Deborah rushed over and helped her up. "Are you hurt?" she asked, looking her over.

"Nay." Erin stretched out her arm and turned it over to look at her elbow. "I'll have a mark tomorrow is all."

Deborah rubbed the elbow and shook her head. "You'd think us little more than children."

"Ah, the bucket!" Erin ran over and saved it from its tilt against the spinning wheel. A slow stream of water had been pouring out. "Have haste," she said, "pull down vervain and bayberry leaves. We'll banish the bad luck."

Deborah took the herbs off the drying pole and squatted next to Erin, who turned Deborah's hand over and rubbed the vervain between their palms, letting the brownish-green and purplish-blue bits drop into the puddle. They did the same with the bayberry, rubbing the leaves between their palms, watching the pool disappear into the earth floor.

All at once Deborah felt the room tilt sideways then right itself again. She heard a familiar voice say, *"God shall not allow you to take her away!"* Startled, she dropped Erin's hand.

"What is on you?" Erin asked.

In the wet earth, Deborah saw her mother's face, hard and accusing. Her long red hair waved against her white linen gown. The beauty of that loosened hair, which Deborah had rarely seen, rendered the memory all the more unpleasant—it was a mock too painful to reckon. She covered her eyes but saw the awful scene again.

Catherine had Granna backed against the wall, the older woman looking aghast and beaten. Her black and grey hair stood out in wisps as if she'd coated it with whale oil, combed it out, and let it dry. Catherine spoke with a condescension Deborah had only heard directed toward her. "You shall no longer teach her," she told Granna. "Keeping her out all the night." Catherine's voice faltered, then gathered itself. "My daughter shall not be made to suffer your life."

Cowering behind the table, Deborah wanted to run out the door but couldn't leave her grandmother. She had never seen her mother so angry, defiant, and powerful. Catherine turned toward her and Deborah ducked. "What did you in the wood?" she demanded. "What did you?"

Granna asked, "Do you not remember your own first bleeding, daughter?" Catherine whirled around to face her but Granna spoke first, "Your church hath deviled our goddesses and gods, yet they do exist. In rivers, in oaks, in you, in me."

"That is heresy," Catherine whispered angrily. "You shall kill her, Mother. Doth that matter naught to you?"

"Witch trials are rare now."

"The laws against your kind remain, and may again be enforced with fury. No, you shall never again teach her!" She pounded her fist on the table. "God shall not allow you to take her away!"

Granna lunged forward and Catherine leapt out of her way, not realizing Granna went for Deborah, who was on the floor, rocking back and forth, her hands over her ears. "'Tis all right, child," Granna cooed, embracing her granddaughter.

"'Tain't all right," Catherine said. "Look what you've done to her."

"I haven't done it, Catherine, we have." Granna stroked Deborah's hair. "The child is trapped betwixt us."

The scene slipped away, the voices and figures reabsorbed into the past. Warmth flowed into Deborah's legs, up her torso, and into her face. Erin was kneeling before her, her hands cupped on Deborah's knees.

"You've returned." Erin smiled. Deborah opened her mouth to speak, but Erin said, "No," and picked up the hemlock broom near the threshold and swatted at the hearth. "*A thaispeánadh*, cease your torment!" she said, then put the broom aside.

Deborah returned wearily to her chair and sat down. She held the birch perpendicular to the floor and leaned her forehead against it, wondering why it was so difficult for her to simply learn her craft, why she still felt divided against herself at times. But Granna told me why, she thought, as did the vision—'tis this cleft within me, my grandmother and mother fighting for my soul. Yet there is a promise in it, as Granna said. For out of the struggle flows my faculty to heal others.

She watched Erin begin a bread dough of corn meal and rye flour. Might

I speak of this with her? she wondered. We must share at the least a similar background, given her otherworldly whistle and now the banishing of bad luck. But what if she is merely superstitious? No, I cannot risk it just yet.

A shadow fell in the doorway and Deborah started, then smiled as Japhet walked into the room. He wore his work clothes: a beige linen shirt, brown fustian breeches, and a wide-brimmed suede hat which he took off to wipe his brow.

"Hard at work, thou be?" he asked, reaching for the birch, but Deborah moved it away. "Ah, forgive me, wife. I shan't touch it till 'tis there. A new broom for a new house." He went to the hearth, picked up the old hemlock broom and made a sweeping motion. "I could use this when the pine floor is in."

"That broom will make wood for the fire and naught else," Erin said.

"Ah, yes. Thou hast no need to trouble thyself about it. I shan't court bad luck by bringing it in." He sat on a stool next to the bucket, dipped up water, and drank. "I know not why some deem not to sip it, this is the sweetest drink. Those at work on the house take ale and hard cider all the day. I fear one will fall from the roof and require thy services."

Deborah laughed but saw that he was serious. "To be sure 'tis not as bad as all that," she said, surprised, for nearly everyone drank fermented beverages on a daily basis.

He dropped the empty ladle into the bucket and looked around. "Soon 'twill be time to put up the loom. After we've brought in Mary's harvest, I shall set to work. Then thou shalt see what a fine weaver thou hast married." He smiled.

"Shall I then?" Deborah retorted, her voice jolly. "Put me to shame, will you? Three months of my spinning you'll draw together in as many weeks."

"Thou wouldst have me at the loom year-round? Then who would plant the rye for her bread?"

She followed his gaze to Erin, who stood before the window rolling out the dough. Her arms filled her sleeves with every forward, bending motion. Her elbow didn't seem to be bothering her.

"When we are in the new house, there will be a separate room for that work," he said.

"Methinks I prefer this." Deborah gestured. "One large room. 'Tis warmer, I should think."

He frowned at her. "There will be two rooms, Deborah, and both will share the hearth. The house will please thee, I should think. Glass in the window and wood on the floor and a mulberry-painted door!" He stalked away and paused at the threshold, bright sunlight before him, the darkness of the cabin behind, then walked through, silhouetted, into the day.

She followed him as far as the door. He advanced across the field with long, quick strides, holding onto the top of his hat. Soon he neared a stand of oaks and disappeared within them. "He becomes angry, of a sudden," she said, watching the trees as if expecting him to reappear.

"He wishes to please you is all," Erin said. "And believes he hath not when you question him so."

"Hmph."

Erin rested the backs of her floured hands on her hips and squinted at Deborah. "'Tis the truth you know, once the babe comes, he'll not concern himself so much."

Deborah leaned back against the doorjamb, wondering how Erin had known. She hadn't even told Japhet yet, had wanted to wait until she was farther along.

"I *knew* 'twas so," Erin said. "When I put my hands on your knees, I thought, She's with child now, not yet two months." She frowned. "But you ought not to have fooled with the birch."

"Yes," Deborah agreed.

Erin pushed a few stray hairs off her forehead, leaving a dusting of flour. "Firstly, I'll make you a red raspberry leaf tea. 'Tis early to drink it to effect but–" She paused. "I go on when you know about the leaf. Have you convinced Grace Kirkbridge to take it as often as you would wish her to?"

"At the last, yes, she drinks enough now. 'Tis good, for soon I shall add to it a tincture of partridge berry—for her last six weeks—which will speed and ease the birth. But I knew not you use herbs as well, Erin. Are you a midwife or healer?" she asked cautiously, a short pause between each word.

"Nay, nay. I know only a bit of this and that." She poured the remaining water from the bucket into a small three-legged iron kettle and put it in the embers next to the stew. Then she reached up to the drying pole and pulled down dried raspberry leaves. "I pinch three for the child that hath never tasted the leaf, and one for the mam." She paused in mid-reach. "That's how it goes now, doth it not? Mam hath one for e'ery three of the child's.

And so will it go, Deborah. Henceforth, 'tis you and me 'gainst all the children you will bear."

"The way you talk, you are an old woman. You have not borne any, have you?"

Erin laughed and shook her head. As she crushed the raspberry leaves between her palms, she began to hum, then dropped the dry bits into the kettle. After three handfuls, she sang,

> "Nine sisters of the isle so deep
> Guardians of the apple sleep
> Keepers of the cauldron
>> weep.
> A child is come
> A child *will* come
> Let the way be sweet."

As a fourth handful fell from her fingers, sparks kicked up from the fire, which with the sun coming in the window lit her palms in yellow and orange. Deborah saw a female child's face appear in the crumbled leaves just before they hit the boiling water. "A girl it will be," she whispered in awe and touched her belly. It still didn't seem possible that a life was there, that she would bear a child. She looked up at Erin, who was smiling at her.

"A girl 'twill be," Erin agreed. "I saw her as well. Come along." She took Deborah's arm and led her to the room where Erin slept at night and all the blankets and skins were stacked by day. Erin sat on the bedding and motioned for Deborah to put her head in her lap.

"There is much work . . ." Deborah resisted.

"Come along," Erin said. "Only till the tea brews. You must rest when you are able."

'Twould be pleasing to take my ease, Deborah thought. She lay down with her head on Erin's thigh.

"There now," Erin said.

Deborah let her mind float. It went out with the tide and lapped against the rock where the green woman sat, smiling at her. Deborah opened her eyes and sat up.

"Your mother again?" Erin asked.

"No." Then she realized and turned to face Erin. "I did not tell you of that."

"I saw her in the puddle."

"You saw her?" She stared at Erin as a chill went through her. "You saw her and you knew I was with child and you saw the girl child in the leaves?" She was dumbfounded, but realized what this meant. Erin *must* be some kind of witch.

Tears came to her eyes. She was not alone, just as Granna had promised. Then she noticed that Erin wasn't having a similar experience, but was looking at her as if she were a child who had finally succeeded in reaching the latch and opening the door. But Deborah didn't feel proud as the child would; she felt daft, as if she'd been searching for a lost key and found it finally on a chain around her own neck. She blushed and looked away from Erin.

"If not your mam, who did you see?" Erin asked gently.

Deborah took a deep breath, met her eyes again, and told her the truth. "I saw a woman on a rock. My Granna wrote of this woman in a book she gave me. She was once called Great Fish, Mother of all. Now, she is known as Marian, a merry-maid. She hath a fish's tail." Deborah flinched and waited nervously for Erin's reaction, which was a slow, dawning smile.

"The Great Fish," Erin said, "that is our salmon, the wisest and oldest of creatures. As well, a'times the Morgen—the nine sisters I sang of—appear as mer-maids. But I have never seen them myself. You saw her?"

She seemed impressed and Deborah smiled. "Yes, thrice I have seen her now."

"Hmm, I did once see *cú doimhne*, depth hound, the black dog. 'Tis an image of the God. I was at a circle of standing stones and thither he leapt from one to another. Some say he is to be feared, but he seemed full of joy to me."

"Have you seen him again?"

"Small glances from the edges of my eye, but not so clearly as 'twas there. Though he hath come into my dreams."

"Why do you think you saw him?"

"Why?" Erin asked. "Because I was looking when he leapt." She got up and left the room, whistling.

Deborah looked after her, noticing the yeasty aroma of bread dough that lingered behind. Erin came back a few minutes later with a saucer and the porcelain cup Richard had given Deborah. She put them on the dirt floor next to her, then sang of the sisters again. When she reached the last line, she sang, "A child is come. A child will come, let *her* way be sweet." She poured tea from the cup into the saucer and handed it to Deborah, then leaned over and kissed her forehead. "May your way be sweet."

A man's voice said, "I cannot tell if thou art unwell or very well indeed." Japhet pushed off from the doorpost, where he had been leaning, and walked into the room. He smelled like the earth itself, musky and rich.

"Back so soon?" Erin quipped. "You have heard the news on the wind, then."

"Erin!" Deborah darted a glance at her, and she smiled mischievously in return. Well, Deborah thought, when should be a better time to tell him? "I am very well, Japhet, methinks you will say."

"I'll return to the bread." Grinning, Erin pushed past Japhet.

He glanced after her, then approached Deborah. She stood and held both his hands. "We have been married how long now, husband?"

"But three short months."

"Well, you are blessed indeed."

He looked perplexed, then his eyes went wide and he squeezed her hands. "Is it true?"

Deborah nodded, smiling.

"A child? So soon? I can scarcely believe it." He reached down and tentatively touched her belly.

"'Twill be a girl," Erin said from the doorway.

He turned to her. "Thou know'st this, Erin? The tea leaves tell thee, mayhap." His tone was light but sarcastic. "'Tis true then what they say: All Irish women are conjurers at heart?"

"Not all," Erin replied, smiling.

Japhet chuckled but eyed her suspiciously as well, then turned back to Deborah and looked down at her belly again. "A child," he whispered.

"A girl," Deborah said, smoothing the hair back from his sweaty forehead. "Our own daughter."

17

EBORAH LEANED over the deer hide, using her bare hands to rub tallow into it. She had already soaked the hide, removed its hair and flesh, then soaked it again. It still didn't look like leather to Deborah, but hairless and stretched over a large block of wood, it appeared less and less like the buck she'd shot a week before.

She had never used a gun, but when a loud noise outside startled her awake, she reached for the powder flask like a veteran, primed the loaded hunting piece as Japhet had taught her, then walked out the front door.

The moon was quarter-full, and she could hardly distinguish the hen house, only fifty yards away. She stood still, waiting. A rustling began, too close to her chickens. They weren't squawking though. Was she too late? She took a step and paused, then another and stopped to listen, the cool October air prickling her flesh, a clenching flutter in her stomach. Then behind a tree she saw a four-legged beast, its head bowed toward the ground. She didn't think to make a noise to frighten it away. She aimed the gun. The animal raised its head. She fired. They both fell to the ground.

She picked herself up, cursing, and heard Japhet calling over frantic clucking and flapping sounds. "Hither," she called back and walked toward the animal. "Hhhh," she breathed in sharply through her teeth. The animal was a deer, not a panther or wolf. It had only been grazing and was now shot through the chest. She dropped to her knees and lay the gun on the ground.

"Art thou hurt?" Japhet asked, coming up behind her.

"No."

He held a candle lantern up to the deer. "I didn't hear thee till the shot. 'Tis a fine buck. Bit too young to shoot, but . . ." He glanced at her stricken face, then added cheerfully, "I knew not thou wert a crack shot. I'll go after a knife to finish him." He headed back toward the house.

"I thought my hens were in danger," she called after him, looking into the buck's half-open eyes. A rear hoof pawed the ground as though trying to get itself up. She touched the wound gingerly and the deer's flesh jerked.

Japhet returned at a quick pace. "Whatever thou thought, we will have ample dried venison and buckskin come winter." He slit its throat, then held the knife aloft, blood dripping on the dirt. "Never killed a deer before?"

Nauseated, she braced her arms against the ground and shook her head.

He found a suitable fallen branch and lashed the buck to it while she watched. Then they carried it, neck slack and bobbing, to the smokehouse behind the cabin. When they were rounding the side of the cabin again, he put his arm around her waist. She paused by the grease-papered window where the hearth's light shone dully through.

"I know something of what thou must feel," he said. "We Friends do not bear arms against, so when Friends arrive from England some resist at the first a gun used even for hunting." He pulled her forward again. "But as thou hast learned, in this New World thou must sully thyself or starve."

He opened the front door and they saw Erin wrapped in a blanket on a stool by the fire, her hair mussed and backlit.

"Thy mistress hath provided us with meat and leather," he said proudly.

"Ah, 'tis good," Erin replied. "I knew not you could handle a gun."

"My wife knows much which is yet unrevealed." He smiled. "The hens were so alarmed by the blast, I warrant there will be two batches of mattress feathers this week."

Despite herself, Deborah smiled at the image of her poor balded birds. Then she scowled. Japhet's good nature was infectious, but not always appropriate.

"What is on you?" Erin asked.

Deborah sat down on a stool. "In England when we had need of meat, we ate the flesh of our own sheep or fowl. But as Japhet suggested to me, here we must be as animals ourselves. I told him I was but protecting my hens when I picked up the gun. But I knew 'twas no dangerous beast.

Though I did not allow myself to think it, I knew 'twas a deer and I desired its flesh." She looked from Erin to Japhet. "I am not pained because I have done it. I am pained because it pleased me, the stalk and the kill."

The memory of that night still unsettled Deborah. She wiped her hands on a cloth, then went inside to get more tallow, kept warm in a large kettle on the hearth. Erin was using a smaller amount of the melted fat to make rushlights. She pulled a wick made of rush, peeled so only one narrow strip of its skin held the pith together, through a shallow, three-legged, oblong pot.

Deborah ladled tallow from the kettle into her wooden bowl, then returned to the hide, lucent and orange in the late afternoon sun. She glanced toward Mary's house and saw her and Grace Kirkbride approaching. Grace carried something, perhaps a plucked turkey.

"Look at thee, Deborah," Mary said when they reached her. "Is this the buck thou shot?"

She nodded, uncertain whether she deserved to feel proud of her deed.

"Didst thou ever think ere thou left England," Grace said, "that thou shouldst lead so rugged a life? That puts me to mind of Elizabeth Haddon. She is a Friend who sailed hither alone at the same age as thou, Deborah. Her father was unable to leave England to manage a tract he had purchased, so Elizabeth came alone, saying Divinity had called her to serve as physician and provide a home in the wild to traveling ministers. She runs the estate by herself, they say. 'Tis south a ways from here."

"The New World hath made heroines of all women," Mary said. "Those who survive."

"Survival alone doth not make one a heroine," Deborah said.

"That it doth!" Mary protested. "With all that opposes us, survival is the most heroic of all acts. In the main, Deborah, thou art too modest. Humility is unbecoming in the female sex. 'Tis a virtue in the male, reared as they are to rule, but we ought cast it aside."

"Ah," Grace said, "but is there not a spiritual humility we must all seek?"

"Yes, yes," Mary agreed impatiently. "But truly, Deborah, I refer to thy gift for healing. 'Tis a pity we have physicians here, for thou wilt not be permitted a wide enough berth to fully develop thy ability. Wert thou in the wild or e'en in Leeds where there are no physicians, to be sure, then thou wouldst one day be a great healer."

"Why are there no physics in Leeds?" Grace asked. "To be sure, there is need."

"That may be so," Mary replied, "but there are few Friends there. Given their stature, only those physicians persecuted for their religion come to the New World. That is, lest they be quacks or have otherwise run afoul of the law."

"You speak kindly of my skill, Mary," Deborah said, "but I would rather remain in Burlington. I am allowed a place for my tinctures and salves. Dr. Grant e'en took some off me last I was at market."

"As well he ought," Grace said. "This speaks to the reason I have come." She gave Deborah the turkey. "I wish to thank thee for the salve thou made for Jeb. His wound hath healed with no scar. He would have brought the fowl himself, but I told him I desired to come and see thee." She turned about in a circle. "Am I not the very image of health? The partridge berry hath had its effect. With my last child at this late stage I shouldn't have made a journey such as this."

Deborah stepped closer to look into Grace's eyes and mouth, and probe her belly. "Yes, you are very well, you and the babe."

"Now, if you might give me an herb to stop them from coming at all." Grace laughed. "I jest, for I would ne'er wish for such a thing, though I hear they exist."

They did, but Deborah thought she would be unwise to admit it. Such use by midwives had led several to be killed as witches.

She said, "And what of your eldest son, Caleb? Hath there been any reoccurrence of his cough?"

"Nay. Thy syrup soothed it. He is a lively one. Would I had a girl of age, though. Those boys do tire me. Jeb now teaches Caleb to smith. No animal shall go near him. He tried e'en to shoe our hound."

Deborah heard the cabin door slam and turned around, still laughing. Erin walked over, clad in a green linsey-woolsey gown, her hair tied back with a green ribbon.

"Grace," Deborah said, "you shall at the last meet my servant, Erin."

"Good day." Grace gave her a quick nod, then addressed Deborah. "Jeb recently bought the indenture of a servant, but I trust he will not be as the last—intemperate. Thou art Irish, Erin?"

"Yes, I am," she answered somewhat curtly.

"Thou speak'st English tolerably well," Grace said. "Patrick's from west of Shannon. He speaks nary a word."

"I'll carry the bird to the smokehouse, *ma'am*," Erin told Deborah, taking it from her and carrying it around back.

"Did I affront her?" Grace asked as she watched her go.

"She is more vexed at Deborah, methinks, for calling her servant," Mary said. "Though her occupation is honorable, methinks Erin ranks her servitude with the oppression of Ireland. Makes a bitter pill, to be sure."

"Prithee tell the maid I intended no slight. I must return now." Grace kissed Deborah good-bye.

"I will go as well," Mary said, and they left, raising the hems of their petticoats and gowns as they crossed the field to her house.

Erin returned to Deborah's side and waited until the other women were out of earshot. "I heard what Mary said as I walked to the smokehouse. She is clever. For as Mary suggested, I speak English *tolerably well* because our farm was snatched by you English and we were made tenants upon it. Pappa could have had equal to one-third his holdings west of the River Shannon, but he said he ne'er should leave his fertile fields, e'en if he no longer had title to them. He said as well we children must speak English, so as not to be swindled of the rest of our possessions, and he arranged to have us taught."

"I am sorry for you," Deborah said. "Something similar hath occurred in England as well. The common land for farming and grazing is snatched and the people forced into foul cities and poorhouses. It happened in this way for my father when he was a boy. Much of his family perished, so he went to sea. After he married my mother, he could have remained upon the farm, but did not. I remember he told me the land had cast him off and ne'er would receive him again. He was lost at sea when I was a child." Deborah looked down at the hide. "I know you shan't be free for nearly five years, but I do wish for you to be pleased with your life here. And despite calling you servant, I do think on you as a friend." She looked at Erin again, feeling embarrassed and uncomfortable. "I still do not know what is proper."

Erin smiled. "Methinks you do know what is proper, but do not honor it much of the time—for which I am grateful, although your husband may not be." She winked and Deborah knew she had heard Japhet's complaints. "I forget as well," Erin went on, "that I am not the only one who aches. But 'tis a bitter pill as Mary said. Had our land been not snatched, I should be thither in its lush green. 'Tis so lovely, Deborah, a'times I cannot believe I have left it." She made a choking sound and covered her mouth with the back of her hand.

Deborah put her hand on Erin's shoulder and felt her soften under it. They stood in silence, then Erin put her hand over Deborah's and patted it. "Let us not speak more about it." She stepped away and wiped her eyes. "I have finished with the rushlights. I'll bring you the rest of the tallow and help with the hide."

She returned with the kettle. They turned the hide over to its non-grain side and rubbed in the fat. They worked hard, and Deborah realized that only a few months back she would have been weary already at this task; she *was* much stronger than she had been when she arrived. She paused for a moment and watched Erin, who was as tall as Deborah, but stockier and stronger. Not ungainly, though, Deborah thought. She is hardy and lithe at the same time. She is lovely.

Erin glanced at her, and Deborah blushed. She began to rub the hide again in earnest, but soon her thoughts returned to Erin. She asked, "I have ne'er inquired—how was it you made the whistle on the ship?"

Erin laughed and dipped her hands into the tallow. "My Aunt Gwen taught me. She was a witch."

Deborah glanced around as if they could be overheard. "You say the word so freely."

"Yes?"

"Were witches not hanged or burned in Ireland?"

Erin kneaded the hide some more before answering. "I have heard of one ... two. But 'twas by the English, Deborah, not the Irish. Why should we kill she who keeps us well and speaks with the fairies? Should be like killing your mother while you're yet at her pap."

"But was your aunt not feared?" Deborah pressed. "Because she could do what others could not."

"My aunt was loved, Deborah." She paused. "Give me leave to tell you the difference in the main between the English and the Irish. You fear what you cannot understand, while we hold it dear."

Deborah stared at her, thinking she might be right. To be sure, she said to herself, I fear it a'times.

She made a spiraling stroke on the hide. "My grandmother was a witch, though she dare not speak the word aloud where others might hear. She was called 'wisewoman' because she cured with plants. The book of which I spoke is a book of receipts she gave me ere I left England, which hath stories in it as well. It hath a passage I wish to read to you. 'Tis a horrid tale, but 'twill explain why I saw my mother in the puddle. And why we have been frighted from the word 'witch.' Shall I read it?"

"Aye!" Erin said. "I intended to ask you of the book when you spake of it before. You can read, then?"

"Yes. The Goddess Brigid taught us and we have passed it down."

"Brigid?" Erin seemed surprised. "I ne'er heard you English speak of *Bríd* excepting as saint."

"She was known mostly in the north but no longer, except among the Catholic, as you say." Deborah smiled. "Brigid is also the name I took at my first blood."

Erin smiled back with a look of trust. "Go and fetch your book. It seems we hold e'en more in common than we knew."

Deborah returned quickly. She looked around to be sure they wouldn't be surprised by an unexpected visitor, then sat with Erin against the broad trunk of an oak tree. She put her knees up to hide the volume in case someone did happen along, then turned to a page near the beginning.

Long ago e'erie Woman was sacred, One withe Mother. And e'erie Man was sacred, One withe her Son. But as Time passt Woman and Man forgott they were Divine and came to holde Awe for those fewe who remembr'd and call'd them Priestess and Priest. Deborah you askt me howe we came to be fear'd and hated. This is howe. A newe Churche came acrost the Sea and grewe strong in the Cities. It banish'd the Priestess and rais'd the Son above Mother. Mary they call'd her. In the Countrie the Churche had not this holde, and we Priestesses, then known as Wicce, continu'd Brigids Charge to Render, Heal and Shape. But the Churche did come at the last into the Countrie and fann'd into Fear the Awe the People helde. And withe the turning of Speech from Wicce to Witch so we were caste downe.

You Deborah love all and wishe to believe they have Goodness in their Hearts. You saye the Clergie and Physicians believ'd they fought their Devill when they kill'd those who remembr'd Brigids Charge. But I saye to you if that is so why did they use Trickery as you wille see.

You aske as welle if there were not those of us who us'd our pow'r in harmeful ways and I saye to be sure it must be so for who shou'd not use all pow'r when attackt. And to be sure, some might use pow'r in harmeful ways when not attackt but that parte is as small as anie other in our people. For if a Smithy uses his Hammer to smote his Neighbour dead doe we then hang all Smithys? So shou'd it be if a Witch doth harme withe Poison or Hex. Onelie she shou'd be punish'd and onelie if the Harme was for no juste Cause as 'twou'd be for the Smithy. You must remember this as welle, whate'er hex a Witch castes comes back on her three times o'er. So thinks she long ere she takes suche a Riske.

Another Word ere the Tale begins. The Churche then the State increase its Wealth withe our Deathes. For the Witch and her Familie must paye for her Execution withe their Properties. Thusly did my Uncle lose his Farme after my Aunts hanging and remove him selfe to London.

Deborah paused, once again shaken by the words. It seemed as if Granna were there, speaking to her.

I was but nine years and my Mamma did take me to a distant towne where her Sister had married and remov'd and was accus'd. She stoode upon the Pillorie alongside her Accuser Reverend-Doctor Hanks. Still I recall the Name. She was naked to her Waiste and bent over. She lookt as one who had neither eaten nor slept for Dayes.

The Reverend-Doctor helde aloft her Confession which he said admitted to Intercourse withe the Devill. I knewe that to be a lie so I cried for what they muste have done to win her Marke on that Page. My crying ceast presently for Aunt Madeline rais'd her Head. She snatcht the Paper and tore it in twain calling out in a Voice I shant forgett. I remain true onelie to Brigid greatt Mother of the Isle of Britain. The Executioner took his Rope and smote it acrost her Back. A fewe cried out in the Crowde and my Aunt felle silent.

The Reverend-Doctor spake again of her devillishness saying she had Medical Skille no Woman cou'd have. Thus it must come from the Devill. He said some had complayn'd to him they wou'd perish without her Curings and spake to him of her Goodness. He said as God would wille it a Pricker was in Towne to prove again before her Deathe she indeed be a Witch.

The Pricker helde aloft a Needle and said Witches have Markes so the Devill shou'd know howe to finde them. These Markes doe not bleede when they are prickt. He stabb'd that Needle into a Mole on my Aunts Face. When he pull'd it out there was no Bloode upon it or her. He putt the Needle in his Waistecoat pockett as some in the Crowde shouted for her Deathe.

As they putt the Noose about my Aunts Neck, the Needle slippt out of his pockett and felle to the Flor of the Pillorie. My Aunt opened her Eyes and lookt at me. I heard her voice inside my head saye The Needle. I saw it there on the Flor and took it up and presst it to my Thumbe. It did not prick me. I stabb'd into the Wood of the Pillorie. When I pull'd it awaye I found no Marke. I stabb'd again. No Marke was there. The Needle was a Tricke. It felle away when presst. The Pricker look'd downe at me and gave a start and strove to grabb my Hand. I strove to toss the Needle to the Crowde but he caught my arm and lifted me. I droppt the Needle and he droppt me. I ran and he call'd after me, Seize that Childe. She is another Witch.

I ran thro Legs and about Bodies. Some strove to grabb me but many more did not. Some e'en gave a pushe this waye and that. Methinks the Reverend-Doctor did see their Help for he ceast his call for me and prayed God shou'd save my Aunt Madelines Soule. I heard the snapp of her Neck as Mamma took me upon her Mare.

Deborah closed the book and stared off into the distance. Her and Erin's knees were touching. "Such rarely occurs now," she said haltingly, "because they have killed most all the true witches, and so many who were not. I am all who yet remains from our line, and Granna sent me hither to carry it to the New World. To fulfill Brigid's charge." She looked at Erin. "I am frighted. I am not stalwart as was Granna. And I wish to be loved by my neighbors, not viewed with suspicion."

Erin put an arm around her, and Deborah rested her head on her shoulder. "You will be loved," Erin said. "You are." She said this softly, almost under her breath.

Deborah sat up and faced her, felt absorbed by her pale blue eyes, felt a thrill move through her chest and sex. "Who are you?" she whispered.

Erin laughed, and the quivering ceased. Deborah blinked several times as if to clear her vision. She wasn't sure what had just happened. The smile on Erin's face seemed knowing, but Deborah couldn't tell if she had experienced the same thing and was afraid to ask.

Erin said, "I am neither more nor less than what you see. You fear Mystery, Deborah. Behold it."

"Behold it?" She moved away, suddenly angry. "I thought I did till you arrived. Now I feel I know naught. I fear my grandmother hath not taught me enough to survive. And I fear I have listened over-well to my mother and shall a'ways be frighted."

Erin nodded thoughtfully. "I know not what to say 'cepting you seem to lie upon the road. You have will, Deborah. Shape your fate."

Her advice seemed to echo Granna's dying words. "Build a bridge to bear my weight," Deborah said.

"What is that?"

"Granna said it to me ere she died."

"What more did she say?"

Deborah shook her head. "This is one reason I ask who you are—you inquire of me as if you a'ready know what I shall reply. As if you merely bid me remember."

Erin smiled as though found out. "You are on to me, then? I jest, Deborah, but 'tis the truth in part. A'times I know the answer ere I ask, but mostly I do not. Just then, I heard an old woman's voice and so I thought 'twas your Granna and was important. So, I ask again, what say she to you?"

The words came as if given: "I shall not be alone."

Erin smiled and leaned over and kissed her cheek. Her breath was warm and smelled of chocolate. When she pulled back, she had tears in her eyes. "Do not fear me again," she said.

"I– I shall not."

"Let us finish with that buck ere Japhet returns." Erin started to get up.

Deborah caught her arm. She wanted to explain it wasn't only her keen hearing and knowing that she feared. Erin looked perplexed, didn't seem to be reading her thoughts this time. Deborah released her. "Yes," she said and stood up. "I 'spect Japhet will be along presently."

Erin stayed outside with the hide while Deborah returned the book to its hiding place in the trunk. She closed the lid, then sat on it, thinking back to the desire she had felt for Erin. No, that cannot be, she thought. I felt joy because I am no longer alone, because Erin is a witch like me.

MOTHER
1708

18

ERE IT WAS again, skulking in like a burglar while Deborah tried in vain to sleep. She braced herself and hoped it would pass quickly—the feeling she had made a mistake; the feeling that after four years and three children, she still did not love her husband. She liked him, respected him, thought him a fine man, but she did not *love* him as she thought she should.

She groaned and turned over, then sat up. Her three-month-old, John, stirred in his walnut cradle. Robert, her nineteen-month-old, slept peacefully in the trundle bed at the foot of their bed. Her daughter Mary slept in the other bedroom with Erin.

It was midnight she guessed. John would be ready for another feeding soon, and Deborah knew she should sleep while she could, but wakefulness had become habit. A habit which remained unchanged by skullcap or any other tincture she had made.

Once she asked Grace if she ever had trouble sleeping, and Grace had looked at her with surprise, then said she was made so weary by the children and her work that she fell asleep the second she lay down. It wasn't that she wasn't fatigued, Deborah tried to explain, but gave up. For the truth was that though her exhaustion the next day was difficult to tolerate, if she wasn't plagued by disturbing feelings she usually liked being awake at night. She enjoyed the silence and the solitude, the time to think.

But not tonight. Tonight she was unsettled.

Japhet smacked his lips and pushed off the quilts. Something in the gesture reminded Deborah of sleeping on the dirt floor of the cabin. She smiled, grateful for their four-poster bed. Although it had been tedious to make the mattresses, she sang through every bit of the work since it meant she was that much closer to sleeping in comfort.

Every day that first year when she went out to feed their fowl, she gathered all the feathers she saw. She picked over them carefully, discarding those that were too bald, and once a week washed her collection in the stream. On baking day at Mary's, after the bread was taken from the oven, Deborah put the clean feathers in. When they were dried, she added that week's collection to the canvas bag hanging in the corner of the cabin.

She made four mattresses during the year before the house was completed: one for herself and Japhet, one for Erin and Mary, and two small ones for the cradle and trundle bed. While Deborah gathered, spun, sewed, and stuffed, Erin plaited straw, fashioning paillasses to go beneath each feather mattress.

Mayhap I should sleep better on the dirt floor after all, Deborah thought grimly. She got out of bed, then climbed down the narrow twisting staircase to the main room, a combination living and dining area. She took her cloak off a peg by the front door and walked onto the small flagstone porch. It had been a mild fall so far, barely distinguishable from summer except for the colored leaves. She held her cloak without putting it on and looked at the full moon. 'Tis the reason I am troubled, she thought. When the moon brims, so do the heart's secrets.

She stepped off the porch and looked back at the house. Japhet disdained the new architecture popular with the Anglicans in Burlington and had modeled their home after the older ones in Burlington County. This house was larger and more carefully constructed, but still reflected their simplicity, square shape, and brick pattern. Up close in the daylight, the bricks were irregular: pink, orange, and red, but from even a short distance they appeared to be a uniform russet.

"'Tis lovely weather, is it not?" Japhet asked. He had stepped into the open doorway. "We might sleep out-of-doors on such a night as this, if we desired."

"To be sure," Deborah agreed, both sorry and glad he'd come down. "Couldst thou not sleep?"

"I woke when thou left." There was a catch in his voice and Deborah waited. "Do I disturb thee?" he asked.

He sounded so young and kind she walked to the doorway and put her arm through his. "No," she said, smiling up at him. "Shall we have some chamomile?" He squeezed her arm affectionately and they went back inside.

After hanging up her cloak, she walked through the main room into the kitchen. A shared massive stone fireplace extended nearly the length of both rooms. At the cooking end of the hearth Deborah hung an iron kettle on the trammel—a chain and hook device suspended from a lug pole moored inside the chimney—which held food vessels in position over the fire. She reached over her head to the drying pole and pulled down a few sprigs of chamomile.

When she brought in the tea, Japhet was asleep with his head on the table. A tallow candle burned close to his black hair. She moved the flame, sat across from him on a stool, and scooped honey from an earthen jar. He raised his head and wiped sleep from his eyes.

Deborah stirred her tea. "Mary tells me she's begun to use cotton wicking for candles rather than pith. Next she fashions some, I'll watch how she does it."

"Once was a time in Burlington," he said, stretching, "when most settlers used split pine knots for light. Soon as I could wield an ax, 'twas my chore to chop them. They were difficult to start. I'd toss them into the fire and let them sit awhile, then have care whilst I fished them out with a tong. They gave out much smoke but 'twas a pleasing odor. I hear they were about right for the must of the caves in which the settlers first lived."

"Mam," came a sleepy voice. Their three-year-old daughter stood on the stairs.

"Come hither, Mary," Deborah said. "Pappa will tell us again the story of the first Friend settlers of Burlington." She smiled teasingly at him. "Thou wert about to tell it again."

"Thou know'st me well."

Mary tromped over and climbed onto Deborah's lap. She took a sip of her mother's tea and made a face.

"More honey, my sweet?" Deborah laughed.

Mary nodded, then watched the gooey substance drop from the wooden dipper her mother used.

Japhet took a sip of tea and began. "William Penn collected on a debt owed his father and received the grant of Pennsylvania. And though the Crown said 'twas his, he did not concur till he had purchased it fairly—some might say, again—from the Lenni-Lenape who were its rightful owners. Few others did suchly, Mary, which is why there are wars with the Indians in other colonies. And which is why the Lenape shall not make a treaty with a white man unless a Friend be present.

"But before Penn received Pennsylvania, he became a proprietor of this colony, known then as West Jersey, which was a Friends colony until we were united with East Jersey and lost control of our government."

"Jersey," Mary said sleepily, pushing her head into Deborah's breasts, putting her thumb into her mouth.

"Methinks thou speak'st above her head," Deborah said lightly, pushing Mary's brown hair out of her eyes.

"Better above it than below," he said indignantly. "Thou wouldst prefer I tell her one of Erin's fairy stories?"

"At the least, she doth not fall asleep for them."

Mary sat up and looked at her parents glowering at each other. "Tell the story, Pappa," she said.

"So I shall." He smiled at her, avoiding Deborah's eyes, and began again. "Now, to the early settlers. A few brought frames of houses with them on the ship, all ready to be assembled, but most did not, and thus had no houses in which to live. Some lived with the Indians in their villages, but the majority preferred to remain with their fellows so they dug caves into the banks of the Delaware River. Some of those caves were as large as this room. They built up the sides with sod or saplings and laid crude chimneys of stick mortared with clay and grass.

"The rugged conditions in which all settlers found themselves—regardless of their stations in England—were a great leveler, and thus was our old way turned upon its head. For those best suited for life in this New World are of coarse, not gentle birth."

"Well said." Erin descended the stairs clad in her white morning gown, her waist-length hair loose. "You could write pamphlets like your father." She slid onto a stool at the foot of the table.

"I have asked thee not to speak of my father," Japhet said bitterly.

"Goodness, *Master*, but you are in a pique this night."

"*Erin,*" Deborah said.

He looked sharply at Erin. "'Tis very well for thee thy indenture was not purchased by one who would cast thee out for thy impudence. For thou hast proven time and again thou know'st not the meaning of the word 'Master.'"

"*Japhet,*" Deborah said.

"As you are a Friend," Erin retorted, "I should think you would not know it either."

"And that is my folly," he said, "for thou takest advantage of my tolerance a'times."

"I am pleased to hear only a'times. But as this is the first I have heard you speak directly of displeasure with me, now on nearly the eve of my leave-taking, prithee, how would you have me be, then?"

"Firstly, thou hast more than six months left of thy indenture, so do not rush so out the door. Secondly, how I should have thee be is not as my wife would have it, thus on that score 'twas of little use to upbraid thee. But since thou hast asked, I should have thee not come down in the mid of the night when we are sitting at table. However, I am certain," he looked at Deborah, "that my wife would have thee join us, even prefer thy company to mine. Therefore I am the one who will bid adieu."

He stood up and looked with guarded appeal at Deborah. She thought he seemed to want her to prove him wrong, but felt too much hostility in the request to oblige him. Not that she blamed him for his hard feelings. For it was true she preferred Erin's company to his. With Erin she bared her true soul and felt at home. And because Japhet surely sensed this and resented Erin for it, Deborah sometimes found herself trying to soothe relations between them. But never had Erin goaded him as she had tonight. Is this how 'twill be for the rest of her time? she wondered with dismay.

She finally answered in a voice she hoped was neutral, "I'll be along."

With a frown, he glanced at Mary, sleeping against Deborah's chest. "We have much work tomorrow with market the morrow next."

"I have not forgotten, and I shall be along as I said. I'll bring Mary when I come."

"All right, then," he said in a resigned voice and went upstairs.

Erin moved to his stool, then sipped the tea he had left behind.

"I do wish you twain would not quarrel," Deborah said.

"'Tis because of you. We are jealous of the other." She grinned.

Deborah lowered her head. It upset her when Erin joked like that, reminding her of the desire she successfully kept buried most of the time, a feeling, she realized again, that was not as distant as she had hoped.

She said, "Thou art my friend, and Japhet is my husband. You twain have no call to be at odds."

"Yes, yes," Erin said, then smiled. "And soon I shall no longer be your servant."

Deborah tried to return the smile, yet was miserable at the thought of losing Erin and could only grimace.

"But we shall be neighbors and true friends then," Erin said, obviously puzzled.

"Yes, to be sure." Deborah knew her effort at enthusiasm appeared as insincere as it was, so she couldn't bring herself to look at Erin. She stared at her tea, then sipped it, but it was too sweet for her now, so she pushed it away. "Goodness, but the moon hath entered our house this night."

"Because we have not honored her, she comes unbidden through the back door."

"*Erin.*" Deborah raised her head and said in a low voice, "I told thee we must have more care. Wait till he is away for our rituals."

"You told me." She reached over and took a sip of Deborah's sweet tea.

Deborah watched the candle burn, noticing its scent of cooking fat. "All right. The moon will be full again tomorrow. We will tell Japhet we are gathering herbs, and then after we have plucked some, we will cut our wands."

"Good." Erin smiled.

"Now, I am going to bed. Come, Mary, 'tis time for thee to sleep on thy mattress." Mary stretched up her arm and accidentally hit her mother in the nose. "Lord!" Deborah exclaimed, brusquely pushing her daughter's hand to the side.

Mary looked up, about to cry, then glanced over at Erin, who was grinning. Mary started to giggle, crossing her hands over her mouth.

"Should I fall down the stairs you twain would fall to fits," Deborah said.

"Oh now," Erin chided.

Deborah eased her daughter off her lap and stood up. "Art thou coming, Erin?" she asked, still feeling cross.

Erin took a long, last sip of Japhet's tea, then Deborah's, and got to her feet as well.

Mary wasn't allowed to touch the candle, but as usual she stood right next to it to watch her mother put it out. Deborah licked her forefinger and thumb and pinched the wick. The flame died with a sizzle.

Only moonlight gave the room a pale glow. Erin was in the right about the moon, Deborah thought. She shall not be slighted. She hath laid my heart open like a book, which I fear now I cannot close.

19

HE SUN was setting when Deborah parked the cart near a field which bore an abundance of meadowsweet. She had come to rely on the herb because it cured so many ailments. Her teas treated inflamed stomach conditions, from overeating to ulcers, and also relieved headaches and women's discomforts. She used it in a tincture to treat ague, gout, and chickenpox, and as a wash to clear up rashes.

She and Erin carried large baskets and were dressed in loose gowns that allowed easy movement. They weren't picking at this hour to hide their activity—for nearly everyone in the community used Deborah's medicines and she was a common and welcome sight in the area's fields and woods—but because Deborah preferred to gather herbs at the end of the day. To do so at any other time would interfere with her duties as wife and mother. And though Japhet was proud of his wife and boasted of her cures, he wouldn't be happy if it meant he had to care for the children or prepare his own dinner.

His cousin's remarks had proved accurate. Deborah's medicines were widely used but her other healing skills were not. Except in the case of a birth, her neighbors called for Dr. Grant in an emergency. And while cousin Mary still objected to that situation, Deborah did not. It afforded her the time she thought she needed to more fully learn her craft.

Now the surroundings were too dark to see clearly. Deborah returned to the cart to retrieve a candle lantern, then continued to pick, sharing the light with Erin. She squatted to cut a particularly stubborn stalk.

"Mayhap the next time we gather herbs we ought bring little Mary along," Erin said.

Deborah looked at her with puzzlement, for though neither she nor Erin could exactly articulate the reason, they both agreed Mary was probably not Deborah's heir to her wisdom and knowledge.

"Why, Erin?"

"You have had two sons, one after the other. What if you are not blessed with another girl?"

The thought seemed ridiculous, for it had become increasingly clear to Deborah—with the birth of three healthy children—that she was meant to have many. Surely, one of them would be the girl she awaited.

"I cannot believe I should be left barren on that score. She will come. I have only to be patient."

"You may wait for a thing that will never be, and then have nothing. Mary may not be the one you seek, but she could learn some of our craft."

Deborah cut another stalk. Erin's proposal seemed risky or at the least unwelcome, for the only time they could talk freely about their religion was when they were away from the house gathering herbs. If they started to bring Mary along, they would either have to silence themselves or risk her repeating what they said to her father. She was surprised Erin hadn't thought of that, or perhaps she trusted that the girl could be silent.

"No, Erin. I should rather wait my entire life for the right one than risk being found out. Dost thou truly believe Mary could be shown the edges of our work without breathing of it to another?" For that, Deborah thought, would be my undoing. Although well tolerated as a female healer within a certain range, she thought her pagan religion would not be. In truth, she wasn't certain how the Friends would react. They were known for their tolerance—West Jersey had insured religious freedom—but witches were quite another matter, were they not? She never wanted to test it.

"Methinks children keep secrets better than their reputation bespeaks," Erin said, "but to be sure I see the need for your caution. And 'tis your daughter, after all."

Deborah noticed the longing in her voice and was surprised. Erin had never talked about having children. But of course with her indenture nearing its end, Deborah considered, she would have such thoughts of her future—which likely will include the Kirkbride's servant, Patrick. A burly young man with dark hair and eyes, he had courted Erin for a few months. Deborah shuddered as if from the cold.

Erin put her arm around her. "We have nearly picked it clean, have we not? Let us make our way to the buttonwood." They returned to the cart.

As Deborah drove up to the Witches' Tree, she was impressed as always by its size and animation—its massive crooked branches reaching out like arms to embrace the river. She handed the reins to Erin and looked around. No candles shone in any of the nearby houses and no one was about.

Deborah climbed down from the cart, pulled two crates from it, then walked warily toward the tree as if approaching a wild horse. She put the crates down, pressed her palms against the trunk, and looked up into its branches.

A low roar rose as if from the tree's roots and entered her hands, filling them with a sap-like weight that moved through her body. She raised one foot, just to see if she could, and a charge like lightning shot upward through her. As she grabbed the tree to steady herself, she felt hands on her waist. Erin kissed the back of her head and moved to her side. Holding hands, they reached around the tree's massive trunk. Two rough, wrinkled hands took their free hands and closed the circle. Isaiah had joined them. A short distance away at the cart, the horses neighed and stamped their feet.

"Ah yes, 'tis very good thou hast come," Deborah said.

"Indeed, lass," he answered, "the tree calls me to all such occasions."

They put their foreheads to the trunk and she again felt the sap-like weight. When she lifted her foot this time the density slowed the lightning charge, protracted it, enabling an alchemy of the two, from which music rose. She opened her mouth to let it out. "Ahhhhh . . ."

Erin and Isaiah joined in the call which aligned them with the sacred elements of life: air, water, fire, earth, spirit. Overhead, the branches began to shake and Deborah heard the cry of a bird. They followed it with their voices which rose, striking a high, almost strident harmony. They reached their arms into the air. The song's crescendo lifted up and out, as if it had substance, into the indigo sky.

Deborah dropped to her knees and touched her forehead to the ground. Her breath settled; her heart pounded in her throat. All this was forbidden, dangerous, but impossible to resist. She got to her feet again and asked, "Hast thou the blade, Erin?"

With the sheathed knife between her teeth, Deborah stood on the crates, stacked like steps, and began to climb the tree. Erin helped, mounting the crates as well to push Deborah until she had reached the lowest branch and straddled it. The limb was broad and Deborah sat for a few moments, catching her breath, steadying her nerve. An intersection of more branches spread out only a few feet away. She braced her hands in front of her for leverage and support, then crept forward. When she reached the dividing point, she grabbed a sturdy limb above and pulled herself to a squat. Slowly she stood, gripping branch after branch over her head, and then began to move farther out.

"Have care," Isaiah called. "Have care."

Finally she saw it: a reddish-blond and grey mottled beauty about three feet long and an inch in diameter. Every half foot or so, a stub as if of a new twig emerged. The promise of spring, she thought.

Still holding onto support above her, she stepped out a little more, seized the desired branch near its base and yanked down, making an almost clean break. Quickly, she cut the wood still attached, then sliced the side of her palm and rubbed her blood on the wounded places on both tree and branch.

She was suddenly aware of light and looked through the branches to see the rising moon, yellow and full. She held her branch toward it, powering the wand, feeling again the radiant link among all life, remembering again why she practiced these rituals. Her medicines would be blessed. Her link to Granna had been renewed. She felt beyond any doubt that she was part of the lineage that bore wisdom from the time of Brigid's first priestess. She knew Brigid would never leave her or fail her, for she had been entrusted with the care and survival of sacred knowledge. She was merged with a body larger than herself, and nothing would change that. In this moment, the possibility of persecution didn't worry her. One way or another, Brigid would ensure that her truth survived.

Deborah kissed the wand, more certain than ever that she should not attempt to teach Mary. Were we in olden times, she thought, Mary would be a good pagan, but she would not be a witch. Brigid hath not chosen her, hath not marked her with large healing hands or unusual perceptions. Mary is a lively, lovely girl but not a healer, and not a witch.

Deborah tucked the wand under her arm, sheathed the knife and put it between her teeth again, and started to climb down.

Erin and Isaiah each grabbed a leg when they could and helped her the rest of the way.

"'Tis lovely, is it not?" she asked, holding up her treasure.

"As are you," Erin said, looking into Deborah's eyes, seeming to regard her as more than friend.

Deborah stood, staff in hand, wanting to embrace Erin as a lover. Yet, she thought, what if I mistake her meaning, and she recoils? The hesitation cost Deborah the opportunity. Erin turned aside, then bent down to check the buckles on her shoes.

There will be another moment, Deborah thought, and one when we are alone. She climbed onto the stacked crates after Erin, and helped her begin her climb.

20

HE MARKET in Burlington wasn't nearly as large as the one in Leeds, England, but Deborah often felt like a child there, not exactly lost, but awed by the eclectic selection of merchandise, mostly homemade and homespun. She and Japhet preferred walking around to sitting behind a table, so as usual they had left their barter in the cart while they searched for what they needed. They had brought linen and wool spun by her; rugs he'd woven and chairs made of stripped planks and limbs; corn, rye, and wheat; and her medicines for various ailments such as coughs and nausea, as well as salves for cuts and burns.

Little Mary held onto Deborah's gown and yanked her this way and that, darting for anything colorful. It usually pleased Deborah that her daughter's longing for color was so much like her own, but today she was tired from too little sleep and having a hard enough time keeping baby John quiet in her arms. She snapped at Mary to be still.

Japhet was losing patience as well, so they split up. He went in search of sugar, salt, seed, and flour. Deborah and Mary looked for a blanket.

"Thither!" Mary shouted, forgetting her mother's admonition and pulling her to where a young Lenape man sat surrounded by wares.

"Good day," Mary said politely, her hands clasped in front of her.

"Good day." The man nodded at her.

Deborah noticed his long, slender hands when he gave Mary a doll.

"Mam, may I have it?" Mary showed her the doll. Its corncob body was dyed reddish-brown and dressed in deerskin, but its hair was blond, made of fresh corn silk that hadn't yet browned.

Deborah did a quick calculation. "Thou may'st have it, Mary. And there is a blanket for Robert." She gestured.

The man spread out the light blue cloth on top of others in a pile, then picked up a pair of moccasins and pointed them at her belly and then at John, who was sleeping now. "For young mother," he said.

Deborah rubbed the soft deerskin. They will feel fine, she thought, but will my neighbors find mirth in my dressing like a woodman? She glanced around.

Mary touched the shoes. "They are soft, Mam."

The man pushed over a crate for her to sit on. Balancing John in one arm, she slipped on the moccasins, then walked around. They had the summer comfort of bare feet with the winter warmth of leather.

She sat down again, staring at her feet. Though the farm produced well, with no sons of age there was only so much Japhet could plant and reap. Still, they were not poor by any means. She walked around again. I have had no new footwear since I arrived, she considered, more than four years now. "I will trade *my* linen for them."

"Yea!" Mary raced in a circle around her and the man.

"Mary is my sweet girl." Deborah laughed. "Wishes her Mam to wear these."

She brought over the cart and bartered a chair and linen for the moccasins, blanket, and doll. After the exchange they left the cart there and went to find Japhet to show him what they had traded.

He smiled at the corncob doll and held the blanket against his face. "'Tis a fine one," he said. Then he reached for the moccasins and laughed.

"The Lenape told me they are good for a woman who hath recently borne."

"Did he now? I fancy thou wilt cut quite the figure in them," he teased.

"I suppose I shall." She snatched them back.

"Deborah, Deborah Leeds," a female voice called out.

Deborah turned to see Elizabeth Basnett approaching. "I hoped to see thee today. Good day, Japhet." She nodded at him. "I am in need of more of thy slippery elm root lozenges. My winter sore throat hath arrived early."

Deborah stepped closer and tilted back the older woman's head so the sun would illuminate her mouth and throat cavity. "I see no undue redness or white spots by which to be further troubled, so I shall give thee lozenges for thy relief." She let go of her head. "Come along with me."

Mary took her mother's hand, and the three of them headed back to the cart. "The throat might ache for many a reason," Deborah said, "even for not having enough sleep, but it might also herald great illness." She counted out eight lozenges and wrapped them in a thin cloth. "Thou must be vigilant about it and call for me or Dr. Grant if these do not ease the pain, or if it persists longer than two days, or if thou hast other ailments."

Elizabeth accepted the lozenges and promised to deliver two chicks to the farm in recompense. As they parted, she asked, "Shall I see thee at Meeting?"

"Y– yes, to be sure." Deborah watched her leave, feeling anxious as she often did in the face of such questions. It wasn't that she disliked the meetings, for she usually found them pleasing. The quiet contemplation that comprised most of them was calming and left her free for her own thoughts. In the four years she had gone to meetings with Japhet, she hadn't found anything in their beliefs that directly countered hers. They were a good, tolerant, generally peaceful people, who had many ideas she admired. What troubled her was being reminded of her pretense. For although she had never officially joined the Meeting, her membership was taken for granted. She attended regularly with Japhet, dressed plainly, and had adopted their speech. And though since the first Women's Meeting she had never felt forced to act contrary to her principles, it was still an act—an act of self-preservation, but a deception nonetheless.

Mary tugged on her arm. "Yes," Deborah said, glad to be released from disturbing thoughts, "let us find thy father."

As they crossed the market area, Deborah saw Japhet standing with a young couple she didn't recognize. He waved, then left them to meet her.

"They are the itinerants I told thee about," he said, "who fashion a bedstead for Jeb and Grace. I . . ." He hesitated. "When they are finished they will come to our farm. Then thou shalt have thy wet nurse and I a hand."

Deborah stared at him, shocked he had taken them on without consulting her. They *had* talked about hiring more servants, especially a wet nurse to help her with the boys, but he had chosen them without her agreement. She was livid.

They walked over to the pair. Mary whirled around behind her mother during the introductions, and Deborah nodded at them, trying to be polite. They were very young. Johanna couldn't be more than eighteen, and Ethan twenty. Despite their roving life, Ethan was stout, straining the seams of his homespun blue breeches and linen shirt. Johanna was thin, too thin, from nursing and inadequate food, Deborah surmised. She wore a dark blue gown, stained with milk on the front, and a white apron. Her dark brown eyes were large and bulging. Deborah looked again at the stain and wondered how long ago Johanna had lost her child—if indeed she had. How sorrowful it must be to lose your own, she thought, then hire out and suckle others.

Johanna started, then squinted questioningly at Deborah as if she had heard something that surprised her. My thoughts? Deborah wondered. Could she have heard my thoughts? Intrigued, Deborah watched as Johanna reached into the basket she held and pulled back its cloth. The sun made a rainbow glint on the lone fish lying within. Deborah gasped, remembering the girl on the dock at Philadelphia who had held her entranced. Is Johanna that girl? she wondered, noticing the resemblance.

Johanna revealed nothing, her face impassive. She said, "Lovely fish at market—Mrs. Kirkbride will be pleased," then put the cloth back.

"Whence have you twain come?" Japhet asked. "Jeb ne'er told me."

"Massachusetts," Ethan replied.

Johanna bent over and reached out a hand to Mary, who still cowered behind her mother. "Soon, little one, we shall be great friends. She's a lovely girl, Mrs. Leeds. And look at this one." She touched John's cheek. "You have yet another at home? I trust I shall be a help to you."

Deborah swallowed, still thinking of the fish, and could only nod.

"Well, Ethan," Johanna said, then motioned to her husband that they ought to be going. They said their farewells and left.

The ride home seemed bumpier than usual. After a particularly deep rut that sent Deborah off her seat, she snapped, "Why didst thou not consult with me?"

Japhet kept his eyes on the dirt road. "We spoke on it a'ready. Thou said thou wouldst have a wet nurse. Thou know'st there are none in Burlington just now. Ethan and Johanna happened along, so I hired them ere did someone else."

"And thou hadst no leave to consult with me about it?"

"I did not think 'twould vex thee. Besides, with Erin's indenture o'er in a manner of months, we will have need of another servant."

That hurt and he seemed to know it. He winced, resentful enough to take a jab at her, Deborah noted, but not cruel enough to enjoy it.

"Be that as it may," he said, "thou art in the right. I ought to have discussed it with thee. But I cannot go back on my word, nor do I wish to. Ethan is highly regarded by Jeb, and Grace told me she will be loathe to let Johanna go. She says she keeps her children well occupied—not an easy task, as thou know'st."

Deborah nodded, satisfied by his apology. She allowed herself to imagine sleeping an entire night without nursing. Heaven, she thought. "It shall be good to have them, but do not e'er again think it unimportant to consult with me."

"I shan't," he said, but didn't look at her. Deborah had a fleeting feeling there was something else he hadn't told her. She was about to ask when they hit another deep rut and John woke up wailing.

"Shh, shh, my boy," she said, holding him tighter. He went searching for her breast. "Not on this bumping road, little one." She held him up, making faces to distract him. An image of Johanna suckling him came into her mind and left her uneasy. She held him close again. "All shall be well, John," she consoled herself. "Mamma simply doth not wish to let thee go."

For the remainder of the ride the image of the girl with the fish lingered in her mind. Even if she and Johanna are not one in the same, she thought, 'tis at the least an omen. But of what? Good or ill? Mayhap Johanna hath been sent as some form of replacement for Erin. No, that cannot be. No one could replace Erin. They loved each other as sisters, as more than sisters. Then what? She received no answer and let the query go. To be sure, she thought, 'twill be revealed soon enough. For there is something of import to her arrival. Of that I have no doubt.

21

DON'T NEED the hindrance of some Puritan child," Erin said. "You tell Japhet I don't want her. You tell him I shan't have her."

"Erin, she is not a child. No! Robert! Stay clear of the fire. Mary, hold his hand, I told thee. Take him to the crib." Addressing Erin again, Deborah said, "Thou know'st I need a wet nurse."

"Not if you would wean Robert. He is nearly old enough."

"Granna said a child ought wean itself. 'Tis the better way, methinks."

"But why do you have to choose a Puritan? You know they hate the Irish, and they've hanged a Quaker or two in Boston as well."

"That was long ago. If she were so hateful she should not be amongst Friends now, should she?"

"I'd not trust that."

Deborah watched Erin furiously scrubbing potatoes and decided on another approach. "I will tell her she is to take direction from thee."

Erin stopped and looked up. "She shall not be pleased," she said, and couldn't hide her smile.

Oh dear me, Deborah thought, she will torment the poor girl. Robert wailed suddenly, and Deborah turned toward him. "Mary! Allow him a look at thy doll. Remain with him and he shan't harm it."

"Yes, he shall." Mary pouted but handed the corncob doll to her brother.

"When do they arrive?" Erin asked.

"When they finish the bedstead. Another two weeks at the least, I should imagine."

"Hmm." Erin put down the knife and wiped her hands on her apron. "Mary," she said, "come tend the turkey ere it burns."

Mary snatched her doll from Robert, and he wailed again. Deborah glared at her daughter as she went over and picked up Robert and sat down on a stool. She removed her modesty piece and lifted out a breast, closing her eyes as Robert quieted and began to suckle.

Sitting on a low stool before the fireplace, Mary used a pointed stick to turn the turkey, which hung from a toe-string looped around a spike on the inside of the mantel. Below the bird was a drip pan which caught the fat and juices. The luscious aroma filled the room.

While Mary turned the turkey, Erin basted it, then poured the drippings into a three-legged iron skillet which sat in the embers. After putting the drip pan back beneath the bird, she scooped flour into the skillet to make gravy.

Mary started to get up, and Erin said, "No, remain. Poke at it."

John was crying now, so Deborah put Robert in the crib and picked John up from his cradle in order to nurse him.

"You also should not need the girl," Erin said, "if you'd refuse Japhet at the proper time and take the herbs. Then your children would be a bit farther apart."

"Erin," Deborah said, offended. "I wish to have many children. I'm meant to have them."

Erin looked sharply at her, but didn't say anything. Their disagreement over how direct a role fate played in their lives had grown tiresome, but Deborah felt contentious. "Most things *are* fated," she said. "I am meant to have many children, and to be a healer, and to meet thee, and to practice our craft, and..." The rest she didn't know, but it was there, waiting for her. She could feel it.

"'Tis done," Mary said.

"No, 'tis not!" Erin snapped. "You remain there."

Deborah raised her eyebrows at Erin, disapprovingly, and Erin turned back to her work. Deborah switched John to her other breast and with her free hand shook a gourd rattle against the crib's floor. "'Tis a snake, Robert, run, ruun, ruuuunn." He reached for it, squealing. She shook it next to one ear and the other, then against his belly while he laughed and pushed it away with both hands.

John started to squirm away from her breast. "'Tis enough?" she asked. "Robert, play with the snake and when I'm done with thy brother, I shall sit right here and mend." She handed Robert the rattle, burped John, then put him back into his cradle.

"You spoil Robert," Erin called from the hearth.

"Damn, Erin, what harm is it to please my children if I might? Besides, thou art the one who gave him the rattle." Deborah grabbed Japhet's grey worsted coat and her sewing box and sat down on the floor next to her sons. As she started to mend the coat, she wondered why Erin was so riled about Johanna. *I should think she would be pleased to have the help.*

"'Tis done," Mary said again.

"Mary," Erin said evenly, "if you leave that bird 'twill burn and we shall have no dinner. Sit there, it will not be so very long."

Mary thrust the stick at the turkey.

Erin grabbed the gravy skillet's long handle and moved it away from the hottest embers. Turning her attention to the potatoes, she used a wooden masher Japhet had made and prepared them for her dumpling batter.

"Art thou wet a'ready?" Deborah asked, smelling urine on Robert's diaper. She would have to finish the mending later. She hung the coat back on the peg and put Robert on the changing blanket on the floor. He wasn't quite done, though, and peed in the air when she untied his diaper. She chuckled and wiped the spray off her face with a clean cloth, then wiped him with it. His rash was almost healed, she was glad to see, and spread on more of her calendula, comfrey, and meadowsweet salve. He lay quietly, watching her, one finger in his mouth. She slipped a fresh diaper beneath him and tied it, remembering how Mary had hated to be changed. She would cry and fight and make Deborah feel like a beast. Then a moment later she would stand, dry and smiling, her rage forgotten.

"The bird needs basting again," Erin said in a conciliatory tone, turning to look at her.

Deborah nodded, but wasn't quite ready to make up. She thought of Johanna and her milk-stained gown. *The poor girl looks as one who wants for a good home, and I warrant Erin will not e'en attempt to be kind to her.*

She put Robert back in the crib, washed her hands in a bucket, then went over and basted the turkey, juices sputtering as they hit the drip pan. "Shan't be long now, Mary," she promised.

After adding the drippings and more flour to the gravy, Deborah stirred it with a long wooden spoon and stared absently out the window. Strips of venison hung drying from an apple tree. A pile of leaves lay below it. Never mind the warm weather of late, she thought, winter is nigh.

Smelling of smoke, Japhet appeared in time to eat. The harvest brought in, he had been smoking meat in preparation for winter. They sat on stools and dug in with neither formalities nor forks. Deborah shared a wooden trencher with Japhet. Erin and Mary shared another. They piled them with turkey and gravy, and ate the dumplings and broth out of the kettle. Deborah cut portions off the bird with a knife, then ate the meat with her fingers. They did not speak and were done in less than a quarter of an hour.

Japhet left again to smoke the venison strips hanging in the tree. Deborah fed Robert bits of dumplings and gravy while Erin cleaned up.

"How 'bout some chocolate?" Deborah asked Erin, when Robert had had his fill.

Erin turned to face her and smiled. "Aye, that'll do."

"Good." Deborah stooped to add more wood to the fire. All will be well with Johanna, she thought, once Erin grows accustomed to her. To be sure, she will come to value the help. Deborah put one last log on the fire. Sparks shot out and landed on her gown. She hurriedly brushed them off.

"You recall that Patrick is calling this even, do you not?" Erin asked.

Deborah closed her eyes. She had forgotten. She poured the rest of the day's milk into a pot, aware that she hadn't responded yet, wishing that talk of the Kirkbride's servant did not bother her so.

When she looked over at Erin she felt her heart clench. She forced out the words, "Japhet and I will go up and leave you twain the main room."

"I thank you." Erin smiled.

Deborah couldn't return it. She picked up the long bar of chocolate Japhet had bought at the market and sliced strips into the milk. The repetitive motion gradually put her at ease. She watched the chocolate melt and thought of Richard. How was he faring in Providence? Was his arm fully healed? Had he found a better life?

"Prithee add sugar and watch that it doth not scorch," she told Erin without looking at her, then walked outside and around back toward the smokehouse. It was odd to feel the rocks beneath her moccasins but sense no pain, like the invulnerable feeling she had toward summer's end, after going barefoot for three months.

The smokehouse was just ahead. She halted at its open door with a sudden visceral memory of standing in the doorway of their smokehouse as a child while her father prepared meat not long before his last voyage. She remembered feeling timid and nervous, watching a man who was her father but whom she hardly knew.

Japhet stepped into the doorway. "Would– wouldst thou like some chocolate?" she asked.

"Yes," he said, "bring it when 'tis ready if thou please. I cannot leave as yet."

He went back inside, and she stood there with a vague feeling of loss. It faded with nothing more revealed. She walked around the side of the house toward the kitchen door. Mary sat in the crook of an apple tree, where the trunk first split into branches, playing with her doll. Deborah kissed her cheek, then looked up into the branches, some stained with deer blood. The sky beyond was cloud-filled, darkening.

"We may have a storm tonight, Mary," Deborah said and helped her down. "Thou art grown so heavy, so big."

"Big girl," Mary said to her doll.

Deborah glanced at the ominous sky again. There was a feel to the air she didn't like. Loss again, she decided, then the meaning came clear. There will be much loss this winter and beyond.

She took Mary's hand, tighter than she intended, and Mary grunted. Deborah relaxed her grip, but only a little. "Come along, now," she said. "Let us go have our chocolate."

They walked then, Mary glancing anxiously at her mother, into the kitchen. Deborah noticed her awareness and stopped to hug and reassure her. She pressed her nose against her daughter's. "Now go wait at the table, little one, and I'll bring thy chocolate!" She playfully pushed her away. The girl raced into the other room.

Deborah went to stand by the hearth, and stirred the drink. Loss, she thought, that was certain. But of what or who?

22

T WAS LATE, about three in the morning, and Deborah couldn't sleep. She sat in the dark on a wide stool by the kitchen window, drinking chamomile tea from her porcelain cup, watching the first snow of the winter season come down.

"*Deborah.*"

She heard Erin's whisper and turned to see candlelight flickering in the main room as Erin walked through it toward the kitchen.

"I could not sleep as well," Erin said quietly when she reached her.

Deborah tried to look into her eyes, but they were shadowed by the candlelight. Erin rarely suffered from insomnia. If she honestly couldn't sleep, something must be wrong. "What troubles thee?"

"I will tell you plain. Patrick hath asked me to marry him, and I have agreed—when my indenture is up."

Though Deborah had suspected this was coming, she felt a sudden, crushing pressure in her midsection. She hunched over, couldn't speak, tried to catch her breath. I'm losing her, she said to herself. I'm losing her.

She struggled against this. I am not, she told herself. We might still be friends, share our lives. But then with a force that shook her, she realized she'd no longer control Erin as mistress over servant. She opposed that thought. I do not believe suchly. I *never* thought on her that way. Yet when she looked at Erin, she knew it was true. Erin had been an indentured helper, beholden. With her freedom, she may not wish to be a friend.

"Speak to me, Deborah. You knew this would come. You knew about Patrick, and my term nearly due."

Deborah felt overcome with memory and emotion. She remembered Erin teaching her how to swim after they'd cleaned the chimney with the goose. Erin standing nude before her in the water. So lovely she was and is.

Deborah covered her mouth with her hand. No, she thought, her throat tightening from the tears she would not let come. Prithee, do not go. She wanted to say this aloud, but her throat burned so much nothing would come out. Oh, Brigid, she pleaded, finally letting the tears come, do not take her away from me.

In a moment Erin stood directly in front of her, pulling Deborah up off the stool, holding her, her breath hot on Deborah's neck. Deborah pulled back to look at her: Erin her beloved, the only one who knew her true heart. She pinched out the candle, reached her hands through Erin's coarse, thick hair, and kissed her suddenly, passionately on the lips. Erin surprised her by responding, by grabbing handfuls of Deborah's back, by playing her tongue along their lips.

"Erin, I love thee," Deborah said at last, pulling back and pressing her head into Erin's shoulder. "Prithee, do not go."

All at once Erin pulled away, went toward the window, and Deborah saw another flickering movement approaching from the main room.

"Japhet?" she whispered, starting to panic, but saw it was Johanna with a confused look on her face, seeming not to comprehend what she had almost witnessed.

"'Tis all right, Johanna," Deborah said, her voice shaky. "I am sorry we woke thee."

Johanna looked as if she were about to say something, seemed to want to speak. She glanced at Erin, who glared at her, and Johanna remained silent.

"'Tis all right," Deborah repeated. "We have matters yet to discuss, but we will hope not to disturb thee again. Go now, to bed."

Deborah watched the light flicker back to the main room where Johanna and Ethan slept on blankets before the hearth. The candle went out. The only light now came from the accumulating snow outside.

Deborah led Erin to a darkened corner of the kitchen and pressed her against the wall. They kissed gently, allowing their passion to build. Their hands caressed each other's necks, breasts, hips. They sank to the floor in a fast embrace.

"Erin, I love thee," Deborah whispered, again and again.

"I won't leave you," Erin replied each time. "Deborah, I will never go."

No footsteps intruded, no light shone, nothing interrupted the soft rustling of their skirts. They tumbled back in time to the reign of the Goddess, when such love was not forbidden, when all acts of love's pleasure honored her.

23

EBORAH LAY the yarn leader onto the fanned-out fibers of a rolag of fleece and twisted them to the left. As she held the joining between her thumb and forefinger, she gazed out the window at the bare apple tree, thinking about the other night, how she and Erin hadn't been alone since, how they had hardly spoken. "Japhet is in the fields," she said, starting the wheel spinning, "and I sent Mary and Robert with Johanna to fetch water."

Erin stopped chopping potatoes, put her knife down and brought the back of her hand to her forehead.

"I did not intend . . ." But Deborah didn't know what she had intended—to speak about it, to kiss again. She stopped the wheel with her hand, her heartbeat quickening.

"It cannot happen again," Erin said.

Deborah stared at the wheel, wondering if Morgan the Fate were somewhere spinning this scene, every rotation of her wheel taking Erin farther away.

"I have been thinking on this," Erin said, "we cannot . . . it cannot happen again."

There didn't seem to be much to say. Deborah was still staring at the wheel, thinking, I have lost her. This is the way it will go.

"I do not regret it," Erin said softly, and Deborah looked up. "But I am marrying Patrick, as I said I would."

"Thou said thou shouldst never leave." The words seemed to have come from someone else.

"I said I would never leave and I am not. I am not leaving you. We will be friends. Our children will play together. I shall come over for tea." And then she hushed because Deborah was hitting her forehead against the spinning wheel, and crying.

"Deborah, my sweet, *mo chailín fhionn*." Erin came over and squatted in front of her, placed her hand between Deborah's head and the wood of the wheel. Deborah rammed it once, then raised her head and looked up.

"I'll not forget the magic we made." Erin put a hand on Deborah's cheek. "And 'twas magic, *a mhuirnín*. You know you never repeat a spell."

She got what she seemed to have wanted, a smile out of Deborah, who shook her head and said, "I know not what I thought—that we would live together in a cabin beside town?" Then she recalled the Quaker women who did just that. Who lived, traveled, and sometimes ministered together. But they're simply spinsters, she thought, they do not as did we.

"I have heard," Erin said, "'twas no sin ere the Church came, and e'en in its early days. Love was love, no matter the beloved be man or woman."

Deborah looked at her, thinking, then why not now? Why can we not leave our mates and love as we did? As we do?

Erin said, "I do not believe 'twould be for the best." She got up and returned to her work.

Deborah watched her, feeling as if something had broken, thinking that it would be a long time, if ever, before things would be the same between them again.

"A thing broken then mended can be stronger than before," Erin said.

Deborah shook her head. It didn't feel that way to her. I have lost Erin, she thought. She's gone.

"*Mam!*" Mary opened the front door and she and Robert tumbled in. "We saw a spider, a big one. Johanna said 'twas a devil and she killed it."

Deborah hurried to the door and saw Johanna coming up the path with the water buckets. She went out to meet her. "What didst thou tell Mary?"

Johanna continued in her laden stride to the house. She put one bucket near the front door and the other by the hearth.

"What is a devil, Mam?" Mary asked.

"Did not Johanna tell thee ere she killed the spider?"

"No."

Johanna sat down to take over Deborah's spinning and seemed not to be listening. Erin was muttering under her breath.

"There are no devils 'cept in the minds of frighted people," Deborah said. "Did that spider fright thee?"

Mary nodded. "It came down." She made a spinning motion above her head.

"Johanna," Deborah said, "thou know'st now that spider was no devil, doth thee not?"

She didn't answer or avert her gaze from her work.

"Johanna, 'twas no devil which thou saw," Deborah insisted. "'Twas a spider, an earthly creature just as thou and I."

Johanna didn't glance her way but said, "Yes, missus."

Deborah looked at Erin, who shook her head and mouthed, *Be rid of her now!* But when Deborah turned her gaze to Johanna, she felt she understood the fright Johanna must have had when the spider seemed to be threatening Mary. She understood the impulse to call evil the things that terrify.

She continued to watch Johanna's quick, able fingers feeding the fleece, and realized it was more than understanding she felt. It seemed as if she had known Johanna for a very long time. The impression didn't make much sense to Deborah, but she knew it was true. Johanna and I are linked, she thought, in a manner I do not yet grasp.

"'Tis all right, Johanna," Deborah said. "We will not speak of it again." The woman looked at her and smiled, grateful it seemed.

Deborah ignored Erin's burning gaze and headed for the door. Robert followed her. She closed the door behind him and watched as he waddled to a stump and tried to climb upon it. "My big boy," she said and picked him up. He reached for her breast. She sat on the stump, untied the lacing of her bodice, and began nursing him.

She looked up and saw Japhet coming in from the fields with his cloak slung over his shoulder. As she watched him, she tried to summon her old feeling of awe at the beauty of his stride. She saw it. She saw the grace of the movement, the gliding over the ground. But it didn't touch her. It didn't move like fingers over her skin. It didn't quicken her heart or stop its beat. It didn't make her want to press him against the wall.

24

"OTHER LEEDS! *Mother Leeds! Prithee come hither!*"

Deborah jerked awake, leapt out of bed, and pulled on her morning gown and shoes before running down the stairs. The front door was open. A gust of wind caught it and slammed it against its hinges. Shielding her face from the blowing snow, she walked out into the storm, trying to recognize the small figure who had opened the door and called in, who was now mounting a horse which twisted anxiously from side to side.

"Who is there?" she called.

"Caleb. My mother is ill. Prithee come quickly. Dr. Grant is there as well."

Erin met Deborah at the front door and asked, "Who is it?"

"Grace Kirkbride," she said. "Prithee remain with the children. I know not how long I shall be." Deborah ran up the stairs to her room as Erin went to hers.

Japhet was getting dressed. "I heard 'twas Grace," he said, "and thought thou mightst desire a driver."

He had never accompanied her on a visit, but then she had never been called in the middle of the night for a non-birth emergency. He would be useful, she decided. She could concentrate on Grace while he drove.

"Yes, Japhet," she said. "Prithee come along as well." She started to get dressed for the fierce weather.

"I'll bring the horses around," he said when he was fully clothed. He left the room, leaving the door open.

Deborah heard Mary's soft crying behind her. She turned and bent over, eye-level with the girl, then glanced at Erin who stood solemnly in the doorway. "Thy father and I must go to see Caleb's mother," Deborah said. "Thou shalt be good, shalt thou not, and go back to sleep?" She pushed Mary's hair out of her eyes. "If we are not back by morn, help Erin and Johanna care for thy brothers. Shalt thou be a good girl?"

Mary nodded, her eyes downcast. Deborah stood up straight and from a peg grabbed her safeguard, a long over-petticoat that protected her clothing from the weather. As she tied it on, she glanced at her daughter again, who watched her, still frightened. "Don't fret, little one," Deborah said, and smoothed her daughter's hair again. To Erin she said, "Prithee take Robert to thy room. I'll carry John down to Johanna."

Erin picked up Robert, who was sleeping. "Come along, Mary," she said, then looked at Deborah. "I hope Grace shall be well." She left the room.

Deborah sighed as she watched her go. Two months had done little to ease the strain between them. She picked up her bag, lifted John in his cradle and carried him downstairs. Johanna was sitting up straight, staring wide-eyed at the door. Ethan lay with his back to her.

Deborah put down the cradle and called her name twice. When Johanna didn't respond, she snapped her fingers in front of her eyes.

Johanna started, but still seemed to be watching a distant scene. In a small voice she said, "Mrs. Kirkbride is frightfully unwell."

"Yes, yes, she is. I go now to help her." Johanna didn't respond, so Deborah bent over and put her hands on her shoulders. "Thou must care for little John whilst I am gone. Dost thou hear me? Put those other thoughts from thy mind. John hath more need of thee than Grace."

Johanna blinked several times as if slowly coming back to herself. "Yes, ma'am," she said. "Yes." Then she seemed to realize what had just happened and began to shudder with fright.

Deborah felt precious time passing. "Johanna," she said sternly, "tend to my son or I will cast thee and Ethan out."

Johanna started again and the shuddering stopped. "Never fear, missus, never fear." She pulled away from Deborah's grip and leaned over and stroked John's cheek.

Deborah glanced up the twisting stairs and saw Erin's feet. That is good, she thought, relieved. Erin shall be watchful; I need not fear. She took a few slow steps back toward the door, watching Johanna who was now cuddling John. I must have haste, she told herself. She grabbed her hat and cloak and left.

While Japhet drove the horse cart on the dirt road dangerously pocketed with ice, Deborah tried to clear her mind to sense what was wrong with Grace. The last time she had seen her—two weeks ago—Grace had seemed a little pale and nervous and Deborah gave her a simple tonic. Did I overlook something? she wondered, stricken.

Over the sound of the horses' clop, clop in the mud and ice came a preternatural singing of birds. Sweet, low, and melodious, the song entered Deborah's chest and left through the nape of her neck. Rhiannon's birds, she thought with dismay and alarm. Mayhap it be too late.

When they reached Grace's house, Deborah jumped from the cart and slipped on the ice, going down on one knee. Before Japhet reached her, she stood up and limped inside.

Sharp, sickly-sweet camphor scented the air. The Kirkbride farm was small but prosperous, and the normally tidy home was in disarray. Caleb's five siblings, ranging in age from one to eight, sat before the hearth. Erin's fiancé, Patrick, held one of the twins on his lap. Jeb had been pacing, unashamedly clad in only his breeches, and brightened when he saw Deborah. He grabbed her arm and practically pulled her up the staircase.

"She's been such as this since early even," he said over his shoulder on the stairs. "Kept sayin' she weren't unwell, only resting. Would not give me leave to send for the doctor or for thee. Would not allow me to stay with her. At the last, I called for Dr. Grant, who is with her now. Soon after his arrival, she asked for thee." He stepped aside to allow her into the room, then went back downstairs.

Deborah approached the bed, her breath catching as she saw Grace was close to death. Her sunken, vacant eyes opened and closed in a slow flutter. Her skin was grey. Deborah stood next to Dr. Grant and touched Grace's clammy cheek.

The doctor was a Quaker, about thirty-five, with dark balding hair. With a curt motion he indicated for Deborah to follow him to the stairs. "She is bleeding to death," he said in a low voice. "I have done all that I am able. She said she wishes to be with thee alone, so I will take my leave and wait on thee down the stairs."

Deborah heard something accusative in his tone. She wondered about it, then said, "Very well." After he left, she went back to the bed and gently lifted Grace's hips. The linens underneath were drenched with blood. Her genital area was heavily bandaged with cloth soaked red. She lowered Grace's hips gently and started to unwrap the bandages to replace them, then realized it was of no use. "My dear friend," she said.

Grace's eyes opened wide and she was suddenly lucid. "Don't tell Jeb. Promise me." Her voice was a harsh whisper, the whites of her eyes ghostly, their blood vessels empty.

Deborah knelt beside the bed. "Grace, why?"

"Promise me, then hide the needle."

"I will not tell him, Grace. I promise."

Grace's eyes again began their slow flutter, her lucidity gone. Deborah looked under the bed and found a bloody knitting needle made of horn. She wrapped it loosely in cloth, put it in her bag, then took Grace's face in her hands. Her eyes opened wide again, this time in fright.

Deborah saw it also: a woman with open arms, and bright light. "Have no fear," Deborah said. "Go to the Mother. Allow her to take thee into her arms. Listen. Listen to the call of her sweet voice. She will love and keep thee, Grace. Go to her. Find thy peace."

And then Grace let go—that's how it felt to Deborah—she had been struggling and she simply let go. She died. And Deborah began to sing a passage song.

> "Morgan the Fate calls her children home
> > to sleep in the orchard
> > to rest not alone.
> Morgan calls her children home
> > to eat of the apple
> > to live not alone."

She continued to hum the melody, noticing the small smile on Grace's face and her eyes now touched with wonder. She closed Grace's eyelids, then kissed them. "Farewell," she said.

Slowly, she got to her feet, picked up her bag and limped down the stairs. Caleb stood at the bottom and stepped back when he saw her. Jeb started to push past his son, then froze. He backed away, then turned his face to the wall.

Deborah walked out the door into the snow, a brilliant blue-white in the light of the half-moon. She put down the bag and raised her arms into the air which sparkled with ice crystals. Snowflakes melted in the blood on her hands, forming red rivulets which ran down her arms.

"Deborah," Japhet called. He approached her from the house with a bucket of water and a cloth, the doctor a few paces behind.

She dipped her limp hands into the warm, comforting water. "The snow hath almost ceased," she said. "After I have sat a time with Jeb, I desire to go to the buttonwood." She dried her hands.

"We will go, then." He took the bucket and cloth and returned to the house.

The doctor remained, standing with his hands in his coat pockets. "Thou knowest I have regard for thy simples and salves and use them myself on my patients." He paused to look her steadily in the eye. "I will ask thee plain. Didst thou do this? Didst thou give her herbs to murder her child?"

"No," Deborah replied, shocked. "I did not e'en know she was with child."

"Neither did her husband." He turned around to glance back at the house, then faced her again. "I have said nary a word against thy herbs, but if they brought thy neighbor to her death–"

"I told thee I had nothing to do with this. She did herself the injury with a needle."

"Didst thou find it?"

"Yes, under the bed. I have it now in my bag and will show it to thee." She took out the bundle and handed it to him. As he unwrapped the cloth, she said, "My sole fault lies in not knowing she was with child, in not know-ing she would attempt this." Her voice broke.

He looked at her, not yet convinced.

"What dost thou think?" she asked indignantly. "That I gave her herbs, then came in and used the needle, then left again? Thou mightst ask Jeb if I was here earlier. Or dost thou think I gave her herbs which had no effect, so she finished it herself? Had I given her herbs she would have called for me at the first, not lain abed, calling for me only at the last." He nodded his head, conceding the point. She added softly, "She did herself this injury."

Dr. Grant focused on her, and she knew what he was thinking: If Grace had come to her first she would have gotten the result she desired. And she would still be alive. He cleared his throat and looked away, part of the decreasing school that still left the full range of women's mysteries to women, as long as no harm was done that he heard about.

Deborah looked over his shoulder toward the house. "What didst thou tell Jeb?"

"Only that she miscarried. I desired to speak with thee ere I said any more."

"And what shalt thou tell him now?"

He folded the cloth over the needle, then gave it to Deborah. "In a case as tragic as this," he said, "the truth holds no purpose. Better she be remembered as devoted wife and mother. She will answer to the Lord for what she hath done." After Deborah put the bundle back in her bag, he offered her his arm. "Shall we go in now?" he asked.

She accepted the courtesy. As they walked back to the house, it occurred to her with a chill just how differently this might have gone had he been a doctor of a different school.

Deborah and Japhet drove to the river in silence. The road was still icy and the wind cold, but the storm had lessened. When they arrived at the sycamore, Deborah quick-stepped toward it, favoring her twisted ankle, and leaned her face against the trunk. She couldn't get Grace's ghostly eyes out of her mind.

"Deborah," Japhet said, coming to her side.

She turned and stared out over the river. A shadow moved across the water, disappearing into the trees on the other side of the Delaware. She shook her head. Why, she asked herself, why did Grace not come first to me?

Japhet put an arm around her and she leaned against him. His wool cloak scratched her face. "So it is with everyone," she murmured. "Everyone goes."

"Thy Japhet stands here in the dark and cold with thee."

She smiled up at him, then said grimly, "Erin will soon marry Patrick. She is leaving– us." She had almost said "me."

"Mayhap thou wilt prefer it. She is more friend to thee than servant."

He said this kindly but Deborah thought, of course he hath noticed Erin and I are estranged. And he takes pleasure in that. She realized she wasn't being fair to him but pulled away and said, "Await me at the cart, if thou please. I shall be but a minute more."

She knew he felt the slight. He took a step back, but stood there a moment, his face hidden by the shadow of his hat. She could still feel his hand on her, warming into her shoulder. I never meant thee harm, Japhet, she thought.

He turned away and walked slowly toward the road.

She pressed her forehead against the tree to which the first Quakers in Burlington had moored their ship. Craning her neck, she looked up into the limbs and wished she could moor here as well. Remain with her buttonwood, escape her life awhile.

A shadow crossed her vision and lighted on one of the biggest branches. She stared at the owl perched there with large blinking eyes and a blooming sprig of heather in its beak. How can that be? she wondered, then whispered, "Granna?" The owl looked down at her. "Tell me what I must do."

The bird spread its wings and flew away. Following its spiraling path, Deborah looked toward the river. The heather left a purple streak like a comet in the sky, still sparkling with ice crystals. Then falling suddenly, like an arrow reaching its mark, the owl disappeared into the woods of Pennsylvania.

She watched the bird's entry point as if expecting its return, all the while knowing it would not. She had received her answer; comprehending it was left to her. Oh, for a religion with certainty, she thought half-jokingly, with clerics who tell you what to believe. She sighed heavily, then returned to the cart.

25

PRING CAME, staccato and bright, a month after Grace's burial behind the Quaker Meeting House. With the season came the elucidation of the owl's message, Deborah believed, an invitation from Mary to accompany her to the Yearly Meeting in Philadelphia. They would stay with Eleanor Woodford, an old friend of Mary's mother's.

"The change will serve thee, I should think," Japhet told Deborah as she finished packing her valise.

She noted something false in his voice and asked, "Dost thou desire me to go?"

"No, but..." He paused, and Deborah knew he was considering how Grace's death had shaken her confidence. She couldn't stop thinking she should have noticed that Grace was feeling desperate.

"Methinks it shall serve thee to be rid of responsibility for a time," he said, then the false pleasantry returned. "We shall manage without thee."

She squinted at him. He was hiding something from her, something that worried him. "What is it, Japhet? What troubles thee?"

"Naught." He smiled. "Naught is the matter. I merely wish thou wouldst become thyself again." He glanced toward the doorway where Erin stood, her hands in her apron pockets. "I will take this down for thee," he said. He picked up her bag and nodded at Erin. She stepped out of his way.

"No need to trouble yourself about the children," Erin said, coming into the room. "Johanna will see to their nursing, and I to the rest. You shall only be gone a few days." Then she raised her eyebrows with a silent question: How long, Deborah? How long till you allow us to be friends again?

Deborah wanted to say soon; soon she would accept that they were merely friends. But "merely" betrayed her true feeling. When being friends was honestly enough, then it could happen.

Erin nodded and left the room, her wooden heels clicking down the stairs.

Deborah followed, but as she reached the threshold she felt as if something had been forgotten. She looked around at the room's furnishings: their four-poster oak bed; John's maple cradle near the window; their pine desk with a quill and ink she had made. She walked to the cradle, rubbed John's tiny fingers and touched his cheek. How can I leave thee? she thought.

Carriage wheels crunched outside on the dirt and gravel. Japhet was downstairs calling to her. "Farewell, little one," she said and kissed him. "Mamma will be home soon." She turned toward the doorway and saw Johanna standing there.

"I thought I should take him down now," she said pleasantly, gesturing toward John.

Deborah picked him up and handed him to Johanna, who cradled him lovingly as if he were hers. "I trust he shall not be any trouble," Deborah said. "He is well used to thee."

"Oh, yes, you have no need to worry. John will be well without you a few days." He reached up a forefinger and touched her mouth. She nibbled it playfully.

Deborah averted her gaze. Although the two women shared the nursing of the boys, she found it difficult to watch Johanna with John. She feared he might come to think of her as his mother.

"That will not be," Johanna said.

Deborah darted her eyes to the wet nurse who now cooed to her son, seeming not to realize what had just occurred. She did read my thoughts, did she not? Deborah asked herself, remembering Johanna's intuition the night of Grace's death. She continued to study the wet nurse's manner, searching for signs of the instability that had also been present that night. But Johanna seemed perfectly sane, and Deborah had to leave now to catch her ferry.

"Farewell," Deborah said. "I shall see thee ere long."

Johanna looked up at her and smiled. "I wish you a fine journey."

I need not fear, Deborah told herself, but I shall whisper a word of caution to Erin ere I go. The two women headed amiably toward the stairs.

Charles Snowden and cousin Mary stood next to Deborah on the ferry, watching her feed scraps of bread to the gulls. One after another would fight for a turn to swoop toward Deborah's outstretched hand, snatching the bread she held. Her concerns about Japhet had faded, and now she was beginning to feel excited at the thought of having a few days where there was nothing she had to do. *Nothing*, she thought, amazed.

"I hope thou wilt not have overmuch idle time while Mary is in Meeting," Charles said.

Deborah laughed out loud. "I was just thinking on that. It will not be a problem, methinks." She threw a handful of bread into the air. About twenty gulls dove toward the shower of food.

"Eleanor's daughter Rachel," Mary told Charles, "will take Deborah about Philadelphia. She is a lovely woman of uncommon intelligence, twenty-six, little older than Deborah but unmarried. She is a minister." Addressing Deborah, she said, "My hope is you twain will find each other pleasing."

Deborah nodded, watching as the last bird, a runt, searched for scraps in the ferry's wake. She reached into her apron pocket and held out one last piece. The gull bobbed toward her and back timidly a few times, then made an arching dive, snatched the bread on the upswing, and flapped rapidly away.

Besides the gulls, Snowden's Ferry had no more to recommend it on this trip than on others Deborah had taken. But the winds favored them and soon she arrived in Philadelphia, a city which always impressed her with its numbers and its benevolence. She supposed it was the result of the Quaker government, a gentleness she sensed that was difficult to articulate. It wasn't that she regularly came upon genuine acts of charity; but rather as if the air conveyed a feeling of well-being which its citizens seemed to feed on and give back.

The streets, however, were a different matter. They were either dusty or muddy, such that a woman might wear her safeguard at all times. On this cool spring day they were a quagmire, but with effort Mary and Deborah managed to stay clear of the worst as they hired a coach.

After a short ride, they pulled up to the Woodford house, a mansion, really—with three stories and nine rooms, Mary told her—plus an attic with three dormer windows and a basement kitchen. The brick was laid in a Flemish bond pattern, the alternating header glazed a brilliant blue-black. A belt of white marble about a foot high circled between each story.

Eleanor Woodford invited them in and Deborah saw a floor made of highly glossed yellow pine. In the parlor off to the left were finely papered walls, upholstered furniture, and a fireplace faced with blue marble. In front of them rose a mahogany staircase.

A diaphanous figure appeared on the first landing and moved gracefully down the stairs. The woman's blonde hair, pulled back in a loose bun, had a carelessly put together look. Her calm demeanor was accented by a small but generous smile.

"This is my daughter Rachel," Eleanor said.

Rachel paused at the bottom of the stairs, then stepped forward with her hand extended. Deborah took it, surprised by its firmness. She is no haunt I warrant, Deborah thought. She is a woman of purpose.

"It pleases me to meet thee," Rachel said. "I have heard much about thee from Mary."

"And I about thee."

"Mayhap thou wouldst show our guests to their rooms, Rachel," Eleanor said. "Our rooms are the warmest in the house, so Deborah, thou wilt share Rachel's room, and Mary will bed with me. My husband is away."

Two servants came from a room off the foyer, picked up the luggage, and followed the women upstairs. Rachel left Mary to settle into Eleanor's room, then walked with an animated step to the next. "It is here," she said, stepping back, allowing Deborah and the servant with her valise to pass into the room.

Sunlight shone through thin white damask curtains, patterning the opposite wall with a wavy design. On a pedestal table under the window stood a doll modeling London fashion: an orange satin gown with trained overskirt turned back and hitched up over the bustle to show off the petticoat. Stiff starched ruffles extended from the mouth of each sleeve. A tall frontage sat atop its coifed hair.

"This room was my older sister's ere she died," Rachel said. "I have scarcely changed it. But mayhap when my twelfth quilt is finished, I shall lay it on the bed."

"I should love to see it," Deborah said. "Though I have lived amongst Friends for some years I have yet to master thy quilt-making."

"Thou hast other skills, I hear. Thou art a healer?"

Deborah nodded without enthusiasm. As Rachel pulled a trunk out from under the bed, she remembered Mary telling her that Quaker girls began making quilts at age twelve. When they had completed their twelfth quilt, they were considered ready to wed. "Thusly could a woman prolong a maiden state indefinitely," Mary had quipped, "or hurry toward an engagement."

Rachel pulled off the quilt's protective cloth. A maize star with five rounded points leapt from a circle of alternating blue, violet, plum, and lilac squares. The background beyond was solid black.

"'Tis extraordinary!" Deborah said. "From only a short distance, the circle looks as if it were one purple color, not four differing colors, just a shade apart. What was the model for the five-pointed star?"

"A dollar-fish."

"I have ne'er heard of such a creature."

"They are found at the sea." Rachel picked up a sand dollar from the table by her bed and gave it to Deborah. "Thou mayst keep it. I have others."

"I thank thee." With her index finger, Deborah traced the pentacle etched onto the sandy surface, then put the piece on top of her bag.

"Come now, let us go down for tea." Rachel put the quilt back into the trunk and pushed it under the bed.

Eleanor was waiting at the bottom of the stairs. "I thought we had lost you twain," she said pleasantly.

"I showed her my last quilt."

"'Tis lovely, is it not? We all marvel at my daughter's skill with the needle. Last quilt, thou sayest? Dost mean to say thou shalt marry Philo?"

Rachel blushed. "I will not marry him, as I have told thee. I am but nearly finished with quilt-making for a time. If a man appears I wish to marry, I shall be ready. But I wait not on him, Mother, to be plain." She walked out the back door to the brick-terraced garden.

After a moment, Deborah followed her. The air was cool, and she wished she had brought her cloak. Ivy climbed the brick wall and framed the bench where Rachel sat. She picked up a plump grey tabby next to her, set it on her lap, then gestured for Deborah to sit.

"My mother wishes I were an ordinary girl," Rachel said when Deborah was settled. "I tell her I did not ask to be called to minister. Sometimes I, too, wish I could have only my own household and family." She smiled. "But most of the time, I do not. Travel suits me. And nothing pleases me more than the feel of words flowing from my mouth like water down a stream, or sparking like a fire."

Deborah smiled as well, but was disturbed to feel envy. Until she had arrived in Burlington, she had never even considered that she could choose not to marry. *Could* I have? she wondered. Could I care for myself without a family of wealth and a like-minded community about me? She felt angry and empty and touched her large breasts which were heavy with milk and painful. I must pump them soon, she thought.

"Mayhap we might take a coach about the city center tomorrow," Rachel said, "then dine at the Blue Anchor. 'Tis one of my favorites. 'Twas the first building William Penn saw as he docked, and they say 'tis the oldest tavern in Philadelphia."

"I know the Blue Anchor," Deborah said. "I should like to eat there again."

"'Tis settled, then." Rachel stood up, taking the cat off her lap and placing it on the bench. Felicity opened one green eye for a moment, then promptly went back to sleep.

26

OMEWHAT unthinkingly," Rachel said, as she and Deborah rode about Philadelphia in a hired coach, "I once told my mother I revered Queen Kristina." She smiled. "Ever since, she hath pushed me to marry."

"Kristina? I do not know of her."

"This Queen of Sweden was known as 'Pallas of the North' and was quite a dashing figure, they say. She had been highly educated as if she were a male heir to the throne, and she took to learning as a bird to air. She was a brilliant scholar, fluent in many languages, and corresponded with the great minds of the day. And that was but the tame side of the Queen. A superb hunter, she dressed in men's clothing, eventually abdicating her throne, as none had ever before done, because she refused to marry. She left Sweden, traveled to Rome, and most scandalous of all, became a Catholic."

"Heavens," Deborah said.

"Yes, some say as well she loved no man, only one woman. And others say she followed a priest to Rome and corrupted him. I believe neither story. Methinks she was bold is all, and few can tolerate a woman bold. Ah, there is another worth a look. Driver, stop a moment."

Rachel pointed to a woman standing on a makeshift platform surrounded by a large crowd. Tall and beautiful, she was curiously clothed in both men's and women's attire. She wore petticoat and waistcoat and a silk cravat. Her thick black hair, undressed, fell loosely past her shoulders. Her voice was hypnotic and unearthly, neither feminine nor masculine, but a mixture of the two. "And the Lord sends the rain to remind us of the covenant with Noah, just as the Lord sends the blood to remind woman of her covenant with the Lord. For as God is the creator in heaven so are women the creators on earth. For is it not so that the great mystics and even the scriptures praise God as 'Mother'?..."

The driver urged the horses forward.

"She is quite compelling," Deborah said, looking back.

"Yes," Rachel agreed. "More and more now there are others in Philadelphia like her, ministers of every faith—mostly those none have ever known before. They ride in and ride out. Few remain long enough to build a proper meeting house. I suspect there is no place that is home to them because none would take them in."

"Is not that the life thou leadest?"

Rachel looked sharply at her, then sighed. "The truth of it is I fear the end of our holy experiment. More and more non-Friends arrive with sentiments unlike ours. I fear one day soon we shall be outnumbered in our own government. Ah, we are here."

It seemed like such a long time ago that Deborah had eaten at the Blue Anchor with Erin and Japhet, she was surprised to see it looked just the same: small and listing, surrounded by whortleberries.

"I find Philadelphia a remarkable city," Deborah said when they were seated. "It hath a kind of gentleness which I cannot describe, though I try e'ery time I come."

Rachel raised her eyebrows. "Thou hast seen only one side, I fear. In the caves at night all manner of baseness occurs: overmuch drinking, gambling, even whoring. They call them 'tippling houses,' these unlicensed taverns. 'Tis the price we pay for our fame methinks, and the tolerance of our government."

A young boy put down two trenchers laden with venison, mashed potatoes, and bread. Rachel laughed. "They feed me such as this whene'er I appear. Mayhap 'tis the reason I come."

Deborah took a bite of venison, glancing at the dogs in the cage turning the spit.

"Thou hast two children?" Rachel asked.

"Three."

"And as many servants, I trust."

"Soon I shall have but one. My servant and dear friend Erin is marrying. Her term is nearly up and she seems overjoyed to go." Deborah felt a stab of disloyalty; she knew she was being unfair.

"Who should not yearn to be unyoked, no matter how beloved her mistress?"

Deborah frowned. "Thou art in the right," she said. "Once I strained at holding servants at all, now I cannot let her go."

"Dost thou fear the loss of her as friend or servant?"

"Friend," Deborah admitted.

"If you twain love one another despite the difference in your stations now, then to be sure when she is free, your love will only grow."

"Yes," Deborah said without conviction. Japhet had told her that at the buttonwood, and Erin had said the same several times. But it didn't help. She was hurting still in a place reason could not reach.

"I am thinking," Rachel said, "about thou once straining at holding servants and methinks that is the way of us all. Thy situation is perhaps not the best example of this, but mayhap we rail against in youth what we know we shall become. I ne'er wished to be a minister. I even used to poke fun at them—they seemed so fervent and fixed. And now I am just the same."

"I think not," Deborah said. "I don't find those qualities in thy manner. Mayhap thou objected so to ministry because thou knew there was another way, a joyous but pensive message thou must put forth."

"Joyous but pensive," Rachel repeated. "I like that."

Deborah smiled. "But continuing . . . is not it so as Friends say, that if persons remain close to the Light, they will not wish to rail, but will follow the path they see there?"

Rachel pursed her lips, considering. "In the main that is so, but would it were so simple. 'Tis true we humans have goodness at our core, and 'tis best to expect such in each one, yet if we deny other forces that are there as well—not necessarily evil, just human—so shall we be ensnared along the way. A balance is the better, methinks, with the heart forever leading the way and the mind checking the steps. And that is precisely the function of the Meeting. We are the mind checking the steps of our members, being certain they don't confuse the Reasoner for the Light."

"The Reasoner?"

"'Tis much spoken of in our Meeting, especially among the female ministers. 'Tis the voice which can lead us astray. Oftentimes it tells us women we are unworthy to speak publicly. In the male of our membership the Reasoner is more of a passion. A man may find himself called to an act, but upon reflection discovers 'twas but his own vain imagining he was following."

Deborah heard a commotion at the door and glanced up. Two men were greeting each other. One left and the other walked in and glanced in her direction. "No," she said, "it cannot be." She got up and walked quickly toward the bar where he was headed. His back was to her now, so she tapped him on the shoulder.

His hair was longer, his face more lined, but there was no mistake. "Richard!" she exclaimed. The shock ran through her body. "Richard."

He leaned back against the bar. "My God, Deborah. Deborah Smith."

"I– I know not what to say." She wanted to throw her arms around him but held herself in check.

"I can hardly believe it." He reached out and took her hand. "Deborah Smith, uh, Deborah . . ."

"Leeds."

He released her hand suddenly, as if realizing Japhet might be there, and looked around the room. "Art thou seated?"

"Yes." She pointed at their table. Rachel was turned sideways in her chair, watching them.

He nodded in her direction, then smiled at Deborah. "I will beg leave— I'm cook here—and join thee." He shook his head. "I knew I should see thee again, somehow." He went behind the bar.

Deborah walked back to her table, embarrassed at the attention they'd attracted. As she sat down she noticed Rachel seemed amused. "I met Richard on my passage over," she explained. "He left the ship at Philadelphia but said he would go to Providence."

"He looks as one who hath led a rugged life," Rachel said, straightening her bodice.

"He is coming now."

After Deborah introduced them, Rachel stood up. "I'll leave you twain to speak. I see neighbors 'cross the way. Pardon me whilst I speak with them."

When she was gone, Deborah looked long at Richard. "All these years," she said, "I have wondered whether thou got safely away."

"There were times when I wondered it myself."

"Thou hast such a look. What happened to thee?"

"Worry not. I was brought to no ill. I shall tell thee, but firstly, may I?" He pointed to her mug of cider.

She pushed it over. "But before the tale, thou must tell me about thy arm. I can scarcely believe I forgot about it at our greeting."

Smiling proudly, he raised his left arm over his head, brought it down again, crooked it at the elbow, straightened it again, then picked up her mug of cider.

"Richard!"

"'Tis weaker than the right, but I move it about still and knead it as thou taught me." He took a sip from the mug and put it down.

Deborah reached for his left arm and held it. It was strong and firm and muscled. No one would ever suspect it once had been unusable. She released him, tears coming to her eyes. I healed him, she thought.

He watched her, confused and concerned, so she explained. "Not long ago, I lost a neighbor for whom I cared. It pleases me to see thou art well."

"I am well because of thee." He smiled and asked gently, "Art thou ready for the tale?"

"Yes," she replied, glad to think of something else. "Pray tell."

"After I left the ship," he said, "and when I was but a few hours at the Pewter Platter, the first mate from the *Willow* came a-looking for me. The captain must have sent him to e'ery tavern in town. I was up the stairs when he arrived and stood just out of sight, but where I might hear. He asked my widow friend about me, curiously saying my arm may or may not be injured."

Deborah nodded. "The captain guessed I had healed it and helped thee to desert."

Richard put his hands on the table. "What harm did he to thee?"

"I– I stopped the captain—before he harmed me." He looked at her, his eyes a mixture of anger and dismay. "Prithee continue with the story," she said.

He seemed to struggle with himself: wishing to press her further and not wanting to know. Finally, he went on. "The widow told the mate a man of my description had come in and apprenticed himself straight-away to a sotweed planter in Virginia. I remember still, he laughed and said, 'Just what the bugger deserves.' He left appeased and I more than relieved. I tarried at the Pewter Platter for three days, till 'twas clear the *Willow* had set sail and none remained to clap me. Then I set out on a coach for Providence to find my sister. But ere we were very far along, the coach was beset by highwaymen. They shot the driver and tied us five passengers to trees."

"How horrid, Richard! But thou said thou wert not harmed?"

"Nay, nay, only terribly frighted. I thought I had escaped the ship only to meet my end there. Then one skinny rascal approached me and fixed me long in the eye. He was queer-looking: very slight and smooth-faced. A mere boy, I reckoned. The lad took my purse and the pistol my friend had given me, then lifted my left arm and let it drop, nodding significantly to the other men. The four highwaymen whispered amongst themselves, then a brief quarrel broke out. In the end the boy untied me, mounted his sorrel, and demanded I seat myself behind. As best I could manage, I climbed aback his horse and we rode away.

"When we were a ways off, we halted. My captor fired two shots into the air, then whipped the horse to a full gallop. It was all I could do to hold on, but I dared not ask him to slow the beast. After nearly an hour we came upon an inn, and the boy bade me wait outside. Without much trust in my horsemanship, I believed 'twas wise to obey. When he returned, he pushed me up the stairs to a large room, set me in a chair, and paced the room a few times, deciding what to do with me, I supposed. 'I saved your life,' the boy said, 'you know that, do you not?' I nodded, hoping 'twas so. He put his and my weapons on the bed. 'I desire you to help me in kind, but of your own will.'"

"With the guns out of his hands, I felt bold and said, 'You must first tell me what 'tis, ere I agree to it.' A red flush came o'er his face, and I feared I had spoken too freely. He paced the room a few more times then stood in front of the looking glass with his back to me. He took off his hat, shook out his shoulder-length brown hair, and turned around. It was another moment ere I understood. 'Twas no boy standing there, but a woman, a girl really. I was so stunned I could not speak at the first."

Richard shook his head as if experiencing his amazement again. "Then I asked the girl, 'What is it you wish?' She—Molly was her name—told me a long tale which began with her arrival in Massachusetts with her parents. Soon after, her father had quarreled with someone he ought not to have and they were banished from the colony. They roamed about for a time, finally befriending some Indians and living amongst them three years."

Deborah leaned forward, curious to hear how a banished girl had become a bold robber.

"One day a band of white settlers attacked the tribe. Molly fought with the tribe, but the settlers had guns and soon o'erpowered them. She climbed a tree and hid there, at the first to have better aim with her bow, but then remained, watching as the last of her family and tribe were slain. When the settlers were gone, she climbed down and took the clothes, purse, and weapon off the body of a young white man. Then she caught one of the tribe's horses, cut off her hair, and left. She rode about disguised as a man for some weeks ere she met up with one of the highwaymen. Two others soon joined them, and they began robbing coaches. Molly never revealed her true sex to her fellow outlaws, fearing what they'd do."

Richard sat back in his chair. "'Tis difficult to imagine she was ne'er found out, but I have heard of other women disguised as men, hiding their sex to do battle, their fellow fighters none the wiser. In any case, she said she took no mind to the thieving, but couldn't abide by the killing and began plotting her escape, since 'tis unlikely they would have permitted her to take her leave. When she saw me, she said, she had found her opportunity. I was traveling alone on the coach to Providence—whither she had recently heard distant relations of hers had settled—and my injured arm rendered me harmless, she thought, and provided her with a story."

He leaned forward again as he arrived at the crux of the matter. "She told her fellow highwaymen she knew me, that I had killed her parents. She said she knew I was he because she herself had injured my arm with an arrow. And now she wished to take me to the wood and avenge her parents' murder before only the eyes of the Creator. For this pleasure she gave up her share of the loot, save my lean purse. She reasoned they would not come after her when she did not return. They would think I had killed her and escaped. Molly then asked if I would ride with her to Providence, and I agreed. She had quite a sum from other robberies and gave me back my purse. A bit farther on, she bought women's clothing and another horse, and we rode together, posed as man and wife.

"When we arrived at Providence, I learned my dear sister had died of consumption. Molly's relations were pleased to see her, as they had long thought her dead. I tarried a time with them before making my way back to Philadelphia."

"Goodness," Deborah said, "have the rest of thy days been filled with such as befell thee then?"

"No." Richard smiled. "I have lived these years a humble cook. Ah, but I do have news of Captain Hughes. Nearly one year ago, remember the young tar whose hand thou tended after he burned it on the ropes?"

"Yes. Jacob was his name."

"Well, he came hither. We had a warm reunion and he told me about Hughes. The captain turned to slaving. On his second voyage to Guinea his crew mutinied, shot him in the gullet, and turned pirate. Jake heard this from a tar who had it from one of the crew in Newgate. Hughes is dead." Richard drank from the mug. "And just was his death for the harm he intended for thee." He held the cider out to her.

Deborah took the mug but put it down. She couldn't drink to anyone's death. She lowered her head, remembering the spadefuls of dirt covering Grace's coffin.

"How goes it in Leeds?" Richard asked. "'Tis the name of the town, is it not, where thou said thou wouldst reside?"

She looked at him with surprise. "We live not in Leeds but in Burlington. We have been only across the river all these years."

"Aye," he said, "a bitter irony, methinks." He sighed, then smiled. "I kept the note thou wrote me, e'en though I could not read it then. Dost thou remember what thou wrote?"

"No," she admitted.

"The words 'I shall always remember you.' I carried the note in my pouch till it threatened to tear. I keep it now in a box."

"And I drink from the porcelain cup."

He cleared his throat. "Thy husband, he is good to thee?"

"Yes," she said, blinking, "Japhet is kind enough and fair."

Richard nodded, cleared his throat again, then looked over his shoulder in the direction of Rachel, who still sat talking with neighbors.

"She is a minister with the Society of Friends," Deborah offered.

"These Friends are a mystery, are they not?" he asked. "They have some queer ways, but are good people. I have lived amongst them now these many years and picked up their speech."

"As have I," she said, glad the conversation had moved away from their past attachment. "I go to Meeting with my husband. I admire their belief that God speaks to all, that we are all equal regardless of our sex and our stations. Howe'er, action doth not always meet entirely with word. There is much controversy over slaving. Some wish to issue a formal condemnation of the practice, but others say nay despite horrid testimonies about it—children taken from mothers' breasts, husbands and wives fore'er separated, ill usage by masters. 'Tis difficult to believe anyone could resist a condemnation, but those who do say they dispute the authenticity of the reports. But 'tis the truth they own slaves themselves or have dealings with those who do and don't wish to affront them. Regardless, I do feel certain the Society will condemn the practice one day."

Rachel looked over and Deborah nodded, indicating she was welcome to return. As she approached, Deborah was impressed again by her graceful carriage. Like Japhet, she seemed to glide over the ground, but her stride was slower and even smoother. She moved like a slim vessel easing into port.

"Mother will worry if we don't return soon," Rachel said, looking from Deborah to Richard. "If it pleases Deborah, mightst thou join us for dinner on the morrow?"

"Yes," she said to him, with a grateful glance at her. "Do come."

"I thank thee." Richard smiled at Rachel. "To be sure, I shall come."

The next day after a dinner of pork, squash, pie and beer, the three of them took a walk away from town. Deborah wore her scarlet cloak with the hood up and strolled arm-in-arm with Rachel, while Richard walked beside. As they walked along a dirt road she noticed him gazing at Rachel with more than passing interest.

"'Tis a pity, Deborah," she said, squeezing her arm, "that thou must leave so soon, when I have just begun to know thee."

"Yes," Deborah agreed.

"Ah, there 'tis," Rachel said abruptly and released her arm. She went over to a nearby flowering cherry tree.

Deborah felt eyes on her and looked at Richard but couldn't read his expression. Sorrow that I am leaving? she wondered. Regret? She found herself wishing he still had strong feelings for her. She heard a twig snap.

Richard turned toward the sound. "I'll assist thee with that," he said and walked over to help Rachel break off a small stem.

Deborah watched them laughing as they struggled with the cherry tree. It had been years since she had laughed like that. Rachel was older than she, yet it seemed she was just beginning her life. And Richard . . . She remembered their kiss.

The flowering branch was finally free of the tree, and Rachel presented it to Deborah like a bouquet. As she took it, she felt nauseated and held her belly.

"Art thou unwell?" Rachel asked.

I might have stayed at home in England and worked the farm and made the woolens, Deborah thought. Or I might have left with Richard. I need not have become a healer. I need not have married Japhet. I never knew I could simply choose not to marry.

"Let us get thee home," Rachel said. "Canst thou walk?" She put an arm around Deborah.

'Tis late for regret, Deborah told herself. Stand up on thy own. Thou art a healer. Thou hast lovely children, a husband who cares for thee, and Erin *is* thy friend.

Still holding onto her belly, she raised her head. Richard offered his arm. After a moment's hesitation, she took it, then accepted Rachel's as well. They walked back in silence. When they neared the house, Deborah gently pulled away from them and stepped ahead, unable to bear their touch any longer. She went down the alley next to the house, through the iron gate and into the garden. There she sat on the bench next to Felicity, dropping the cherry branch beside her. Rachel and Richard looked so beautiful as they approached she wanted to scream or cry. Instead, she lowered her head and pet the cat.

"I know I have not the knowledge to suggest a remedy," Rachel said to her. "But do ask Gertrude. She will make up any thou mightst require."

Deborah nodded in thanks and turned to Richard. She wanted in that moment to turn back time, to be the young girl she once had been, to *choose* her life and mate.

"Richard," she began, wanting to say something meaningful to him. What? she asked herself. Do I pretend I would abandon my family, and Erin? Do I believe this is not a passing fancy?

He was watching her, waiting, and she felt oddly released. As if seeing him again had been inevitable. As if she had to meet Rachel in order to realize how her life had been shaped by others. And knowing that, what now? Could she choose anything different? Did she have any choice but to accept the responsibility of her children? To accept that Erin desired her only as a friend? No. Could she choose whether or not to be a healer? To develop her craft? Those also seemed given. So what was the purpose of this revelation? Japhet, she thought, her stomach clenching. Something about him?

She moved forward hastily and kissed Richard's cheek, aware of his whiskers against her lips. Then she turned away and walked into the house, closing the door tightly behind her.

27

DEBORAH KNEW something was amiss the moment the cart drew up to the house. A pile of wooden crates stood beside it. Someone was leaving.

Erin appeared in the doorway carrying John and rushed toward her. "So glad you are home," she said.

Deborah climbed down and waved good-bye to Mary, who left. Before she had a chance to question Erin, Japhet walked around from the other side of the house. The color drained from his face when he saw Deborah, but he stepped forward and kissed her cheek.

"What *is* this, Japhet?" Deborah asked. He looked as if he hadn't slept well since she left.

"We are leaving Burlington," he said flatly.

"What?"

"We are removing to Leeds."

"Dost thou mean to tell me that I go away for a matter of days and return to hear we are leaving our home?" She looked around in disbelief.

"We must remove. My father hath called for his land."

"His land? What dost thou mean, his?" Then she understood and her voice rose. "Thou never bought it from him? Thou told me thou hadst settled with him."

Japhet's face reddened. "I did, or so I thought it at the time. He refused to sell, Deborah, but wrote saying I might build and remain, and gave me some funds. He was not pleased I chose to remain, but was glad I was here to care for his niece. He believed he never would return to Burlington, and knowing how despised he was by Friends here, I thought it so as well. But now he says there are no reliable routes 'twixt New York and Leeds, and issues of his almanac have gone astray on their way to the printer."

"We shall all live here together. We need not remove."

"Mary's house is too small for him, my seven brothers and sisters, and her. They could not live there. Besides, once he learns I am a Friend he will cast us out."

"He cannot be that vengeful. He hath not cast out thy cousin Mary."

"She is not his eldest son." Japhet took a deep breath. "Neither hath she deceived him."

Deborah leaned against a stack of crates, steadying herself for what he was about to say.

"I never told thee, but shortly ere thy arrival I was baptised at St. Mary's Church and sent him a notice, so he'd have no reason to fear I would become a Friend. Methinks it pleased him to imagine his son as a thorn in the side of the Society."

"Thou feigned an Anglican baptismal? I cannot fathom thou wouldst do that, Japhet. I cannot believe anyone would!"

"It sounds incredible I know, but 'tis the truth. I had to convince my father I would not become a Friend or he should never have allowed me to remain. When those at St. Mary's later learned I had joined the Society, I told them only I had found another way. My father would never believe this tale—he would see the truth of the matter."

This is no jest, Deborah thought. He kept all this from me, and now he means to say he shall allow his father to chase us from this land, our home. "How long hast thou known of his intentions?"

"I have had the letter two weeks. I said naught because I did not wish to trouble thee ere I spoke with a lawyer. He says we can do naught about it. 'Tis my father's land and he desires it. But Deborah," he urged, "he hath given me a thousand acres—nearly the entire town of Leeds—including a house with furnishings and a farm with livestock. I have the deed, which he sent with his message. He might simply have kept that land, but he wishes to be fair and to remain in this house. He is an old man now with few years left."

"No," Deborah said.

"Once he returns, he would learn of my trickery and toss us out," Japhet repeated. "But the deed—I have the deed to his land in Leeds."

"Sell it."

"What?"

"Sell the land."

"I could not do that. He told me he named the town after me."

"*Japhet.*" She rolled her eyes. "The name is his as well as yours."

"Regardless, if we sold it whither would we reside? Here? I could ne'er live in the same town as he." He put his hands on Deborah's shoulders and leaned toward her. "'Tis a working farm with livestock, and 'tis mine: nearly an entire town." His eyes glazed over.

So this is what it is, she thought. The land baron desires to go. "No," she said again.

"'Tis the best I could hope for, and 'tis done." He repeated quietly, "'Tis done, Deborah."

"I shan't go."

"What?"

"The children and I will stay. We'll live with Mary, or Erin. Daniel Leeds may take our home, but he shan't push me out of Burlington!"

"But Deborah," Japhet said, clearly surprised and shaken, "thou must go."

"Must I?"

"Thou– thou wouldst abandon me?"

"Thou art the one removing."

He dropped onto a nearby crate and looked up at her. "Whither wouldst thou have us go, then? I told thee we could not live in Burlington with him so near. So whither?"

Deborah did not know.

"There is no place. No place to go but Leeds!" He stood and picked up the crate he had been sitting on. "We are going," he said angrily, "and soon. My father's letter stated he would leave in a matter of days hence. We must be gone ere he arrives." Japhet headed for the rear of the house, then said as if an afterthought, "Thou wilt change thy mind."

Deborah watched him until he was out of sight, then walked slowly toward the house. When she reached the door, the mulberry door she had fought for so vehemently, she dropped to her knees and wept.

LEEDS

28

VERY DAY, leaving got a little easier. Deborah was leaving because she couldn't bear to separate the children from their father, and didn't think her healing work could support her and her family. But these were only arguments she used to convince herself she was being sensible. There was really only one reason she was leaving—because Japhet had outmaneuvered her, by arranging for Erin to go as well.

There hadn't even been a big quarrel about it. Erin's hand had brushed her shoulder—that was all—a touch on the threshold and Deborah's tears stopped. She picked herself up, climbed the stairs with Erin following, then allowed herself to be tucked in bed and her temples rubbed until she slept.

The last thing Deborah remembered that night was Erin coming back in after supper, putting a trencher of food on the floor and saying she was going as well.

What? Deborah thought. What?

"Patrick and I," Erin repeated, "we are going to Leeds. Your husband hath given us a fifty-acre plot out there—the twenty-five he promised me and the twenty-five Jeb promised Patrick." She kissed Deborah on the forehead. "I am going, Deborah. I am going to Leeds."

Driving three horse-carts on a trail meant for single travelers was slower than walking. Little Mary's arm cuddled Robert as they lay stretched out on the seat beneath a blanket, their heads resting on their mother's lap. John slept also, swaddled against Deborah's chest, covered by her scarlet cloak.

Ahead of them, scythe, axe, and spade flashed rhythmically as branches and young trees fell under Patrick's swing, and Japhet and Ethan cleared away underbrush and dug stumps. They weren't the first white settlers to widen this ancient Lenni-Lenape trail to the shore, and they would not be the last. Flora had a penchant for retracing her steps.

It was the third day of their journey, and Deborah still couldn't believe Japhet had been capable of such deceit—to feign a baptismal, lie to his father, and lie to her. Then when he is undone, she thought, he expects me to go easily with him. And when I refused, he connived to convince me with Erin—or take her from me—by not only giving her land in Leeds, but to Patrick as well.

She became angry again as she watched Japhet's strong, scythe-wielding arms. Yet he is not an evil man, she decided, continuing the argument she had had with herself every day. His father likely would have turned them off his farm in Burlington if Japhet had admitted he had become a Friend. She also conceded that once Daniel returned to Burlington, he would soon learn of his son's religion and disinherit him. Japhet had leapt at a thousand acres in the east because he knew that was all he would get. When faced with nothing or ownership of a town, who would not choose the town?

But who was this Daniel Leeds whom everyone, it seemed, either hated or feared? This man who had been the first Surveyor-General of West Jersey; who sat on the Assembly for many years; who had been a councillor until recently and was now a supreme court judge; who while a councillor had convinced the governor, Lord Cornbury, to prevent three Friends from taking their duly elected Assembly seats for eleven months, until they successfully refuted his accusation that they didn't own the requisite amount of land; who had benefited from Cornbury's patronage until a year ago when the governor was recalled by his cousin, Queen Anne; and who still published one of the first annual almanacs in the colonies.

Japhet once told her about reading the minutes of the Men's Business Meeting during which they attempted to raise funds to publish a rebuttal to one of his father's tracts. They referred to him during the meeting as *that malicious Instrument of the Devill, Daniel Leeds.* And this from men who did not use those words lightly, who did not even believe in the Devil, or at least not with the passion of other Christians.

Deborah had wanted to see the face of the man who provoked such rage. She was curious if father and son shared the same fine black hair and long, French nose. But she never got her wish. Three carts left Burlington: Deborah and Japhet's, Erin and Patrick's, Johanna and Ethan's. They drove south, then northeast to join the main path to the shore. Though Japhet hadn't said so, Deborah knew he chose such an out-of-the-way route to avoid his father.

Although the Lenape trail was narrow and strewn with stumps, it was congenial in the way it skirted hills and circled streams rather than cutting across. There *were* a few stretches, like the one they presently traveled, wide enough to simply drive through—even after dark, with the assistance of moonlight.

Deborah managed the reins while the children and Japhet slept. She turned to look at the cart behind. Erin waved from the driver's seat. Patrick was asleep as well. Deborah picked up her wand from the back, then pointed it at the path ahead. "Be good to me," she whispered. She lowered the wand, looked up toward the full moon, and remembered the night she had cut it from the Witches' Tree. How can I have left it? she thought. How can I have left cousin Mary and Isaiah?

She glanced down at the trail and saw a group of Lenni-Lenape men just ahead. Where had they come from? Quietly, she drew the horses to a stop. More astonished than frightened, she didn't wake Japhet but sat passively as the reins were taken from her hands. The men led the carts a short distance to the center of their small village. Japhet and the children finally woke when Johanna began to scream.

Perhaps it was the late hour but no one else reacted, not even Ethan, who simply looked at Johanna as if she were mad. She fell silent and stared around her, clearly confused as to why no one else was afraid of the enemy.

The travelers were invited to sit by a large fire. "Have they any dolls?" Mary whispered to her mother after they had accepted the invitation.

Several children sat together on the other side of the fire. "Go and ask," Deborah coaxed. She watched as Mary walked slowly over and joined them.

A woman handed Deborah a shell bowl of hasty—a corn porridge she had made herself many times—topped with strips of dried meat and oysters. As she ate, Deborah watched Johanna and Ethan still seated in their cart, both now refusing to get down. Johanna cannot help what she believes to be true, Deborah thought, nor the way it binds her.

She remembered a conversation about Johanna she'd had with Erin while helping her dress the morning of her wedding. It took place two days before leaving Burlington, and Deborah had just told Erin that Johanna and Ethan were coming with them to Leeds.

"I cannot believe what I hear," Erin said as Deborah tied on an ivory, quilted silk petticoat borrowed from cousin Mary. "You have an opportunity to be rid of Johanna and you invite her in?"

"Why should I not, Erin? I need a servant." She said this more bitterly than intended but didn't apologize.

"There are many who could be servant to you," Erin said. "Japhet hath released me a bit early, yet I have agreed to remain for bed and board till Patrick hath built our cabin. You might choose another girl after you have arrived in Leeds. Or you might return now to Philadelphia and purchase another redemptioner. You need not keep Johanna."

Deborah stood at Erin's back and started to lace the ivory silk stays. "Why dost thou despise her so? She hath done naught to thee. She doth her work well with nary a word, despite thine ill usage."

"I do not use her ill. Ow!" Erin looked accusingly over her shoulder.

"'Twas not done with purpose," Deborah said, then loosened the lacing.

"Hmm. And what of the spider she thought was a devil?"

"I own that troubles me," Deborah said without looking up. "But I feel sorrow for her. She lost her child and now hires out, with no place that is home to her."

"Your pity will be your undoing."

"Overstating the matter doth not help thy cause."

"She is mad as a hatter, Deborah."

"Save for the spider, she is only unsound when she hath a vision. She is a seer but hath nothing on which to tie it. We are able to know our sight for what 'tis. But she can see it only as sin or curse and is frighted by it, if she is aware of it at all. Canst thou understand how that must be? 'Twould be the same for me had I had no Granna. I desire to give her what Granna gave me—a place where she might develop and shape her sight, so that it will not fright her so."

"You desire to give, I hear, but doth she wish to receive?"

"I know not," Deborah admitted. Erin's words unsettled her, but she felt strongly that she should at least try to help Johanna.

She finished lacing the stays in silence. "There now." She helped Erin step into the pale olive, satin gown and caught a glance at them both in the looking glass. Except for the rags in Erin's hair, she was beautiful. "Mary was in the right that the olive shows thy dark hair to better advantage than my white gown."

Erin ran her hands down the satin, then looked at Deborah in the glass. "Am I passing fair?"

Deborah stepped forward and faced her. "Thou art lovely."

Erin smiled and tears came to her eyes.

Deborah had rarely seen Erin moved to tears and it felt as if a quill were going through her heart: the dull tip slow to penetrate, the pain unbearable. She bit her lip and started to work on Erin's hair. Slowly, she unrolled each rag, stretching the curl out long, then pulled the cloth free and let the curl bounce back into a shoulder-length ringlet. She couldn't help thinking how comely Erin was, how much she wished this day weren't happening. When she felt Erin's eyes on her, she glanced again toward their reflection.

"I thank you," Erin said, "for assisting me to dress. There is no other I would wish with me this day."

The quill plunged deeper. Deborah tried to smile but couldn't. She ducked completely behind Erin as her own eyes filled with tears. Untying the next rag, and then the next, working quickly, she tried to think of nothing else but the movement of her hands: untying, unrolling, pulling the cloth free; untying, unrolling, pulling it free. Soon she began to feel better. She wiped her eyes and nose with her hand and moved back into view to start on the other side of Erin's head.

When she came to the last rag, she attempted levity. "I thought helping thee dress would be the proper manner in which to end thy servitude. 'Tis, dost thou not agree?"

Erin smiled and ran her fingers through some of the curls to fluff them out. "But what of Johanna?" she asked. "Will you not leave her behind?"

"No, Erin," Deborah said, yanking away the final rag. "Johanna is coming along."

Sitting now around the fire, watching Johanna's terrified face, Deborah saw her as an insect in a web, unwilling to trust her own senses, unable to believe these Indians could be offering a friendly respite on their journey, refusing to consider what she'd always known to be true could be wrong.

Then Deborah heard a voice inside her head, "You are not so different, as you say." I *am* not so different, she agreed with the voice. I know what 'tis to be frighted by visions. The girl with the fish was an omen, telling me 'tis my fate to help Johanna make peace with her sight. I must do the best I am able. Regardless of Erin's ill feeling, Johanna Conrad must stay.

It was sunset on the fifth day when Deborah smelled the sea. "We are here," she whispered to Japhet, asleep next to her. She turned around and Erin waved and nodded. She smelled it too.

Suddenly, Deborah felt a sting and slapped her arm, but missed the insect that bit her. She swatted at her forehead, and this one she smote and watched fall into her lap; a light brown, skinny fly with a pointed head.

The horses neighed and thrashed their tails, then took off. All around buzzed a swarm of biting flies. "Begone ye demons!" Japhet yelled, dashed fully awake. He held the children close to him with one arm and waved his hat, but his efforts were futile. The flies formed a cloud around them.

The trail was wide enough here for them to pass easily, but still the cart lurched and bounced, threatening to break apart. Japhet pushed the children onto the floor and covered them with a blanket. Deborah braced her feet and clung to the reins as she struggled for control, hoping the other carts were still intact behind them.

The path grew wider and wider, then became a road. The frantic horses veered off and headed across a field. Deborah was certain now the cart would break apart and abandoned all pretense of command. She handed the reins to Japhet, gripped the seat with one hand and held onto John with the other. He screamed, still swaddled against her chest. She noticed a dirt road running parallel to them and signaled to Japhet. He yanked the reins harder, trying to drive the horses toward it, but without success. She remembered her staff and grabbed it, then leaned over and hit the horses repeatedly on the rump. Together, they urged the team to the road.

As they rounded a bend, they saw a two-story farmhouse with four smoking barrels in front, and drove the horses toward it. The team stopped finally, heaving and lathered, at the porch. Erin and Patrick, and then Johanna and Ethan pulled up alongside, out of breath and dazed. No one said anything, and they all stared stupidly around them. On either side of the large porch and below the two front windows, barrels blazed.

The door opened and a woman rushed out. "You are not the first to arrive suchly," she said cheerfully as she helped them down. "My husband shall see to the horses."

They followed her inside. Though there was nothing striking about her looks—she was of medium height and build, about thirty, plainly dressed in grey—she seemed to Deborah the very image of a savior.

"We rarely have the mosquitoes and biting flies so early in April," the woman said over her shoulder, "but we do have them May to October, to be sure."

She led them to the hearth and bade them sit. A baby girl was crying in a crib. Robert squirmed off his mother's lap and walked over to the infant.

"Thou likest my little Abigail?" the woman asked. She picked Robert up and put him in the crib as well.

Then she brought over a small wooden bucket containing a bitter-sweet smelling liquid, which Deborah later learned was a mixture of camphor, calendula, sassafras, pennyroyal, and bergamot.

"Had I a lemon," she said, "'twould do just as well for the bites, but to keep them at bay, this concoction is all a person needs against the mosquitoes and biting flies of these shores." She dipped in several cloths, started to hand them to Deborah, then gave Japhet a puzzled look.

He stood up and smiled wryly. "Hath it been so long thou knowest me not, Alice Higbee?"

She absently gave the cloths to Deborah and said, "Japhet Leeds. Is it thou? Why didst thou not say so?" Affectionately, she gripped his arms. "But ..." She pulled back and studied him. "Thy sober dress, Japhet. Art thou a Friend?"

He grinned.

Alice burst out laughing. "Thy father, he doth not know?"

Japhet shook his head.

She laughed again and wiped her eyes. "Welcome," she said. "Thee and thy family, welcome home."

Deborah watched them, unable to share in their warm humor, still bitter about Japhet's deceit. And yet, she considered, though the biting flies and frighted horses would seem a bad omen, here they were greeted and given comfort. In sooth, mayhap it be a hopeful portent for our new life. Mayhap all will be well.

29

S IF HE REALLY were moving back to Burlington to die, Daniel Leeds had left nearly everything behind. The rooms Deborah entered were amply decorated with sturdy furniture, some of it quite fine, such as the tent featherbed with a canopy of green damask and a matching quilt in the master bedroom. At the sight of it she felt a pang of guilt—which seemed ridiculous under the circumstances—for she had stripped their house bare, leaving only the most basic furniture and her home-made mattresses, which had been difficult enough to give up. To convince her to do so, Japhet had to show her the deed and his father's letter, which stated that since transport was arduous both families must leave their houses fully furnished. Deborah finally abandoned the mattresses and, for safekeeping, placed the deed in Granna's rosewood box.

Japhet gestured at a large oak wardrobe across from the tent bed. "It will replace pegs for hanging clothes," he explained.

Deborah opened the wardrobe's door and frowned. She wasn't certain she would prefer to have her clothing hidden away. She did like the mahogany butterfly table and its two chairs, painted red and black. Sitting down in one, she put her arms on the rests and smiled.

"Shall we go now to the parlor?" he asked.

She followed him down the winding staircase. Erin and Patrick remained upstairs. They were looking at the room they would sleep in until their own house was built. This room and the third bedroom upstairs contained simple bedsteads with straw mattresses.

The parlor was bright, with three windows, two of which faced the limbs of apple trees. In the corner by the rear window was a six-legged, folding trestle bed. Its valance, hangings, and coverlet were a matching ivory crewel-work with a widely-spaced floral design. At the front of the room stood a pine settle with a tall back of five fielded panels which dropped nearly to the floor.

"If thou and our neighbors agree," Japhet said, "I wish to hold the Friends Meeting here, with the bed tucked away, of course."

Deborah sat on the pine settle and imagined the room on a Sunday morning, light trickling through the trees. It would be lovely, she thought. Despite herself, she liked the house and what she had seen of its surroundings. She was also starting to feel excited at the prospect of being a healer in an area with no doctors. As cousin Mary had said years before, she would be free in Leeds to fully develop her skills. Except for Alice Higbee, Deborah had learned, she and Erin would be the only ones with such knowledge and experience. Mayhap we might all assist each other, she thought.

Japhet left the parlor. After examining the bed's crewelwork more closely, she went into the main room, a combination kitchen, living, and dining area with a massive fireplace. In front of it stood an oak stretcher table with long benches on either side and two joint stools at the far end. Japhet was sitting on one of the stools and turned to face her.

"I recall meals here," he said. "We eight children and Pappa and his wife. I a'ways thought the room small—'twas why I desired another for the cooking—but it appears large with no one in it."

He smiled but Deborah couldn't return it, not yet. She heard a squeal behind her and saw Patrick chasing Erin down the stairs. He caught her half-way and kissed her. Erin pushed him off, then raced to the bottom, laughing. There she halted and blushed. Patrick scooped her up and started to carry her back to their room.

"'Tis time for the blessing, *now*," Deborah said, frowning at Patrick. He put Erin down.

Japhet walked across the room and clapped him on the shoulder. "Let us take our leave, Paddy, we don't wish to stand in the way of *this*." He snickered as both men headed outside.

Deborah went to the door and called after him, "I bless this house to protect us from thy father's influence. To be sure 'tis necessary, since thou canst not be trusted to face up to him."

Japhet turned to look at her, a mixture of shame and anger on his face. She responded to his hurt and stepped toward him onto the small porch. He turned away again and kept walking. I shan't have thy pity, his last look seemed to say. Thou ought to be pleased I even offer it, she thought, then sighed and looked out over the land.

The Leeds homestead crowned a rise which Japhet said was the highest point along the coast between the Atlantic highlands and the Virginia capes. Of this Deborah couldn't be sure, since pine, oak, cedar, and birch trees blocked the view. In a marsh beyond the woods, their cattle grazed on salt hay. Apple trees planted by Daniel circled part of the house and grew down the rise in a southwesterly direction toward the fenced-in garden, where Deborah planned to grow vegetables for the family and medicinal herbs. Past the garden was the barn and beyond that the fenced fields where Daniel and his sons had grown corn—where Japhet and his sons would grow corn and wheat. The air all around smelled faintly of fish.

Erin touched Deborah's arm and suggested, "Let us go to the cart."

"Yes," she agreed.

They stacked what was needed for the blessing onto the seat of a heavy oak chair and carried it to the door. Deborah set aside everything except for salt, a large shell, and a loaf of bread, then took the chair in to the middle of the main room. She filled the shell with salt and put it on the floor. Then she squatted evenly on her haunches and placed her palms on the pine. "I did not wish to remove, but I am here now. May we never hunger and may we ever prosper."

She called to Erin for the rest of the items, and together they went through the house, pushing open every window and securing the iron latches on the bottom. When they returned to the main room, Deborah was to begin with Earth—the element of the tangible, the felt and seen—but she sensed that something wasn't right. Staring into the bowl of salt, she said, "Erin, we have done no workings together since..." When Erin didn't respond, Deborah glanced up. She had never seen Erin look so sad. "I do not mean to say I will not," Deborah said.

"But do you say you cannot?"

Deborah wasn't sure, but knew that she wanted to. She wanted things between them to be back to normal. She wanted to stop feeling betrayed and shattered. "I will make the attempt," she said finally.

She picked up the bowl of salt and carried it to the northern corner of the room. "By the will of Earth, we purify this house," she recited. She tossed a pinch of salt into the corner. As it fell, the grains caught the sun and twinkled like stars for a moment. She glanced at Erin, who smiled.

They moved to the next corner, dropped salt into it, and said together this time, "By the will of Earth, we purify." They did the same throughout the house—leaving salt in every corner, saying the phrase together, their will and words united to purify and bless.

When they were done with Earth, Erin filled a cup with water from the well bucket, dipped in her fingers, and flicked the water in each corner of the house while saying, "Wash away that which is left behind. By the will of Water, we cleanse."

For Fire they lit a honeycomb candle on live coals Alice had given them and carried it about the house. "Powerful one, Fire," they said, "burn away the old. Let us begin anew."

Then came incense—a blend of yarrow, Johnswort, basil, and juniper berries in a shell—to represent Air. As Deborah watched Erin light it with the candle, she had the startling feeling that she was changed—that she had set out to purify the house and without noticing it had cleansed herself. She felt at peace, at ease. She put her hand on Erin's shoulder and squeezed it, thinking, is not that the way with magic? It always comes back on thee.

Erin turned to look at her and smiled, fanning the incense with her hand. "Shall we?" she asked.

Deborah took her arm and they went through the house, fanning the smoke into each corner. Once more their voices joined, "All that remains unwanted, Air, cast out on thy wind."

They returned to the main room, put the incense on the floor and headed outside. Erin went first, carrying the shell of salt. The air had become a bit humid and her hair was frizzing. When they reached the bottom of the front steps, she turned suddenly and pinched salt at Deborah. "By the will of the former servant, I purify you," she said.

Deborah laughed and grabbed for the shell but Erin yanked it away and ran. Deborah took off after her down the rise and caught the back of her gown.

"You have me. You have me," Erin said, panting.

"Thou art not as quick as thou once was."

"Mayhap not, but I might still fool you!" She leapt forward and threw the rest of the salt at Deborah.

After a stunned moment, Deborah dropped to her knees and scooped up the white crystals and tossed them at Erin, who, squatting now, was throwing back what she could gather. Soon they were tossing only dirt.

Deborah put up her hands and said, "Stay, stay. No more." Erin nodded in weary agreement, and they retraced their steps into the house, where the incense was still burning.

Suddenly, Erin grabbed Deborah from behind and said, "I had this in my apron pocket," and dropped a small handful of salt down her bodice. Deborah whirled around prepared to chase Erin, expecting her to run away, but Erin remained, gave Deborah a look that stopped her, a look that said, I have chosen Patrick but I love you.

Deborah reached out tentatively and put her hands on Erin's hips. Erin did the same. Pale brown flecks dotted Erin's blue eyes. Her lips were large and brownish-red.

Standing like that, squared off as years before with the broom, they leaned back and walked clockwise, pulling their torsos together, clasping their hands behind each other's waists, their heads arched back. They increased their speed and soon were spinning, like an upended wheel. They turned until they nearly dropped, hugging at last to keep from falling, holding on until the ground stopped spinning. Erin stood straight and kissed Deborah's lips. "Thou art Goddess," she said.

Fascinated by the flecks she had never noticed before in Erin's eyes, Deborah whispered back, "Thou art Goddess."

30

REEN SILK swayed as far as Deborah could see. Smooth miles of spring marsh grass grew from black mud and were grooved with roads of brackish water. She tossed in her fishing line, lifted her grey calico gown, and sat heavily on a log. Salt came off on her hand when she touched the grass. Overhead the gulls shrieked constantly. They swooped toward the shore, their black heads darting, looking for food.

She sat at the base of the creek where Lenape from the west used to come each summer to catch crabs and gather oysters. They set up wigwams along the shore and feasted till fall. What they could not eat they dried and smoked to carry back to their villages.

It was from the Lenape that Alice Higbee had learned about the medicinal properties of the local plants she used to treat her neighbors, and which she shared with Deborah and Erin. The Lenape stopped coming to Leeds, Alice explained, after Daniel Leeds shot at them his first summer there. Each June, even now, she waited for them to return. But they never did, and probably never would.

To the south lay Absecum, where cousin Mary's father, William, and her siblings had settled. Japhet had been uneasy about seeing his uncle again, since William was an Anglican as well, but when they met again—nearly a year ago now—he was pleased to learn that William and Daniel were not on the best of terms. They had squabbled over a land deal, it seemed.

Deborah moved her fishing line back and forth in the water. Nothing was biting today. Erin approached and stood next to her. "'Tis the best place, is it not," she remarked pleasantly, "when the flying pests sleep."

Deborah smiled up at her and shifted her weight a little. A pain—like a severe menstrual cramp—moved through her. She gripped her thigh until it passed. "'Tis only wind," she told Erin, seeing her worried expression.

"Wind?" Erin frowned.

She obviously didn't believe the explanation any more than Deborah believed it herself. But since this was only her eighth month and her other children had been on time or late, Deborah had been trying to convince herself that the widely-spaced pains she'd had all morning were from too much cranberry sauce in the middle of last night. Abandoning the pretense, she held an arm up to Erin. "Wilt thou assist me?" she asked.

Erin helped her, and they took a path through the dense woods which led to the Leeds house. Another contraction came on when they reached the front porch. Deborah leaned heavily on Erin and moaned.

Erin pushed the door open and called in, "Mary, run and fetch Alice. Johanna, come hither."

As the pain subsided, Deborah became unsettled, fearing this birth would be more difficult than her others. During those earlier pregnancies, she had taken a tincture of partridge berry during the last six weeks to ease the birth. But since this child was early, she had only been taking it for two weeks—not enough time to fully prime her muscles for contractions. But it doth me only ill to dwell on that, she thought, and so tried to comfort herself with humor. Just like his father, she joked to herself, Japhet's namesake will bring me only grief.

Johanna took Deborah's other arm and helped her into the parlor. Robert and John played on the floor with a toy their father had made—six wooden blocks of different shapes on a long hemp string.

"'Tis all right, my sons," Deborah said as they stopped to watch her. "Mam must lie down awhile." She collapsed onto the bed.

Erin took the boys into the main room. Johanna was about to go as well when Deborah said, "Prithee, remain a moment."

Johanna's face was downcast but her upturned gaze accentuated her protruding eyes. Deborah wasn't sure why she had called her back. Somewhat confused, she said, "I thank thee for thy good work."

"I only desire to please you."

"Yes, Johanna, I know. And thou dost." Johanna smiled.

Erin entered the room with a mug of red raspberry leaf tea and a cool cloth which she put on Deborah's forehead. "Johanna," Erin said, "I have started the water to boil. Make your mistress a tea of birth wort and red raspberry leaf. The herbs lay on the gateleg. As well, heat more water for the cloths. Robert, John," she reminded the boys who stood in the doorway, "I told you to remain in the other room. Go now." To Johanna she added sternly, "Keep them out."

Johanna took Robert's hand and tried to pull him away from the parlor. He started to wail and so did John. She bent down to quiet them.

"If you would not treat them roughly, they would not cry," Erin said, then gave Deborah a look of exasperation.

"Missus, no," Johanna said, obviously feeling unjustly accused.

"Don't concern thyself, Johanna," Deborah soothed. "Go now, boys. Don't make me leave my sickbed. Do as thy nursemaid bids thee." After they left, she said to Erin, half-joking, "Methinks thou wouldst be pleased with no one in thy old position."

Erin seemed about to object when Alice walked in with five-year-old Mary. "I was on my way to check on thee," Alice said. "Thus I arrived so quickly. Give me leave to have a look."

"Mary," Erin said, "your brothers are with Johanna by the hearth. Take them up the stairs and remain with them."

Mary appealed to her mother with a pleading look.

"Give Mam a kiss firstly," Deborah said. Mary ran over and hugged her. "Thou art my best girl, thou knows that– uhhh . . ." She let go of Mary and tried to get up onto her hands and knees.

"Go on," Alice told the little girl, keeping her voice calm as she helped Deborah to the position she wanted. "Go to the main room."

Mary didn't move. Deborah wanted to chide her, then was only aware of her own chant-like moan, the pain, and a calming hand on her head. When the contraction finally passed, she saw that the hand on her head had been Mary's. There hadn't been anything especially healing in the hand, but it had met a need for touch.

"Mam, may I stay?" Mary asked.

"It may fright thee," Deborah said, panting. "I shall call out in pain."

She wasn't sure what to do. Her own mother never would have allowed a child in a birthing chamber, but Granna might have, depending on the child. Deborah made her choice half-way between them. "Thou mightst remain awhile. I do desire thy help. Prithee run now and bring Mam a cup of water."

Mary grinned and skipped out of the room.

The two women helped Deborah lean back and bring up her legs so Alice could examine her. "Thou art far along," she exclaimed. "How long hast thou been laboring?"

"A few hours of calling it wind," Erin said. Deborah nodded, sheepishly.

"Healers are the worst patients," Alice said. "And thou mightst have another healer in Mary."

"I think not," Deborah said. "She is a good daughter, but no healer."

Alice raised her eyebrows but said nothing. Mary came back into the room, reverently holding out the porcelain cup.

"Ohhh," Deborah cried, motioning for Alice and Erin to help her back onto her hands and knees. "Ohhhhh."

"Drop it down," Erin said, referring to the sound. "Drop it to your belly. From there, Deborah, good, bring it from there."

Deborah pressed her head against the mattress and rocked forward and back. She wasn't aware of much more than the heavy movement of her body, the low, full cry she made, and the wracking pain, indeed worse than with her other births. When it eased, she sat up again, sweating, unable to focus on anyone there. Alice mopped her forehead and Erin encouraged her to drink the tea Johanna brought in, but soon she had to change her position and motioned for help. With the assistance of the other women, she sat with one leg crossed before her, the other hanging off the bed. Johanna stepped back, knocking into Mary, who was clearly frightened.

Alice noticed as well. "Johanna," she said, "take Mary into the other room."

Mary looked at her mother, no longer seeming like she wanted to stay but rather afraid to leave.

"Thou wert a great help," Deborah said, gasping, "but go now. Mam shall be well."

Mary didn't seem convinced but followed Johanna out of the room. Erin held the mug again for Deborah to sip and said, "Listen to your own words; you shall be well."

Deborah smiled a little. With the pain subsided, she believed her. But this babe was early, she thought.

Erin began to hum. The melody soothed Deborah and she leaned back against the pillows. Alice put a dropperful of black snakeroot tincture under her tongue.

Johanna caught sight of it as she walked back into the parlor. "You must not ease the pain of birth!" she exclaimed. "As the Lord commanded, pain is punishment for Eve's sin."

"You are my punishment every time I look at you," Erin said. "Be gone, you ignorant Puritan wench."

Johanna stood still, looking at her hands. "I intend no disrespect Mrs. Leeds, Mrs. Higbee, but 'tis true. You must not ease the pain of birth."

"God grows the plants which ease our suffering," Alice said gently. "He intends for us to use them."

Deborah felt a contraction rising again. She closed her eyes and began the chant from her belly which had helped to keep the pain bearable during previous births. From within the dark of her closed lids, she saw the waters of the Little Egg Harbour River. She was standing in it, waist high.

Then she was in the room again, on her knees, pressing her head into the mattress, in full pain. "Damn me," she shouted angrily. "Damn me. Damn, damn, damn, damn."

"Down, down," Erin urged her. "Bring it down."

The pain eventually eased, but Deborah remained, panting on her hands and knees. Sweat from her face dripped onto the quilt. She reached out for water, and Erin handed her the cup.

"Johanna, prithee make up a bed on the floor," Alice said. She wiped the cool cloth over Deborah's face and neck. It felt luscious. Deborah sat up again slowly, put down the water cup, then sipped at her tea.

"Let us have another look," Alice suggested, when Deborah had had a few sips. She and Erin helped Deborah lean back.

"Soon, Deborah," Alice said. She smiled encouragingly from between her legs. "Shan't be long now."

Deborah's waters broke with the next contraction, and the women helped her out of bed and onto the floor. The pain was just as intense—the pounding in her back, the burning vise-grip in her belly, and something else. Something was boring down her legs. She tried to look at them to find the source, but was disoriented and uncertain where to look. "Erin," she called out, because she couldn't find her either, couldn't hear her encouragement or feel her touch.

Erin moved from her side and got directly behind Deborah, pulling gently on her shoulders to encourage Deborah to lean on her. It helped. The leg pain eased, and then the contraction. Deborah collapsed onto Erin.

"Good, Deborah," she heard Alice say.

Deborah was motioning for more water when the pain began again. Unbearable, back-breaking, womb-burning pain. She thought she would die, then wanted to die.

"We're on now," Alice assured her. "Stay, don't push. No! Not yet or thou wilt tear." She kneeled in front of Deborah. Erin was still behind. Johanna was at her side. "Raise thy legs, Deborah," Alice said. "Good. Johanna, help her. Help her keep them up."

"NOOO!" Deborah screamed. The boring leg pain was back. She was dying. She couldn't bear it. No one could. "NOOOO," she screamed again. "I cannot do it! I cannot. No! I cannot!"

"Yes, thou canst, Deborah. Thou canst bear thy babe."

"No, I cannot. I cannot do it!"

"We're here, Deborah. We love you, Deborah."

"NOOO! I'm dying. I'm dying. I cannot."

"Now, Deborah, 'tis time to push. Push now. Push hard, Deborah. Push."

"No, I cannot. Stop. Stop. I cannot do it!"

"Yes, you can, Deborah. Push, Deborah. Push!"

"ERRR. I cannot! Devil take the child! ERRRR. NOOOO!"

"You're there, Deborah. 'Tis coming. 'Tis coming. Push harder, Deborah. Harder now. Push!"

"ERRRRRRRRR . . ." Suddenly, she was in the river, holding her child, a tiny boy. And Johanna was walking toward her, hands extended, taking her son out of her arms, suckling him. Deborah reached for him, but Johanna only laughed. Deborah looked down. Her breasts were flat, barren.

Then she was in the room again, hearing Erin's cry of delight, and felt a squiggly wet form on her chest. The pain was gone, as if it never had been there at all. And she was crying, reaching up to touch her baby boy. There was no river, no barren breasts. Alice and Johanna were beaming. And there was Erin, holding her from behind, peeking over her shoulder at her son, telling her how handsome he was, how strong he looked.

When Johanna reached for him with a damp cloth, Deborah thought, I have no cause to be troubled, for she is but my servant girl. And the river, only my fright taking form. Although she told herself this, she did not loosen her grip upon her son.

"Leave us to that," Erin snapped at Johanna. "Gather up the cloths."

"We thank thee," Alice told her, "but we will tend to the child."

The smile was gone from Johanna's face. She said, "You ought be wary what you wish for, Mrs. Leeds. The Devil listens especial to the cries of women."

"Leave the room!" Erin pushed Johanna's shoulder.

Deborah looked quizzically at Alice. She didn't know to what Johanna was referring.

"Dost thou not see, Johanna?" Alice asked. "Thy mistress doth not even remember. Deborah, in thy pain thou said, 'Devil take the child.' But Johanna, a woman is not to be held accountable for what she says with the strain of birth upon her. Hadst thou a child thyself, thou wouldst know how 'tis to bear."

A palpable silence fell over the room. "Prithee, forgive me," Alice said, but Johanna turned away.

"I know no matter what be upon you," she replied, "you ought ne'er wish for the Devil." She left the parlor.

"Do not listen to her," Alice said as she eased little Japhet off Deborah's chest. "'Tis a fine boy. And he will be a fine lad, just as the others."

Deborah woke the next morning to see Johanna at her bedside in the parlor. Her dark hair was out of the knot she usually wore at the back of her head and hung loose to her waist. Deborah sat up a little.

"If you please," Johanna said, "I beg your forgiveness for my impudence—reaching for your babe, saying the things I did. I know not what I was thinking. You are kind to me and I do not deserve it."

"Don't be troubled, Johanna. Come, sit with me." She sat up a bit more and moved over gingerly to make room on the bed.

Johanna sat down and regarded her, seeming young and frightened. Of what? Deborah wondered. "What *wert* thou thinking when thou said'st those things?" she asked gently. Johanna looked down at her clasped hands. "Unburden thyself. It will put thee at ease to speak of it."

Johanna raised her eyes and said quietly, "I looked at your son and he reminded me of my own departed girl—so tiny—I could not help myself but to reach for him. But ere that, when you called for the Devil it frighted me."

"Dost thou understand I was not wishing for evil? I knew not that I had even spoken the words. I have no wish for the Devil. I do not even believe in him."

"But the Devil comes to those who do not believe in him." She glanced away. "And to some who do."

Deborah waited, hoping for more, but the woman was silent, staring at the cradle where little Japhet lay. If I push at her, Deborah thought, she will only become more frighted. I must continue to earn her confidence.

"The Devil will not come hither," Deborah said. "With my next harvest I'll put a circle of garlic upon the door. That shall keep him at bay, yes?"

Johanna looked back at her and nodded but still seemed distressed. "I see things," she said quietly. "I have the Devil's sight."

Deborah leaned closer. "God gave thee thy sight, Johanna. He wishes for thee to use it to help thy neighbors, as do I. We can all see—only some more clearly than others." She reached out and touched her hand. "If thou allowed it, it could serve thee and others in thy life." As she heard herself speak words Granna might easily have said to her, she again felt determination to free Johanna from whatever bound her and to help her accept her vision as a gift. For 'tis true, she thought, there but for the grace of Brigid go I.

Then Deborah realized she hadn't heard what Johanna just said. "What was that?" she asked.

"I am frighted."

"Dear, thou need'st not fear thy sight. I wish thou couldst understand 'tis an honor to bear such vision."

Johanna bit her lip and looked out the window. "Prithee, might we speak of something else?"

"Yes, we may. But if thou dost e'er desire my help—any time of the day or night—thou hast only to ask and I will come to thee."

Johanna pleased Deborah by smiling at her, by seeming grateful.

Deborah seized the opportunity. "I have been wishing to speak with thee on a different matter. If thou shouldst give me leave to give thee a tincture, it could help thee bear a babe. Then thou couldst have a child of thy own." Immediately, she realized her miscalculation.

"No, Mrs. Leeds. No." She got off the bed. "The Lord doth not desire me to bear." She left the parlor with a hand over her mouth, passing Japhet on her way out the door.

Damn me, Deborah thought. Damn.

"She is a nervous one a'times," Japhet remarked, glancing after Johanna. He walked to the cradle and peered in at his newborn son. "How is my little boy? Japhet, aye?" He looked at Deborah and smiled.

"I have not changed my mind," she said. "Thou ought to have a name-sake—I have told thee before."

"So thou hast. And how is the mother?"

"Weak yet, but well with the care of Alice and Erin and Johanna."

"I am glad to hear it." He touched his son's cheek. "One day, little man, thou and thy brothers will work by my side in the fields and I'll no longer have need to hire drunken hands." He looked at Deborah. "They are at their flasks of applejack all the day. I let some go by midday now, for they are of no use to me after. I tell them they can drink water in the New World, that I have done so all my life, but only Ethan believes it. Wilt thou tell them they can drink water here to no ill effect? They might listen to thee."

"When I am walking, Japhet, I shall. Though I doubt they will listen. Molasses beer doth its own healing at the end of the day."

"'Twere it only at the end, or only molasses beer, I should not mind."

"Methinks thou ought be easy about it. Nothing we say shall persuade them. The superstition runs too deep." Deborah shifted her position and groaned a little, her body still quite sore.

"Listen to me go on like a man possessed when thou liest there abed." He sat down beside her and took her hand. "Thou dost not know what it means to a man to have a son, another son." His eyes were moist.

She squeezed his hand, thinking she did know, and that despite how much she loved her sons and believed during her pregnancy this child would be another one, she was disappointed she didn't have a girl. She longed for the daughter who would inherit her wisdom, who would become the next healer and priestess. Her dear Deborah Fae.

31

IX YEARS LATER, by the birth of Deborah's seventh child, the family was well established on their farm, which despite the challenging sandy soil, had begun to prosper. From his brother Felix, Japhet bought two hundred acres which adjoined his current holdings, and he planned to acquire additional tracts. He still complained about hired hands who drank, and was sorely vexed when his cousin Jonathan opened a tavern. Deborah thought it better for imbibing to occur at a licensed establishment than in the wood, but Japhet would not be consoled. He told her his only comfort was four younger sons who would one day join the two older boys working beside him and he'd no longer have to rely on hired help year-round. At ten and eight, Robert and John couldn't do heavy labor and only worked afternoons. But Japhet always had a tale to tell about them at the evening meal—once about their efforts to lift a salt hay bale too big for them and falling into it instead; of being chased across the pasture by a bull they shouldn't have approached.

In the mornings Deborah taught the older children to read and write, while Johanna cared for the younger ones. She and Johanna had reached a quiet time, as Deborah called it, with Johanna having no episodes of seeming madness nor extraordinary perception. That suited Deborah for now. She was consumed by the daily work of running her large, ever-growing household as well as answering calls as a primary healer in the area. Still, she might have pressed Johanna if she weren't afraid of losing her. Soon after Erin's departure to her own house, Deborah realized she couldn't get along without Johanna. It's true they could have purchased another indenture, but she agreed with Japhet that it was difficult to find loyal and competent help. In addition, the children loved Johanna, and she adored them, especially young Japhet.

Deborah continued the children's lessons right up to the birth of her seventh child. The delivery had gone smoothly to a point, but her new son was quite large and she had torn. She was still in bed—downstairs in the parlor—a week later, allowing herself to heal, her infant yet unnamed. Increasingly, she found herself impatient with Japhet. She had suggested several names, but he kept insisting they weren't right. It was a particularly sore issue as she still didn't have a daughter she considered her heir.

"He has six sons," Deborah exclaimed to Erin, who had come by to visit. "Six sons, and he cannot find a name."

"Do you think him ungrateful or dull?" Erin asked. "For mayhap he is so much in awe of his good fortune that he seeks in vain for a name that could be worthy of such a blessing." She grinned.

"Thou jest," Deborah replied, "but there might be something of truth in it. In sooth, I know not what keeps his tongue still. But enough on that—thou art truly radiant."

Erin turned in a slow circle, finally pregnant. After a barren first year she began taking various herb combinations, finally conceiving after yet another year. In her fourth month she lost twin girls and was so devastated she refused to take any more remedies. She also stopped coming to visit. It was too difficult, she'd said, to see Deborah's large brood, then go home to her empty house. Thus Deborah rejoiced when Erin became pregnant again and reached her fifth month. Now she was six months pregnant, at a good weight, with no reason to expect anything less than a healthy child, which Erin and Deborah both thought was a girl. That belief further allayed Erin's feelings of failure, and she resumed her daily visits.

Japhet entered the room, his face red and sweating as though he had run in from the fields.

"We were just speaking of you," Erin said with a coy smile.

He ignored her teasing tone and asked, "Wouldst it trouble thee, Erin, if I spoke with my wife?"

"She only arrived moments ago," Deborah said. "And with such a heavy load it took her twice as long to walk it." She winked at Erin.

"Oh, never fear," Erin said, "for I like to keep moving. And Japhet hath something of import to say. Farewell."

As she left, Deborah frowned at Japhet. It was unusual for him to appear in the middle of the day, except for dinner, but she didn't care. She was tired, still in pain which kept her awake most nights, and had been looking forward to Erin's visit.

"What is it?" she asked curtly.

He looked at her with a mixture of disappointment and irritation. Then he pulled up a chair to the bedside and asked solicitously, "Art thou any better?"

"Yes, yes I am." She softened toward him. "I hope to be moving about in a matter of days."

"We shall be glad for it."

Indeed, Deborah thought, certain they weren't faring very well without her. But Japhet had forbidden the children to speak of their difficulties—a fact she learned from six-year-old Japhet the first day of her confinement. She found it a relief, actually, that she didn't know precisely how they endured without her, and was rather enjoying taking her ease. Every morning Mary read to her from the Book of Esther in the Old Testament. Deborah hadn't realized the Bible contained such women of note. When she tired of correcting her daughter's pronunciation she read other parts of the book herself. She was fascinated to discover references to distant goddesses—Diana of Ephesus, for one. She also wondered about the whore of Babylon in the Book of Revelation, who seemed to her a vilified goddess, but John the Apostle had looked upon her with awe. She thought it an interesting reaction for a Christian.

"I have arrived at a name for our son," Japhet said. "It shall be Daniel."

"Daniel!" She sat up straight and winced in pain. "Daniel?" All at once she understood. "Japhet, no, thou dost not attempt to win thy father's favor again. Dost thou?"

But she knew that was exactly what he was trying to do. It was evident in the flush on his face and his downcast eyes. For of course, soon upon arrival in Burlington, Daniel had learned of Japhet's "convincement," as cousin Mary put it. She had written of her attempt to ease her uncle's rage by accepting some of the blame for Japhet's conversion herself, saying it was due to her influence. The other Quakers covered for Japhet as well by giving contradictory dates as to when he had become a Friend, or saying they couldn't recall, or like Isaiah, pretending not to understand the query. Daniel had almost as much difficulty with the Anglicans. Most said Japhet turned Quaker soon after his arrival; others couldn't remember or thought it was much later, each likely marking the date as the first time they saw Japhet leave the meeting house.

Armed with nothing conclusive, Daniel fired off a pointed missive, to which Japhet never responded. He answered a second letter immediately—which threatened to sue him for the farm on the grounds of fraud. Japhet asserted strongly that he hadn't received the first letter and admitted he had become a Friend, but after a year or so in Burlington. He insisted he never intended to deceive but didn't want to aggravate his father. Then he prostrated himself, begging not to be turned off the farm, telling Daniel all about his grandsons as well as his own prosperity. He also sent along a promissory note for an amount equal to one-tenth of each future yearly income, hoping it would be sufficient to prove his contrition. The offer was accepted, although without overt forgiveness, and all went well for a few years. Several months before, however, they had received another letter which went on at length about the ill-tempered Friends of Burlington. Japhet expressed concern that his father's bad feeling would extend to him and he might reopen the issue of the farm's ownership. He said he had to find some way to appease his father for good. And this was it, Deborah thought. Name his next son after him.

"Japhet, why dost thou not tell thy father the entire truth and take the consequences? 'Twould be preferable to this misery."

"Deborah, I cannot. For he might then sue me for the farm and prevail. And then in what manner would we live?"

"We would live as most others do—as best we are able. And we'd still have our bit of land from Felix."

"I am no idle gentleman farmer bringing in slaves to do my work," he said indignantly. "I toil on my land."

She frowned. "I did not intend to suggest thou wert idle. I merely say we need not be as prosperous as we are in order to live well." She took his hand and leaned closer. "I fear for thee, Japhet. Thou art a good man. To deceive again and again must rend thee. If thy father dies ne'er hearing the truth, I don't think thou wilt survive it."

He flinched and pulled his hand away, then put his fingers to his temples and pressed hard. "Were it only me," he finally said, "I might do as thou hast suggested. But we have six young children and now a seventh. Only Mary is old enough to send out to service, but thou hast need of her thyself, especially if we could no longer hire servants. No." His voice hardened with assertion. "I cannot risk being unable to care for my children. I won't have them suffer for my deceit. We will name the boy Daniel, which will appease my father. 'Tis but a small price to pay, methinks. And now, if thou please, that is all we will speak of it."

Deborah found that she couldn't fault his reasoning, and she certainly hoped it would work. She had no desire to be turned off their land. But what of our newborn son? she wondered. Can Japhet truly love him? Will he not a'ways look at the boy with shame and so barely regard him at all? Yes, that is how 'twill be, so I must be both father and mother to him. I will give the boy the favor he will miss from his father.

"I understand," she said. "Daniel Leeds. 'Tis a fine name."

He smiled at her. "I don't deserve thee." A strange look came over his face and his hands returned to his temples.

What ill news now, she wondered. I will not bear much more.

"I cannot ease my burden of deceit with my father, but I can do so with thee. Forgive me, Deborah. Forgive me for using Erin to take thee from Burlington."

Instantly her old feelings resurfaced, stronger than ever before. She hated him. She despised this coward of a man.

He stared at her, obviously not expecting the harsh response he saw on her face. But to his merit—Deborah thought later—he went on. "I was in the wrong not to remain and face my father. I was in the wrong to use Erin against thee. Thou know'st of this, but I have not confessed all. I knew thou wouldst not come to Leeds without Erin. I knew thou wouldst not come to Leeds . . . for me." He looked away and cleared his throat. "I was filled with rage and wished to injure thee as thou hadst me. I wished to take thee away from thy home. And so I connived with Jeb to give Patrick my land."

Deborah closed her eyes. She thought she had forgiven him long ago, but felt overwhelmed with feelings of anger and contempt. Still Japhet went on, obviously needing to unburden himself more than requiring her good graces just now.

"Thou hast been a fine wife for me and mother to my children. From the first I saw thee by the wharf in thy pale purple gown, I loved thee. So comely thou wert and witty besides. I was so pleased to have thee as my wife, and I hoped thou wouldst grow to love me. I know thou hast in thy way, but it pains me, I must say to thee, that thou ne'er will love me as I do thee."

She stared at him, stunned, her anger burning off. Of course she had sensed his jealousy of Erin, but hadn't realized the depth of his feelings. She didn't know he felt unloved. Yet what he said was true. She wouldn't dishonor him by denying it, by rushing forth with false sentiment. For she would never love him as she loved Erin. Nor the way he loved her. She reached out and touched his arm.

"I have thy pity," he said, "but I need thy forgiveness."

"Forgiveness," she echoed. It occurred to her that she ought to be asking for his forgiveness. His deceit had been known for years, but hers remained hidden. She felt that she was a coward as well. He had pretended to be an Anglican. She still pretended to be a Friend, and hadn't told him of her infidelity with Erin. He was unwilling to confess to his father, and she to him.

Japhet waited, hoping for release. Of course she would give it, then at least one of them would have partial peace. "Thou hast my forgiveness, Japhet. 'Twas long ago, and thou wert hurting. I forgive thee," she said softly, surprised to find she really did.

He squeezed her hand and smiled.

Looking into his grey eyes, she wanted to say something to honor and match his honesty. Was there nothing she could confess? Might not I tell of my time with Erin, she asked herself. No. 'Twas a long time ago and would only add to his wounded feelings. Nothing to be gained by telling him, and everything to lose. She reconsidered telling him about her ancient religion, this secret surely the highest wall between them. He is a man who knows fear because of his choice of religion, she thought. Is not he capable of understanding mine?

Sudden terror shot through her chest, and she saw a vision from years ago. She was running, being pursued through woods—these woods, she realized, these pine and sandy woods. Her throat closed and she choked on her saliva. She started coughing, deep and hard. She coughed until she could breathe again, nodding repeatedly to Japhet that she would be fine. He rushed to the other room and returned with a mug of water, which she drank down when she could. He left again to refill it, then returned.

As she drank, her throat returned to normal and she knew she would tell him nothing. He sat beside the bed, the creases around his mouth made deeper from worry. Half-seriously, she tried to rub them away, thinking they were the mark of a good man lying to his father. She glanced at the looking glass to see if there were any such stamp on her, but she was no more lined than any other thirty-one-year-old woman. There must be some trace of her deception, she thought, but didn't know where. Then it seemed to her that she and Japhet were a perfect pair, for they were both capable of living with deceit. Though how well and for how long, she wasn't sure.

Deborah stood beside Johanna, waiting for Ethan and Japhet to bring around the cart, trying one last time to prevail upon her to stay. She had used every argument she could think of, but Johanna would not be moved. She glanced back at the children who filled the doorway of the house. Deborah had bid them remain while she tried to change Johanna's mind. I am to blame for her departure, she thought, but 'twas a horrid choice—my dear little Daniel or Johanna. How could I have chosen otherwise?

She made another effort. "Prithee, Johanna, shalt thou not reconsider? We love thee and require thy help. Thou art one of the family. Didst thou not hear young Japhet crying long into the night?"

Johanna grimaced, then said in a seemingly dispassionate, tinny voice, "'Tis time to remove."

"I thought thou wert happy here."

"I was, to be sure."

"Then why, why dost thou remove?"

Johanna shot her a glance as if to say she knew very well why.

Deborah was taken aback, then asked, "Dost thou not understand why I must nurse Daniel? I explained it all to thee."

"Missus, you must understand as well. James is nearly weaned and my milk steadily decreases. I leave now or I lose it. And if I lose it, I shall likely ne'er gain its full return." Her voice choked and she was silent.

Tears came to Deborah's eyes and she ached from her terrible decision. If she allowed Johanna to take over nursing Daniel, she would remain. But what would become of her son? In the month since his birth, Japhet had spent hardly any time with him, and as if sensing what Daniel represented, the other children seemed almost to shun him as well. I must hold Daniel dear to my breast every day, Deborah decided again. I must choose my boy, my son, over her. I must allow her to go.

Johanna took both her hands. "Prithee don't cry, for you do what is right."

Deborah's heart felt leaden with regret as she looked into Johanna's large, compassionate eyes. I have failed, she thought, when I might have reached thee. Why did I think there would always be time?

"Mayhap we shall find another employ not so very far away," Johanna said. "You know I cannot bear to be away from them." She glanced toward the house and bit her lip.

Deborah looked at her children still piled in the doorway, their expressions hopeful, fearful, and expectant, surely thinking of their mother as a woman who performed miracles. But this one would not be. She heard Daniel crying in his cradle upstairs, and the squeaky wheels of Ethan's cart. She shook her head no at her offspring, then Johanna walked toward the house to say good-bye.

The children flew at her, young Japhet in the lead. She spread her arms wide and caught all six of them in a loving, awful embrace. Deborah couldn't watch. She went in the opposite direction, down the rise, then kept going, unable to face her children's grief and disappointment. She entered the barn, passing under her drying herbs, bunched and hanging from the rafters, and headed directly to her mare, Polly, who tossed her head in greeting. She burrowed her fingers into the horse's mane and hung on, letting herself sob. All the missed chances, all the thwarted attempts to heal Johanna rose within her. A part of her asked why it mattered so much. Why this one servant girl? At the moment Deborah couldn't answer. She only knew this was a tragic loss.

When sated and exhausted, she returned to the house. Johanna and Ethan had gone. She went to her children still in the yard and gathered them to her breast.

32

IGHT MONTHS pregnant with her ninth child, Deborah slowly climbed the winding staircase which led to the Covenoven's bedroom. Two years after the birth of Daniel, she'd finally had another daughter, Sarah, who was now almost two. Although thrilled with another girl after six boys, she didn't think Sarah would inherit her legacy. Nothing unusual had occurred during the birth and she'd had no portentous dreams. But most telling of all, she felt, was her lack of reaction when Japhet had suggested her name. If Sarah were her heir, her Deborah Fae, then something inside of her would have flared in protest.

She paused on the stairs to rest as an image of fifteen-year-old Mary caring for the younger children alone came into her mind. She still winced every time she recalled Johanna's departure and her failure to reach her. After they left, Japhet had said he thought they would soon return because plantations to the south relied so heavily upon slaves. They might require a wet nurse, he argued, but they would be loathe to hire Ethan. But after four years with no word from them, everyone else had given up hope. But I have not, Deborah affirmed again. Not as yet.

She gripped the rail and pulled herself forward, then into the bedroom, where Alice Higbee Mathis—recently remarried after the death of her first husband—leaned over Paul Covenoven, wiping his face. Though not diminutive herself, Alice seemed elf-like beside the man whose large stature and abundant dark hair had earned him the nickname Bear.

Deborah joined her at the bedside. "Dost thou feel no better?" she asked Paul.

"A bit," he replied groggily.

"I gave him a decoction of sassafras and dry-cupped his feet," Alice said, "but the dropsy remains."

Deborah examined him and agreed that he was still bloated. "Methinks we ought attempt a different treatment," she said.

"White ash," Alice suggested.

"Yarrow as well," Erin said from the doorway. She walked in holding the hand of her four-year-old daughter Ana. "It worked well with Esther Cordery last month."

Deborah and Alice looked at each other and nodded. "I'll begin it," Alice said, and went downstairs to the kitchen. Paul turned onto his side and fell asleep.

Over the years, the women had become quite a trio. There still were no male physicians in the broader area known as Great Egg Harbour, nor in most rural parts of the colony. As cousin Mary had said, given physicians' high status abroad, only those oppressed for their religion would emigrate. Traveling men claiming to be doctors did sell cures from their carts. Some had apprenticed, some not, but all were largely regarded as quacks. Deborah had been pleased to find conditions in rural New Jersey just as Granna predicted, and true to her description of olden England villages, where women were regarded as the primary healers.

Deborah and Erin stepped to the other side of the room so their talk wouldn't disturb Paul. "How is my sweet little sweet?" Deborah tousled Ana's brown hair, straight like her father's. Ana peered up at her with the perceptive, black eyes of a prophet. "We have no cause to doubt about her, do we?" Deborah said to Erin, for it had been clear from before Ana's birth—starting with Erin's vivid dreams and confirmed when Ana began to talk—that the girl was born a witch.

"Tell your auntie Deborah what you told me yesterday," Erin said softly and raised her eyebrows. "About your Mam." Ana turned her head away. "Come now, you need not be shy," Erin coaxed. "Tell her."

Ana crooked her finger, motioning for Deborah to come closer. Deborah eased into a chair. At eye-level with Ana, she said, "Now, dear, pray tell."

Ana whispered in her ear, "I had another Mam." She pulled back as if that were enough.

"What dost thou say?"

She cupped her hand around Deborah's ear and tried again, "She was a white Mam, and it was cold."

Deborah looked up at Erin. Ana called people with blonde hair white. Was she talking about Sweden? Settlers from there lived in the area. Had they talked with her about their homeland? Deborah turned back to Ana, thinking about the spiral of life, death, and rebirth. Mayhap a person can remember an earlier time, she thought, though I never have.

"Did this white Mam please thee?" Deborah asked quietly.

"Not so much as her!" Ana ran over and hugged her mother's hips.

"Well," Deborah said, "as I say, no need to have any doubts about her."

"I shall begin to teach her very soon," Erin said.

Deborah felt a twinge of envy as she smiled and nodded her approval. She put both hands on her large belly and gently probed, feeling for the head. Might thou be the one I await? she thought.

Alice returned with the tea, still steeping. "Japhet is down the stairs," she said. "He asks for thee to come."

Deborah didn't like the sound of this. Something must be wrong. The children? she wondered in alarm.

"Go," Erin said. "Alice and I will tend to Paul."

Deborah descended the stairs as quickly as she could, and Japhet met her halfway. "What is the matter?" she asked. "One of the children?"

"Nay, nay. Come and I will tell thee." He helped her down and outside. "Jedidiah English rode by to say a letter awaits me at the tavern. Shalt thou accompany me?"

He didn't have to voice his concern. They looked at each other as if certain who had sent it.

Deborah dug her fingers into his arm while he drove, her mind racing with possibilities, the most likely involving Japhet's Uncle William, who lost his son Jonathan two years before. In his grief, he sold the tavern and his plantation, then removed to a portion of his brother's farm outside Burlington, which Daniel had given him in settlement of their dispute. Although Japhet had never been especially forthcoming with his uncle, perhaps while commiserating with him about Daniel, Japhet might have let something slip that if repeated would arouse his father's suspicions that Japhet had willfully deceived him.

When they arrived at the tavern, now owned by Jedidiah, they walked quickly to the table where the mail was always stacked. On top lay a letter addressed to Japhet Leeds, yeoman. He picked it up, paid the postage to Jedidiah's wife, Emma, and they walked back outside.

Deborah watched Japhet's face turn red, then drain of color as he read silently. He leaned back against the cart. Deborah took the page from him.

My deare Cousin,

What a sad Daye this is for me when I must needs write to tell thee of the Death of thy Father, Daniel Leeds. I maye say onelie that he went in his Sleep in the House thou built which he so loved. I know this wille strike thee hard, for as thou knowest, he ne'er forgave thy Convincement and e'er suspected great Deceit. I have no desire to burthen thee, but thou must knowe this ere thou arrivest. For certain of thy siblings share his same feeling. We shall hold Service without thee for thou won't receive this in time. Tho I trust thou wilt come posthaste. Despite all, thou art his eldest Son. I have been told he did not leave thee out of his Wille. I have not been welle my selfe, but seeing thee again shall revive me. My love to thee, Japhet, and to Deborah and the Children. Isaiah sends condolences as well. Methinks that kind old soul will outlive us all.

Mary Leeds

Deborah stared at the words, thinking they conveyed what she had always feared, that Daniel would die before Japhet cleared his conscience. She put her hand gently on his arm. "Oh, Japhet, I am so very sorry for thee."

He raised his head and looked at her, his face as grey as death itself. "I am going thither," he said. "The harvest is brought in. Robert can work the loom. I must go."

"But what could he have left to thee that should be worthy of the trip?" As the words left her mouth, she realized he wouldn't journey to claim his inheritance. He goes to meet his fate, she thought, as we all must.

She cupped his face, looking into his blank eyes. He shan't survive intact, she thought. Some part of him—even now I feel it—some portion I cannot reach shatters.

@@@

Deborah lay in the parlor bed nursing her newborn daughter, running her hand over the wisps of fair hair. "Is it really thou, my darling?" she whispered.

She had asked her that many times in the days since her birth. During the event, only the babe's head had passed through the birth canal to air, and both she and Deborah paused as though catching their breath. Erin had held up a mirror so that Deborah could see. The sight of the infant's big head protruding from between her legs seemed so incongruous that Deborah wanted to laugh. "My Deborah Fae," she'd said—involuntarily—and started to push, then out slipped the girl easily, as if called.

Deborah Fae squirmed away from her mother's breast. "Art done, little one?" Deborah burped her, thinking about her promise to raise her children as Friends. She knew it was unrealistic to believe she could raise a pagan family these days. To stay safe they would have to pretend at some religion, and she felt certain the Friends were the best she could hope for.

But this child could be my heir, Deborah thought, clutching her. And yet, I have no choice; she will attend the Friends Meeting. And I must be wary as well of my knowledge, revealing only what she might understand and keep secret. I may teach her openly about herbs and healing. Just go gingerly with the rest.

"Come now, Mam must rest." She got up and placed her daughter in the cradle. As she climbed back in bed she heard a noise and glanced toward the doorway. Japhet stood watching her. After weeks of absence he had finally returned from Burlington.

"Japhet!" she exclaimed, then noticed he looked haggard and thin. "Art thou unwell?"

He approached the bed, his expression distracted as if not realizing she'd recently given birth. "Cousin Mary is dead." He collapsed beside her and burst into tears.

Deborah wrapped her arms around him. She held one hand on the back of his head and waved her children away from the doorway. "There now," she said, rocking him. Her tears fell into his black hair. She couldn't believe the news. How could Mary be dead?

His crying ceased, and he pulled away from her. The grief, so present a moment ago, had vanished.

She reached for her handkerchief on the table and gave it to him. "Japhet, what happened?"

"A horrid accident."

When he didn't go on, she said, "Prithee, Japhet, tell me."

"'Tis a horrid tale from beginning to end." He blew his nose with the handkerchief, then dropped it onto his lap. "She and I had been with a lawyer all the day with my brothers Felix and Titan. My father left *this* farm, our farm, to Felix. Well, he could not do that, could he? He merely wished to create a row 'twixt us. And we did have one. Felix was angry, as were all my family, for my dear father willed our old farm outside Burlington to me."

"No."

"Yes. It makes no sense at all, unless he were trying to create strife. Felix and Titan have been dutifully publishing Pappa's almanac and there is no sound reason to remove it to Leeds again. Trade routes 'twixt here and New York are no more improved. The almanac still would stray on its way to the printer. In the end, Felix agreed to abandon his claim on this farm if I gave him our old farm."

Japhet said this carefully—Deborah was glad to notice—acknowledging the impact the information might have on her. She nodded. "What else was there to do? Thy father mocks us from his grave. Leeds is our home now, Japhet. Thou didst what was right."

He breathed an obvious sigh of relief and took her hand. "I am glad to hear thee say it. But now I fear I must speak of the tragedy. Art thou ready to hear?"

"Yes." She pulled back her hand and braced her arms against the mattress.

"Mary, Felix, Titan, and I were in a tavern, toasting our agreement with molasses beer. Titan drank quickly and overmuch. He was bitter still that I was mentioned at all in our father's will and began a row with me. I walked away from him at the last, onto the road, but he followed. I had crossed to the other side when I heard him shout, then heard the sound of hooves, neighs, and more shouts. I turned . . . I turned and saw my dear cousin trampled." He picked up the handkerchief again and compressed it into a ball. "Titan stood there, in drink, swinging at the horses, in truth urging them on, while Felix and the driver attempted to calm them and free Mary. 'Twas a horrid sight, Deborah. Horrid. Felix later told me Titan had raced after me into the path of that carriage, and Mary grabbed him and pushed him to the side, but lost balance herself and tumbled beneath the hooves."

"Japhet." Tears ran down Deborah's cheeks.

"The image of it doth not leave me," he said. "Every time I close my eyes I see Mary under the horses and my fool of a brother swinging his arms, assuring her death. I ran across the road, pushed Titan out of the way, then helped pull Mary free. While Felix went for Dr. Grant, I held her in my arms as she drew her last breath."

Deborah covered her eyes as she envisioned the scene. Mary, she thought. Dear, dear, Mary. What a horrid end for a fine woman as thou.

"'Twas the drink, Deborah." Japhet's voice changed, became deeper and filled with transcendent passion. "Dost thou know how many deaths and injuries are caused because of spirits? We do not need them! Water is sweet in the New World. We can take it and cider as well. We must be rid of devilish drink."

Deborah stared at him. The animation in his voice seemed unnatural, misplaced. It hails from that damned, shattered place I cannot reach. Still, she tried. Over the next minutes she tried to direct the conversation back to cousin Mary, Japhet's brothers and father, their new daughter, but he ignored her attempts and didn't even seem to notice the interruptions. Eventually, he left the room.

Deborah climbed out of bed, picked up her daughter, and held her close. "Thy father will return to himself in a matter of days," she said. She looked anxiously toward the doorway, then added softly, "I do hope 'tis so."

33

SEVEN MORE YEARS had passed. Both Japhet and Deborah were in their early forties, and Deborah had borne three more daughters. The youngest, Hannah, was a year old.

Despite Japhet's travels to preach against intemperance, the farm prospered with the toil of their sons and a ready supply of labor—for the population grew steadily. The Friends' religious tolerance, which had drawn settlers of all faiths to West Jersey, still had effect. Great Egg Harbour was developing a reputation as a place where all Protestant sects commingled in peace. And with several large plantations owned by Quakers, who were now officially discouraged—though not yet forbidden—from owning slaves, itinerants might find work and eventually buy their own land.

Though the farm produced well, Japhet's absences took a toll on the boys. At twenty-one, Robert, the eldest, assumed his father's role while he was gone. John and young Japhet, separated from Robert by only a few years, resented his authority, while the younger sons Nehemiah, James, and Daniel accepted it without question. However, Daniel complained often about their bedroom, which was too small for six young men. He would say at the least the older boys had their own beds. He had to share a straw-filled mattress with James, who talked in his sleep. Deborah sympathized with him, but could do nothing about a room filled with five bedsteads and able to fit no other. The girls occupied a smaller space, just as crowded, with Hannah allotted the trundle and her four older sisters sharing two bedsteads. Mary and her new husband, Samuel, slept in the parlor.

Deborah had forbidden the children to use the main room for sleeping, but suggested Daniel might rest there if he hid all his traces. Of course the other boys soon figured out where Daniel went in the night, and it likely confirmed their suspicion that he was somehow different and also their mother's favored son. If they were up and peeking, they sometimes saw her follow Daniel down the stairs. On those nights she sat with him on the bearskin rug before the hearth, telling him stories—a pastime he had never outgrown. His favorite was the ongoing tale about the cook and the minister—the cook whose arm Deborah had healed, who later deserted his ship, was captured by highwaymen, then returned to Philadelphia, where Deborah saw him again and introduced him to the minister. The next chapters Deborah filled in with cousin Mary's old letters. The cook and the minister courted for several years, finally married, and by the time of Mary's death had had two children. That ending hadn't satisfied Daniel, so Deborah briefly considered inventing one filled with dangerous adventures, which ended happily, but such hyperbole seemed an insult to her old friends. Instead, she made up a real life for them, one that was possible, though not necessarily true, each chapter prompted by a question of Daniel's. Did Richard ever return to the sea? Was Rachel still a minister? Did they have any more children? And so on, the story grew.

On a blistering August day, Japhet tied the horses to the hitching post in front of the general store and wiped his brow with his handkerchief.

"Canst thou leave off this day, Japhet?" Deborah asked as she climbed down from the cart. "'Tis too hot to stand so in the sun."

Japhet held his hat angled against his side as if it were a Bible. "Thou knowest I must speak firstly in my own town, ere I speak in another where I am known not." He said this simply, without exasperation, and walked toward the tavern.

She squinted from the sun as she watched him go. After twenty-three years of marriage, she felt she still didn't know him—especially since he'd started preaching. He seemed a different person now—overly earnest and unyielding—a man, she had to admit, she did not like as much. It didn't help that he traveled so often. Even though the Society did not recognize him as a minister, he went about the colony on his own, speaking against the evil of spirits. His leave-takings had increased from once or twice a year shortly after cousin Mary's death to three or four times annually, each trip lasting several weeks. He missed the births of Deborah Fae, Dorothy, and Ann, but was home when Hannah was born. With six boys and six girls, they both agreed they wanted no more children. "We have our own twelve disciples," he'd said proudly after the last birth, "not e'en Jesus required more."

"Come along," Deborah said to Deborah Fae who still sat in the cart outside the Mathis store. "Let us see how we shall spend our coins this day."

They entered and saw no other customers among the crates, sacks, and wooden boxes. Deborah rang a cowbell on the table near the front door. Alice's husband, John, emerged from the rear storage room, wiping his hands on an apron. A short man with pale red hair, he had the trusting smile of a child, but an astute mind for business. At a time when peddlers were the norm in rural areas, he thought instead that a good living might be had for a store owner, and he was right.

"'Lo, Deborah, Deb," he said. "What is it today?"

"Salt, to be sure," she replied. "Molasses . . . and sugar."

"Very well." He walked off and returned with a sack over one shoulder and nodded at Martha Thompson as she came in. Unlike other Quakers, she always dressed in a fashionable manner, today in a scarlet satin gown with a wide hoop.

"Saw thy girls yesterday," he said to Deborah as he put the sack down. "They all came in, 'cept the little one, hand-in-hand." He reached up to a shelf for the molasses and sugar.

Deborah smiled at the paper-doll image of her young daughters. Others besides John commented on her fertility as well as her children's placement according to sex: Mary, six boys, then five girls. No one in the area had borne so many live children, and those few with almost as many had lost two or three.

"Hath Mary removed as yet?" John asked.

"Nay, she and her husband take to the parlor," Deborah answered. "They will remove to their own land soon as we hire a maid. Were it not for my need of her, Mary would have left a'ready. If thou hearest of someone for hire, prithee give us a shout."

"I will," John said. "But what of the girl thou hadst before? Couldst thou hire her?"

"The pop-eyed wet nurse?" Martha interrupted. "Thou wert wise to be rid of her. I would not allow her near my children. That is, my child," she added with an angry glare.

Deborah frowned sadly at Martha. Two years before, Deborah tended the birth of Martha's son, who died soon after. The delivery had gone smoothly, mother and babe seemed well, so Deborah, Alice, and Erin left. Later that night, the newborn died of an unknown cause. Martha never accepted their explanation that sometimes tragedies can't be prevented. To this day, she blamed them for her son's death.

Deborah had given up trying to convince her and ignored the taunt. "We were not rid of Johanna," she said. "In sooth, I would be pleased to have her and Ethan again. They reside south a ways. Japhet hath seen them during his ministerings. He asked them to return the week last, but they are pleased with their present employ."

John shook his head. "Thy husband enjoys a quarrel, doth he not? Going to the heart of applejack, and that spirit they call lightning, with his message against drink."

Martha smirked and Deborah saw an expression on John's face she had come to expect. A look which said, I understand Japhet's loss, but hath he not taken his stand against drunkenness a bit far?

"I don't pretend to know how the Lord would use my husband," Deborah said. "That's 'twixt him and the Light."

John reddened and glanced away, then carried the items to the cart.

Deborah followed him, helped Deb climb up into the seat beside her, then took the reins and drove toward the tavern. The sun, high overhead, gave off relentless heat, and sweat rolled down Deborah's back. But as they approached, she felt the chill she always sensed when she heard Japhet's haunting, resonant preaching voice.

"One night," Japhet was saying, "Margaret Peele tended her youngest boy, Jeremiah, who was unwell. After midnight her husband strode in, loud and stumbling. Finding no wife in his bed, he made a roar like a very beast. Margaret's blood went cold, she said, and all the children save Jeremiah leapt out of bed and cowered 'gainst the wall. She began to pray aloud. Her husband, full of a wrath which only spirits can give a man, grabbed his wife's arm. She pulled away from him and stood with her back to the bed, shielding Jeremiah."

Japhet looked around, meeting his neighbors' eyes. "Now did this man fall to his knees and beg forgiveness from the wife who had served him faithfully and well? Did he wipe the tears from his ill son's face? No! He was so o'ercome by the drink that he raised up his right hand and smote his wife across the face."

A few listeners gasped and Japhet paused. "Margaret was dazed and injured," he went on, "but still had her wits. She was filled with that bear-like instinct that moves a woman when her children are threatened. She pulled herself up off the ground and took up the nearest heavy object, a box iron, and hit her husband on the head. He fell to the floor.

"You may ask why she married such a brute. But my friends, when he doth not drink—which is rare now—he is gentler than a lamb and harder working than a mule. 'Tis the applejack that darkened the man's soul. 'Tis applejack and Jersey lightning that threaten our colony. Some men drink because they wish to know God—they wish to know ecstasy. But my friends, we cannot know God, we cannot see the Light of God through a fog. E'en one taste of molasses beer throws a blanket o'er the Light." Japhet spread his hands and walked back and forth. "My friends, we must smash our stills. Now, this very day."

Many in the crowd left. Japhet raised his voice. "We all are tainted by the evil which afflicts Margaret Peele's husband, and we must rid our colony of it. 'Tis not the man who is evil, but the spirits that go into the man. . . ."

Deborah saw movement out of the corner of her eye and nodded at Paul Covenoven's approach. When he reached her, he said, "Can Japhet find a place other than the tavern to speak? Jedidiah told me he shall swear out a complaint—I barely succeeded in calming him. Prithee carry Japhet away ere Jedidiah hath a change of heart."

Deborah sighed and shook her head. "No man's law shall stay my husband, Bear, as thou well knowest. His passion listens not to me, nor any person. He will come to me only when he is done and not before."

Paul turned to look at the dwindling audience. Deborah noticed a carbuncle along his hairline. She put her hand on his shoulder and drew him toward her. "Paul, how long hast thou had these boils?" He shrugged. "Thou hast not been taking the dandelion root tincture I left with thee. Thou must do so, Bear, and eat the garlic thy wife now grows. I can chase the boils away, but thou must assist me in keeping them at bay. I have told thee before they attest to a lack of hardiness. I shall come by this even with a poultice, but thou must take the herbs I give thee."

"I sorely despise the taste of that tincture."

She smiled, thinking he sounded like one of her children. "Thou mightst take it with a bit of honey. Thou must accept the cure till I can be certain there will be no recurrence."

"If I must," he agreed with a frown.

They turned their attention to Japhet, alone now except for his sons Japhet and John and a woman with her back to Deborah. Japhet was drenched with sweat, his head high. "E'en molasses beer we must be rid of," he declared. "'Tis our only hope for grace."

Paul ground his teeth together and kicked at the dirt. "Tell your husband for me, there is well enough sorrow in life without adding abstinence to it!" He stomped away.

Deborah watched him go, thinking he was really angry at her. She snapped the reins and drove the cart closer to Japhet.

"Fear not, Mr. Leeds," the woman before him said, "your powerful words shall soon have sway." She looked around, saw Deborah, and smiled.

"Oh, my, Johanna, is it thou?" Deborah exclaimed. "I was talking about thee only minutes ago. I knew not thou wert in the town."

"We have come to accept your husband's offer of our old positions," Johanna said. "At the first we refused, as we were pleased where we were. Then I remembered your dear children, whom I suckled as my very own, and I had to return. I cannot believe I have been gone eleven years. You, young Japhet, are fully a man now." He smiled warmly at her.

Deborah noticed how stalwart Johanna seemed, her frame full and strong. "I am pleased thou hast returned. We do have need of thee. To be sure, Japhet told thee Mary waits to remove. She married Samuel Somers."

"Yes, Mr. Leeds told me. As well that you have had many girls, including one not long arrived." She looked expectantly at Deborah as if to confirm what Japhet had been instructed to promise her—that she would nurse Hannah.

"Quite so, and she doth keep me awake all the night. To be sure, the hungriest of all my children. I shall be pleased to have thy assistance." Johanna beamed, then directed her attention to the girl seated next to Deborah. "This is my third daughter, Deb," her mother said.

Deb looked at Johanna with intense curiosity, as if finding her as compelling as Deborah always had.

"You are the image of your mother," Johanna said. "Such fetching hair you both have—the color of fresh honey." She smiled at Deborah. "I have told your husband I shall go after Ethan and come straightaway to the farm. Farewell, then."

As Johanna walked away, her bare feet kicking dust up behind her, Deborah marveled how at ease Johanna had seemed and how hale. I am glad for it, she thought.

"Canst thou believe it, Mamma?" young Japhet asked. "My nursemaid hath returned."

"Yes, son, and we are pleased. Come, let us take our leave. Thy father must have need of victuals."

Japhet climbed up to the driver's seat and took the reins. The boys piled into the cart. Deborah noticed a nervous sensation in her belly. "So Johanna and Ethan have returned," she said. "We do indeed multiply, do we not? Every day another child from our loins, and another body from the east, south, west, or north."

Japhet gave her a look which froze her where she sat. He seemed years older, weary and grave. "We're all called hither by the Lord," he said, and started the drive home.

34

HE FRIENDS MEETING had already started at the Leeds house when Alice and Deborah arrived after treating a neighbor. Alice took a seat next to her husband toward the back of the room, and Deborah sat at the front in a chair placed so she could look out the window. The seat beside her was empty. Japhet was away again.

Although she still didn't consider herself a Friend, she continued to find them a congenial and admirable group. She felt fortunate she'd never had to make a ritual declaration of faith or be baptized, as other sects expected. When they first arrived, she stood next to Japhet while he presented a letter of introduction from the Burlington Meeting and asked to join the local Meeting. No one, including Japhet, would have any reason to suspect she had not been equally sincere. She still conformed to the external aspects that marked her as Friend—attending all meetings, speaking and dressing as they did, behaving toward them with genuine good will. As for the internal—she practiced her own version of quietism. She was as contemplative as they during meetings. No one knew she didn't pray to their god.

From upstairs came Hannah's faint cry, then the sound of Johanna mounting the steps to quiet her. Reflexively, Deborah touched her breasts, surprised as usual to find them empty of milk. She wanted to be certain Johanna remained this time so allowed her to completely take over the nursing. A few months had passed since her arrival, and Johanna seemed settled in and content.

Erin wasn't pleased with her return but had promised to temper her words and treat Johanna civilly. Unless, she added, Johanna earned a good tongue lashing. Deborah eagerly accepted the promise, knowing it was the most she could expect.

Although Deborah had thought it might be difficult to watch Johanna nursing her daughter, except for brief twinges in her breasts sometimes when Hannah cried, she enjoyed her new freedom and mobility. She could dash after three-year-old Ann without supporting her bosom. And she could wear her better clothes with no fear of staining them. It's true her breasts sagged quite a bit, but she didn't mind. She eagerly anticipated the time when she would start holding her monthly blood within and thus collect wisdom, like Erin, who also had welcomed the onset of menopause. For it was the case that even years after Ana's birth and with no other pregnancy, Patrick still had hoped for a son. Erin had said she used to hide her monthly from him, since more than once she found him close to tears after coming across one of her rags. She confessed to sometimes crying as well at the reminder of her failure to conceive. Thus she rejoiced when she began to have mild hot flashes and night sweats, for soon Patrick would have to accept he would never have a son. And not long after, she was free of his—as well as sometimes her own—crushing disappointment each month.

Hannah's crying had stopped. Deborah looked out the window at the tree, recently emptied of fruit. In order to facilitate connection with the Light, most Friends kept their eyes closed during the meeting, unless someone were speaking. But Deborah found herself more at peace gazing at the bees among the apple blossoms; or in summer, watching the fruit plump then turn red; or after harvest, counting the leaves as they yellowed and fell. Then came the fallow period when everyone else moved into the main room by the hearth. But unless it were bitterly cold, Deborah kept her seat by the parlor window, bringing in the tree's bare branches with her breath.

She heard a noise in the rear of the room and shifted to look for her children. Recently, they had taken to sitting in a line against the back wall in their specially designed chairs. Following local tradition, each family fashioned its own chairs for the Meeting. The Quaker commitment to plain dress and simple living still allowed a few frivolities, which kept the soul supple, and they reveled in fine crafts: dress clothing made of the best fabric they could afford, and finely wrought furniture for the Meeting.

The Leeds's chairs were pine with tall scalloped backs and lobed arm rests. When each child could handle a knife, he or she was free to carve the rest of it. Fifteen-year-old Nehemiah, the family artist, adorned his with lions' heads and manes that swept up the chair's back and down the legs. The Philpotts, relatively new in town, had the roughest-hewn chairs—yet uncarved and not much distinguished from sections of trunk. They owned neither cart nor carriage, so the family carried their chairs to the Meeting. The Corderys brought their armless, rush-bottomed chairs stacked in a cart. The Smiths left their fine oak chairs at the Leeds house. They had enough at home.

"Friends," Jedidiah English said and stood. "I am compelled to speak about one of our own who hath strayed from the Light."

"Good Friend, I must protest," Esther Cordery said. "Thy complaints are inappropriate. Speak them at the business meeting."

"Nay, for the Light compels me to speak."

"Methinks 'tis thy pocketbook which compels thee," John Mathis said with a laugh. "We know of thy complaints."

Jedidiah flushed but did not yield. "Japhet Leeds sullies the name of our Society with his speeches. We ought read him out of Meeting."

"He doth not speak in our name, so how doth he sully it?" young Japhet asked.

"Thou speakest to the heart of it," Jedidiah replied. "We are able to exert control over our ministering members by issuance of the traveling minute. And though Japhet is not a minister, he acts as such and finances his own travels. Thus, because he hath the means to do so, he flouts our authority."

"I insist we cease discussion till the business meeting," Esther said again.

"Nay." Deborah stood and faced the others. "Let us speak now while connected to the Light. But let us *be* connected to the Light. Jedidiah, thou fearest for thy livelihood and none present find any fault in that. As do we all, my husband moves from his own will as well as from the Light. I know many of you believe Japhet hath fallen prey to the Reasoner, that he hath confused its voice for the Light's, but I say to you my husband had a vision that he would be called upon to speak. He believes he follows a direct leading of the Holy Spirit."

She glanced at Jedidiah, then addressed the group at large. "'Tis the truth, as Jedidiah says, that one without means could not minister without the consent and assistance of the Meeting, but Japhet settled that long ago. He is not a Friend minister and never claims to speak in the name of our Society. Thus, we have no call to comment on his message." She paused to press the point on Jedidiah. He pursed his lips, considering, though judging from his expression was obviously not convinced.

"I own," she continued, "I know not if he hath strayed. But have we not all strayed from the Light? Have we not all fallen prey to the Reasoner's strong and luring voice? Let us be charitable and wait for my husband. For if he hath in sooth gone afield, I know he will correct his course. Jedidiah, hast thou truly suffered from my husband's preachings?"

"No," his wife Emma replied.

Jedidiah frowned at her, then agreed, "I have not, in sooth. But Japhet preaches with a righteousness as if he hath ne'er done wrong himself, and we all know of his deceit to his father."

"Friend Japhet hath confessed his deceit," Justine Smith said, "which is all we might ask. And further, methinks he hath not strayed. I find no pride in his words, and are his stories not horrid? Do they not call out for attention? He says as well 'tis the spirits which are evil, not any person, not e'en the most heinous of whom he speaks."

"Mayhap I could be lenient for a time," Jedidiah said, "but the others, I know not. Jonas Vale was in my tavern saying God hath given us spirits and Japhet is devilish to deprive us of them."

John Mathis laughed. "Jonas sees a demon everywhere when he drinks applejack."

"Very true," Justine said. "Jedidiah, thou mightst calm thy revelers. When they speak against our brother, tell them Japhet is wrong if thou please, but tell them he wishes only what is best for the colony. If thou, who hast the most to lose, art charitable, then so shall they be. Though in sooth thou hast lost nothing, for I have seen thy tavern fills faster when Japhet speaks."

Jedidiah tried to suppress a smile. "Friends, I thank you all, for you have been most kind to listen to me this day. I will wait for Japhet to return to the Light, and I will calm others if need be. And in sooth, 'tis only when the spirits flow too freely that anyone speaks against Japhet. Deborah, prithee forgive my words against thy husband."

"No harm to it," Deborah said, relieved that Japhet had been discussed at Meeting when all were calm, rather than at a business meeting where passions sometimes flew.

She sat down, pleased she had helped her husband, but disturbed as well, wondering how long Jedidiah would remain appeased, and if the Friends would continue to defend Japhet. Why cannot he simply remain at home? she thought. Why must he carry his message about? Yet, is not he correct that strong spirits can bring harm? But to deny beer and ale as he hath, which nearly everyone drinks daily, *that* he will never win.

When she looked out the window again at the apple tree, her chest tightened in alarm. She glanced around the room. Everyone sat quietly, their eyes closed. Her fear faded into a prickling of goose bumps: a premonition. She prepared herself to receive it—imagined she was a heavy cauldron, solid on the ground and wide, able to contain whatever would come.

But nothing came. No images, no words, just a portentous feeling about this meeting. What? she asked, enlarging the cauldron. Chills moved through her and she knew the premonition had nothing to do with Japhet. This meeting presaged something about her.

35

T WAS TWILIGHT, that sliver between day and night when the other worlds reveal themselves. Deborah squatted by the marsh's edge, the water before her a lustrous pinkish-grey, lit by the remaining colors of the sun.

She wove silver thread into a scarlet woolen cloak she and Erin had finally finished for Ana, who was fifteen and, for a few months now, a woman. Ana had anticipated her first blood ritual for a full two years before the event—asking when she would get her cloak, when she would meet the Goddess Danu.

Soon, Erin had told her, soon. When the first frost touches the fields, when the birds leave their nests, when she had shown by her blood that she was a woman.

Ana had touched her sex. "Will blood really come from here, Mamma? Shall I not bleed to death?"

And since that cold October eve, Ana had joined Erin and Deborah as a full participant in rituals marking the holy days of the year. Deborah realized she was probably overly cautious, but she still didn't bring eleven-year-old Deb to any rituals. She wanted to be sure she groomed her daughter carefully and didn't push her before she was ready.

Deborah pulled one final stitch in the cloak, folded it carefully, and put it into her basket. She rubbed her hands together to warm them, then noticed a dead fish on the ground to her right. That is odd, she thought.

Erin came up and squatted beside her, gesturing at the basket. "'Tis good you have finished with the cloak, for soon you would have no light, and your fingers would be frozen together as well. 'Tis cold!"

"Indeed. Where is Ana? I thought thou wert bringing her with thee." Deborah leaned over and picked up the fish. It felt fresh to the touch and had no odor of decay.

"She will be along in a moment. I have the coals here with me. So, you had time to finish the cloak and catch us some supper?"

Deborah smiled. "I only just saw it here. Why would someone catch it, then leave it to waste?" She examined it closer. "No marks suggest 'twas dropped by a bird." Neither was there any indication of a hook. She shivered but not just from the cold.

"Maybe the fairies left it for you."

Deborah raised her eyebrows. She didn't put as much stock in the little people as Erin did. Yet it was strange, the fish just appearing there. She passed it from hand to hand. "Granna's final words to me spoke of fish in Brigid's well. I know not if I fully comprehend it, but she said they were sacrifice, which is what we give and are given."

"I do wish I had known your Granna. And you my Aunt Gwen. But 'tis only you and I, orphans in the New World, building our joined house bit by bit."

"That sounds like a thing I would say."

Erin smiled. "I do feel a bit of melancholy this even. I know not why."

They heard a rustling behind them and turned to see Ana step from the path holding a candle lantern. "At the last," Erin said. "We are nearly frozen waiting on you."

Deborah stood up to greet Erin's daughter, a wasp-waisted young woman with long, dark hair worn down. "Thou art so tall, Ana, taller than thy mother, now. Just like my boys, nearly all of them greater than their father. Come, let us go." She still held the fish. Deciding it was a gift she should accept, she placed it in her bucket and gathered up the rest of her things.

They walked northwesterly along the road while the last pink light of the sun faded and the sky turned to night. When they came to their path they entered the woods. Erin led, carrying an iron box of hot coals, followed by Ana with the lantern, then Deborah with the bucket and her basket of ritual items.

After a mile or so, they came to a stream. Ice had formed at the bank. Deborah broke it with a rock and filled the bucket, the fish floating on top. They walked on again until they reached a small clearing within a grove of pine. Flat rocks marked the four directions around a fire pit.

From her basket, Deborah took a bowl, filled it with water, put the fish in it, and positioned it next to the pit. Ana began decorating the stone altars with dried flowers, food, and feathers, while Erin and Deborah brought wood from a pile outside the clearing, then built a fire together using the hot coals.

When the fire was going well by itself, the women stood in front of it and joined hands. They envisioned themselves as what they were, a direct continuation of the earth, the blood within them like the warm waters within the earth; waters they brought into their bodies with each in-breath, hot fluid which rose upward, holding them, powering them as it coursed through their legs, their torsos, their arms, their throats, where it emerged as song, a chant reaching into the air, embracing starlight, then dropping upon them like rain.

When each woman felt she was ready, or could tolerate no more, she sank down and pressed her palms, forehead, or cheek to the ground—giving back what she did not need, giving back what she could not sustain.

With her heart pounding, her cheek against the ice cold ground, Deborah felt changed, felt truly one with the earth. She was the grasses, the trees, the hills. Here and now she was alive as at no other time, her perception sharp and clear. Every flower was a smile of the Goddess, every storm a display of her power. You didn't have to read a book to know her, and you didn't even have to *believe* in her. You needed only to be open to your senses and to your own experience. For she lived in the quiver of the belly at a lover's touch, in the making of bread, in the trusting hand of a child slipping into yours. These were her rituals—her reminders that she was present, that she would never abandon her children and welcomed their each and every return.

Deborah opened her eyes and looked up. Erin and Ana stood, waiting for her. She got to her feet, took their hands and squeezed them, feeling so full of love for both of them that tears ran down her face.

"*Mo chailín fhionn*," Erin said and smiled, "might I begin?"

Deborah wiped her wet neck with the sleeve of her cloak and laughed. "Thou must or I will surely freeze, as thou said before, from all this water."

Erin laughed as well, then faced the fire. "On this night," she said, "we gaze into the flame of *Bríd* and see what should be our future course. If we are willing, we speak what we see and take of her waters. When we speak, *Bríd* listens and holds it true."

"A long shadow covers our craft," Deborah added, "such that we hide in this wood when once on this day in February, those on the British Isles joined to honor Brigid, goddess of poetry, smithcraft, and healing. Much which hath been lost will never again be known, until once more the wheel begins to turn and earth touches sky. Then She of Many Names will emerge with the Dancing God to shape the world anew."

Erin unfolded the scarlet cloak she and Deborah had made and put it around Ana's shoulders. She pulled up the hood and kissed her daughter's forehead.

Deborah took handfuls of barleycorn from her apron pocket and sprinkled them around the stone altars. "I draw the circle round our hearth. I draw the circle round. Let those we honor be welcome hither. Let those we don't *be gone!*"

She clapped her hands and returned to the center, emptied her pocket of the barleycorn and threw the remainder over their heads. Erin and Ana stepped in and stood beside her.

"Thee, Ana," Deborah said, "sacred to Danu, whose title thou bearest, shalt thou behold the flame of Brigid?"

"I will," Ana answered. She asked Erin, "Mother, sacred to Eriu, whose holy name thou bearest, shalt thou look into the flame?"

"I will." Erin addressed Deborah, "Dear Brigid, who art sacred to she whose holy day we keep, shalt thou look into her flames and see?"

"I will," Deborah said.

With that they spread their cloaks upon the ground and knelt before the fire. Deborah luxuriated in the heat warming through her gown and let her mind drift. The familiar violet doors appeared. Deborah passed through them. In the luminous world beyond she saw the green woman sitting on her boulder offshore. The woman stretched out her tail across the waves and Deborah crawled to her. They held up their hands and interlocked fingers.

You are no longer fearful.

No, Marian.

The woman smiled and moved to the side, revealing a hill behind them. Shall you come?

Yes, Deborah answered. Then she found herself in a clearing where an old woman warmed herself by a fire.

Take my hand now, the crone began, look into the flames.

Deborah stared at the fire. The vision she saw years ago on the ship rose again before her eyes. Events from over the past hundreds of years recurred: Granna planting in her garden; a hooded woman on her knees in a cave, wailing; a young woman gathering herbs while her mother waited in a clearing; a hundred women joining hands and jumping off a cliff with a city burning behind them; an old woman walking to a pyre, hands bound, jerking away from those grabbing at her.

And then the incident that terrified Deborah—she was being pursued through these woods. No! she shouted. I will not allow that to be me.

What then is thy charge? the old woman asked.

I will not run.

Deborah opened her eyes and put her hands on the ground. When she looked up, Ana caught her eye and smiled. Soon, Erin opened her eyes as well.

They rose and stood together again. Ana stepped forward to the fire and held her hands over it. "*A Bhríd*, I have opened to thy direction and speak what I must do. I will remove to Little Egg Harbour where I will apprentice with Dame Albina and learn thy art, midwifery."

Erin groaned and turned her face away.

Ana took water from the bowl and ran her wet hands over her face and neck.

Erin walked toward the fire. "I now know the meaning of these words: Ana, I give you leave to go. I know you must go thither to find your own way, but I bid you return. Your work here is not done." She took of the water, then stepped back.

Deborah walked forward and held her hands over the fire. "Before Brigid, Erin, Marian, and Ana, I speak my charge: I will not run." She took water with both hands and wet her face, hair, and gown.

Erin held her athame over her head with both hands, its silver blade piercing the dark sky. "We have spoken before each other and before thee, *a Bhríd*." She plunged the knife down into the frozen earth. "So mote it be."

CRONE
1734

36

ACK AND FORTH Deborah went with her bucket, from the barrel under the rain spout to the bathing and laundry trough where the soiled clothing lay. It would have been more efficient to bring the trough over—or keep it by the barrel as Deborah had repeatedly told her children—but everyone else was occupied and she didn't feel up to that kind of exertion.

In the nearly eight years since Hannah's birth, Deborah had not conceived. Japhet spent even more time traveling, a total of several months a year now—although he always made it home for the harvest. Robert had married Alice's daughter Abigail and they lived in a cabin on the Mathis homestead. Since his departure, John and young Japhet assumed their father's place and ran the farm when he was away. Nehemiah was courting a young woman, Elizabeth Wood, and an announcement was expected soon. Mary lived on the Somers plantation with Samuel and had a daughter herself. Since Deborah's girls were of an age to offer skilled help she was free to concentrate even more on her healing work, sometimes traveling a fair distance and remaining away several nights. Recently, Ana had her called to Little Egg Harbour to aid a young Quaker woman dying for no known reason. Deborah spent two weeks there and finally cured her but never did give a name to the malady.

Much to Deborah's relief, Johanna had remained with the family. After Hannah was weaned, Deborah suggested to Johanna that she hire out to others in the area—so as not to lose her completely—but Johanna refused, saying her time as a wet nurse was done. Over the ensuing years, Deborah had succeeded in gaining more of Johanna's trust, but still hadn't convinced her to embrace her visions. Nor had she learned the nature of the terrible secret Johanna carried.

Deborah poured one last bucket of water into the trough, then went to her knees on a piece of canvas. She picked up John's grey cotton stockings to wash them, but heard soft crying and looked up to see Johanna bringing Hannah out to her.

"Mam, it hurts," the girl said. She had one finger in her ear.

Deborah moved her hand aside and looked in. "Thou hast a red, red ear, Hannah. Prithee bring a large clove of garlic and a knife," she asked Johanna, "and Hannah's doll."

When Johanna returned, Deborah peeled half of the clove, carved the bare end into a blunt point and put it just inside Hannah's ear. The clove was large enough not to slip down the canal, and the pointed end let the juices heal the infection. She told Hannah to keep her hands away from her ear, and made her sit next to her and play with her doll, to be sure she obeyed. Then Deborah resumed her washing.

She knelt on the canvas again, placed John's stockings over a rock in the trough, and rubbed them with a beech ash and quicklime soap. As she reached for the horsehair scrub brush, she noticed Johanna standing stiffly in the doorway. "What is it?" she asked.

Johanna gave her a horrified look and ran into the house.

Immediately Deborah took Hannah inside where Sarah was slicing carrots. "Be certain Hannah doth not touch her ear," Deborah told her older daughter.

"I will not, Mamma," Hannah protested. "Sarah need not watch o'er me."

"Good," Deborah said, "but remain here regardless." She addressed Sarah again, "Whither did Johanna go?"

"To the parlor," Sarah replied.

Deborah found her on all fours. She approached quietly and squatted behind Johanna, putting a hand between her shoulder blades. Johanna began to sob as if her heart were breaking. Deborah gently increased the pressure on her back and whispered Johanna's name several times.

Gradually, the sobs ceased and she turned to face Deborah. "Something hath happened to the Friends going to the Yearly Meeting," Johanna said.

"What?"

"I know not, but 'tis bad. It may not have happened as yet." She started to cry again, murmuring that her worries were not about the Friends.

"What is it, Johanna? What else troubles thee?"

She jumped up and backed away. "I did not see these things till I came hither, nor in the years I was gone. 'Tis you–" Then suddenly abashed, she stared at Deborah. "Missus, I know not, I . . ."

Deborah rose to her feet unsteadily, shaken by the outburst. "'Tis all right, Johanna," she said. "Thou wert frighted by what thou saw. But Johanna, 'tis not me. Thou seest these things, and have all thy life, I warrant."

"No, missus, ne'er have I seen such things as I do here. They are from the Devil."

"Johanna," she said gently, "I have told thee thy sight is a gift from God, like my healing. He desires us to use our gifts to help others, in his service. Else why should he have given the sight to thee?"

"No." She shook her head. "I ne'er saw these things before."

"Be that as it may, now thy sight can help thy neighbors. Tell me what hath happened."

She looked down at the floor. "I know not."

"Methinks thou dost."

Johanna frowned. "There hath been a fall at the crossing of the Little Egg Harbour River, or will be."

"I will go now, Johanna. I thank thee. Thou mightst have saved a life this day."

She hurried to the kitchen area and removed the garlic clove from Hannah's ear. It looked better but would need another treatment that night. To Sarah she said, "Run and tell Erin to bring her cart to Swimming Over Point, where there hath been a fall. Johanna shall watch o'er dinner till thy return." She decided not to send for Alice, because she didn't want to have to explain where she had gotten the information if Johanna proved wrong.

Deborah quickly saddled Polly. As she rode toward the river crossing, she tried to remember who had planned to attend the meeting. Justine and John Smith, their thirteen-year-old daughter, Elizabeth; Esther Cordery; and Peter White, who had bought Uncle William's old farm.

Deborah neared the river. A grey morning mist hung over its waters. She saw a small crowd and rode toward it. Justine lay on the ground, but a couple of people waded clumsily in the thigh-deep water, as if searching frantically. Deborah jumped from her horse and rushed to her neighbor. Esther was giving Justine cider from a flask. She moved aside as Deborah knelt and looked into Justine's eyes.

"Canst thou hear me?" Deborah asked.

"Elizabeth . . ." Justine said.

"Her arm is broken, methinks," Esther told Deborah, "but 'tis Elizabeth we fear for." She gestured toward the river. "Their horse threw them and no one hath seen the girl since."

"I'll search for her," Deborah said, "then return to set thine arm." She knotted up the hem of her calico gown and waded in to her knees. The men searched in the tall marsh grasses along the edge so Deborah continued downriver. Mosquitoes covered her. She wet her hands and wiped dozens from her arms, face, and neck, keeping her eyes trained ahead.

A sudden movement in the marsh grass just ahead caught her attention, and she rushed toward it, flushing out a pair of ducks. "Damn," she exclaimed, and kept trudging through the water, becoming increasingly concerned. The current wasn't terribly strong, but if Elizabeth had been knocked insensible, she might already have drowned. Deborah picked up her pace.

Finally, just past a bend in the river, she saw a figure clinging to a log not far offshore. She waded toward it and grabbed the girl from behind, loosening the log from its mooring in the process and sending it away. She shifted Elizabeth to hold her in her arms like a baby, and pushed through the grass toward shore.

Once on the bank, she lay Elizabeth along a rise, her head pointing down. Deborah collapsed beside her. The girl wasn't breathing, so Deborah pinched Elizabeth's nose, tilted her head back, clamped her own mouth over the pale lips, and blew. The girl's chest rose. Deborah stopped to gulp a breath. The chest fell but did not rise again.

She straddled the girl and pressed firmly below her breastbone until she began to vomit water, then quickly turned Elizabeth's head to the side and continued pressing as water gushed from her mouth. Now, she thought, there's space aplenty for air.

Again, she knelt beside the girl and blew into her mouth, although no one had ever taught her how to give breath to one who had lost it. As with much of her healing, she did it instinctively. She blew again and again and again. Elizabeth choked and vomited more water, then coughed again and drew breath. Deborah sat back, panting. Elizabeth breathed on her own, coughed, then inhaled again.

A familiar male voice said, "'Tis the damnedest I e'er saw."

Deborah looked up and saw Jonas Vale, Paul Covenoven, Erin, and Peter White.

"I ne'er saw such as that," Jonas said again.

"God be praised," said Peter White.

"You saved her," Erin said.

Peter knelt to wrap a blanket around the girl, then Paul lifted her. Erin put her arm around Deborah and they all walked back.

After a ways, Deborah slowed her pace to put some distance between them and the others. "Why is Jonas here?" she whispered to Erin.

"I passed him and Paul on the way and they wished to help."

"Oh, dear."

"What is the matter?"

"Never thee mind, mayhap there be no need for concern." Deborah then quickened her pace to catch up to the men.

John Smith ran to meet them. "Mother Leeds brought your girl back from death," Jonas exclaimed to him. "I witnessed it myself." Paul lay the girl on the ground next to her mother. "She put her mouth to hers," Jonas went on, "gave the girl her own breath. Like she was–"

"God hath blessed us with thy gifts," Esther interrupted. The others nodded approval.

Deborah tucked the blanket tightly around Elizabeth, then turned her attention to Justine's arm. Peter and Paul went back toward the river to look for lost belongings. Deborah put a knotted kerchief in Justine's mouth and said, "Bite hard, for the pain will be fierce, but brief." Justine tensed as Erin pulled steadily and firmly on the arm to separate the bones and Deborah eased them back into place.

"I shall make a casting when we return," Deborah told Justine. From her bag, she took two kerchiefs, wrapped the arm tightly with one, then made a sling with the other. "After thou and Elizabeth rest a moment, we'll get you twain to the cart. Elizabeth must needs remain abed a few days, and may yet fall very ill." She sat back on her haunches, coughed in exhaustion, and looked at the water. It seemed so benevolent now—the mist gone, the sun shining on its brackish current.

"I wish to know," John Smith asked, "how did you four arrive so speedily?"

"Mrs. O'Hara told us Mother Leeds said there had been a fall," Jonas replied, then looked quizzically at Deborah. She cursed herself for not having come up with a ready answer.

"That is indeed queer, for it happened but minutes ere your arrival," John said.

"Shh," Justine said, "do not question it so. The Lord watches over us all, and we know he speaks especially in Mother Leeds's ear." She reached out and took Deborah's hand. "Bless thee." She closed her eyes. "God bless thee for saving my daughter."

Deborah looked John steadily in the eye, hoping to underscore his wife's words. It seemed to work. He cleared his throat, glanced away, then asked, "Shall I fetch the cart?"

"Yes, I thank thee for it," Deborah replied, then risked a look at Jonas.

He had been staring intently at her and now turned his gaze away as if frightened. "Just a moment," he called out to John, then left to help him.

Deborah fixed her eyes on Erin, implying that she would explain everything later, even though she knew that Erin would never understand why Deborah was unwilling to tell the others Johanna had had the vision. She knew as well that Erin would soon end her promise of silence and good will.

37

EBORAH LISTENED to Johanna's knife hitting the chopping block. Johanna was deft with a blade and usually cut vegetables quickly, but today she was slow, brooding. They were alone by the hearth—which was rare—making beef stew. Deborah had sent the girls outside to spin, card, and do the wash on this warm spring day. Despite Johanna's initial distress, in the few weeks since the accident at the river, she seemed to feel pride that her vision had likely saved a life. She had started to ask Deborah questions about her own sight and healing ability. The new attitude thrilled Deborah, and this morning she had awakened with a feeling that today might be the day Johanna asked for help.

"Missus." The knife stopped and Deborah held her breath. "Is it true you once healed a withered arm?"

"Yes. Did I never tell thee of that?"

"Nay, I think not. I heard Daniel speaking about it." Johanna looked at Deborah, expectantly, hopefully. "I have horrid dreams. Will you give me something for them?"

"Certainly. I have a tincture that shall help thee. But to rid them completely thou must do more."

"Must I?"

"Yes." Deborah waited for some kind of outburst, but Johanna seemed no more apprehensive than anyone else would be at the prospect of starting a treatment. "Wilt thou give me leave to attempt it? It might fright thee a'times."

"You have been so kind to me."

"Shall we attempt it, then?"

"Yes," Johanna said and smiled.

Surprised and encouraged by the ease with which she agreed, Deborah asked, "Shall we begin now?"

"Yes."

Upstairs, Deborah collected several wool blankets, including her red one, then went outside to fetch Sarah and Deb, who were doing the wash. "You twain go in and continue dinner," she told them. "Johanna and I shall be away for a time."

Sarah walked directly into the house, but thirteen-year-old Deb lingered. She was in a coltish phase—skinny, all legs and arms and long, thick hair. She glanced at Johanna waiting just inside the door, then threw her arms around her mother. "I am glad," Deb whispered in her ear, then hurried toward the house.

Deborah watched her go, pleased that she seemed to understand what they were about to do. She didn't talk to Deb of her hopes to heal Johanna, but Deb was a sensitive girl and seemed to know Johanna was more than a servant. Deborah still didn't bring Deb to rituals, although she had begun to teach her about the Old Religion—and much to Deborah's relief and delight, her daughter seemed eager to learn more.

Deborah smiled broadly at Johanna. "Shall we go?"

They went to the stream just short of the ritual grove and sat on the wool blankets among the bank's oak and willow roots. That first day they did little else but watch the water's drowsy flow. Johanna fell asleep, wrapped in Deborah's red wool blanket, her head resting on an oak root.

A few days later, on an unseasonably cold day, they returned to the stream. They sat on two folded blankets and wrapped two others around them. When they were settled, Deborah asked, "When didst thy family arrive in the New World?"

"They came firstly to Boston some fifty. . ." Johanna seemed puzzled, but Deborah just nodded and urged her to continue as if that were the point. "Fifty years ago. They built themselves a prosperous farm. My pappa was one of two boys. The eldest drowned in a lake. My pappa's pappa was a cruel man, said it ought to have been my pappa who drowned in the stead of his brother. Mam was the one told me this. Pappa rarely spoke to me, 'cepting for my nightly Bible lessons." She stopped and stared at the creek, her large eyes black with pupil.

Deborah spoke to put her at ease. She talked about England and life aboard the *Willow* and healing Richard. Johanna eventually lay down, curled onto her side, and fell asleep.

For the next few weeks when they went to the stream they spoke only of the present. Both lay idly on blankets, raising themselves on their elbows periodically to drink cider from a leather flask. "Thou art not my servant here," Deborah would remind Johanna every time she suddenly apologized for forgetting her place. But that didn't happen as often as Deborah had expected. She felt Johanna's growing comfort with this arrangement. And here by the stream, she seemed to allow her mind to rest.

As they walked home after a particularly peaceful afternoon, Deborah spread her arms in elation. 'Tis truly having effect, she thought. Johanna becomes more content. Everywhere she looked she sensed the promise of harvest, in the tiny green apples, the warming soil.

The moment Deborah had waited for came on the Summer Solstice. They put their feet in the cool water, and Johanna smiled at Deborah as if they were friends, as if she had always trusted her.

Deborah smiled back and said, "Thou wert telling me of thy Bible lessons."

Johanna brought her feet straight up out of the water and held them there, ankles dripping. "Every night we would meet after supper and Pappa would bid me repeat the passage I had learnt the night past. A'times I spoke them well and he listened and nodded. But ofttimes I could not remember all the words and I would stumble, and he would silence me and fix his eyes upon me and say, 'O, full of all subtlety and mischief is the Devil.' Then he would bid me begin again. If I faltered a second time, he beat me with a rod."

Johanna dropped her feet into the water with a splash. She looked at them and spoke no more, yet did not seem downcast. When she turned at last to face Deborah, to her pleasure Deborah saw Johanna as she once had been—a lively, spirited girl, gathering flowers, singing to bees—a girl of vigor, imagination. Deborah leaned forward and cupped her face. "I see thee, Johanna," she said.

Johanna wrapped her arms around Deborah. "I thank you, Mother Leeds." Her voice choked. "I thank you."

38

T was Hannah's turn at the spit. She sat on a three-legged stool and repeatedly pulled a twisted string which turned the flank as it untwisted. The pork was nearly done—no longer splattering juices into the drip pan.

"I'll see to that," John said, and Hannah returned to the children's trestle table. She sat on the bench between her older sisters Ann and Deb, and across from Millicent, Mary's three-year-old daughter. Johanna and Ethan sat on joint stools at one end.

Deborah and her grown children and their spouses were gathered around a gateleg table piled with cornbread and butter, ears of corn, and cranberry sauce. The apple pie and fresh cream came from Robert's wife, Abigail.

"When will Pappa return?" Mary asked, dipping a piece of corn bread into the bowl of cranberry sauce.

"He said he would be gone but two weeks," Deborah answered, "and it hath been more than twice that now. I suspect he remains in Monmouth. With his cousin William's wife gone now, I mark it must be hard on him. Thy Pappa likely helps him bring in his harvest."

"He might have remained to help *us*," Daniel said, scowling into his trencher.

"Thou art a sloven imp, Daniel," young Japhet said. "Thou dost no more work than the rest of us, for all of thy complaints."

"Children," Deborah said, "we are here at this evening feast to welcome Nehemiah's fiancée, Elizabeth Wood, into our family. Let us not show our worst to her. And let us toast them now." She raised her cider and touched cups all around.

"I make another toast." Mary's husband, Samuel, took out a buckskin flask. To the shocked looks of everyone at the table he said, "'Tain't applejack I have, but molasses beer. Japhet Leeds ought not go so far as to forbid such gentle nectar."

Mary looked straight ahead, avoiding everyone's gaze.

"'Tis ridiculous," Samuel went on, pouring beer into his cup for all to see. "Who hath e'er heard of such a ban?" Looking around again he asked, "Who shall join me?"

No one responded. Nehemiah glanced toward the door as if he considered leaving with Elizabeth. Finally, Robert gulped down his cider and held his mug toward Samuel.

"There 'tis," Samuel said. "Who else shall drink with me?"

Mary held out her mug tentatively, followed by Daniel, then Sarah. Before Samuel had finished filling them, Deborah held hers out as well.

"Mamma!" several of her children exclaimed at once.

"Samuel is quite right," she said. "Molasses beer ought be the drink with which we wish Nehemiah and Elizabeth future joy." She clinked her mug with the other beer drinkers and took a sip. Outside the open windows she heard rustling pines and smelled the faint aroma of smoke. Something seemed amiss although she couldn't sense what it might be.

"Mother," John said, "forgive my forthrightness, but methinks thou hast injured my father."

"Aye, that is so," young Japhet agreed. "Hath he not eloquently extolled the virtues of sobriety and the dangers of drink?"

"Sons," Deborah said, "'twas but one sip and a sip thy father would not have denied but a few years past. I have done him no injury. Indeed, I shall tell him what hath transpired this night and methinks he'll not judge me harshly."

From the looks on their faces, she knew they didn't understand how she could say such a thing. She wasn't certain either. For surely Japhet would be vexed. His conviction to rid the colony of applejack and other spirits had never lagged over the fourteen years he'd been speaking about it.

But his health concerned her more than his fervor. He was aging quickly, as some said his father had toward the end. She implored him before this last trip to stay home, to cease traveling. He refused, but moved by her caring had kissed her warmly the morning he was to depart. They returned to bed, enjoying each other intimately for the first time in two years. Later as he was leaving, she felt a new love for him, somewhat motherly—fearing for him—but also lustful. She wanted him back, now.

Japhet must have felt it as well for he had turned his horse around and come back to kiss her one more time. He'd touched her cheek, his eyes moist, his grey hair now only singed with strips of black. "Two weeks, Deborah," he promised, "and I'll return. Mayhap 'twill be my last trip." He snapped the reins and rode away, his lank body twisted toward her, one hand on his hat as if in salute.

The vivid memory held Deborah's full attention until she heard a voice say, "Mamma." Deb stood by her side. "I hear something."

The horrified look on her daughter's face was so familiar Deborah upset her stool as she raced for the door.

"What is it?" Mary asked.

"Deb's always hearing things that aren't there," Daniel said, laughing.

"The barn!" Johanna cried out.

Deborah flung open the front door of the house. Deb ran ahead down the stairs but tripped and fell hard onto the ground. Hastily, Deborah moved her out of the way, while her other children raced past. Nehemiah, Abigail, Elizabeth Wood, and Johanna remained behind.

"Johanna and I will tend to Deb," Abigail told Deborah. "You are needed there."

Deborah couldn't see down the rise to the barn but saw smoke rising.

"I'll fetch neighbors to help," Nehemiah said, then looked stricken. His colt was in the barn.

Elizabeth touched his shoulder and told him gently, "I will go." She ran to where her filly stamped nervously at a hitching post. Nehemiah bolted in the direction of the barn.

Deb staggered against her mother, unable to stand. "I will help you twain get her inside," Deborah told the others. She pushed Deb's hair out of her eyes and said, "Thou wilt be well, my fair one, 'tis but a turned ankle." The women helped the girl up the stairs, then onto her bed.

As she propped Deb up with pillows, Deborah glanced out the window toward the barn. Brilliant orange flames shot above it.

"Go along, missus," Johanna said, "we will tend to her." Abigail had already begun to unbuckle Deb's leather shoes.

Deborah kissed her daughter's forehead. "Thou wilt be well," she repeated. "Do not trouble thyself about the barn. We will put the fire out." Deb turned her face away.

"Go along, missus," Johanna said again.

Deborah felt a vague sense of unease about leaving her daughter but pulled herself away, then hurried downstairs and out of the house. When she reached the rise she slowed, feeling compelled to note the color of the flames and the odor she couldn't place. Soon she discerned the terrible, dying screams of their livestock. "Polly!" She remembered her mare, and broke into a run. Were they unable to rescue her?

When she reached the barn, she had her answer. It was completely engulfed. Their chickens and geese raced about frantically, but the other animals were trapped. She realized with dismay that there was nothing they could do to save them. They could only prevent the fire from spreading to the carriage house, the crops, and the main house. Then she saw that John had already thought of that. He was soaking the ground around the barn and pulling back flammable debris.

The rest of the adults had formed a bucket brigade with Robert at the head. Mary was filling buckets at the well and handing them to the girls, who carried them to the back of the line.

Deborah hurried to the front, then suddenly remembered her dried herbs and staggered, losing her balance for a moment. Almost her entire supply had hung from rafters or were stored in wooden boxes in the barn.

"Mother, get back," Robert shouted between coughs. "'Tis too dangerous for thee."

"Elizabeth hath ridden for help," Deborah said.

"As did Daniel, in Mary's cart. Get back, Mother, I mean it."

"I cannot run as fast as the girls. Hannah!" Deborah called to her daughter who was spilling half the water in her bucket as she ran with it from the well. "Let thy sisters carry the full buckets. Come hither and take them back the empty ones." With a glance at Robert, she added, "I'll remain here."

She stood next to her son and took every other bucket, which allowed them both to plan their throws, or pause to cough. The line did move faster, but soon she began to feel faint from the heat, and exhaustion forced her to slow down until she threw one bucketful to every three of his.

"Sit down, Mother, ere we have to carry thee away," Robert said, poised to throw.

Deborah ignored him and took the next bucket Samuel handed her. She tossed it, then felt light-headed and brought her hand to her forehead, willing herself to remain upright. Suddenly, the heavens seemed to open as Abigail put a wet cloth on her neck.

"Deb shall be well," Abigail said. "Johanna tends her now."

Deborah stepped out of line, realizing as the coolness of the cloth spread up to her throbbing head that Robert had been right; she needed to rest. She hung gratefully onto Abigail and let her mop her sweaty neck and chest, then took the cloth and buried her face in it to suck the water down her raw throat.

She heard shouts and looked up to see several neighbors arriving. They leapt from their mounts and carts, ran down the rise and formed another bucket line. Neighbor upon neighbor pulled up. Erin and Patrick arrived. Elizabeth Wood reined her nervous filly this way and that, directing the volunteers. Deborah's eyes filled at the community effort. She felt that profound but seemingly ludicrous joy common to tragedies—the overwhelming realization that people really cared, that they will hurry to help a neighbor.

She tied the wet cloth over her nose and mouth and rejoined Robert at the head of the line. With the additional bucket line, it wasn't long before the fire was completely out, but the barn was leveled. When Hannah realized their efforts hadn't saved her goat, Frosty, she ran toward the smoldering mass. Nehemiah caught her and pulled her back, holding her while she struggled, then sobbed.

Paul Covenoven, now the constable, walked up to Deborah. "I'll be along tomorrow," he said. "Touch nothing ere I return." He shook his head, then looked her in the eyes. "I am sorry for you."

His sincerity moved her, and she clasped his hand. "I thank thee for coming, Bear."

After he was gone, Erin came over and put her arm around Deborah, and they watched as the others left, all expressing condolences and offering to help raise a new barn when Japhet returned. Japhet, Deborah thought with a start, what will he say?

When Erin had left as well, Deborah returned to the house. Her children were devouring the rest of their meal. She smiled wearily at the scene, relieved that the crisis was over for now, but still felt troubled. Her scurrying fowl came to her mind, and she remembered that John had secured the barn just before the meal. How did they get out?

She pulled herself up the stairs, pausing to gaze into the looking glass on the wall. A ghostlike image peered back. Her smudged face bore deep lines, her gown was torn and smoke-blackened, and her hair was a snuff blond, heavy on the grey.

She continued on to the girls' room. Deb sat up too fast and winced from the pain in her ankle. "Mamma!" she exclaimed. Her cheeks were blotched and her eyes swollen. Her blond hair hung in her face.

Johanna had been looking out the window and whirled around, guiltily it seemed to Deborah. "I will leave you be," Johanna said, then left the room.

Deborah drew back the quilt to look at Deb's ankle. She was impressed by how securely Abigail had wrapped it.

"Mamma, forgive me," Deb said.

"Thou hast done nothing, pumpkin."

"Yes I did." She stared at her bandaged ankle. "I made the fire. I saw it."

"No, Deborah Fae! Thou saw the fire, but thou didst not make it. Thou must understand. Seeing is not the same as bringing about." She looked into her daughter's unconvinced eyes and it came to her. "What did Johanna tell thee?"

"She said– she said 'twas a curse to see and 'tis so. 'Twas horrid, Mamma. I heard a sound and saw the fire and I– I kept seeing it, but I knew not how to say so. I knew not what was happening." She choked and began to cry, jerking back and forth.

Deborah sat on the bed, then shifted around behind Deb, holding her, rocking her gently. "Oh my little night owl," she said, "soon thou wilt know, seeing 'tain't always the curse it seems just now to be."

She adjusted their positions to lie together side-by-side. Deb's crying stopped, and after awhile she began to snore. "I will take care of thee, my sweet girl," she whispered in her ear. "As Johanna or even I never was cared for, I will take care of thee."

39

EBORAH DIDN'T WANT to do it—she was coughing, exhausted, and several of her children needed tending—but she awoke the morning after the fire with a feeling of urgency. If she didn't attempt another healing with Johanna, the shock of the fire might undo or greatly harm her progress, if it hadn't already. And so, after she vomited for the third morning that week, they left.

As they headed down the road for the stream in the woods, Johanna started to walk with a staggering step.

"Art thou hurt?" Deborah asked.

"No," Johanna said without altering her gait.

It occurred to Deborah that she might be imitating Deb, which gave her an idea. "Johanna, wouldst thou be troubled if Deb came along with us? We shan't be able to go to the stream, then, but she could hobble to the creek by the house. 'Tis still early, no one will trouble us."

"I should like that," Johanna replied, and turned to go back.

The two women helped Deb down the stairs and along the path to a small clearing in the woods, just shy of the creek. They helped her get settled onto a log, then spread out Deborah's red blanket on top of another one on the ground. Johanna lay down and closed her eyes.

Deborah realized nervously that this healing was vital—and her hands shook as she took dried marigolds from her bag and surrounded Johanna with them, for protection. When they were in place, she sat at Johanna's head and began to rub her temples.

"Missus," Johanna protested, and started to sit up.

"Shh, 'tis part of thy healing. Lie down. Thou know'st by now I shan't harm thee. Thou hadst a nightmare last night?"

"Yes." Johanna again closed her eyes.

Deborah's hands moved to her neck. As Granna had taught her, she was feeling for the key, the place that when touched would spurt forth the truth to one willing and able to receive it.

"I was in a room," Johanna said, "and Deb was there but 'twas not truly her." Once more she began to sit up. "Where is she?"

"I am here on the log."

Johanna lay back down, then grimaced. "'Twas my pappa."

Deborah waited a few minutes for more, then moved to Johanna's side, placed her hands on her stomach, and saw it clearly: a boot poised to strike Johanna's pregnant belly.

"Oh, Brigid," Deborah said before she could catch herself. She held her hands still and looked at Johanna's face—her eyes tightly shut, her black hair peeking out from under her mobcap—and saw the tale unfold.

Johanna was young and with child by some sweet-whispering rogue, her long torso and loose gowns hiding the fact from her parents until into her seventh month. And when she could no longer hide it, she pled for forgiveness and mercy, but her father raged. He beat her and kicked her repeatedly in the belly. Killing the Devil's child, he said again and again. She finally got away from him by crawling under her bed. At last, he left. Her mother then took her to the local midwife, and the babe was born dead. The next day her mother returned with a bundle of clothing and told her to go, to never come back.

After her mother left, Johanna saw milk on her gown and realized it was her sole means of support now. She called in the midwife, who showed her how to keep it flowing, and said if she didn't pump her breasts they would dry up. Johanna did as instructed, but did it desperately, painfully: both hands encircled one breast at a time, thumbs on top, fingers below, squeezing inward and toward the nipple to imitate the rhythm, the back and forth of a baby's sucking. And she was successful. Despite the blow of losing her baby, she kept her milk and became a wet nurse.

Later she met Ethan, told him of a young husband and newborn taken by a distemper, and off they went to marry. She hoped for another child, hoped at last to bear another girl child, her Prissy. But with every barren month she knew more clearly that she was being punished by God. For she had allowed the Devil into her bed, and the stain of his seed would never go.

Deborah slowly removed her hands from Johanna's belly and shifted to sit behind her again. She put Johanna's head into her lap and placed one hand behind her neck and the other on her forehead. With her imagination she drew two pentacles, one above and the other below Johanna, and imagined these pentacles as hands, holding Johanna lovingly, protectively, the five points interlocking like fingers. Then she filled the hands with pink, the color of health. Pink cheeks on pale skin, pink tongue. When the color dissolved on its own, she followed it with blue, the color of the watery womb of the Great Fish, the first Mother. She tried to end with yellow—the color of the sun, the first flowers of spring, hope, and rebirth—but wasn't successful. The color streaked, then faded immediately every time she added it. Johanna's closed eyes fluttered as if in deep sleep, but she was aware enough to fight, to deny hope. Deborah stopped trying, for now. She unclasped the pentacle hands, removed her own hands from Johanna's head, and told her to lie still awhile before getting up.

Deborah sat back and glanced over at Deb, who was leaning as far forward as her sprained ankle would allow, her arms outstretched in front of her, palms down, receiving her own impressions. My sweet little Deb, she thought. My namesake and heir. I will begin now to teach her in earnest. There is no reason to delay.

Johanna opened her eyes and stretched, then sat up. She smiled at Deborah gratefully, but Deborah felt certain she wasn't aware of what her body had revealed. Poor, poor child, Deborah said to herself, mourning silently for her terrible loss.

She reached out and straightened Johanna's mobcap and ran a hand gently down her face. Johanna stopped the hand and held it, then brought it to her lips. "No one hath been more kind to me," she whispered, "ever in my life."

Deborah nodded and said softly, "When thou art ready, my dear, we shall return home."

40

ONSTABLE COVENOVEN didn't return until the second morning after the fire. He'd had ague accompanied by a cough, he explained as he and Deborah headed toward the ruins of the barn. She carried her pick over her shoulder, and he led his horse which bore his tools.

"Thou swallowed smoke, Paul," she said. "Thou always think'st thou hast a dying fever and thou art always well the day next."

He paused to cough into his handkerchief. She reached for the cloth and he surrendered it. She sniffed the phlegm, then poked at it with her finger. "Save for some soot, 'tis a clear stream." She put one hand on his forehead and the other behind his neck and peered into his eyes. "No fever today."

"No."

"Show me thy tongue. Any sweat last night?"

"No."

"Swallowed smoke, like the rest of us. Thou shouldst have seen this house yesterday. We were all coughing, and some of us stayed abed."

Paul tied his mount to a tree, took his spade to the southwest corner of the barn where Deborah's collection of herbs had hung, and began digging. "Methinks this is where it began," he said. "I thought so that eve."

She started to join him when her eye caught sight of a piece of cord under a nearby tree. It looked like the hemp string she used to bundle her herbs. She walked to the tree and discovered a small bunch of dried stalks that had once been part of her herb collection. The bundle appeared to have been trampled. Most likely while we put the fire out, she thought, but why was it outside the barn?

"Did you find something of note?" Paul called.

"I think not." Deborah dropped the bunch into her apron pocket, then joined him and started to dig for the cause of the blaze, moving aside pieces of charred wood and the remains of farm implements. After awhile she leaned on her pick, sweat soaking through her gown, and wiped her face with her handkerchief. Nehemiah and Hannah probed the other side of the barn where the stalls had been, looking for the bones of their animals.

"Have a look at this." Paul held up a blackened, silver brandy flask.

"Applejack?" Deborah asked.

"Any of your boys out here ere the fire?"

"No," she remembered. "Everyone was inside at table. And none I know takes their applejack in a silver flask." She took it from him and traced its ornate etching with her finger. "'Tis indeed a fine piece."

Paul righted a nearby metal trough, then bent over. "Well, well," he said, and scooped up two handfuls of charred hay. "You kept your hay where?"

Deborah pointed. "In the loft by Hannah, near the stalls." She looked again at the hay and the flask. "Someone made a bed here?"

"Appears so."

He continued to dig in the ashes and soon found a well-made copper lantern. He wiped soot off the bottom and read, "London 1725."

"Not ours," she affirmed.

"No, and now I know how your fowl escaped unharmed. The barn door remained open behind the man when he ran from the flames. And your other livestock did not succeed in breaking down their stalls."

Deborah winced at the image of her terrified mare, rearing, kicking in vain.

"And Deborah, 'twas no poor itinerant who slept here. Our man is a man of means." He scanned the ruins. "Likely he was in drink and coming down the road, and deigned to rest in the first barn he found. He saw your house from the road, came closer, marked everyone occupied with a late feast, and headed for the barn. Wasn't too drunken to make himself a home.

Lit his lantern, made the bed of straw, and fell to sleep. Must have knocked the lantern o'er. I suspect the poor soul awoke with his bed ablaze and ran away quick as he might."

"With no regard–"

"Fearing the consequences."

Deborah stabbed her pick into the ashes and tried to imagine the barn as it once had been. Four horses, two goats, four milking cows, her herbs. She looked up at Paul just as he turned aside to slip a lozenge into his mouth. "What is that?" she asked.

"For my cough."

"Thy cough? Who gave it to thee?"

"Dr. Hyme."

Deborah shook her head. "Thou know'st better than to buy pills from itinerant quacks."

"He's not itinerant."

"What?"

"He's a new neighbor of ours. Yesterday I was witness to a deed transfer for a parcel bought from John Mathis. He'll live in the cabin next to the store." Deborah leaned against her pick. "He's no quack, either," Paul added. "He hath a degree from Edinburgh. I saw the certificate."

"Thou saw it?"

"When he gave me the pills. I was coughing and feverish and–"

"Give me one, Paul."

She wiped ash off his spade, wrapped the lozenge in her handkerchief and put it on the metal edge. Then she stomped on the lozenge and ate the broken pieces. "Slippery elm," she confirmed, "same as I gave thee last month for thy aching throat. Scabwort, all right, and horsetail grass, a good tonic though I'd not use it for a simple cough. What was his price?"

"He's a genuine Doctor of Physic, Deborah, he's no quack. Showed me his tools, finely wrought silver, some of them." Paul turned away and walked over to his horse.

Deborah looked beyond the ruins to the corn which stood as tall as a man. The tassels shone like water. Beyond the corn were the woods and fields where she and Erin had gathered much of the herbs. They are gone, she thought.

The constable mounted and turned to her, reins in hand. "'Tis a pity

I have no one to apprehend," he said, "for our man, to be sure, is long gone." He turned his horse and headed for the rise.

"Bear," she called after him, "send for me, thou hearest, if thy cough worsens." She watched him go, feeling as if she were in another world, distant and shrinking.

When he was out of sight, she saw he had left his spade behind. She took it in both hands and swung it around over her head. Then low and level, as if skimming a stone, she threw it toward the center of the barn. It landed, completely submerged, in a heap of ashes.

41

READADH CHUIGE," Erin said to Deborah. "Do not continue to trouble yourself about that quack. Were he a genuine physician he'd be in England."

"Paul said he hath a degree from Edinburgh and fine silver tools."

"Tools, fools. He's a man, is he not? No man is a better doctor than a woman. We have nothing to worry about. Now, pull!"

Deborah pulled, Erin pushed, and together they dragged the bathing trough from outside into the main room of Erin's three-room house. Ana was still apprenticing in Little Egg Harbour, and Patrick was at the tavern.

Deborah poured three large pots of hot water into the trough. "Alice told me Paul went to see him again. I have cared for Bear twenty years. I know his body as well as my own children's. Now this doctor shows him silver tools and he calls for me no longer."

Erin spit air between her teeth. "I *never* trusted that man, Deborah. What do you expect from a constable? They think they owe no one a thing."

"Would he were the only one, Erin. Yesterday, I stood aside the general store and watched two of our neighbors walk in to see the good doctor. Two who always have come to us."

"Who?"

"Jonas Vale and Paul's brother, John."

"Let him have the ingrates. If he doth not kill them, they'll be back."

"I think not," Deborah said as she poured in more hot water. "While I would not have included horsetail grass for a cough absent of blood, slippery elm root and scabwort were in that lozenge as well. He is no quack."

"He must be. You say he's no dissenter, so he's either running from gaol or, like the rest of his sort, he finally killed enough that they've banished him to the New World." Erin emptied three buckets of water into the trough. "Worry not, Deborah, and get in. He will show himself by next spring, and we shall be here, welcoming the return of those we tend."

Deborah took off her clothes and stepped into the water. "Ahh," she said with pleasure, holding the side of the trough. "'Tis much too hot for thee." She eased herself down, then relaxed. "A near scalding soak is wondrous, Erin, thou must simply enter it slowly."

"I shall wait. Warm is wondrous enough for me. Come forward now and I'll see to your back while it cools. Then you can see to mine."

Deborah leaned forward and rested her cheek against the edge of the trough. "Nothing better," she said as Erin scrubbed her back and neck.

"You say you saw Alice?" Erin asked.

"Yes. She is no worse. 'Tis not a bad fever, but it hath remained. I told John leave her be and send for us if it worsens tonight. As well, I told Alice I shall go see her again on the morrow. I do wish Japhet would return. The boys need his help. Lammas hath passed and harvest is nigh." She sat up straight. "Come in now, Erin. More scrubbing and I shall fall to sleep and drown." She turned around and stretched out her legs.

Erin laughed. "You issue an invite then take up all the bath."

"Only whilst I might, never fear. There is always room for thee." She drew up her legs after Erin had undressed and stepped into the water. Erin smiled mischievously, then plopped down, splashing Deborah as well.

Deborah laughed, wiping water from her eyes. "At thy age, Erin."

"I shall go thrashing to my grave." Erin turned around, parted her hair in the back and pulled it over her shoulders. Deborah rubbed the soap over Erin's broad back. "I saw Johanna outside the Mathis store," Erin said. "She seemed," Erin glanced briefly over her shoulder, "different."

Deborah sighed. "I did not tell thee of the healing because I knew what thou wouldst say."

"With good cause."

"Erin, prithee be kind to her. I have come far, but it could be turned back at any time. If thou art kind, 'twould help her. She hath had a sorrowful life. If I can bring her peace, I should be pleased." Erin turned around to face Deborah and frowned. "Thou lookest at me as though I withhold some portion of this," Deborah said. "But I do not feel at liberty to reveal what I know, though if I did, thou wouldst agree she is in want of kindness."

"I sense," Erin said, "that you are a mole above ground, blindly moving about. And Johanna is a hawk, about to swoop."

"That is a wild image." Deborah shivered, then sank lower in the water to cover her shoulders. "Methinks Johanna is more the innocent babe just learning to walk. She falls down often, to be sure, but is certain to succeed. 'Tis the doctor who is the hawk." She shivered again. "Another minute and I shall have need to get out, this bath is too cold for me." She looked toward the hearth and wished they had put on another kettle of water.

"I told you we need not worry o'er him," Erin said. Deborah sighed heavily. "What?" Erin asked.

Deborah shook her head. "I got on well with the doctor in Burlington, but 'tis different now. I don't wish to defer as I once did. I will not defer. Yet, e'er since the fire and learning of his arrival, I feel– I feel that we are passing away."

"Who do you mean by 'we'?"

"Thee, me, Alice, female healers. 'Tis what occurred in England, and elsewhere I should imagine. Now at the last it hath removed hither."

"Deborah, if a few neighbors leave to be maimed by Dr. Hyme, so be it. You are loved and admired, *a stór*. And so am I and Alice. Our neighbors will not scorn us. Were he a Friend doctor like Dr. Grant, 'twould be another matter. But he is Anglican, they say. And so are those three who went to him, are they not? The Friends and Anabaptists will come still to we who have served them long and well. Heed my words and give your mind a rest."

"I know not." Again Deborah shook her head.

"Come." Erin held out her arms.

Deborah turned around and let Erin hold her from behind. The rise and fall of Erin's chest was comforting. Erin crossed her hands over Deborah's stomach. Desire for Erin, which Deborah hadn't felt in years, crept over her.

"Do you e'er think," Erin asked, "of how it should have been had we remained in Burlington—if I had remained with you?"

"Yes," Deborah admitted.

"A'times I wish we'd had the courage."

"We?" Deborah sat up, gripped the sides of the tub, and turned to face her. "I might have done it hadst thou been willing!"

Erin was silent, then said, "'Might' is the word. But since you yet bear such ill feeling about it, listen to how it would have gone. If we had not ceased after that first time, we would have been found out ere long, and I cast out in disrepute with no land and no means. Japhet would be convinced 'twas all my doing, e'en that I'd bewitched you, and if you denounced me, he would allow your return." She sighed as if the next was difficult to say. "I did not believe you would abandon your children and leave with me. I believed you'd denounce me." She looked away from Deborah's gaze. "Later when you said you would not go to Leeds, I did not think you would hold to that. Then Japhet came along with his plan, and it seemed the better way for us to remain together."

Deborah nodded in sad agreement. "I should like to believe I'd not use thee so ill, but I cannot say thou art in the wrong about it. I cannot imagine my life without my twelve children."

"Nor I without Ana."

"'Twould have been a different story, though, to be sure, if Japhet had left without me. If thou and I had remained together." She smiled. "I hear Rhode Island is the home for castoffs."

Erin moved closer and grabbed her shoulders. "Patrick is my mate, but you share my soul. We *are* together. And so we shall always be."

Deborah leaned in slowly, her eyes not moving from Erin's, and Erin met her. They kissed, drew breath, then kissed again. Deborah wrapped her arms around Erin, then glanced toward the window. She thought she saw something and pulled back from Erin, as she watched the window for movement outside.

"What is it?" Erin turned to look.

The shadow of a branch swept past. They turned to each other, chuckling, then kissed once more.

"I could ne'er have lived these years without thee," Deborah said.

"While there's breath yet in my bones, my sweet," Erin whispered as their lips touched, "you'll ne'er be rid of me."

<h1 style="text-align:center">42</h1>

EBORAH STOOPED to pick yellow chamomile blossoms. The herb always made her smile; the way it grew stubbornly in the road, heedless of boots and horseshoes. This walk to Alice's was one she loved in all seasons, but especially late summer. It was still hot and a chore to move about in the afternoon, but there was abundance in the land. It was a time of reckoning and reaping, learning what you have sown.

Deborah approached the front door of the Mathis house and peered in. "What is this?" she exclaimed in horror.

On a daybed Alice lay with leeches dotting her chest and arms. A strange man wearing a curled, powdered periwig stood by her. Deborah rushed over and stared at the worms. They had nearly drunk their fill. One by one, they were dropping off.

Deborah peered into Alice's eyes while she checked her pulse. It was only a little fast. Her color was normal and her skin warm and dry. To Deborah's relief, she seemed not to have suffered a significant loss of blood. She still had a fever but it wasn't threatening.

"John Mathis," the man beside her called out, "carry off this woman."

Deborah turned to face him. This is the good doctor, she thought. A paper-faced man, frail looking, and poorly fed of late. He ought to drink dandelion root tea to begin.

John walked in slowly, embarrassed. The doctor demanded, "Who is this woman thinks she can come 'twixt a physician and his patient?"

"Thou art mistaken," Deborah said with forced calm. "Alice is *my* patient and Erin O'Hara's. We three—Alice, Erin, and I—care for our neighbors. We are the physicians and our patients enjoy good health. Thus hath it been for twenty-five years. And before us, Alice was the lone healer. We need not thy doctoring, nor thy leeches, nor thy pills. Now leave this house ere I forget my manners."

"Methinks you forgot them long ago, Madam. I did not ask to administer to this woman. The gentleman summoned me." He gestured toward John. "Said his wife required a genuine doctor, since the area is blessed, at the last, to possess one."

Deborah glared at John, who was backing out of the room, then faced the doctor again. "I will tell thee only once that thou art not to treat my patients unless they themselves come to thee."

He started to gather up the leeches and other tools, his hands covered by cotton gloves. "Madam, she may not have called me but she gave her consent. She is a wiser woman than you."

Deborah looked questioningly at Alice, who seemed a bit baffled by the argument.

"Prithee join me upon the porch," the doctor said, "where we might discuss our differences." He put the last of his belongings into his leather bag. "I assure you, Mrs. Mathis shall be quite fine without us."

Deborah looked at Alice again. The doctor was correct; she was in no danger. "I'll return in a moment," she told Alice, who nodded in reply. Deborah followed the doctor outside, leaving the door open a crack.

"Madam," he informed her, "perhaps you do not understand I am a well respected physician. I am certain you have done your best, but you have not been graduated from medical school. You do not know as much as I."

His statement came as no surprise and Deborah replied confidently, "I know people are afeared to go to hospital in England, for most do not come out again, but perish of illness they did not enter with. I know you doctors amputate when there is no need. I know you use tools for their own sake when herbs would do." And she thought but did not say, I know you murder female healers, signing the paper to call them witches, then happily snatch their patients.

"I own our practice is young, and all loss of life is bitter. But to be sure even you must see there are times when the death of one ultimately serves the good of many."

"Not to the bereaved, the children left in squalor."

"A mother's view," he said, and dismissed her with a wave of his hand. "So, you have proved my point. There is no reasonable comparison 'twixt me and you."

She glanced down at his covered hands and the truth hit her. She looked him in the eye and said, "Thou mightst be correct, for were I the cause of a fire, I would free the trapped livestock and remain to put it out. As well I would never run away with an old woman's herbs." She grabbed the doctor's right wrist. "What should I see were I cruel enough to tear this off thee? A bad burn, I warrant." She dropped his arm.

He leaned back against the rail, seeming stricken for a moment, then stared down at his clenched fingers.

"I see," she accused, "thou thought a common, ignorant woman would not guess who had burned her barn and taken her herbs."

He raised his head and smirked. "A person can burn oneself in many ways." He peeled off the glove, wincing, and revealed a burn not a week old. "Foolishly, I reached into the hearth and touched a log." He turned his hand over a few times. "'Tis a pity about your loss, but I assure you I had nothing to do with it."

"I am not impressed by thy pretense, and I am certain 'twas thee. Thy arrival coincided with the fire. The constable and I found in the ashes a copper lantern that is not ours, as well as a silver brandy flask. No one in the area hath such a fine flask. After the fire, I found a bunch of my herbs outside the barn. Methinks thou snatched as many as thou couldst ere the fire forced thee out, and then dropped one as thou ran. And the final proof is that burn upon thy hand."

"Proof?" Hyme laughed. "I think not. You make a better scribbler than a healer or constable. 'Twill be your next profession." He eased the glove back on. "Carry your fiction to Constable Covenoven—my patient, I might add—and see if he doth not agree with me. I will take my leave now, but think on this: your Mrs. Mathis allowed me to bleed her. As she did, most in your position find 'tis better to step aside while you yet may." He marched down the porch steps.

"Thy threat gives me no fright," she called after him. "Thou shouldst know thou hast found thy match."

Her bravado faded with each step into the house. Alice was sitting up on the daybed, her greyish brown hair in a twisted knot on top of her head. Deborah asked, "How couldst thou let him bleed thee?"

"He was here, Deborah, at the behest of my husband, and he made such grand assurances I desired to see it through. Thou know'st I always wish to learn a new treatment. I knew as well thou wert coming along soon to check on my condition. So if he failed in it, thou wouldst administer to me. If he did not fail, I'd have another treatment I did not know before."

Deborah sat on a nearby stool. Alice obviously didn't feel threatened by the doctor's presence. But then, she thought, Alice doth not hail from a lineage of murdered healers. She did not watch her grandmother's friend be hurled to her death against an oak tree. She is not a witch.

"All told," Alice said, "methinks the treatment did me neither good nor ill." She lay down again. "Dost thou truly think he burned the barn?"

"I do," Deborah said. "He all but owned to it when he fell upon the rail in surprise at my words." She pulled the stool closer to the daybed. "But let us cease speaking of this. Allow me another look at thee. How dost thou feel?"

"Weak, faint yet. Hath Japhet returned?"

"No, but never thee mind. Rest now and give me leave to have a look."

"Thou wouldst want cold Indian sage tea for fever. 'Tis there on the pedestal table."

"*Alice*," Deborah said, "I am the healer here. Must I remind thee of this as well?"

43

EBORAH STOOD at the hearth stirring mutton stew when Sarah came in from the parlor and asked, "Why is Johanna packing her trunk?"

The question seemed to have come out of nowhere. For an instant she had no answer, but then put the wooden spoon on the chopping block and hurried to the parlor where she found Johanna on her knees, packing her and Ethan's belongings. "Johanna, what is this?" Deborah asked.

"We are leaving, Ethan and I." She spoke in a strained sing-song. "We work now for the Smiths. 'Tis for the best, methinks."

Deborah knelt beside Johanna and took her arm. "Prithee, what is the matter? Did someone shout at thee?"

"No. No."

"Pray tell me why, then?"

Johanna put the last of the clothing in and closed the lid. "I thank you for your kindness."

She stood up and turned to go, but Deborah rose quickly and caught her arm again. "Why dost thou remove? What of thy healing? Thy nightmares are gone. Everyone says thou look'st well. Even Erin said so to me. Let us continue and thou mightst be fully healed."

Johanna glanced down at Deborah's clutching hand, then looked her in the eye. "I cannot be healed from one whose sin is greater than my own."

Deborah remembered the shadow at Erin's window and let go of Johanna's arm. She thought she might faint, and stepped over to the pine settle and slumped down.

"Missus, I will not tell a soul, you may depend on it. No one hath shown me greater kindness in my life, and I know the burden sin can be. God's judgment is swift and sure—'tis that which you will face."

After Johanna left, Deborah thought of things she could have said to convince her that she had misinterpreted what she saw. Things that may have absolved her and Erin but driven Johanna back into confusion. She wouldn't do it.

She was still sitting on the settle when Johanna returned with Ethan. He hoisted the trunk to his shoulder in silence and carried it outside. Johanna waited till he was gone, then leaned within inches of Deborah's face. "I saw you with the Devil. I saw him take you against your will. I saw you fight and flail against him to no avail. I saw him o'erpower you, as he once o'erpowered me. I saw you, Mother Leeds." She turned and ran out the door.

In the garden Deborah was sitting on a piece of canvas, not weeding as anyone watching from afar might assume, but just sitting, staring at the carrot tops, when Erin arrived.

"Quiet, are we?" Erin asked. She sat next to Deborah on the canvas.

Deborah faced her and grabbed her hand. "Johanna saw us in the bath," she said, her heart pounding. "Now she hath removed to the Smiths." She couldn't bring herself to repeat the rest of Johanna's words.

"No," Erin whispered.

"She says because of my kindness she'll not breathe a word of it."

"She owes you that. Do you trust it?"

"I know not." Deborah shook her head back and forth. She felt that everything she had built was bursting into flames as her barn had, with scarcely enough time to breathe between events. 'Twill be like this, she thought, till the end.

"Deborah, she is but a servant girl. She knows no one would believe her tale over one such as you. She will not speak of it. Come, I have brought my carders. Let us card some wool."

Erin helped Deborah to her feet and they went up to the house and sat on the porch steps. Deborah evenly distributed a small amount of teased wool fleece across the bent wires of a paddle-shaped carder she held in her left hand. Holding the handle pointed away from her, she drew a second carder down it as if combing. As usual, the motion gradually put her at ease.

"I am now more troubled by the doctor than by her," Erin said. "Let us have haste and hex the bastard."

Deborah combed a few more times. If ever I were tempted, she thought, this is it. "Thou know'st a hex comes back on thee. Even he is not worth such a risk."

"He's a bad wind, Deborah. I can feel it."

"I grant thee that." Erin squinted at her, questioningly. "But he is the future," Deborah said.

"How is that?"

"I have been thinking on what thou said before, that 'tis true some of our neighbors will come still to us, but thou and I and Alice, we are biding our time. To be sure there are no medical schools or societies in the New World, yet there will be, and soon. I thought I shouldn't see his kind in my lifetime: an educated physician, with no known cause to run, leaving England to journey to the New World. But they're arriving now. He is but the first here. We *are* passing away, Erin, and we can do nothing to stay the course. No hex shall cease what began so long ago."

"I shan't go without a fight."

"With fight or not, we shall go. If not now, then soon. And we must prepare Deb and Ana for what they will face in their lives. There's no other New World to send them to. They must remain and live as best they are able."

"Midwifery," Erin said.

"Yes. Men will never take o'er that. Even should a wife be willing, what husband would let another man betwixt her knees? When Ana returns in January she'll begin to teach Deb, as will Alice, if all are willing."

"After Ana returns in January," Erin said quietly, "she will bring forth your child." Deborah put her carders down. "Why did you not tell me so yourself?"

"Erin, I am nearly fifty. I cannot be with child. I have not borne in eight years."

"What *is* this?" Erin asked and put a hand on Deborah's belly.

"I know not," Deborah said, but thought that she did. My fate, Erin, she said to herself, 'tis my fate.

They began to card again in silence. After awhile they heard a horse trotting up the path and waited. Japhet appeared. Erin quickly gathered her carders and wool and kissed Deborah good-bye. She waved hello to Japhet as she passed him.

He dismounted and embraced Deborah. She thought he seemed much weaker than usual, and pulled back to look at his gaunt face. "Thou hast been unwell, hast thou not?"

"Worry not, my dear. I am well now." He smiled. "My darling wife, how wonderful 'tis to see thee at last."

"I am glad to see thee as well. We were all worried, Japhet. What kept thee away so long?"

"I shall tell thee." He glanced around. "It pleases me so to see our farm again." He walked toward the rise as if to admire the view, then stared down toward where the barn had been.

Deborah joined him, put a hand on his arm as they looked upon the blackened ground.

"How did it happen?" he asked.

"Paul says a transient, a well-heeled transient slept there and knocked o'er his lantern." She hesitated. "I believe 'twas the new physician who arrived at the same time. I confronted him, and he hath a burn of that age, but he doth not own to it."

"Whoever is responsible, was he in drink?"

"Paul found a silver flask."

"To be sure, 'twas applejack. That dreaded drink! Were we to rid ourselves of that one substance we should all endure so much less suffering and destruction on earth. When shall we learn that we might all be closer to heaven if we smashed our stills and . . . "

Deborah stopped listening. She put her hand on his chest and pressed evenly in and down. The glow around Japhet faded and the corners of his eyes and his shoulders fell. He looked at her, and she removed her hand.

"Was anyone harmed?" he asked.

"No, but only the fowl survived."

"Hannah's goat?"

"She and Nehemiah have taken it most ill."

Japhet looked down the rise again, then put an arm around her waist. "Let us go in." They stepped into the house.

"Pappa," Hannah shouted, abandoning her place at the hearth and running into his arms. "Pappa, thou art home!"

The other girls gathered around. "Did Mamma tell thee about the fire?" Hannah asked. "I helped put it out. We all did, save Deb."

"Thou didst? You are all good children."

"Deb hurt her foot," Sarah said. "She fell."

Japhet looked at Deb, who nodded.

"But she is well now, Pappa," Hannah said. "Do not go away again. Don't go."

"Father!" John raced into the room and embraced him. "We saw thee from the fields." Young Japhet, Nehemiah, and James soon followed. Daniel remained in the doorway.

"In a moment Robert and Mary will appear," Japhet said, "smelling my arrival on the wind." He winked at Deborah, then added, "I have something to say to you all." He cleared his throat. "I shall travel no more. I tarried to help my cousin William with his harvest and fell sick thereafter. I did not have thy mother's care so I languished for some time. I came soon as I was able. Forgive me, boys, for you have had to do without my help." His eyes rested on Daniel, still in the doorway.

Japhet turned back to the others. "Children, I have a thing of interest to us all." He went outside to his saddlebags and brought in a rolled-up drawing.

Deborah held the bottom of the paper as he unrolled it. Three black eagles, their wings outspread, were arrayed on a silver shield with a red band across its center. Above the shield was a crest which bore a mythic creature, something like a dragon, but with a cock's head. None of them had ever seen the likes of it before. Under the drawing was written "LEEDS."

Deborah was the first to speak. "What is this, Japhet?"

"Our coat of arms, given to some ancient Leeds, William knew not whom. Though he did tell me our line in England goes back to 1150, to Peter de Leeds."

"What is a coat of arms?" Sarah asked.

"'Twas an honor bestowed upon our ancestor, but 'tis a kind of protection as well. The charge on the crest—the creature you see there—is called a cockatrice, a serpent-dragon said to have been born from a cock's egg, which you know cannot be since cocks do not lay eggs. Our ancestor once wore the image on his helm. 'Tis likely he wished to fright his enemies in battle, as if the creature itself would come alive and fight alongside." He looked at it again. "My father wrote about this coat of arms in his almanac, but I ne'er knew we had this rendering. William got it from our grandfather and thought I would wish to have it."

"I don't like it," Deb said.

"Why, pumpkin?" Japhet asked. "'Tis but a drawing."

"*Mam.*" Deb looked plaintively at her mother.

"The drawing will go in the parlor, methinks," Deborah said, and Deb stared at her. "Above the trestle bed. We'll take it down during Meeting."

"Yes, 'tis the best place," Japhet agreed. "Who will help me hang it?"

Young Japhet went with his father, and the rest of the children scattered to their work. Deborah took Deb's reluctant hand. They walked outside and began to pick apples from the lowest branches.

"The apple bears the promise of immortality," Deborah said. "Thou know'st Avalon? Apple-land. Paradise. 'Tis whither we shall go till we return again." She retrieved a knife from inside the house, then cut the apple across the middle and held up one half to reveal a five-pointed star.

"In each apple is hidden Morgan's pentacle—for protection." She took a bite and leaned against the tree. "I knew there was some reason I put this in my pocket today. Morgan shows her pentacle here as well." She pulled out the sand dollar Rachel had given her years before and handed it to Deb. "As thou become wise, daughter, thou shalt understand the promise in thy sight."

Deb looked at the sand dollar, then placed it in her own apron pocket. She picked another apple and balanced it on her palm. "Why shalt thou allow the picture to be hung in the house?"

Deborah plucked a few more apples. "The book my Granna gave to me is up the stairs just now, but I will tell thee one of its stories. This one is about sacrifice, which means to make sacred. Long, long ago 'twas the king who served the people, and not the other way around. He was chosen by the priestesses and served for five or seven or nine years as consort of the Goddess. He was honored as such and accepted his role. At the end of the term, he was sacrificed, made sacred, one with the Goddess, and his blood used to fertilize the crops. Now, I own 'tis grisly to our minds, but think how 'tis in our day. In the stead of the king giving his life for the people's good, the people give their lives for him and call it 'war.' 'Tis the same thing in reverse. For most battles are but a fight between rulers— or should be. But 'tis the soldier who fights and dies and is honored for his 'sacrifice.'"

She picked another apple and rolled it from hand to hand. "All martyrs, including Christ, know before that they will die, but they continue in their act, believing they give themselves for a greater good, and so are made sacred for it.

"Thou asked me why I allowed the coat of arms to be hung upon the wall. If the events of late have taught me nothing else, Deborah Fae, 'tis that we cannot escape our fates. We might only choose well." She ran her fingers through her daughter's hair, holding the fair strands up to the sun. "'Tis better a'times to set the inevitable into motion, then fight, pray, and hope for the best."

44

EBORAH WALKED up the steps of the store where Martha Thompson stood talking to Justine Smith, and Johanna waited beside her new mistress. When Deborah smiled at Johanna, she averted her face. The slight went unnoticed by the other women who paused in their conversation to greet her. Deborah observed that despite the brisk December day, Martha wore no cloak. Displaying her new azure satin gown, Deborah thought, with its yellow quilted silk petticoat.

"Thy new gown is handsome," Deborah said, reaching out to touch the sleeve. "Didst thou purchase it in Philadelphia?"

Martha moved away, seemingly offended by Deborah's familiarity. Then she stared at Deborah's swelling belly. "I heard 'twas so," she commented, "but I did not believe it. Thou carry'st *another* babe."

Deborah laughed out loud and patted her stomach. "Thou need'st not be so grim about it. I love my children, every one."

"And thou ought not gloat," Martha said. "Not all of us are so blessed." She turned toward Justine again. "As I was saying, Pennsylvania was a disappointment. The roads out of Philadelphia are nearly impassable, and I saw more heathens than ever before. When I told my companions the government ought send them west as others have done, they said that might come to pass, for Penn's sons don't court the Indians' favor overmuch, as did their father."

"Methinks William Penn was in the right," Justine said, "for is not an Indian a brother or sister, and ought we not love all equally? Besides, were it not for the generosity of the Lenape toward the first settlers, we should all have perished our first winter, even our first fortnight."

"P'shaw," Martha scoffed. "Thou ought praise no heathen for God's providence. He called us to this land, did he not? He should not have abandoned us. If the Lenape had not helped us, the Lord would have revealed another way. I'faith, our success is testament to that. And what of the Indian race? It dwindles, as well according to God's will."

"I cannot believe thou bearest such sentiments," Justine said.

"Even their old king concurs," Martha continued. "He spoke prophetically before his death, 'The English shall increase and the Indian decrease.'" She put her hands on her hips. "Providence hath blessed us in a wonderful manner with their decrease."

"Decrease?" Deborah asked. "Thou meanest death. And lo, methinks thou doth not understand the meaning of the king's words. He spoke only of what hath occurred and what will occur, not of the rightness in it. Indeed, mayhap all that hath been done to displace the Indian is not God-guided, but sin–"

"Sin!" Martha echoed. "*Thou* speakest of sin. Thou who, if I must say it, plays the witch with thy cures."

A shiver ran through Deborah and her breath came fast. She was suddenly aware of a small crowd that had gathered around them. Some stood by her and others by Martha, and just as many watched from the middle with Justine. She took a deep breath to steady herself. "Thy attempts to besmirch my name take nothing from my words. I put it to thee in a different light. How canst thou, as a Friend, say the death of the Indian race is good?"

Martha looked around at those she deemed to be supporters. No one said a word. She looked back at Deborah, her eyes narrowing as she smiled. "I hear there is a genuine physic here at the last." She gathered her skirts. "What a godsend he must be."

Deborah watched Martha bustle away to her cart, then turned back to face her neighbors. Jedidiah mumbled something about the store and went in. Jonas glanced at Deborah's belly and hurried away. Johanna nodded, as if understanding something, and went down the stairs. Esther Cordery patted her shoulder in support, then left. Soon only Justine remained.

"Do not trouble thyself about it," she said to Deborah. "Thou told her." She kissed Deborah's cheek, then went after Johanna.

So this is how it goes, Deborah thought, I care for them, and they discard me like scat. She felt exhausted suddenly and decided to return for provisions another day.

As she reached her cart, Dr. Hyme ran out of his cabin, calling to her. He was healthier looking, but still a bit thin.

"Good day to you, Mrs. Leeds," he said as he approached. Deborah nodded. He cleared his throat, then straightened his yellow silk cravat. "I have met with members of the medical community of Gloucester County and written a resolution barring untrained persons from practicing as physician. There will be a meeting of the inhabitants of Great Egg Harbour Tuesday next at the tavern, where I shall read the resolution and we shall vote."

Deborah leaned against the cart and stared at him.

"The crone is speechless. 'Tis rare, to be sure."

"Why canst thou not leave matters alone?" Deborah asked. "Neither Erin, Alice, nor I have brought any harm to any persons. Why canst thou not treat those patients who choose to come to thee, and we will treat those who come to us. 'Tis reasonable, is it not?"

"It is not. Not when the area hath one of my caliber."

"I was a healer in Burlington ere I came hither. I had ne'er any quarrel with the physics there. Why can it not be the same with thee? Alice was the lone healer when Erin and I arrived, and she bore us no ill, nor we toward her. We had treatments to teach the other."

"Therein lies the issue. You have nothing to teach me."

Deborah bridled at his arrogance. "Methinks I do. I will say this to thee again: Thy ilk reaches too readily for a knife when a gentler cure would do. Too many of you seem indifferent to the suffering of patients, for they languish while you improve upon your methods. I own there may one day be value in those methods, but on the whole they are now little more than butchery. And the worst is that you doctors do not own to it. You arrive with great pageantry to a township or village, denounce the wisdom of the healers there, then steal from them what you might—my herbs for one."

He shook his head. "A lovely speech, Madam. I must amend my prior remark about your new scribbling profession, for I think it more accurate to say you share your husband's talent. 'Tis a pity he is not a well-liked fellow, is it not? As for your herbs, I assure you, they are in better hands." He smiled tauntingly. "Wherever they may be."

Deborah reached out and grabbed his cravat. "Thou burned down our barn!" she shouted.

Several of her neighbors rushed over. He pushed her hand away and straightened his neckpiece, then turned to the onlookers. "The burden of a thirteenth child overcomes her." He turned away and walked toward his cabin. Over his shoulder he said, "One would think, would one not, that a pious Friend such as Mother Leeds would stop at twelve?"

Deborah held onto the cart, her heart pounding, her breath short and ragged. Her neighbors wore confused, indecisive expressions. They seemed to want her to tell them what to think. What can I say to them? she thought as she looked each one in the eyes. Either they remember who hath cared for them well these many years or they cast me aside.

She climbed into her cart, snapped the reins, and drove home.

45

APHET TOOK ON Deborah's cause as if defending his own livelihood, and was successful in stalling the meeting for a month. He learned that Hyme had presented his resolution before New Jersey's Assembly a couple of months before, hoping it would pass before anyone in Great Egg Harbour found out about it. But the Assembly had several concerns and decided a hearing was necessary to determine if there was popular support for such a measure.

In the meantime, Japhet talked to nearly everyone in the area, attempting to gather support for his wife, learning who was prepared to join in her censure.

"They're divided in twain," he told her a few days before the rescheduled meeting. Although the delay had given them more time to plan, Deborah was now clearly showing. A fifty-year-old pregnant woman raised the eyebrows of even the most tolerant Quakers, but for those of other faiths it was downright unnatural.

The night before the meeting, Deborah was upstairs gathering items she needed for the ritual of protection she planned to perform with Erin when Japhet came in and sat on the bed. He watched her put candles, thread, cloth, and herbs into her bag.

"Off to a patient?" he asked finally.

"Yes," she lied without looking at him, and closed her bag.

"Deborah," he said, "I fear my campaign against spirits hath harmed thee. As I went about there were those who would not speak to me, and many had to be convinced that whate'er ill will they harbored toward me must not be placed upon thee." He paused and ran his fingers through his hair. "I was wrong, Deborah—not for damning spirits, but for straying from the Light, for following a vain imagining. 'Twas as if I had no say. 'Twas glorious to speak and I reveled in it. And now I own some of it was pride." He looked at her, his face pained. "Should they refuse to allow thee to practice, I shall bear some of the blame."

"Japhet." She went over and sat next to him on the bed. "Thou judgest thyself far too severely. Those who treat thee curtly came still to me for healing, some yet do. In sooth, those angriest at thee have said they pity me. As for thy pride, I am glad thou dost see it. And if thou didst anyone harm, make amends. But that is all thou must do."

"But when I think of what thou hast suffered, and perhaps will, because of my zeal, I am ashamed."

She thought about this, allowing his apology to sink in. She couldn't deny there was some truth in what he said. But he ought not blame himself, she thought. 'Tis my fate I rise to meet. If only I could tell him of it.

Japhet turned to her suddenly and embraced her, and she felt divided— with him and not with him, her secrets a pointed wedge between them. She wanted to tell him about her ancient religion and her lineage. She longed to speak of Millicent and her great aunt Madeline, of Brigid and Marian and Morgan the Fate. She wanted to shout: This is not just my livelihood, and not just the censure of three women. It goes on and on—hath gone on and on.

But she was afraid to reveal any of that, even as he nuzzled her neck, telling her how comely she was, how courageous. She needed him at her side tomorrow and couldn't risk his rejection. Especially not now, with so much at stake. And so she sat there feeling horrid—knowing she was betraying them both—even as Japhet pulled her under the quilt.

About eighty citizens of Great Egg Harbour had squeezed into the tavern, sitting, standing, or leaning wherever there was space. The meeting was being held at midday so that those families coming from southern parts of the area could travel both ways while still light. Deborah sat huddled in her cloak in the front of the room, facing Dr. Hyme, Constable Covenoven, and three Assembly members. She felt bitterly cold despite the large fire in the hearth. Japhet and Erin sat on either side of her, with Patrick, Alice, and John in the front row as well.

One of the assemblymen spoke first and explained that the doctor's proposed resolution to bar untrained physicians had generated considerable controversy in the Assembly. Those residing in cities generally agreed with it, but those from rural areas argued that it would leave large portions of the colony without medical care at all. Some had also asserted that the colony had no precedent for such a measure—and that without a medical society there was no means to enforce it. He said that Dr. Hyme addressed those concerns by rewriting the resolution to allow exceptions for areas without a resident doctor and by vowing to organize a medical society. A majority of the Assembly had remained unconvinced, however, and it was finally agreed to hold a hearing. And who would be better than the residents of Great Egg Harbour, which had the benefit of both skilled female healers and a resident physician? If the people residing there voted for the act, the Assembly would make it law colony-wide.

When he finished speaking, Deborah glanced around at the crowd of Anglicans, Friends, and Anabaptists. Her children lined the back of the room, all twelve of them with their mates, as well as Erin's daughter, Ana, who had recently returned. Their arms were crossed, their expressions resolute, impenetrable.

The doctor stood and read the proposed law.

An Act to regulate the practice of Physic and Surgery within the Colony of New Jersey.

Whereas many ignorant and unskillful Persons in Physic and Surgery do take upon themselves to administer Physic and practice Surgery, in the Colony of New Jersey, to the endangering of the Lives and Limbs of their Patients; among them many possessing an Arrogance equal to their Ignorance. Many of His Majesty's Subjects have been persuaded to become their Patients and have been suffering thereby; for the Prevention of such Abuses for the future

Be it enacted by the Governor, Council, and General Assembly that from and after the Publication of this Act, that except in those districts with no resident Physician, no Person whatsoever shall practice as a Physician or Surgeon within the Colony of New Jersey, before he shall have first been examined in Physic or Surgery, approved of, and submit a Fee of Twenty Shillings to the Examiners.

And be it further enacted that if any Person or Persons shall practice as a Physician or Surgeon or both within the Colony of New Jersey without such Approval as aforesaid, he or she shall forfeit and pay for such Offense the Sum of Five Pounds; one Half thereof to the Use of any Person or Persons who shall sue for the same, and the other Half to the Use of the Poor.

Constable Covenoven asked, "Hath anyone a question to pose Dr. Hyme?"

Elizabeth Wood spoke first. "I noticed thy act uses only the word *he* for those physicians who would be approved and includes *she* for those who would be fined."

The doctor shook his head. "I understand you are betrothed to Nehemiah Leeds and to be sure you are not a neutral party. I use *he* because only gentlemen might attend the proper institutions by which they may learn physic. I say *she* because women are not physicians or surgeons and never will be."

Immediately Esther Cordery spoke. "I wish to know the reason for this resolution. I have attempted to recall one instance in which Alice Mathis, Deborah Leeds, or Erin O'Hara have caused suffering to their patients. I can think of none."

Deborah recognized Martha's snort and heard murmuring throughout the room. What had the doctor done, she wondered. Spread lies about them? For while we are not flawless—she remembered their underestimation of a fever Paul's brother John once had—I warrant we have cured many more than he.

"Constable," the doctor said, "I protest that the women are so forthright. Press them into silence and allow their husbands to speak for them."

Paul laughed. "You have not tarried long amongst Friends. Answer Esther Cordery's question."

Dr. Hyme said, "The purpose of this resolution is as *clearly* stated: to protect you and your family from abuses by those who pretend to know physic."

"I have a word to say on another matter," Esther said. "Granted we are no longer a Friend's colony—though we Friends are a solid majority in Great Egg Harbour—but I take issue with this entire procedure. Within our communities all persons of age have voice in decisions, yet today only men of property are permitted to vote. This offends me, as it ought my community, and would we had the power we once had, I grant it should not be so!"

There was much clapping and catcalls, both yea and nay, and Paul pounded on the table to regain control. "Sit down," he shouted. "Sit down!"

The crowd eventually seated themselves, but did not quiet. Paul said, "This is not a Friends' Meeting, as you say. Only male freeholders will vote." Several people clapped again. Paul brought his fist down on the table, his face red. "Next question!"

Abel Scull stood. "I wish to ask who shall approve the applying doctors?"

"Trained and educated physicians," Hyme replied. "Those details have yet to be arranged."

"Mightst thou be one of them, thus collecting a tidy profit?"

"That is irrelevant. Next question."

"Mayhap since thou hast recently arrived," Peter White told Hyme, "thou dost not understand that thy act maligns three good women, that it strips them of their livelihoods. They have caused no harm to any persons in Great Egg Harbour in the nearly three decades they have practiced. I have been cured of many a malady and was present when Deborah Leeds saved the life of dear Elizabeth Smith. In addition, they have often taken no remuneration for their services. They have served us well. We do appreciate the presence of a university-educated physician. Indeed thou hast patients a'ready. But I do not support this act which brings insult, mayhap e'en ruin, to three good neighbors, and I urge all present, Friend or no, to do so as well."

Much clapping followed, and Japhet squeezed Deborah's hand. She relaxed a little but kept her eyes on the doctor, who waited for the noise to die down.

"You must understand," Hyme said, "I am a trained physician. I received a medical education from one of the finest institutions in the world. I bear no ill will toward these women, but we cannot allow our hearts to dictate our actions. Even if 'tis true they have caused few abuses as of yet, with their limited knowledge, 'tis but a matter of time ere they will—or their daughters." He looked toward the back of the room. "Is not it so that Abigail Higbee Leeds, Ana O'Hara, and even young Deborah Fae will soon follow after their mothers? How can we men of reason allow ignorant women–"

"Silence!" Erin called out. "I will listen no more to this fop, thief, and coward. This *gentleman* set the Leeds barn afire, stole our herbs, and did not e'en remain to help put out the flames which he caused." All eyes focused on him. She continued, "If we are low and ignorant as you say, why have you the desire for our simples? 'Tis clear to me, our new doctor is the only person in this room to have caused injury to persons here."

"Constable," the doctor objected, "we discussed this when Japhet Leeds and his wife brought forth her allegations. You found no evidence that I burned down their barn. And I say to you again, I did not do it."

"I was there," Alice said. "When Deborah accused thee of it, thou wert silent and fell upon the rail."

"Madam, you were in the house," Hyme insisted. "You have no independent knowledge of my response to her ridiculous allegation. And as you are one who must cease your practice by this act, your word is hardly credible."

"To my neighbors it is," Alice retorted.

"I must speak." Jedidiah English stood. "I know not whether Dr. Hyme had a hand in the burning of the barn, but I have been silent these long years while Japhet Leeds strove to deprive me of *my* livelihood. Now, I will unburden myself. Let me state firstly that while I have left the Society for the faith of my father, I bear it no ill will. Neither have I a quarrel with any of its members, save Japhet Leeds.

"I recall well the day Daniel Leeds, bursting with pride, told my father and me that his son had been baptized an Anglican. Japhet deceived his father and as a result possesses the deed to his father's significant holdings, which he lords over us all. This man who ought not speak of others' sins hath decried the drinking of e'en molasses beer, which the Lord in his bountiful wisdom hath given us. Mr. Leeds would have us drink water, then. Mayhap water from the bathing trough."

Laughter and clapping issued from the crowd. Jedidiah paused until it died down. "Like those present, I have enjoyed good health from Mrs. Leeds, Mrs. Mathis, and Mrs. O'Hara. They possess considerable knowledge in the field of physic, and none hath died from their hands unless 'twas clear the Lord should take him. As we all know, this cannot be said of the numerous quacks who journey by. But let us not forget that they have neither been educated in their fields nor have they apprenticed with those who have. They were vital when we had no genuine physician, but that time hath passed. Methinks we ought protect ourselves with this act, enabling only those of the doctor's rank to administer to us." He sat down with a satisfied smile.

Jonas Vale spoke. "I must add to Jedidiah's words. Despite being in need of their services, I have a'ways wondered at the skills Mother Leeds, in particular, doth possess. Who hath e'er heard of one who heals withered arms and brings back from the dead?"

"Mr. Vale raises a point which deserves more careful inquiry," Hyme said. "'Tis long been ascertained in these matters that women derive their skills from, shall we say, unearthly means. My act shall protect you from that."

Mary Leeds's mother-in-law, Hannah Somers, spoke. "One moment thou accusest them of ignorance and the next suggest they have skill that surpasses human possibility."

The constable pounded on the table. "We stray from the matter at hand. Enough have spoken now. Let us vote."

Each property-owning male came forward to use the quill on the table to write 'yea' or 'nay' on a slip of paper which he folded and placed in the constable's hat. When all had voted and taken their seats, the constable read aloud each answer: "Yea, nay, yea, yea, nay, nay, nay . . ."

It seemed interminable and Deborah lost count. She panicked a little, then looked at Erin, who was smiling.

"Nay, nay, yea, nay." Finally the last "nay." Paul stood. "The resolution fails by a count of twenty nays to twelve yeas. We may all leave now."

"Stay," the doctor said, "I must speak again."

"Thou hast spoken enough for one day, Doctor," Daniel called out angrily.

Hyme put a hand on Paul's shoulder. "I must speak, Constable."

"Sit down everyone," Paul ordered with a groan. "Allow the doctor his say."

Dr. Hyme looked around the room. "A grievous error hath been committed this day, not simply an error involving false reason. I have cause to believe that Mrs. Leeds hath poisoned your hearts against me, not merely with the fiction of her barn, but with diabolical influence. For as I alluded to before, it hath been proved again and again that women who possess such powers did receive them through intercourse with the Devil."

Deborah gasped, feeling his lies like the stab of a knife.

"Thy speech offends me," Judith Steelman said.

"Pray forgive me, Madam, I am a physician and well accustomed to delicate matters. I will speak now specifically of the thirteenth child. I have noticed that none in the area do approach Mrs. Leeds in number of live births, and as a physician I must ask why. Why is it that you, her neighbors, have not the blessing she enjoys? I find the answer in that most important book, *Malleus Maleficarum.*" He took a volume from his leather bag, turned to a place he had marked with a feather, and read.

> *Concerning the Method by which Witches obstruct the procreant Function in both Men and Women . . . Obstruction is caused both intrinsically and extrinsically. Intrinsically they cause it in two Ways. First, when they directly prevent the Erection of the Member which is accommodated to Fructification. Secondly, when they prevent the flow of vital Essences to the Member in which resides the motive Force, closing up the seminal Ducts so that it doth not reach the generative Vessels, or so that it cannot be ejaculated, or is fruitlessly spilled.*
>
> *Extrinsically they cause it at times by means of Images, or by the eating of Herbs. . . . By the occult Power of Devils' Illusions Witches by this means procure such Impotence, namely, that they cause a Man to be unable to copulate, or a Woman to conceive.*

He closed the book. "Even Mrs. Leeds's former servant Johanna Conrad hath had no children and Erin O'Hara only one." Erin shouted in protest. He spoke over her, "My father and my father before him were both physician and priest. My great-grandfather was a Dominican and witchfinder. He alone sent three hundred witches, all of them women, to their rightful deaths. I have inherited his eye, my neighbors. You have a witch among you and she sits there. A woman well past childbearing, carrying within her her thirteenth child. The very Devil, no doubt!"

Deborah's son Daniel raced from the back of the room and seized the doctor by the shoulders. "Lying fop," he shouted. "Filthy papist knave!" Paul and Japhet pulled him off Hyme, then Paul ushered the doctor out the back door.

"Who should believe such a tale?" Daniel asked loudly, making sure all would hear. "To be sure, no Protestant. The bloody papist. Reading from a text written by a church that hath seen its last days."

Deborah looked around the room. Many of her neighbors stood in small groups talking. Some argued, others bore accusing expressions. She placed one hand over her belly and held the other out to Japhet. "Might we take our leave now?" she said.

46

LOWING split pine knots circled the grove. Their wafting smoke and sizzling pitch, like butter, gave the air a lemony scent. Deborah sat before the altar in the north, stringing nuts to place upon it. Her callused fingers were stiff and ached from the cold. She glanced at Erin, who in angry silence decorated an altar in the east with feathers from the black-headed gull, the blue heron, and the snow goose.

"When wilt thou tell me what is the matter?" Deborah asked.

Erin sat back on her haunches. "I must tell you? You sat there, giving him leave to say those things about you, rising not once in your defense. In your silence you seemed to invite him on."

"My silence permitted him to bring himself down. He is a papist. From hence all he says shall be considered by others in that light."

Erin slapped the ground. "I despise you English Protestants. So virtuous, so lifeless, arrogant, and cowardly!"

"When did you become Catholic?"

"My country is Catholic, or would be. Even here we quarrel, and you sit distant as the sun."

"Erin, I cannot change the fact I am English. And thou knowest I am not Protestant. Mayhap I ought to have spoken, but I felt as if my fate were being revealed to me. Since I left England I have known something would happen to me. I knew not precisely what, but I knew."

"You speak of your fate like you were a turtle crossing a well-traveled road. Where is your fire? You said you would not run, you did not say you would give him leave to squash you underfoot."

"Erin, I will say again, my silence showed him in his worst light. If I had shouted in protest, he would have had all manner of accusation about it. As it was, he lost and was himself pressed to shout. We won, Erin. Why dost thou challenge me so?"

Erin moved closer. "Because there was more to your silence than you say." She took Deborah's hand. "I know you are with child, but you seem somehow apart from yourself. Do you know something you have not revealed?"

Deborah pulled away and moved to the altar in the west. She decked it with oyster, clam, and mussel shells. Erin held the south altar's candle to a nearby bright pine knot to light it. Deborah said, "I know this child of mine is fated. I shall bear this special child, and be remembered for it."

Erin put the candle on the altar. "Be remembered? You speak of it with pride. The doctor shall take your charge and say 'tis a devil. He hath a'ready said as much. And you, Mother Leeds, will be remembered, as you say, as the mother of a devil. 'Tis the only way this tale will go." She spat upon the ground.

Deborah stared into the fire in the center of the circle. "That is likely true. But thou must remember that the truth, however distorted, shall be preserved as well. For without the tale, our way of life would be forgotten on our deaths. This age, as have all others, will pass away. Then, I tell thee, they will know of us again."

Erin stared at her for awhile, then said, "Those are the words of a martyr."

Deborah stood up. "Come, let us not speak of this. The girls await." When Erin didn't move, Deborah said, "Prithee, the girls must be cold. Let us begin the hand-fast. We can speak on this again."

"Very well," Erin agreed with a frown.

They held hands and with ritual recalled their connection to the earth, then cast a circle around the grove: breathing in the pine-knot smoke, sending it out again—concentric ripples holding them between the worlds, keeping them safe. Erin called toward the woods, "Deborah Fae, Ana Lynn, come hither."

Ana entered first, wearing a red linen gown. Her unbound, wavy dark hair fell to her waist. She was a woman now of eighteen. Deb followed a moment after, wearing her mother's old lavender damask gown. Her wheat-colored hair was twisted and wrapped around her head in a circle. She looked nervous but determined as she stood next to Ana in front of Deborah and Erin.

"Ere we begin," Erin said, "Ana Lynn, Deborah Fae, stand shoulder touching shoulder. Close your eyes and remember why you stand thus. Remember why you make this pact." She allowed them time. "Now turn and face the other and look into her eyes. If you must leave, do so now. There is no shame in walking away if your doubt remains too great. And if either of you are here simply to please either of us, you must go. For 'tis better you should walk into these flames than to forswear on this day."

"Look again." Deborah stepped forward. "Look into her eyes. Think on what 'tis you wish from this binding. Whisper it, then turn yourselves to me."

When the younger women faced her, Deborah said, "Ana Lynn, thou hast agreed to take Deborah Fae as thy assistant, to teach her the art, midwifery. Shalt thou teach her with perfect love and trust? Shalt thou correct her and praise her as she earns it? Shalt thou give her leave to soar beyond thee if she doth so, or to lag even as a snail? Shalt thou feel joy at her gain and sorrow at her loss? Shalt thou welcome her as assistant for two years, at such time thou wilt take her on as apprentice, tell her why thou shan't, or give her leave to go to another?"

"I will," Ana answered.

"Deborah Fae," Erin said, "you have heard the promise Ana hath made. Shall you accept her praise and her correction, even should it bear a sting? Shall you trust she hath your best interest in her heart when she offers same? Shall you permit yourself to know nothing, to watch and to observe, to see as well as listen to your teacher, Ana Lynn? Shall you give her leave to be wrong? To forget your feelings a'times? Shall you remember again and again why you are here? Would you say it now?"

"To learn the art of midwifery."

"Why do you wish to learn it?"

"I am pulled to do so."

"Deborah Fae," Erin continued, "shall you assist Ana Lynn, performing your duties with devotion, in love and trust, learning all that you are able for two years, at such time you are free to go, or to stay if Ana Lynn shall have you?"

"I will."

"Fast hands now to bind your pact."

They faced each other and shook hands.

Erin took a flaxen cord and bound their clasped hands together. "Holy Maiden, Mother, Crone," she said, "in thee whom we have our being, thou hast witnessed this hand-fast 'twixt teacher and student. I ask that thou look'st favorably upon their union. Bless them with health, prosperity, long life."

Erin and Deborah each took the free hand of her daughter, then walked to the fire and formed a circle around it. Smoke eddied above them in a rising cone. Somewhere beyond the grove an owl hooted and was answered by the distant "hoom-hoom" of a bear.

Still holding hands, they began to walk clockwise, slowly. When they had covered the circumference several times, Deborah stopped and sang,

> "Life and death and birth we go
> dancing the spiral 'round.
> Death and life renewed again
> the spiral will never end.
> Circle of life
> We are thee.
> Spiraling 'round
> We are thee.
> Life unending
> We are thee."

The words seemed even more powerful than when Deborah sang them at her first blood ritual with Granna and Millicent, for now she was passing on to her dearest the only treasure they had in a world eager to see them die out.

47

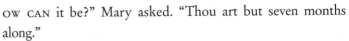OW CAN it be?" Mary asked. "Thou art but seven months along."

Deborah looked up at her from under the apple tree where she had been trying to spin, trying to enjoy the uncharacteristically warm day in late February, trying to avoid the awful truth of her physical distress. She held an arm up to her eldest daughter, glad that she had chosen today to visit. "Help me to the parlor."

Mary pulled Deborah to her feet and took her arm as they walked toward the house. A contraction came on, beginning with a tightening in her uterus that squeezed hot pain down her cervix and into her back. Deborah leaned heavily on Mary until it passed.

"Let us get thee to the bed," Mary said as they passed through the front door. "Deb," she called to her sister cooking at the hearth, "go after Alice and Erin."

"And Ana," Deborah said.

When they reached the parlor, Deborah went down on all fours on the bed, kneeling with her weight on her elbows. Mary brought over three animal skins and stacked them under her mother. "I'll see about cloths," she said and left.

Deborah heard the clanging of kettles as her womb contracted again. She called out, gripping the brown fur—feeling not like someone who had borne twelve live children but like a child herself, terrified, alone.

Mary rushed in. "I have left the cloths to Sarah and brought you water." She stood with the porcelain cup in hand.

Deborah, her teeth gritted and still holding to the fur, couldn't speak. Mary put the cup on the table by the bed. Then as if hearing an unspoken request, she sat beside her mother and dug her fingers into her lower back. The pressure provided an opposing force that somewhat neutralized the pain of the contraction. Deborah sat up, sweating.

"The pains are close together," Mary said. She wiped Deborah's face with a moist handkerchief, then handed her the cup of water. "When didst thy labor begin?"

Deborah sipped. "This morning, but I did not believe it."

Mary wiped her mother's face again. "I remember when I was young I would cling to thee and cry when thou wouldst leave to treat a neighbor, but soon as thou wert gone, I would play physic. My poor brothers and Yonder, they had many a treatment."

Deborah smiled. "Thou wert always a good girl. I am grateful thou art here. Uhhh." She thrust the cup at her daughter, then pitched forward again onto her elbows and knees. "Ahhh. Aahaahaahaahaah . . ."

She tried to picture the pain: hot hands strangling her womb. She imagined pushing them away and her own cool, gentle hands on either side of her womb, kneading it slowly, opening the door for her baby. The pain intensified, shooting through her back and down her legs. She lost the image of soothing hands and began to rock. The pain was huge now. It was everywhere in Deborah's body and she was at its center. Yelling helped. It helped to move her body, to drive her head into the animal skins again and again. But the pain grew so large there was nothing else. She couldn't breathe; she was suffocating. She screamed and screamed and screamed. Terrified. Dying. She was dying.

Mamma, Mamma, Mamma.

Mary's voice finally reached her, and she turned her head to look into her daughter's earth brown eyes. The terror fell away in clumps like fleece. She felt her daughter's fingers then, on her upper back; Mary's mouth by her ear, talking, as she had been all along. The pain drained from her legs, back, and womb. It became small again, menstrual-like. She took a breath.

"Yes, Mamma, thou art all right. Breathe, Mamma. Yes."

Deborah pushed herself up and fell back against the headboard. She felt a wash of gratitude, deeper than she'd ever known before. Gratitude at being alive. She began to weep.

Mary held her. "All shall be well, Mamma," she said. "All shall be well."

Erin rushed in, looking worried and doubtful, as if not wanting to believe Deborah was in labor. She ran to the bed with Ana close behind.

"Good day, Mother Leeds," Ana said, and put her hand on Deborah's shoulder. She nodded at Mary, who got off the bed. "Let us have a look, now, shall we?"

Mary helped Ana and Erin lower Deborah onto her back.

Ana put a horn on Deborah's belly to listen for the child's heartbeat. She frowned at Erin, then checked Deborah's dilation. "We've a bit to go yet, Mother Leeds," she said, her voice strained. "But it shan't be so very long."

As they helped Deborah sit up again, she asked Ana, "What worries thee?"

"Nothing," Ana said. "Do not trouble yourself about a thing. Take some of this." She squeezed several dropperfuls of black snakeroot tincture under Deborah's tongue.

For the next contraction, Mary took her position again, on her knees in front of Deborah, her head beside her mother's. Deborah felt no terror this time, and she never lost her daughter's voice. She said again and again, until she believed it, "I open. Open. Open. Open. Open. Ahhhhhhhhh."

Alice and Deb arrived in the middle of the contraction. When Deb saw her mother on her elbows, calling out, animal-like, she began to cry. "Deb," Ana said, "mayhap you might wish to hold her." Deb choked her sobs and walked toward the bed as her mother sat up again.

Suddenly Erin glanced about and snapped, "What are you doing here?" Everyone looked at the doorway where Johanna stood, fiddling with the sleeve of her gown.

"I was with her and Justine when Deb found me," Alice explained and gave Deborah a questioning look. "Johanna said she desired to help. I thought thou shouldst welcome more hands."

"Prithee," Johanna said, "I wish to remain. I am lonesome for your children and recall fondly the births I tended." Her head was downcast, but her large eyes looked up, exuding sincerity and deference. She might as well have been prostrate.

"Don't permit it, Deborah," Erin said. "Leave, Johanna. We have no need of you."

Deborah reached for her water, still panting a little, and took a sip, watching Johanna over the rim of the cup. Her pleading eyes called out to Deborah, and struck deep. There was something there Deborah wanted. If not wanted, something she had to have. She put the cup down. "I will thank thee for thy help," she said.

Johanna smiled. "I'll go to the well for more water." She left the parlor, her eyes trained ahead, Erin's piercing gaze following her.

Another contraction came on and Deborah went forward again onto her knees. When it eventually subsided, she started to sit back when another one began, just as strong. She took a gulp of air, nearly choking on it.

"We're there now," Ana said.

A third contraction began before the second was over. And then another after that. Deborah felt submerged in the pain. She tried to hear her friends and family, tried to feel Mary's fingers, but she was gripped by contraction after contraction. She didn't think; she didn't know where she was. Occasionally she remembered she was being held. She felt a finger, recognized a voice.

The unrelenting agony went on for nearly an hour. All the while Deborah gripped Deb's and Erin's hands, and Mary held onto her, speaking in her ear. Alice and Ana attempted to hear the child's heartbeat and encouraged her. Johanna was at the hearth most of the time, boiling water for cloths, and helping the girls prepare dinner.

Finally the contractions eased and Deborah sat up. Soon 'twill be over, she thought, nearly mad with pain. Soon I shall bear my child. "But my babe is only seven months," she protested.

"Shh," Alice said, "thou bearest the child. We shall tend to it." She put the horn on Deborah's belly and moved it around, frowning.

"What?" Deborah said. "Tell me!"

"Nothing, I told thee. Do not worry." Alice went over to a corner of the room where Ana was instructing Deb. Deborah looked up toward Erin who stood like a sentinel by the bed. Erin watched every move Johanna made after she hastened into the room and stacked blankets and skins on the floor.

"AAAHHH," Deborah exclaimed suddenly.

"Johanna," Erin said, "bring in the cloths, then go for more water."

"The floor," Deborah said, as her water broke. "Take me to the floor."

"Now, Johanna!" Erin demanded, when she hesitated.

The women helped Deborah onto the floor as she screamed again, then pushed. "No," Erin said. "Be still. Don't push or you will tear."

Ana and Alice crouched in front of Deborah, watching for the baby's head to crown.

"'Tain't breech," Ana said, from between her legs. "Ah, 'tis coming now. I see the head. A comely head of hair. Honey-colored methinks, like your own. Now, Mother Leeds. Push now. Push!"

Deborah didn't have to be told. Her instincts rose. She pushed and growled and pushed and growled and pushed, then suddenly the internal insistence ceased, and she tried to sit up.

"Stay, Mother Leeds," Ana said. "Damn! Don't move. The cord's wrapped about the neck. Don't move." Her fingers flew, unlooping it.

In her mind, Deborah saw her baby looking at her with blue eyes. Another girl. The child spoke, and her face distorted into shards . . .

"Damn," Ana said, "'tis wrapped twice."

. . . the way her dream people did when they spoke prophetically. The babe held her arms out to Deborah, but receded. I go now, she said, I go. Deborah thought she should shout NO, but was silenced by the serenity of the child's presence. I am so very young, the babe was saying, I should never survive. Deborah watched her daughter rise in the room, translucent. She realized then it was the child's spirit who had spoken. My daughter is dead.

"God in Heaven, what is that?" Johanna dropped the cloths on the bed and pointed toward the wall.

"Stay, Johanna," Erin said over her shoulder.

Farewell my child, Deborah mouthed, as she watched her settle into waiting arms. The Mother's arms. Brigid's arms.

"I see a demon," Johanna said. "The Devil!" Alice nodded at Erin, who ran over to Johanna and shook her. "You brute, leave me be," Johanna said and pushed Erin's hands away. "The child is a demon."

"No more, Johanna," Erin warned.

Brigid was tall and blue, shifting shape like fog in the wind.

"The child is a demon. She wished for it years ago. I heard her! And now the Devil comes at the last—for her thirteenth child. What other child should he desire?" Johanna pointed at Erin. "And you. The Devil took your body. I saw you make the child, you and Mother Leeds."

Erin grabbed Johanna's shoulders and threw her against the wall. "You saw nothing, you bedlam wench!" Johanna slid to the floor.

"Erin, come hither," Alice called, and Erin rushed over. She joined the other women in trying to revive the floppy, grey infant. "Come now, little one, don't leave us," Alice said.

The parlor door opened, but no one noticed at first. Dr. Hyme ran to Johanna and gave her a smelling salt. Young Japhet remained in the doorway.

"How dare you enter a birthing chamber," Erin said when she saw them. "Leave now, both of you." She glared at Deborah's son.

"The gentleman was fearful of his mother's health and asked me to come." The doctor motioned for Japhet to help Johanna and took a step toward the women. "That infant will die," he said. "'Tis clear I am needed."

Erin leapt up to block his approach. "Leave this room."

Brigid held Deborah's daughter, and Deborah felt at ease. She felt as if she were both mother and baby, rocker and rocked.

"Leave now," Erin said. "I shan't allow you to come forward."

Brigid began to dissolve slowly, like a drop of dye in water. From within the body, Marian emerged, green and lovely, smiling down at Deborah, the child still in her arms.

Johanna was on her feet again, pointing. "Do you not see the Devil? The tail forked as the night. Her child is the Devil's child."

Dr. Hyme looked in the direction Johanna indicated. "Just as she says–"

Erin ran toward them both, hitting them hard with her body. They crashed into the other room and Erin grabbed the doorjamb to keep from falling herself.

"She is gone," Ana said softly.

As Erin slammed the door shut, Johanna shrieked, "The Devil . . . he touched me!"

"She is gone," Ana said again.

Marian and Deborah's daughter disappeared.

"Fare thee well," Deborah whispered.

Erin whirled around. Both Deborah and Deb stared at the ceiling. Erin picked up a cloth, dipped it in a bucket, then knelt beside Deborah and rubbed the cool water over her face.

Ana handed the dead infant to Mary, who wrapped up the tiny body and left the room. Then Ana began to cry. "No, 'twas not thee," Alice said, putting an arm around her. "The babe was so small. She'd not have lived long."

"What did you see?" Erin asked Deborah quietly.

Deborah glanced at Deb, who knelt beside her, still staring at the ceiling. "Brigid and Marian held my babe."

"Marian?" Erin asked. "Johanna said she saw the Devil." She looked at the coat of arms on the wall and nodded. "She saw Marian and that bloody crest. I ought to have known. Worry not, *a stór*, I'll set things to right." She kissed Deborah's forehead and left the parlor.

Deborah leaned back on the blankets and skins behind her. Ana and Alice talked intently in a corner of the room. When Deborah reached out and touched Deb's arm, her daughter looked at her, too stunned to cry. Deborah put her hand on Deb's shoulder and pulled her down. "Come, my little apple blossom," she whispered in her ear. "There is something thou must do."

Ana and Alice were feeding Deborah chicken broth in bed when Erin burst into the parlor. The constable, Johanna, the doctor, and young Japhet followed.

"I saw it," Johanna declared. "The child was normal at the first, and then became a demon before our very eyes."

"'Tis the crest, you fool," Erin said. "The coat of arms hangs there, above the bed." She pointed at the wall, then gasped. The space was empty.

"I told you," Hyme said, "'twas the very Devil she– I saw. We both bore witness. It had the tail of a serpent, the body of a dragon. 'Twas covered in green scales, with huge bat wings, and the head of a horse."

"No, no," Johanna said, "it had the head of a cock, not horse."

"However it appeared," Hyme said, "we must go after it at once."

"Where are Mary and Deb?" Paul asked.

"The Devil child ate 'em, I warrant," Johanna replied.

"Shall you do nothing, Constable?" the doctor demanded. "This spawn of hers is loose."

"Be still, Doctor, we don't know that as yet."

"If you shall do nothing, I will. Come along, Mrs. Conrad. Let us sound the warning bell." He and Johanna left the room.

Japhet went to his mother's bed. "Prithee forgive me, Mamma, for fetching the doctor. I was coming in from the fields with an injured knee, and as I neared the house, I heard thee screaming, and Johanna came out arunning and said thou wert dying and I must go for Dr. Hyme. And though he is loathsome, he is university educated and, and..." His voice choked. "I thought thou wert dying."

"You made a fool's choice," Erin said. She pulled away from Paul and went to the bed. "Deborah, where is the drawing?"

"I know not."

"You must have seen who took it away." Erin looked plaintively at Ana and Alice, who also seemed mystified. "Deborah," she said more sharply, "this is no idle gossip. 'Twill soon be over, as you said before, if you do not come forward with the drawing."

Deborah looked out the window at apple trees that would soon begin to bud. "'Tis not over, Erin," she said. "I'faith, 'tis only just begun."

48

HEY CAME for her two days later—another midday meeting at the tavern. Deborah was still weak, bleeding, and grieving the loss of her child, but she insisted on walking in on her own, holding to no one's arm, her head high. Paul directed her to a table in the front of the room, and this time she sat facing the crowd. He seated himself at the table next to her along with Dr. Hyme.

Opposite Deborah were Erin, Patrick, and Ana, Alice and John, and Japhet. Deborah's children and their families sat at the next tables back. Behind them were her neighbors, the same who had attended the last meeting. But something had happened in the two days she had lain in bed. The doctor, and Johanna as well she supposed, had riled her neighbors against her. She felt it. People she'd healed, friends and acquaintances she'd had for years would not meet her eye.

Paul stood up. "I have called this meeting because very serious accusations have been brought against a woman we all know. They are grievous charges, and I wish to air them. Dr. Hyme, shall you begin?"

He rose. "The Latin word *doctor* comes from *docēre*, meaning to teach. I expected that the need for someone of my learning would be great in the New World, and so I have found it to be. Since my arrival, nearly all have welcomed me save Mrs. Leeds. Knowing her to be wife of Mr. Japhet Leeds, gentleman and yeoman, I honored her with the respect due to one of her station. In return, she hath slandered me. I know not why she bears me such ill will, save she may know that as an educated physician, I see the harm she may one day cause to her neighbors through her ignorance.

"Since the resolution to regulate the practice of physic and surgery failed due to pity, I agreed to allow her to continue treating all those who wished to seek her out. But I have come to see the situation is far worse than I thought. Mrs. Leeds hath knowledge of medicine beyond what any woman could possess. I have heard stories about her curing of limbs which God had willed to lay dead, her use of nefarious herbs no one should touch, her wanderings into the wood at night in the company of Mrs. O'Hara and her daughter. I shudder to think of the demons they have called forth. Knowing this, my heart was heavy indeed when I went forth to aid in the birth of her thirteenth child."

A hush had settled over the listeners. No one coughed or fidgeted. He seemed to realize he had them in his thrall, and he paused like an orator sure of his audience. With an assertive nod, he went on, "We all know thirteen is the number of the Devil, as it is based on Eve's punishment: thirteen cycles of menses, following the turning of the moon. There are those yet among us who cling to pagan practices, who celebrate this monthly flux, which is actually God's curse on womankind. And we good Christians have sought to rid the world of their evil influence. We formed a most holy Church, but the women in particular did remain in their hamlets, calling forth the Devil in his many guises, assuming knowledge of medicine as well as holy matters none on earth should know."

He raised a forefinger. "Those like my great-grandfather, the witch-finders, did rout out these women and men—for like Eve, woman again tempted man to join her in sin—and did see them burned or hanged. I let it be known at our last meeting that I inherited my great-grandsire's eye. Mother Leeds is a witch and she must be put down."

A collective gasp echoed in the room.

"The man is touched," Peter White said and stood up. "Dr. Hyme, ere thou malignest such a fine woman, thou must first put forth thy evidence."

"Might it be you are blind and deaf? Were you not present when Mother Leeds brought Elizabeth Smith back from the dead? Have you not heard of the fright which John Covenoven did have when he found his dog impaled upon a stake of his fence? And Jonas Vale—rise and tell your story."

Jonas stood only part-way. "Please sir, I am afeared to speak. What if she sends the Devil after me?"

"You must speak," Hyme said, "'tis the only way to be rid of it."

Jonas glanced at Deborah, then looked away. "'Twas but two nights past when I was abed and my wife and I did hear a noise. Thinking it a turkey I took up my gun and walked outside. As you know, the moon was dark, and I could see nothing but a shadow upon my fence. I heard a squealing kind of noise, like a pig, but also like a bird. I felt a chill run up and down my back, the likes of which I have ne'er known. I took a step toward the fence. When I was but feet away, I saw the shadow was a beast. As I watched, it spread great wings and rose into the air with a scream. In fright I marveled at this awhile, but I have seen much in my life I cannot explain, so I returned to bed, telling my wife 'twas a crane and it had got away."

Jonas fingered his cuffs. "When we awoke the next morning, we found two of our hens were gone. I might ne'er have thought of it again save later that day, for no reason at all, the butter soured. Then the doctor rode up to warn me of this beast, the Leeds Devil he called it. 'Twas then I knew it must be he I saw upon my fence. I can only praise God, the Devil did not snatch me!" He wiped his forehead with his handkerchief and sat down.

"Now, Mrs. Conrad," Dr. Hyme said.

Johanna avoided Deborah's gaze as she walked from the back of the room and faced the audience. She held her hands clasped before her. Deborah noticed they shook.

In a quavering voice, Johanna said, "I have known Mother Leeds longer than anyone in this room 'cepting her husband and Mrs. O'Hara. I have been wet nurse to several of her children, as well as servant, as most of you know. I have a'ways thought her to be the kindest sort. But now the doctor hath stripped the blinders from my eyes. She only pretended at being kind so I would be silent about her dealings with the Devil."

Johanna clutched her hands more tightly. "As well, I believe Mother Leeds hath bewitched me. She hath cursed me with the Devil's sight, which I did not have till I came to her, nor in the years I was away. In my time with her, I strove to rid myself of the sight, but she encouraged it over and again." She looked up toward the ceiling. "When I went to her house as she gave birth to the beast, I thought I desired only to help. But now I know the Lord sent me thither to bear witness to the birth whose conception I saw as well. I saw Mother Leeds copulate with the Devil."

"The woman is mad." Deborah's son Daniel jumped to his feet. "We all know that. My mother hath been kind to her—treating her as one of our family, and she repays her in this manner. Copulate with the Devil? 'Tis ridiculous!"

"Constable." Esther Cordery stood up. "As a Friend and a Christian, I am deeply troubled at these accusations of witchcraft leveled against another Friend. Equally troubling is the level of superstition and fancy I hear bandied about as if 'twere fact. I have spoken with the Leeds family and they all say an image of a cockatrice was hung in the parlor. The cockatrice bears the same description as the demon creature which hath been spoken of. The eldest daughter says she took the dead infant and buried it under a tree. I own the birth was a swirling event, but I am convinced the matter is explainable. To Jonas Vale I ask, was it not the doctor who put the idea of a Leeds Devil into thy head? Thou said thyself thou wouldst not have thought of it otherwise."

Many eyes turned toward Jonas, who slumped as if to avoid them. "Friends," Esther addressed the Quakers, "we must not allow ourselves to be swept along by those who adhere to superstitions we have long rejected." She sat down.

"I must concur with young Daniel," Justine Smith said, "for I believe Johanna Conrad to be mad. I agreed to take her on because I did desire the help, and she was pleasing for a time, but e'er since the doctor got hold of her I can do nothing with her. I would say as well it seems the doctor doth worship the Devil himself, for all the power he gives him. Is not the Lord the supreme being? Deborah Leeds hath an extraordinary gift for healing. She saved my daughter's life. But I say to you my neighbors, if her healing is of unearthly nature, to be sure 'tis God-given, not Devil-derived."

"Wise men have long agreed," Dr. Hyme stated, "that any who heals without having studied under a physician is a witch, and witches must die. I would say as well that witches have been found amongst the Society of Friends before." Over protests from the crowd he said loudly, "In the *Pennsylvania Gazette* but five years ago, Benjamin Franklin wrote of such a case near Mount Holly. And there was in Ireland the Reverend Alexander Peden who went along to Meeting with a Friend and saw the Devil himself, as did his companion. Now, I do not say you Friends worship the Devil—certainly not—but only that your sect wants for vigilance of its members, the lacking of which invites him in."

"You are the lowest vermin of the earth," Erin said. "Deborah, Alice, and I are abler than you and you cannot abide it. You burned down the Leeds barn, filched our herbs, failed to pass an act forbidding us to practice, so now you deem to hang her—and me as well, I should imagine. Well, you shan't succeed. These Friends possess good sense, and despite your assurances to the contrary, they know when they have been affronted."

"Dare you deny," Dr. Hyme asked, "that you and Mrs. Leeds go into the wood at night?"

"'Tis no concern of yours."

"What do you there?" the constable inquired.

"We gather herbs," Deborah answered, "and sing praises."

Jonas's sister Grace stood to say, "The Leeds Devil was sent to punish us for turning from Mother Leeds. 'Tis the code of the coat of arms, is it not? The beast on the crest hath risen in defense of his lady. We ought bow before her, not damn her in this way. Only then shall the creature be appeased."

"I concur with a portion of this," Justine said. "Let us send the doctor from these parts. We need not his degree nor his university training. For lo these many years, Friends Deborah and Alice and Erin O'Hara have healed our families and we have known good health. I do not believe there is a creature seeking vengeance, but indeed should we harm this woman to whom many owe their gratitude—and some their very lives—so should we deserve any misfortune that might come down upon us."

"I will say as well, there is no creature," Elizabeth Wood agreed. "'Twas the image on the coat of arms. In the stir of the birth, Dr. Hyme and Johanna thought they saw a beast but saw only the crest, which bears a cockatrice."

"Yes," Alice said, "but I would add that the doctor saw nothing, and Johanna is mad, for she saw a devil in a drawing. Do not forget, my neighbors, there were others in the birthing room who saw none of this. Ana O'Hara, Mary Leeds Somers, Deborah Fae Leeds, and I were all there, and none saw this creature. None save Johanna."

"I saw the beast," Hyme said. "And I know the difference 'twixt a drawing and a devil. It snorted and shrieked and thrashed its dragon tail about the room. I thought it would devour us all ere it flew out the window."

"No," Johanna said, "it followed us out the parlor. I felt its breath upon my neck, then saw it fly up the chimney."

Deborah stood up, and the room fell quiet. She looked at each of her neighbors, remembering the illnesses she had cured, the children she had helped birth. She said, "'Twas no beast which Johanna saw. 'Twas the Goddess herself. Johanna saw Marian hold my babe in her arms. Marian with her fish's tail."

Japhet stared at her. The silence throbbed in Deborah's ears.

"So you hear," Hyme said, "she owns the Devil was in the room."

"The Goddess was in the room," Deborah said.

"They are the same," he said. "What is not of Father, Son, and Holy Ghost is of the Devil. You did hear her admit to it, my neighbors! The Devil came upon the town and took her child, which he had spawned, and turned it to a beast—a creature that shall torment us till we are rid of the mother and it as well."

"I concur," Martha Thompson said. "You heard Deborah Leeds's confession. All the while pretending to be Friend when she's a pagan of the wood. And now there's some beast loose amongst us. Let us take up a party and hunt the creature down."

Esther stood and glared at Martha. "We are a tolerant people, let me remind you. However Deborah speaks now, 'tis clear to me she is yet a Friend. For so hath it been for me as well. When I am alone, my own image of God is female. A woman dressed in white, holding out a lily to me. God is not one sex, but both, and appears in images we hold sacred."

"Woman is not sacred," the doctor said. "She is whore, tramp, defiled. She bears blood and pain of birth because she caused the fall of man."

Exclamations of protest erupted from the crowd. Ana spoke over it, "Woman gives birth to boy and girl as the Goddess gives birth to the world each spring."

"Friends, friends," Justine said, holding up her arms to silence the crowd. "The doctor hath shown himself this day. For the Scriptures say we are all made in God's image. And as our founder, George Fox, and Margaret Fell did teach, both men and women possess the Light. Our Lord speaks to all equally. And we can use our reason to know this is so. Why should the Lord desire to toss aside half his creation? Why did he give me a sound mind if he did not desire me to use it? Friends, we have heard sentiments like his before. We must reject them as well as the one who hath spoken them. We must remember the Light lives within us all. If the Light speaks to Deborah Leeds and Esther Cordery in a female form there is no harm to it. For it is as Esther hath said, the Lord appears to each of us in images we hold sacred."

Peter White stood. "I must own I am astonished by Deborah Leeds's revelation. As well, methinks Martha Thompson was in the right in part, for it appears she is not Friend at all but of the Old Religion." He cleared his throat. "I have long held we no longer hunt witches because men of reason know they never existed. But now I see the troubling truth— witches were persecuted for their faith, as were we. Knowing that as I do, I will protect Deborah Leeds with all I have, as I urge all Friends to do. For should Hyme succeed in damning her to her death because she holds a differing image of God, shall we Friends be not next? Indeed, he hath a'ready said we invite the Devil. And to those of other faiths, I say, if he comes after Friends, what should keep him from coming after you? Anabaptists, were you not, as we, driven out of England by those with his intolerance? And Anglicans, do what is just for your neighbor Mother Leeds, who never hath brought you any harm, who hath served you long and well. And protect us as well, your neighbors, who may be next. To all of you I say, rise up. Friend or no, rise up!"

The doctor stepped back as fifty men, women, and children stood.

"Sit down," the constable said. "We must have order."

"No," Justine said. "We are the charge on our neighbor's helm. We have risen in defense of her, and we will sit no longer."

Hyme shouted, "Fools! You know not what you do."

"Her child is a demon," Johanna shouted. "It shall torment us all."

More people began to stand, some tentatively, others boldly, until nearly everyone in the room was on their feet.

"Listen to me," Hyme said. "I know of what I speak. I am a witch-finder. Give me leave to save you. I shall banish the Devil. I *will* do it."

Japhet was the first. He turned his back on Dr. Hyme and stood still, his hands clasped behind his back. John and Alice and Erin and Patrick and Ana were next, and then the motion rippled toward the back of the room. Seventy men, women, and children stood silent, their backs to Dr. Hyme.

Paul had no gavel but his voice boomed, "There will be no charges filed against Deborah Leeds in this matter. We may all leave."

And so they did, crowding around Deborah, pledging their assistance, expressing sorrow at what had happened that day and for the loss of her child. Gradually, they made their way outside.

After awhile, Japhet pulled Deborah away from the others. "Why didst thou never tell me?" he asked, his voice choked.

In his eyes she saw the pain of years of distance between them. What could she say now to explain? What could she add to what had happened? She pointed back at the tavern. "This, Japhet, this accusation is what I feared."

He shook his head sadly, as if to say she could have trusted him, should have trusted him.

"Thou canst not know how thou wouldst have responded, Japhet. And neither could I. Till thou art in the predicament thyself, thou canst not know who will stand for thee and who will betray."

"I stood for thee, Deborah," he said in a hoarse voice. Tears came to his eyes.

She reached up and touched his hair. His grey eyes felt like home. "I will tell thee everything, Japhet." Tears slipped down her cheeks.

"A feast," someone shouted behind them. "Deborah! Japhet!" They turned around to see who had called them. "We ought to raise a feast," Andrew Steelman said.

"Yes," said Justine. "John slaughtered a hog this morning, and our man-servant roasts it as we speak. We shall bring it over as soon as we might."

As other neighbors who lived close by chimed in with what they had to bring, Japhet put an arm around Deborah and held her tight. "A feast at our farm. 'Tis a wonderful idea. Come around, all of you, when you are able."

They headed toward their horses and carts. Deborah stopped to look for Erin but didn't see her. The smile faded from her face. She pulled away from Japhet and went searching among her neighbors, asking if they had seen her. No one had since leaving the tavern.

Deborah hurried back and entered. There on the floor by the table where Deborah had sat, Erin lay bleeding from the chest. "No," Deborah screamed. "No, no!"

Many people ran in. Some then raced to get the constable. Dr. Hyme must have stabbed Erin, they said. Outraged citizens raced to the doctor's cabin and found him packing his trunk. Paul took him into custody as he indignantly proclaimed his innocence.

Deborah knelt on the floor, her fingers over the bloody rip in Erin's gown as if to apply pressure, but not doing so. Deborah was only partially aware of the other people in the room—she felt the warmth of Japhet's arm around her waist—but couldn't make sense of anything that was happening. Erin was dazed as well, and seemed to be trying to speak.

"Shh, dear," Alice told Erin. "There will be time enough for words. Save thy strength." She eased Deborah's hands away, opened Erin's bodice, and dabbed with a cloth to find the source of the blood. "She will be well," Alice exclaimed. "'Tis but a shallow wound." She put the cloth over the slice and pressed with both hands to stop the bleeding.

"Deborah will wish to nurse her," Alice told Patrick, "so when the bleeding ceases, prithee take her to the Leeds house. I shall stitch the wound there when I am certain the bleeding will not begin again. Oh," she addressed Japhet, "what of the feast?"

Japhet looked at his wife. "We will have it still," he replied. "When Deborah returns to herself, she shall desire the company of her friends."

Patrick lifted Erin gently and carried her to their cart.

"Erin is not dead," Japhet told Deborah again and again as he led her to their own cart.

Deborah didn't hear him. She was listening to Rhiannon's birds singing for her, singing for Erin, singing for them all.

She seemed unable to climb into the cart herself, so several of her sons lifted her into it.

The birds continued to sing as the tragedy that had taken place in the tavern revealed itself in Deborah's mind. Johanna and Erin were quarreling. Erin called her a daft, pop-eyed fool, and Johanna sprang toward her, calling her the Devil. Erin pushed her back against the bar and Johanna grabbed a knife which lay there. She pushed Erin to the floor and fell with her. They struggled for the knife; first Johanna had it, then Erin; finally, Johanna stabbed, aiming for Erin's heart, cutting only her breast instead.

Erin is not dead.

Still clutching the knife, Johanna ran out the back door and seized the reins of a horse at a post. She was riding now toward the Little Egg Harbour River. Her black hair streamed behind her, her mobcap long gone. At the bank, she drew the horse up sharply and jumped down. She picked up a branch, hit the horse's rump, and watched it gallop away from her, toward home. She ran her fingers through her hair and shook it out. Then she took off her shoes and stockings. Without bothering to lift her dress, she waded into the river. She squatted and stabbed the water. After several fruitless jabs, she brought the knife up with a small fish impaled upon it. Holding the fish before her like an offering, she waded deeper. Her clinging gown turned black in the water. She raised the impaled fish above her head and shouted, "I have killed the Devil in Erin!"

Erin...in...in

She took the fish off the knife and watched it flap slowly in her hand. Then she threw it, almost dead, toward the middle of the river. It splashed once, then disappeared. She gripped the knife again and sliced a line down the inside of each forearm. "Pappa! Pappa!"

Pa...Pa...Pa

"I have killed the Devil in me." She waded deeper into the river, her bloody arms out in front of her, palms up, until she collapsed. The brackish current carried her away.

Deborah opened her eyes. She lay on blankets spread over the parlor floor. Deb sat beside her, holding her hand. Erin rested on the bed, Patrick and Alice tending her.

"Mamma." Deb touched her mother's hair, her lips trembling.

Deborah sat up and hugged her. "'Tis all right, my dear heart, weep. Weep now if thou must." Over Deb's shoulder she said, "Patrick, prithee tell one of my boys to go after Paul. Tell him from me that he will find Johanna in the river." Patrick hesitated a moment with a look at Erin, then left the room.

Ana came in carrying three mugs of cider. "Mother Leeds, I thought 'twas your voice. So pleased to see you awake." She put the mugs on the table and stood by her mother's side. "Twenty and five women in there raise a feast for both of you."

Deb helped her mother up and they walked to the bed. "Erin, I nearly lost thee," Deborah whispered, taking her hand.

She smiled wearily. "You will not be rid of me so easily. That daft, troubled—"

"Erin, Johanna is gone now." Erin closed her eyes briefly. "Thou wert in the right about her," Deborah said. "I could not heal her. And it nearly cost me thee."

Erin watched her awhile before speaking. "Some will not be healed, Deborah. They leave this life with their wounds undisturbed."

Deborah didn't know if Erin intended to refer to her also, but the remark penetrated, leaving her shaken. She saw her mother and grandmother inside of her—as they'd always been—fighting for her soul. She had been driven by it, by them. She had convinced herself she'd be made sacred—witch-like, Christ-like—and join the company of martyrs. She had told Deb to destroy the coat of arms.

But it was Johanna who had died. Johanna she could not save. Johanna, the fractured one, who died for her.

And yet, she thought—for this was also true—she had wanted to unburden herself of her secret, to worship openly. She wanted these Quakers, her friends and patients, to stand up in her defense. To save her life, for once.

"There is talk of seeing the doctor on his way," Ana said. "Nearly everyone aims to escort him out of town, if he is not gone of his own come morn."

"What do the others say?" Alice asked. "Are there any who believe this devil creature is about?"

"The Friends say 'tis superstition, nothing to the story in the least. Some, like Grace Vale, now say the creature is a kind of angel, avenging Mother Leeds, and henceforth will appear whenever wrongdoing is afoot. Still others say the creature *was* a devil that will leave with the doctor who invoked him. Some do believe the doctor's claim that Mother Leeds gave birth to a devil child, but they are a small part—none others pay them heed. You are a heroine, Mother Leeds. They say you shall be remembered; they shall sing songs of you."

Deborah looked at Erin, knowing there would be no songs. They had escaped with their lives and their livelihoods. They had defeated the first university-educated physician to arrive in Great Egg Harbour. They would raise their mugs in cheer and triumph. But Dr. Hyme was only the first. They would feast today. But that was all.

THE LEGEND,

continued

THE LEEDS DEVIL terrorized the good people of New Jersey for five years—until enough were convinced to send for a Catholic priest to exorcise the demon.

The priest stood, surrounded by Leeds denizens, and spoke a brave prayer, calling on the assistance of several saints. Then as if the heavens themselves had opened, a great cry was heard. The creature appeared, flapping its long, jagged wings over the priest's head. He clutched his crucifix and prayed louder. Finally, the demon shrieked again—an angry, pitiful scream—and disappeared.

The townspeople looked at one another, but no one spoke.

"God hath banished the Leeds Devil for one hundred years," the priest declared.

A murmur began as they all whispered at once, then a woman called out the question they shared, "One hundred years, Father? Why shan't God banish the Devil for good?"

"One hundred years," the priest repeated, and mounted his horse.

Afterword

I was about ten the first time I heard of the Leeds Devil. Sitting around the kitchen table in my grandmother's house in Absecon, I listened to her and my mother chuckle over the exploits of one of my great aunts. It seems a local newspaper columnist had reported that Texas claimed that the Leeds Devil was really the Texas Devil. That was too much for my aunt. She wrote the paper and informed them—tongue in cheek—that she just happened to be flying to Texas and would return the devil to its rightful home.

Even at that age, I was struck not only by the humor with which my family regarded the Leeds Devil, but the pride. My aunt affirms that the creature was universally known by our family name until declared the state's demon in 1939 and its moniker changed to the Jersey Devil.

I was always proud, too, of the family connection, as well as curious. Most stories about the legend have focused primarily on the child—which makes sense—but the salient question for me has always been *why* Mother Leeds was accused.

I gained some understanding of this when, as a sophomore at the University of Missouri-Columbia, I took a graduate-level history class, half of which was devoted to the Salem witch trials. I pored over resources in the library and realized I had an accusation of witchcraft in my own family.

Soon after graduating, I moved to San Francisco and began hearing about "the Goddess," which I thought at first was a feminist linguistic rendering, like "congresswoman." Then I learned that substantial archeological findings and literally dozens of books provide evidence that a once nearly universal, Goddess-centered religion existed for thousands of years and predated Christianity. I also discovered theories about witches, including that they had been respected leaders of the remnants of that religion, who were persecuted by the clergy. And too that witches were healers and midwives targeted by the rising medical establishment. I began to consider that my ancestor Mother Leeds might have been a witch, a healer, or perhaps both.

In the summer of 1987 I went back-packing in Europe and found in every museum and sacred site the physical evidence of the Goddess-centered religion I had read about. When I returned, I took a writing class in which one assignment was to describe a skeleton in the family closet, so I wrote about the Jersey Devil. My classmates urged me to expand the piece. Since I had covered the basic information of the legend, I wrote a fictional scene, eventually integrated into this book. When they asked for still more, I realized I had a story to tell. So on the Winter Solstice of that same year, while sitting in a café with my dear friend Anah Coates, this novel was conceived. I remain deeply grateful to the members of that tiny writing class: Anah, Lenel, the late Karen Hoggatt, and our teacher, Wendy Williams.

After working on the novel for more than a year, I entered the M.F.A. Creative Writing program at Mills College. I am grateful for the astute, constructive criticism and support of my classmates, and especially thank Wendy Dutton, Judy Myers, and Pier Roberts, who remained perceptive critics after graduation. I am thankful as well to my writing professors, Sheila Ballantyne and Diana O'Herir, Ph.D., for their challenges and guidance. Marilyn Chandler McEntyre, Ph.D., recognized what I was trying to convey and enthusiastically urged me toward it. Dr. Madeline Kahn's eighteenth-century literature class immersed me in the language and mores of the time. She also introduced me to the idea that the truth is preserved even in distorted tales.

Soon after graduating from Mills, I completed the book—or so I thought—and began sending it out. During the time it took to find a publisher, I relied heavily upon the suggestions and friendship of my current writing group, which in several incarnations has included Charlotte Allen, Theresa Dutton, George Franklin, Sheila Harrington, Mary Klein, Craig McLaughlin, Cristina Salat, Susan Shors, and Starhawk. Other insightful readers have been Martha Davis, Ann Flowers, Elizabeth Oakley, Margo Perin, and members of my book group: Marilyn Chuck, Ginny Kirsch, Barb Lester, Gina Nellor, Holly Smith, and Phyllis Usina.

A great source of strength has been the unwavering support of my parents, my sister, Sheila Stratton, and Cybele, who always told the truth. Finally, I thank all those I didn't name: the friends, family, colleagues, clients, acquaintances, and members of the Reclaiming community who over the years have buoyed me with their enthusiasm for this story.

Many people lent their expertise in producing this book. I couldn't have asked for a better editor than Waimea Williams, who was generous with praise as she fixed what needed to be fixed. Elizabeth Oakley has been a never-ending source of encouragement and did a wonderful job copyediting the manuscript; Pat Davis proofread the final manuscript and offered insightful suggestions on an earlier version; Lissa Herschleb painted the beautiful art for the cover; Kara Adanalian did the striking design; and ever-patient John Richards did the page composition. Finally, I thank Julia Chitwood of Bay Island Books for her keen editorial eye and for allowing me an unusual amount of input into the production process.

I am indebted to the experts who read the manuscript for accuracy: Professor Anne Brannen, who also generously provided me with the Irish phrases; Lisa Saiman, M.D., who also gave excellent editorial suggestions; and midwife Carol Thomason, CLC, CNM. Any errors, of course, are my own.

This book could not have been written without the collections and/or assistance of the following libraries, historical societies, and resources: Atlantic County Historical Society (Elizabeth Ehrhardt); Atlantic County Library, Galloway branch; The Bancroft Library; Burlington County Historical Society (Norman Blantz, Ph.D.); The Historical Society of Pennsylvania; Mills College Library; New Jersey Historical Commission (Mary R. Murrin); New Jersey State Archives; New Jersey State Library (Rebecca Colesar); Philadelphia Maritime Museum; Rutgers Cooperative Extension of Atlantic County (Chris Dubois); San Francisco Maritime Museum Library; San Francisco Public Library; Sonoma County Public Library; Tuckerton branch of the Ocean County Library; and the library at the University of California at Berkeley. Individuals who kindly answered specific queries were: Lina Braunstein, R.N.; Mike Lamb; Barb Lester; John M. Murrin, professor of history at Princeton; Carol Scholtz, R.N.; Jean Soderlund, professor of history at Lehigh University; and Jim and Gene Steelman. My grandmother, the late June Toler, and my great aunt Dorothy Hewitt researched and documented much of the family tree.

When I started this book my goal was to find out the truth behind the earliest version of the legend, but I soon learned why no one else had succeeded in doing so. Little to no evidence of a real event exists. What I have written is a novel, a telling of what *could* have happened. I used as much fact as I could find and filled in the gaps with my imagination. Although I remained close to what I could verify, when necessary I took liberties with the plot, especially in regard to the timing of specific events, such as the Yearly Meetings and the arrival in Philadelphia of the androgynous female preacher. In a novel the characters take over, thus some of mine have longer or shorter lives than the real people upon whom they were based. Mary Leeds died in 1727, not 1720; Abigail Higbee wasn't yet born in 1709; and Peter (Paul) Covenoven died in 1730. Alice Higbee Mathis demanded a larger role than simply producing a wife for Robert Leeds—and much later a second wife for John Leeds; thus the portrayals of Alice and her husbands vary from the documented facts of their lives.

Although I peopled my Great Egg Harbour with those who really lived there, all of my characters are fictional creations—in some cases complete fiction, in others a blend of fiction and fact. Because of the preponderance of similar names among the early settlers, I made the following changes: Justine Smith was Mary Smith, Paul Covenoven was Peter Covenoven, and Esther Cordery was Ann Cordery.

My rendering and interpretation of the legend is but one version. The text of the legend comes largely from the first recorded version, which wasn't published until more than one hundred years after the 1735 event. Because of the time lag, I felt free to modify a few elements to make certain points; thus, any factual discrepancies between the legend and the ensuing story are intentional.

Jersey Devil scholars will notice that I omitted the location of Burlington from the legend. That reference has been a source of controversy for decades. If it is commonly accepted that the Leeds Devil was born in Leeds (Point), why does the earliest recorded version say Burlington? One scholar postulated that at the time counties weren't clearly defined, and Leeds was thought to be in Burlington County. My research didn't validate that theory, but it did convince me that the legend of the Leeds Devil originated and lives on in Leeds Point and the Pine Barrens of New Jersey, that Mother Leeds was Deborah Leeds, wife of Japhet, and that they resided in Great Egg Harbour in 1735. I left out the Burlington reference to avoid confusion.

One final point: Deborah Leeds died in 1748.